VASILY MAHANENKO

SHAMAN'S REVENGE

*Books are the lives
we don't have
time to live,*

Vasily Mahanenko

THE WAY OF THE SHAMAN
BOOK 6

MAGIC DOME BOOKS

Shaman's Revenge
The Way of the Shaman, Book # 6
Copyright © V. Mahanenko 2017
Cover Art © V. Manyukhin 2017
Translator © Boris Smirnov 2017
Published by Magic Dome Books, 2017
All Rights Reserved
ISBN: 978-80-88231-39-4

TABLE OF CONTENTS:

CHAPTER ONE

EMERGENCE

"CLIMB ON OUT!" ordered a man's voice so hoarse it sounded like its owner had been suffering from a long-term cold—and treating it with ice cream. "Or are you just going to lie there forever?"

Even though my cocoon's lid had slid aside a while ago, I couldn't summon the strength to get up and return to the real world. Fluorescent lights buzzed before my eyes—a standard fixture of every office, or in this case the facility where ex-prisoners were released from their confinement capsules—and still I went on staring, as if into infinity. My head was such a jumble that I concentrated on the only thing I knew to be true and then held onto it like a lifesaver to keep from drowning—I was free! I, Daniel Mahan, who had incurred the wrath of my entire city, had regained my freedom! I had managed to trade eight years of imprisonment for a mere eleven months of gameplay.

And yet, this realization did not make me happy.

The only thing rattling in my head was the

terrible phrase that Anastaria had thrown into my face: "You're useless now." I tried to clear my mind yet again, but the last thirty minutes of my stay in Barliona kept surging to the forefront of my consciousness.

"Hey—are you, uh, alive in there?" A note of worry sounded in the voice and a bearded face materialized above me. A bandana covered his right eye as well as the scar that began on his forehead and zigzagged like a lightning bolt down to his lower jaw. "You seem to be okay. So why don't you get up? All the other prisoners come flying out like bullets and start kissing the blessed floor of reality, but you're still in there. Did something happen to you?"

"Analysis of patient's functions complete," a robotic voice announced several seconds later. "Patient's organism is functioning normally with no defects detected. Physical state is 88% of nominal."

"Look here, I don't have time to deal with whatever your problem is. I have another dozen releases to attend to today, so shake a leg and get a move on. You were released ahead of schedule, so someone will come for you in about half an hour. You'll have to wait in the reception room in the meantime...Hey! Can you hear me or not?! Make a sound or something!"

"I can hear you, I can hear you," I muttered, clearing my mind as best I could. I didn't feel like going off on this fellow—his life seemed tough enough as it was, so I waited until the restraining bar moved aside, sat up and sighed deeply. Immediately, my head began to spin and stars danced before my eyes, but I forced myself to stay sitting—I was done with being weak. It was time to grow up.

"The shower is ahead and to the left," the man added, moving away from the cocoon. "You'll find clothes there for you too. Anyway, I'm not a nanny. You can figure out what's what on your own. Oh and by the way—congratulations! Obtaining a release before your sentence is up is like gaining a new level in-game. Even two, I'd say..."

With these words, the technician turned around and went off on his business, so I had nothing left to do but slide my legs over to the floor and take my first step in the direction of the door he had indicated. Unfortunately, I didn't have the strength for a second one...

I can't explain what happened, but as soon as I took the second step, my legs gave way, a terrible aching swept across my body, my muscles contorted and a hundred little fireworks went off in my head, giving rise to interesting and strange thoughts: 'Achievement earned: You have left your capsule. That's worth two levels!' Great! Now where is my wave of pleasure?

During the eleven months I had spent inside the game I became so accustomed to experiencing a wave of pleasure from reaching some new milestone in my level or skills that I basically stopped noticing it when it happened. It was only in extremely important cases like when my Jewelcrafting skill would grow by several points that I'd still collapse to my knees in sweet exhilaration, subconsciously preparing my hands for the creation of my next masterpiece. For a prisoner like me, the dose of pleasure meant a lot.

Now, I fell to the floor with a dull groan. I could barely feel my own body—my craving to 'feel' that next level eclipsed everything around me.

"You feeling ill?" the technician's mocking voice pierced the fog around me. "It's okay. Just wait a little. You should feel better in a bit. Happens to everyone..."

My muscles contorted themselves so painfully that all I could do was groan and whimper—my craving of the 'dose' was insane. All of a sudden, I understood very clearly that the old technician was the reason for why I was feeling so ill! It was he who was withholding my dose—it was he who'd pulled me out of the capsule—it was he who...

"Oh! You've really got it bad, eh?" said a surprised voice when I began to growl and crawl in the technician's direction—so that I could gnaw his leg off for him. "Well, all right. You can have another hit. It won't kill you. Enjoy it while you can."

A sharp pain flashed near my shoulder and was followed by a warm and stunningly pleasant wave of pleasure that washed over my body. My muscles relaxed, my bones stopped dancing, my consciousness once more began to perceive the world and I flipped over onto my back completely ignoring the fact that I was lying naked on a frigid floor. My gaze encountered the white ceiling with the aforementioned fluorescent lights which were now full of unicorns wandering here and there picking bouquets of flowers. It's odd—I don't remember Ishni having arms. These unicorns looked more like centaurs with horns in their foreheads...

"I thought you only spent a year in there. How'd you manage to get so hooked?" The technician's one-eyed face blotted out the centaur who had just begun to sing a ditty in the background.

"Reality perception level at 35%. Patient is currently at Dependence Level Black. Recommended rehabilitation period: two months, fifteen days," the medical AI summarized my condition, while I fantasized about letting it have it with a Spirit...

"Level Black?" the technician's one eye spread out to cover his entire eye, confronting me with a horrifying Cyclops. Try and believe an NPC after that! Didn't they tell me that all the Cyclopes had been exterminated? Here's one right before me. "You know buddy, I'm even kind of curious about what happened to you."

The Cyclops stepped aside allowing me to rejoin my happy centaur. He was busy gathering flowers and singing songs—when suddenly he looked up fearfully, tucked in his tail and dropped down to the floor. The Master had come to swim the skies—a black Dragon.

Flourishing his enormous wings in the air around him, the Dragon enthralled and captivated me with his power and beauty. His entire body was filled with strength. He was the true master of this world and no one and nothing could depose him from his throne. Not even the Sirens.

The Sirens...

Anastaria...

Barliona....

I am Daniel Mahan, an ex-prisoner.

The Dragon flapped his wings one more time and vanished, returning the ceiling to its blank white state.

"Reality perception level at 85%. The patient has reached Dependence Level Yellow. Recommended rehabilitation period: fifteen days," the AI reacted immediately.

"Ahem," coughed the technician. "What exactly is going on anyway? Black, yellow. Listen, the doctors will show up in ten minutes. Let them deal with you. The shower is straight ahead. There are clothes there too. I have enough problems of my own..."

I sat up abruptly, experiencing no discomfort whatsoever—neither nausea, nor weakness, nor the desire for another 'dose.' At the moment, my entire consciousness was seized with a single feeling—hate. I never imagined that I could feel this terrible feeling, but at this very moment it was like a massive piston that was pushing my pleasure-deprived organism forward. The hate that consumed me was so immense that if Stacey had appeared before me right then, I wouldn't even think twice and...Although, no—I had no desire to go back to the mines. I had to act more thoughtfully. I had to...I had to seek revenge. The important thing was to think of how. This is what I would occupy myself with once I completed my rehabilitation.

"Reality perception level at 100%. The patient has entered Dependence Level Green. Recommended rehabilitation period: three days..."

"That's impossible!" exclaimed the doctor, once she had examined my medical charts. Gingerly holding the tablet with her thin fingers and long nails, which were decorated with a fairly intricate ornament, the doctor kept looking up at me with surprise as if I shouldn't even exist. Her white tunic didn't do much to conceal the shapely build of a longtime patron of either capsules or fitness centers—and with that said, I'd put my wager on the former. Fitness centers aren't very fashionable anymore. "Daniel, how do you feel?"

"As far as I'm concerned, the AI's diagnosis is all right by me," I shrugged my shoulders, unwilling to engage in any unnecessary polemics. I didn't feel like explaining the reasons for how I'd managed to 'return' to reality—that was between me, the Phoenix clan and no one else. As I showered and dressed, I made up my mind about one ironclad thing—I would have my revenge. It didn't matter when that would be—I could figure that out as I went—but it was clear that I simply could not let the actions of Phoenix and my so-called friends go unpunished. Otherwise I might as well stop thinking of myself as human.

"It says it here, but..." the doctor stuttered looking up at me with her blue eyes. "It's impossible to emerge from Level Black on your own! That's never happened before! In all my twelve years in the practice!"

"There's always a first time for everything," I noted philosophically and changed the subject: "Tell me, doctor, will my hair start growing again? Or am I going to stay bald for the rest of my life?"

"You can simply call me Lucia," the girl sighed, evidently realizing that she wouldn't find out anything from me at the moment. "Your hair will grow back, don't worry. The capsule contained a special solution that blocked its growth, so...Daniel, I'd like to run one more, small test before we head over to the rehabilitation clinic. I need your permission to read your brain signals in your waking state. Are you opposed to this?"

"Not at all. I don't have anything to hide," I replied graciously. If at the beginning of our conversation I had unwillingly associated Lucia with Stacey, and kept looking for some catch, then now it seemed to me that I had known this doctor for a long time and so I didn't want to disappoint her by refusing. Anyway, she's a doctor—who says no to a doctor? Only people who are very ill...

It was explained to me that we would drive the two hundred kilometers between the facility that contained the prisoners and the rehab center in only an hour. According to the doctor, there are seven colored levels of pleasure dependence—from the highest which was black to the lowest, which was green. Furthermore, the lower the level, the further away is the corresponding rehab center. The doctor kept trying to involve me in a conversation about the meaning of life and my future place in this world, so I stared out at the trees rushing past us and turned my attention to my plan for revenge.

And so!

The first thing that I'd have to do would be get my Shaman back. Even if they had to drag him out of the prison servers and transfer him to the public ones. I hardly felt like starting the game again from square one when I had such a monster at my disposal.

The second thing was that as soon as I entered the game, I'd go to Anhurs and demand an audience with the Emperor or the High Priestess—whoever was in charge of marriages. I'd demand a divorce from Anastaria and the return of my personal property— everything that Anastaria had stolen from my bag. I'd need to make sure to see a Barliona lawyer about this matter—are items that were removed from an open bag considered loot or not? If not, I'd hold Anastaria legally responsible, and if yes...I'd rather not think about that...It would be really upsetting to lose my Chess Set.

Third—I'd need to deal with the clan. It wasn't of any use to me anymore, since I wouldn't be able to manage it. The responsibility of leading a gaming organization, even one that had only ten members, placed a burden on me that I simply did not want. When I'd return to the game, I would say farewell to everyone who was left and officially shut down the clan...Though, no, I'd remain in it on my own. It wouldn't do to lose the projections.

Fourth—my two major assets: Altameda and the Giant squidolphin. These two would surely become immense drains on my finances and would only pull me down to the bottom. Considering that Leite—who had practiced and profited with my budget—was no longer in the clan, it would remain up to me to solve the question of money. Otherwise, I'd have to do something I really didn't want to do—sell Altameda to another clan. I couldn't see any other way out.

By the way, how much money do I have left? As I was confirming my exit from the game, the number of 140 million flashed before my eyes. Eighteen months ago, I'd never even fantasize about such a sum, but now...I'd spent a hundred to obtain my release. Some other part of the remainder would go to paying my players' salaries until I kicked them out. So in any case, I should have about thirty remaining. But I won't rely on it. Thirty million...Maybe I should withdraw them, buy myself an excellent house and live peacefully without ever giving Barliona another thought? I could study something, find a job and live comfortably without any Anastarias, Ehkillers, or Phoenixes. What's wrong with just sending them all to hell?

Well for one, the fact that old Greed Toad and Hoarding Hamster won't leave me alone until the end of my days. Even if I could handle each one individually, I'm powerless when it's two against one. I want what's mine and I want to punish those who took it away from me. It'd be nice to exterminate the Phoenix clan while I was at it. And this gives rise to two further questions:

The first is how can a game clan be destroyed at all?

The second is how I can protect myself from the wrath of Anastaria and Hellfire in real life? Somehow I don't imagine they'll welcome my attempts to hurt their clan and, if they don't reach an agreement with me in the game (and it'll be mighty difficult to reach any agreement with me in-game), then they might try to find me in real life.

Should I file a complaint with the law enforcement agencies? I wonder what I'd say in it: "I'm about to kill the leading players of Malabar and am therefore afraid for my life?" At a 75% probability, they'd send me to a mental clinic for tilting at windmills. So that wasn't an option. I need to consider everything as carefully as I can. And therefore, I better return to my initial question: What's the best way to hurt a gaming clan?

Send them all to respawn? Hmm...That's a pretty severe punishment considering the level discrepancy between us. Well—what—was I going to hire mercenaries to hunt and kill the leaders of Phoenix over and over again? You couldn't think of a bigger load of nonsense. So that option was out of the question but could come into play under the right circumstances.

The only soft spot that could hurt the clan, it seems to me, were their finances. I had to do something to the finances of Phoenix, to hamper their funds and then...Although, how could I do this anyway? Gold is considered inalienable property, so hacking into the Phoenix accounts was a shortcut back to the mines. And to steal their Legendary items, I'd need to find people to do it. The only way I could hurt their clan was to eradicate it—it's not like I could besiege their castles...

"What happened, Daniel?" the doctor asked with a note of worry when I hopped up in place and almost hit my head against the car's ceiling. She brought an analyzer up to my eyes which confirmed that my level of reality perception was still at 100% and that I was still at Dependence Level Green.

"It's nothing. Just some thoughts," I assured her, turning back to the window. I don't need to siege any castles. I have Altameda!

At the moment, I was aware of the fact that the full extent of Anastaria's property was confined to a single vessel on the seas that cost ten million gold. Considering the ease with which she parted with such a vast amount of money, it'd be stupid to activate the squidolphin and have to pay taxes—the payoff wouldn't justify the expense. Until the players in the south of the continent earned a positive reputation with the pirates, until they begin to receive ships of their own, an enormous amount of time would pass and it's not certain that any members of Phoenix would even be among them. So a seaborne revenge was unrealistic, but...I have Altameda!

The special thing about my castle is that it can move from location to location. This procedure was free once every three months and cost about ten million otherwise. If I manage to assemble a mob of players that will quash any resistance after Altameda teleports on top of the Phoenix castle, and then send in the loot hunters who will pick the enemy castle apart piece by piece as we did to Glarnis...As I understand it, Phoenix has about seven castles, the strongest of which was Level 29, and the weakest Level 18. It takes a pretty substantial investment to level up a castle that high, so if I manage to reduce all of them to level one...Well, that's a more promising revenge than hunting down those bastards one by one.

Now my desire to get my Shaman back became even greater, since Anastaria had carelessly given me her entire map, which had the Phoenix possessions marked on it. My Shaman had access to the exact coordinates of every castle and therefore had a realistic path to revenge. The next step was finding the people who would work with me.

As well as the issue with my castle...

According to the Emperor's requirement, the owner had to spend three months in his castle. I was dutifully doing just this for an entire month, until I left the game, so now I had another legal question for the game lawyer—can I legally lose the castle due to lapsing in my residency requirement, considering that the rehab period is also required? Logically speaking, Altameda should remain mine in either case, but I will need to make sure. I can't afford any mistakes when it comes to this issue.

Further—I need to deprive Phoenix of their quests. Without scenarios, there's no loot, while the members' salaries still have to be paid. It's unfortunate that I can't accomplish this on my own— the Corporation always needs some leading clan that it can lean on. This means I'll have to work with Etamzilat and Undigit. I'm sure that improving the financial position of their clan is one of the priorities anyway.

What else can I do within the game? It's impossible to destroy a character permanently or harm him for that matter...Hang on! The Cursed Artificer! There's a chance that the Cursed Chess Set is the brainchild of the Corporation and I was forced to create it without a chance to repeat the feat, but it's worth trying. If I manage to bind an avatar to some item with certain very specific requirements, that'll be another nail in Phoenix's coffin.

And as a consequence of this last point, I must meet with Kreel and find out where and how he dug up Rogzar's Crystal. If I recall correctly, this item's description went something like this: "*-75% to movement speed; -50% to all stats; -90% to regeneration of Hit Points, Mana and Energy; -90% to Experience earned. May not be sold, dropped, stolen or destroyed.*" Well, a beauty like that is simply begging to find its way into the personal inventories of Anastaria, Barsina, Leite and various other members of the flaming chicken clan. I need to exploit any avenues available to me.

"We're here," the doctor's voice jerked me from my pleasant musings of revenge, returning me to reality. The main bullet points were in place. What remained was to verify, develop and eliminate the ones that were impossible as well as to brainstorm additional ones. After all, revenge, is a dish best served cold.

It would be a stretch to call the facility that I was delivered to a rehabilitation center. I had imagined a monumental edifice barricaded behind barbed wire—after all its purpose was to contain prisoners, so the windows would have to be barred in order to keep the patients from jumping out, and yet the reality turned out to be very different. A mossy forest, neat and tidy, a manicured lawn, small cottages, people in white cloaks sitting and lounging around the grass, the pleasant chirp of birds—I was looking at a picture of some kind of idyll. All that was missing were robots that would flit from patient to patient delivering food and taking care of any bodily needs, so that no one had to bother about anything. When I came closer, I saw that several people were playing tennis on the tennis courts located behind the buildings. Others were swimming in a pool and some others were working in small workshops, doing carpentry and ceramics. In one of the far off houses I saw a blacksmith, ferociously hammering a piece of iron, and yet I could hear no sounds coming from him—a force field surrounding the building kept the clamor from leaking into the forest. A similar field surrounded the athletic areas, ensuring that the people relaxing on the grass could do so in perfect tranquility.

"This is where you will stay for the next five days," Lucia said with a smile. "Please follow me. We need to register your arrival, implant a monitoring device and determine where you will be sleeping. We will also explain to you the assortment of prophylactic treatments that the analytic programs have prescribed to you—but I won't burden you with tedious information. Please, relax, recuperate and do your utmost to become a productive member of society..."

By the end of my second day in the rehab center, I was howling from boredom. I couldn't think of even a few hours over the past year during which I wasn't doing something—with the exception of the time I'd spent sleeping. There was always some kind of activity going on—a Dungeon, leveling-up my Jewelcrafting skill, or some quests I had to do. And therefore my time in Barliona had rushed past me as if the world was on fast forward. Here on the other hand...

I was lazing on the grass, sleeping, undergoing various procedures, lazing on the grass again, sleeping again, again the grass...Several times I tried to occupy myself by playing a sport, but tennis and soccer were never my favorite, so these activities didn't bring me any pleasure either. I took another nap and lazed around the grass some more, underwent some more procedures and went back to the lawn...The mere thought that I'd have to continue to do this for another three days caused my face to contort. I needed some kind of activity...

"It's occupied!" barked the blacksmith without turning to look at me. "There's only one forge here and I'm not about to leave it. If you have a problem, take it up with the orderlies!"

"I don't need the forge," I replied, frowning from the heat. After talking with the doctor and explaining my problem, I received some useful advice: to try and create something in this world as I used to do back in Barliona. So the next morning I went to the forge, since all the materials I needed were there...and encountered this grouchy blacksmith intent on defending his habitat.

"Then scram! Bunch of weirdos wandering around here..."

Digging around the shelves for a Jeweler's toolkit—which turned out to be a faithful double of the one that I'd had to work with back in Barliona, if you didn't take into account its weight—I darted out of the smithy into the fresh forest air: The force field contained not only the noise but the heat as well. It seemed that the smith was an avid masochist who'd decided to take out all the years he'd spent in Barliona on a hunk of iron. I doubt someone who'd spent less than a year in the mines would settle on this form of rehabilitation.

Sitting down beneath the first elm I came across, I opened my Jeweler's toolkit and felt a sharp pang of nostalgia—despite the fact that I'd crafted literally a couple days ago when I created the last of the Chess Pieces, it had really been a long time since I'd worked with the tools. I can't even remember when now...

My hands, which had until then never actually held the mandrel, smelting pot and other tools of the trade, picked up the spindle of copper wire and in several deft and well-rehearsed movements wrapped the first ring without even having to resort to the mandrel. Regarding the fruit of my labor dumbly, I shook my head and placed the ring aside—the outcome was some kind of cheap trinket, without even a single special characteristic. I'd probably be best off working in Design Mode...

The familiar darkness enveloped me on all sides, and the wire in my hands appeared before me. And so! Ordinary rings aren't much fun, so I'll try to braid the wire, encrusting it with this stone: The image of a transparent gem which came included in the toolkit appeared beside the ring. If the ring won't have any characteristics after this, then I don't even know—I'll have to go see the head Master to ask him what I'm doing wrong. But first, let's make a pretty braid. Or had I learned all those skills for nothing?

"Patient has entered Dependence Level Black!" As soon as I finished my ring and saw that the result pleased me, strange sounds began to reach me through the darkness, constantly repeating again and again: "Patient has entered Dependence Level Black! Patient has entered Dependence Level Black!"

The noise was so irritating that I opened my eyes and blinked as per usual from the light emanating from my hands—I had managed to craft another masterpiece and now there'd be a litany of notifications announcing that I had leveled up. A few steps in front of me stood a brave little company of characters: The dwarf I'd met earlier, who'd kicked me out of his smithy; two trolls who were trying to hit me with their darts; an enormous orc pensively scratching his head; and a smallish gnome occupied with pushing buttons on his arm. An ordinary assortment of bystanders, who had gathered no doubt to examine my new masterpiece.

"*Shargak larange!*" said the gnome, addressing me, I think. Shaking my head to indicate that I didn't understand his language, I was about to explain in Malabarian, Kartossian and some other languages of Barliona that I had picked up along the way that I didn't understand him—when, suddenly, I saw *her* among the trees—the Siren. The two-meter-tall beast wasn't even trying to hide and was pointing her trident right at me, smirking and reveling in her impunity—the onlookers weren't any trouble for her, only a true Dragon was capable of defeating Anastaria.

Eh...What Anastaria?

Another wave of emotion swept over my body raising goose-bumps as it went—the very same Anastaria who...

"Patient has entered Dependence Level Green!" buzzed the analyzer and silence descended upon the forest. I was so filled with my hate for the Sirens and that one particular Siren, that I couldn't calm the trembling of my hands and dropped the ring I had made to the ground. I was shaking through and through. My head was filled with a roar, and yet I was slowly beginning to perceive reality the way it was again. Without any gnomes, orcs or Sirens....Grrr! It wouldn't be enough to kill that slithering hag.

"If you can hear me, nod your head," said the short man I had taken for the gnome.

"I'm not a bobble head to nod at your command," I retorted, trying to come to my senses. "Have I been this way for a long time?"

"About five minutes," the smith said. "Your analyzer began to squeak so loud that we had to throw a dome over you to keep the doctors from showing up."

Only now did I notice that we were inside a force field dome that blocked all sound.

"Thank you," I managed, understanding that if the doctors had seen me this way, I'd have to stay here far longer than five days. They'd send me to the clinic and run tests on me for the next two months.

"If you want to get out of here, don't do anything for the rest of the time you're here. Just sleep," the smith added. "We don't squeal on our own kind. Everyone suffers an attack every once in a while, but if the doctors see you, they'll send you to the Level Yellow center. Trust me—it's worse there. See you around!" The force field vanished and the gang of onlookers went off on their business as if nothing had happened. Big deal—someone entered Dependence Level Black and stopped perceiving this plane of reality. An everyday occurrence around these parts, I guess.

Picking up the ring I'd made and not bothering to examine the quality of my work, I stuck it in my pocket and began thinking. I'm starting to like all this less and less—twice now I had crossed the limit at which I perceived this reality and I still had no idea why this was happening. If it weren't for those last thirty minutes of Barliona which had lodged this hate deep inside of me, I'm not sure that I'd be able to return to a normal condition without lengthy treatment. The only explanation I could think of was that Barliona had become my mind's preferred reality and I was trying to force this world into its mold.

By the way, this gives rise to an inconvenient question—what would happen to me if it weren't for my hate of Anastaria? Let's imagine that I bought my release on my own, selling my castle, the Chess Set and the Eye of the Dark Widow—would the time I'd spent in the game allow me to return to reality, or would I turn into some kind of vegetable that desired only the pleasure of living in its own virtual vegetable patch? I don't think I much like the answer to this question—no, I'd revel in my ability to fly as a Dragon and never even think about any stupid Sirens. Another wave of intense hatred swept across my body, squeezing my chest like a steel vice. Why look at that! So does this mean that I also have to be grateful to that beast for giving me the chance to remain human? Like hell!

I spent the remaining four days of my rehabilitation playing the perfect patient—no sudden movements, words, changes in emotion or conflicts with those around me. I was all daisies, roses, butterflies and all that other claptrap that let the doctors know that I was adapting perfectly well to my new reality. I didn't suffer any further attacks of fantasy, but I also did not allow the fiery hatred I felt for Anastaria to die out, constantly recalling my last thirty minutes in Barliona. My revenge fantasies also took a back seat, since I understood that the only thing I could think of at the moment was childish nonsense. Even the plan of using my castle to attack those of Phoenix was a nonstarter—who could guarantee for instance that Altameda would remain at Level 24? No one. I doubt the devs would simply hand an ordinary player the means to single-handedly ruin the game's leading clans. More than likely, Altameda would be destroyed as it crushed its first Phoenix castle. After all, there'd be a player guiding it—not an angel. Sure, Urusai was permitted to attack Glarnis in this manner. But I doubt I'd be allowed to replicate that feat.

"How do you feel?" the doctor asked at my release. According to the analyzer, the rehabilitation period of the person named Daniel Mahan had ended and he could be safely released into the wild. The official wild.

"Very well, thank you," I assured the doctor. Lucia had hovered around me all those four days, trying to detect any signs of aggression or a fit or whatever else would allow her to hold me for some indeterminate period of time, but I kept my cool. The girl couldn't figure out how I managed to leave Dependence Level Black so quickly, evidently assuming that there had been some mistake—either by the analyzer when it diagnosed me or by the staff as they decided to release me. I really hoped it was the former.

"I have a present for you," I told her, trying to change the subject. "As a memento to remember one of your patients by."

Digging in my pocket, I retrieved the wire ring I had made the first day and placed it before the woman. Over the past five days, I had had enough time to look over my work and so now I understood the indescribable surprise on the doctor's face—before her lay a whimsically wire-wrapped ring, encrusted with several simple sequins within its braided lattice. If you'd ask me to make another one, I'd look at you as if you'd lost your mind. You can't create a ring like this with your hands. To do so you need fairly elaborate equipment, which the Jeweler's toolkit did not contain. And yet the fact stood—in a state of full in-game immersion, my mind had guided my hands to do something inexplicable and created this masterpiece. Had I done this in Barliona—I'd earn a point or two in crafting for sure...

"Please sign here, here and here, Daniel," said the orderly who had brought me from the residence hall. He returned my belongings and handed me the keys to my apartment. "Very good," he added as soon as my squiggles appeared on the document. "I hope we won't have to see each other in real life again. Prison isn't very good for anyone really."

* * *

Having watched the car with the Corporation logo vanish down the street, I sighed deeply and looked around. Basically nothing had changed over the last year—a cozy green garden with a playground full of children playing, mothers with baby carriages discussing the latest episode of their favorite shows as they strolled among the trees, elderly women with unkind faces seeking to uncover an enemy of the people in each unfamiliar passerby—my home had remained the way I remembered it. All that was missing was Sergei who lived up on the fifth floor. At this time of day he was sure to be passed out somewhere under some bush or else staggering to one in a lazy zigzag. Prolonged unemployment and repeated summons by the Imitators had ground down this once-good person, and now he survived on benefits. Or rather, instead of living, he drank and slept so that he could do the same the next day. The authorities kept a very close eye on people in his condition and at the first sign of aggression immediately shipped them off to the Barliona mines, yet Sergei managed to pursue his chosen lifestyle in the most harmless of ways.

"Good day, Daniel," said a young man sitting on a bench in front of my building. "My name is Alexander. Do you have a few minutes to spare?"

I shot a puzzled look at the man, who must have been barely twenty and who was wearing a straight-laced business suit despite the warm weather. One didn't have to be observant or cautious by nature to notice the smallish badge on his jacket which told me that this was a member of the Corporation.

"I do," I shrugged. There wasn't any point in hiding and if someone wanted to speak with me, then why not indulge them? "Can we speak here, or should we go up to my apartment?"

"Preferably up in your apartment. It's a bit hot out here," said Alexander, loosening his tie and demonstrating that Corporation employees are people too and not the robots they seem.

My apartment welcomed us with silence and a layer of dust that covered basically every surface in it. Before departing to the mines, I had turned off the air filtration system, assuming that I wouldn't be in the game for that long—and therefore my apartment had become a fairly depressing sight. I can't say that there was too much dust, but there was enough of it that you would leave your fingerprints on any item you touched.

"Have a seat." I dug up a bed sheet from the dresser and threw it over the sofa, thereby covering the dust at least a little and turned on the air filtration system. As soon as Alexander leaves, I'll need to look up a cleaning service, since I won't be able to manage this mess on my own. "Would you like some mineral water?"

"I won't refuse." The smile that appeared on the man's face was so shy that it seemed as if it couldn't understand how it had found itself among such masculine features.

"In that case, hang on just a minute. I'll put in the order..."

As I assumed, Alexander didn't refuse my offer of food either, so I was pleased with my decision to order dinner for two right off the bat. Like two true diplomats, we were putting off the main conversation until the end of lunch, and instead discussed the heat outside, cars and Barliona.

"Thank you for lunch. In my line of work I frequently don't have the time to eat," said Alexander, becoming utterly human and abandoning the last pretenses of being some kind of machine. "Tell me, Daniel, what are you plans for the next several years?"

"That's quite a period of time you're asking me about," I smiled. "I don't know what I'll be doing tomorrow and you want to know about my plans for the next few years."

"I'll put it differently—are you planning on keeping your character, the one you've been playing with in Barliona for the past year?"

"I appreciate you ducking the words 'prison' and 'mines,'" I quipped sarcastically, but seeing the man's embarrassed reaction, felt a pang of shame—it wasn't this guy's fault that I ended up 'there.' "Sorry, it just slipped out. I thought that these kinds of questions would be asked during the rehabilitation process, not at my doorstep."

"You are correct, but in your case there's been a little snag—a fault in the equipment, which for whatever reason transmitted erroneous data to the surveillance system. In fact, this mistake is quite astonishing in your case. According to our system, you entered Dependence Level Black and then bounced back to Dependence Level Green. The Level Black flag remained in the system, since it is a permanent indicator, so you should have been released no sooner than in three months. It was our systems becoming desynchronized that brought you here and no one got around to discussing the issue of your avatar and the funds at his disposal. And that is precisely why I'm here."

"I see. In that case, I have an answer for you—I would like the Corporation to return the character I was using in Barliona during my sentence back to me. With the same class, name, achievements and reputation. Is this possible?"

"Of course. That's a standard procedure in which we transfer the account over to the public servers," Alexander sighed with relief and produced a tablet. "You only need to sign here and here, and the process will be under way."

"Wonderful!" Placing my signature a second time that day, I returned the tablet to its owner. "In that case, thank you for your visit."

"Tell me, are you *the* Shaman Mahan?"

"What do you mean, 'the'?"

"The one that was the subject of two movies and who was one of the most famous players of Barliona?" Alexander explained, flushed with embarrassment and added: "The one who disbanded his clan..."

"What?!" I couldn't contain my surprise. "What do you mean, disbanded his clan?"

"Well...you...I mean...Everyone knows that the Legends of Barliona have ceased to exist...It's been a week now... You deleted all the players from the clan, leaving only you and Plinto who is currently being hunted by Phoenix..."

"May I inquire where you're getting your information from?" I asked, not quite understanding what was going on. Where was this guy getting these wild ideas? How could I disband that which I had built with such love?

"On Anastaria's site," Alexander grew even more bashful, "there's an interview in which she says that...But what am I saying—let's just look at it together. You have a computer, don't you?"

"Hello, Anastaria," said the host of some show. Judging by the names and clan logos hovering over everyone's heads, this footage was filmed in Barliona. "I'd like to address a question that's on the minds of most players right now—why did you return to Phoenix? Everyone knew that the Legends of Barliona were one of the affiliates of Phoenix, but no one imagined such a massive exodus. Could you tell us what happened?"

"There was a conflict between Mahan and I, and as a consequence the clan ceased to exist. We sold off the clan's strategic resources. Mahan used the majority of the clan treasury for his personal ends and blocked access to the clan castle. You're correct to refer to the Legends as an affiliate of Phoenix, and this was why I offered all the players who were dissatisfied with Mahan's policies the opportunity to switch to Phoenix. As for Mahan, he disappeared. I would guess he transferred the clan funds to reality and is using them as he sees fit. I could be wrong about this. In any case, he, the money, the resources and the castle are all gone. Effectively, the clan has been disbanded. I don't really want to speak about this topic for now—it's a bit

painful for me. I haven't been betrayed this deeply in a long time..."

"An unexpected announcement! Okay—let's put the topic of the Legends aside. Tell me, why didn't you take part in this year's beauty pageant?"

"I felt like I should give the other girls a chance..."

Anastaria began to explain her love of humanity and her desire to help the less fortunate, but I stopped listening. What an asshole! Technically she didn't utter a single lie, but the manner in which she said it all..! Judging by its number of views, more than thirty million people had watched this video over the last five days, which meant that the popular opinion of why the Legends had fallen apart was by now set in stone. No matter what I said—no matter what witnesses I dredged up or videos I showed—the player base would be on the side of Anastaria and Phoenix. That bitch!

"How nice," I seethed through my teeth. "Tell me, is there any way I can get the video recording of my last thirty minutes in Barliona? It shows exactly who betrayed whom..."

"Of course you can," replied Alexander, "if you write a letter that...Hang on, are you trying to say that Anastaria lied? That it all didn't happen the way she claims?"

"That's the thing...But okay, if you don't have any more business for me, I'd like to be alone. I need to think about what we just saw..."

The more I considered what had happened, the more I hated Anastaria—and I hadn't thought I could hate her more. She really was terribly precise—it wasn't enough that they had robbed me and forced me out of the game, but they'd also manipulated public opinion against me. They made it seem that I had used my warriors to earn my release—actually even worse: that I had used them to pocket the clan funds. Even if I manage to prove that Phoenix set me up, the matter of the money will keep players away from me. Who wants to play with someone who's known to have embezzled clan finances? I need to see a lawyer urgently!

So I launched the internet and began searching...

"Unfortunately, no one will be able to help you," said one of our city's leading game lawyers shaking his head. I had spent basically all the money I had left before being sent to Barliona to arrange the consultation in the hopes of receiving an answer to the question of 'How much can I get from Anastaria for her stealing from me?' And yet, the lawyer heard me out, inquired about some details, requested the logs from the Corporation—it turned out that game lawyers could obtain these with the players' permission—then went through them, examined each episode in detail and finally explained that, unfortunately, Anastaria had acted wholly within the rules of the game. I spent an entire day only to receive an answer I already knew: The dummy was me. No one had forced me to unlock my bag to the girl—after all, one of the fundamental laws of Barliona, the one that attracted players to the game, was that anything that could be appropriated became the legal property of the player who'd taken it. As long as my inventory bag was closed, the Eye, the Chess Set and the other items were my property and if they'd been removed by the devs or some hackers, I'd be within my right to be outraged. But as soon as I granted Anastaria access to my inventory, the items effectively acquired a second owner. I had done this voluntarily—there had been no official pressure on me from the current deputy of Phoenix. So all in all, the dummy was me. The same went for her interview—formally speaking, I couldn't lodge any complaints against the girl. Had I used the clan funds for my personal purposes? Yes. Had the resources been sold? Yes. Had our players gone over to Phoenix? Yes, goddamn it! Even if I file a complaint of slander, it'd be impossible to prove it—Anastaria had chosen her words very carefully.

The only silver lining in what the lawyer told me was that according to one of the laws of Barliona, if a player signs out to reality against his will, his required presence at various locations is suspended until his return. So if I return to the game and discover that Altameda has ceased to be mine, I'm allowed to petition a court to regain it—although there'd been no precedent for this, since the

Corporation made sure to follow its laws carefully. Furthermore, I retained priority ownership of the castle over my spouse or my legal brother—Anastaria and Plinto, that is. This was all a bit of sunlight in the general gloom of my situation.

"Hello, Daniel!" Alexander called me on the phone as I was returning home. "I have good news— we've completed the transfer of your character and you may reenter the game whenever you like. By way of compensating you for the recent problems we had with your account, the Corporation would like to make you a small present that, naturally, won't affect gameplay, but will make your experience a little better. I'm referring to your ability to choose the projection selected by your clan—now, your clan members can receive whatever projection they wish, not only the ones generated by the Imitator. We believe that you and your clan members will welcome this feature."

"Thank you. That's very kind of you," I muttered in reply to such a 'generous' offer. Considering that the Legends no longer have any members except for me, the option to change my Dragon projection is about as useful to me as a bicycle is to a dog— theoretically the dog can learn to ride one, but it's probably safer off on its own four paws.

"If you have any further questions, feel free to call me or my colleagues in the adaptation department," Alexander went on. "All the best to you and good luck in your conquest of Barliona!"

The phone beeped, signaling that my conversation with the Corporation had drawn to a close: I had been rehabilitated, returned home, given a present and stamped with the official 'case closed' seal. From now on I was on my own.

While I had been with the lawyer, the cleaning service had come by and returned my apartment to a civilized state, cleaning it to a pristine condition. Everything that could sparkled, and even my time-ravaged wallpaper glistened with a bright new layer. Nothing suggested that this residence had spent a year in utter dilapidation reminiscent of a bachelor's lair. Which, in effect, it was.

Having finished all my remaining chores, I sat down on my bed and began to stare at the gaming capsule. On the one hand, I couldn't wait to get back to Barliona and find out what had happened to my clan during the past week. Was my castle still in one piece? How many people were still with me? What funds did I still have? On the other hand, there was one serious problem: As soon as I return, I'll start 'hearing' Anastaria's thoughts. I doubt I'll find the strength to respond properly to hearing her voice in my head and I really wanted to avoid freaking out. The immediate task was to come up with a way to make Phoenix regret what it had done and teach them that they couldn't get away with humiliating me. And yet, this was not a dilemma that I could solve right this instant.

The capsule offered no answer as to whether I should enter Barliona or not, so I opened my computer and decided to check my mail—I'd been free two days now and still hadn't gotten around to it. I'd never allow myself such a luxury in the past—the various offers to take part in contests came with time limits for registration and if I didn't react in time, I'd lose out.

Greetings, Daniel!

We don't know each other, but we have something in common—Phoenix. Just like you, I ended up a victim of this clan and now want nothing more than to exact vengeance against those bastards. I don't know what you're planning—perhaps, you won't even want to return to Barliona after all that they did to you—but just in case, here's a link to a video. You'll understand why Phoenix wanted to send you to the mines: Watch it and consider it. And if you decide to seek revenge as well—I suggest we work together. It's not important who I am at the moment and what resources I have at my disposal. All you need to know is that I have the means.

Make your decision, Shaman!

Among the hundreds of emails about contests and spam that had made it through my filters, there was this one stunning letter. And the most interesting part wasn't so much the text of the letter, which said plenty on its own, but the very fact that the letter had found its way to my inbox. It turns out that this person was perfectly aware not only of what had happened to me in actual fact, but also that I was Shaman Mahan, that this was my email and, what seemed quite clear to me, where I lived. The sender's address was '2233443322@burnermail.vxn' which told me only one thing—this was a disposable email address intended only to send one letter and receive one answer to it. Very curious...

The letter was so interesting that I decided to ignore the first rule of the web (don't click on any unfamiliar links) and opened the video. Before me appeared the scene of Shaman Mahan's last few moments in Barliona. My heart shuddered when I heard Anastaria's voice again—a wave of hate for the girl and Leite, the leading players in my betrayal, swept over me from head to toe—and yet even through these overwhelming emotions I could see the image, the moral annihilation of the Shaman. Of me. Were I to encounter Anastaria right now, I couldn't guarantee that I'd let her live, even if it meant spending the rest of my life in the mines. Finally, I watched myself sit down on the boulder in a stupor, waiting for the final countdown, and at last dissolve into the surroundings. Shaman Mahan had ceased to exist in the game called Barliona. At any rate, for the time being.

The camera switched to a different angle to show the door to the Tomb swinging open. An enormous slab which Anastaria never managed to destroy, slid aside with ease, opening an ordinary passageway to a Dungeon. However, as soon as the passage opened and the players made their first steps in its direction, a star fell from the sky and turned into two angels—a white one and a black one.

"The Creator has opened the Tomb!" roared the black angel, who—unusually for Barliona—didn't have a name.

"From now unto eternity this Dungeon shall have the 'Original' status!" the second angel echoed. "Any items found in tis location shall be Unique or Legendary! However, this status will apply exclusively to the Creator himself!"

"Where is he?" asked the black angel. "Where is he who must receive the original key from us, the key to the most sought after place in Barliona?"

"He is not here, sentries," Anastaria replied, bowing her head. "Having opened the Tomb, the Creator was overcome with rage and hate for this world and abandoned it forever. You cannot give him the key..."

"You speak the truth!" the white angel exclaimed with astonishment. "How could the Creator begin to hate this world having just managed to open the passage? Who shall receive the key in his stead? Was the opening really in vain?"

"There is one here who is allowed to receive the key," Anastaria went on and pointed at Barsina. "Here she is! Give her the key! She can replace the Creator."

"It is confirmed!" announced the black angel. "Barsina is permitted to receive the key. And yet we are patient! If the Creator does not appear before us within a month, the key shall be given to Barsina and all Free Citizens will be allowed into the Dungeon. However, anyone who attempts to slip past us until that time, shall be immolated! That is all!"

"Please forgive my impudence," said Anastaria, "but if the Creator doesn't appear before the deadline, will the Dungeon lose its status?"

"If the Creator does not appear before us, we shall declare Barsina the Acting Creator! The Dungeon shall retain its status and twenty sentients, including Barsina, will be permitted to enter."

The angels fell silent, guarding the entrance to the Tomb with their immense bodies and, suddenly, Anastaria and Hellfire who had been standing next to them flew toward the entrance. And, importantly, they flew there against their will as if some invisible force had flung them there—one powerful enough to send two of the game's highest-level players flying. Plinto!

Two curt swipes from a black wing and white wing dissolved Anastaria and Hellfire, sending them to respawn, while simultaneously the Rogue appeared behind them, cast a bloodthirsty look at the shocked bystanders who had gathered at the entrance and said: "All right you bastards, shall we dance?"

I'd never seen such a crazed look on Plinto's

face. With his red eyes and black wings he resembled the Patriarch in his foulest of moods. The Rogue, or rather, the Vampire dissolved into the air and the players on the plateau began to vanish one after the other—Plinto began to avenge his leader. That was the end of the video.

Staring at my screen blankly, I struggled to get a grip on what I'd just seen. After a short while, I noticed with some surprise that my hands were trembling and like Plinto all I wanted in this world was to personally grab each person who was there on the plateau by the throat, squeeze out their eyes and look on as the blood oozed from their eye sockets and their bodies withered to those of desiccated mummies. I couldn't care less that there was no blood in Barliona—I'd imagine it myself...Hmm...Never figured myself to be so bloodthirsty, but what Phoenix did deserved nothing less.

When I could think clearly again and the first wave of emotion abated, I tried to consider what I had seen.

And so!

Anastaria wanted me off the plateau as soon as the opening process was underway. She could have gotten rid of me in various ways, but she chose the most radical one—manipulating me to send myself back to the mines. If it weren't for my composure, I would have definitely attacked the girl who'd betrayed me and found myself in the hands of the Heralds the next instant. Phoenix's plan was perfect and had it come off as they planned it, I'd be toiling in the mines for the next seven years, reading notifications about how the great players of Phoenix had completed the Creator's Dungeon. Well, tough luck!

Ridding myself of my feelings about Stacey for a second, I occupied myself with another no less important question—who was the mysterious eavesdropper who'd recorded this video? A second watch-through did not answer this question—everyone I remembered being there was in frame—Clutzer, Leite, Magdey and the raiders. Consequently, the cameraman was one of the players who'd arrived to the plateau with Phoenix. This gives rise to a whole host of new questions, which I have no way of answering at the moment. Or rather, I could answer some of them—at the price of agreeing to ally myself with someone I didn't know...How do I know whether it's beneficial to me or not? Do I really want to ally with someone in order to exact my revenge against Phoenix? Do I really want to spend some part of my life in order to hurt someone? A quick glance at the video, which was looping before me, featuring Shaman Mahan as he was leaving the game (oh! I'm speaking of myself in the third person!), yielded the answer to all these questions—yes! I want this!

Greetings! I enjoyed your demonstration of what you were capable of—a video recorded by one of the Phoenix players, your knowledge of my email address, and your knowledge of my real name. All this tells me that you have spent a significant amount of time or money on one thing—to speak to me. I'm open to a conversation. I can assure you that revenge against Phoenix is the highest priority for me. At the moment, I can't fathom how I could harm them in some way. All of my thoughts on that subject seem rather unproductive. If you have something specific in mind— I'm willing to discuss it and work to make it happen. I'm fully behind depriving them of their hegemony in Barliona.

Having written the letter, I already knew what I'd do next—I would no longer have to face Anastaria on my own. Let's see who this guy is and what his actual goals are. In any event, I could be sure that Shaman Mahan would return to Barliona in the next five minutes! Anastaria won't worry me any longer.

"Character transfer in progress," announced a pleasant feminine voice. Unlike the harsh metallic screeching that I had grown used to in the prisoner's capsule, this voice did not cause shivers to run along my spine. "Object modeling complete. Player data synchronized with capsule. Logical network initialized—Anhurs central square. Character settings activation in progress..."

A loading bar raced across my vision and I found myself looking at the settings screen. My Shaman stood against a backdrop of an enormous volcano spewing lava, smirking at the world before me, err, him. The Thricinian armor did a good job of accentuating my Shamanic class. The tip of the staff of Almis in my hands emitted a bright light. A small projection of a dragon flitted around my avatar, while behind my back, between me and the erupting mountain, stood an enormous dark-blue dragon— Draco. Only a week ago he was merely big—about three meters long, but a manageable size for a pet. Now, however, a mature, full-grown Dragon was looking out at the world from behind my back—from a height of four meters. I shudder to even guess the length of my Totem. I wonder whether he's really grown this much over the past week or whether I'm merely seeing my Totem's final form. Even in my Dragon Form, I'd look rather small beside him.

The settings screen reminded me of my 595 unallocated stat points, and recommended I turn my attention to developing my character, yet in this matter I was still in full agreement with Anastaria— the higher the level, the more complicated it'd be to grow. If there was some problem or necessity, it'd take me a second or two to pump everything into Intellect, but right now it'd be better to leave these stat points untouched. There was no pressing need.

I didn't bother looking at my settings—I already knew them by heart. But before entering Barliona, I opened the inventory tab. This listed everything that belonged to me as a player, including real estate. I'm curious to see what I'll have to work with...

There were 6.6 million gold in my inventory and 36.4 million in the clan treasury—all numbers that made my heart constrict in my chest. While I was sitting in Barliona as a prisoner, I didn't have to think of money at all—even my personal bail—the 100 million—seemed like an insurmountable sum. I couldn't believe that by selling the Eye, my castle, the Chess Set and everything else I had, I'd earn such a sum. Admittedly, the castle alone was worth much more than 100 million, but finding a buyer prepared to pay the fair price...I had my doubts that I'd be able to sell the castle for more than 50 million. People with those kind of means were snug and safe in their own castles, while newbies would hardly permit themselves to spend so much money. It was I—Richie Rich—who could afford to dump almost twenty million on hiring personnel for my castle. Back then, Barliona was my only reality, while gold was simply game currency—not real money. Now, however, with 43 million to my name that I could transfer to reality and forever forget about having to work a job, worry about bills as well as all the other myriad perils of life, I experienced a surge of confidence. I don't need to look for work, traipse around company offices and struggle to prove that my time in the mines had been a misunderstanding that would not happen again. In a sense I had accomplished one of my goals—even two—I had been released from prison and I had enough funds to live on. As a result, I am within my moral and financial right to spend several months on dealing with Phoenix the way they deserved to be dealt with.

The castle remains mine and is located—I even opened the map trying to figure out where it had ended up—right on the border with the Empire of Shadow, not far from Barliona's inland sea. It seemed that Viltrius had had quite a scare, since he'd sent Altameda to the other end of the continent. But all right—I'll wait three months and transfer the castle to a more populous place. The important thing was to make sure it was safe. In this matter, like it or not, a crew of NPCs wouldn't be enough. I'd have to recruit some players.

As a matter of fact—on the topic of players!

Checking one more time to make sure that my personal inventory no longer contained the Chess Set, the Eye or the Squidolphin Scales that I'd found in the Oceanic Abyss, I opened the 'Clan' tab. I looked at it, hummed with surprise, looked at the description one more time and hummed again because the current state of the world did not quite gel with the one I'd come to expect.

The clan currently had 4,388 players, most of whom were at the rank of Recruit. About 400 players were gatherers, another 150 headed by Eric were craftsmen, 50 were raiders headed by Clutzer, while the clan deputy—like the warden of a nuthouse—was Plinto. Neither Barsina, nor Anastaria, nor Leite were listed in the Legends; however I couldn't for the life of me explain how a clan that a week ago had at most 400 players now had four thousand whose average Level was 155. I mean, this must be some hallucination...

The next tab in the Clan section informed me that the financial mechanism that Leite had set into motion had gone on ticking like clockwork even in his absence. Altameda's vaults continued to be rented out for storage, resources and goods were being traded back and forth, and the accounts ledger informed me that 1.8 million gold had flowed into the clan last week alone. Here, it's worth noting that Leite had factored the costs of the castle and its NPC personnel into the daily clan expenses. And still the clan remained in the black!

No, but I must be hallucinating!

Clicking around the various tabs in shock and utterly befuddled since the last thing I expected was this kind of news, I finally reached the 'Properties' tab. Here I had to stop because I decided that everything that was going on was no more than the fruits of my overexcited imagination and I'm really actually lying on the floor next to my capsule, drooling deep in Dependence Level Black. How else do I explain how I managed to become the owner of a town called Bulrush in Lestran Province? According to its description, the reforms that Leite had instituted in the three villages placed in my charge had borne their fruits—during the two months, the villages had grown threefold and several days ago had passed a resolution consolidating them into one municipality. Four days ago, the provincial Governor, with whom I enjoyed Exalted status, approved the villages' petition and the three locations ceased to exist on Barliona's map. Instead, they were replaced by a town which was now one of the major locations for steel smelting in the Empire—after all, the Elma mountain range was a stone's throw away from Bulrush. The descriptive text ended at this point, and yet it was clear as day that I needed to urgently choose an official from among the locals and take care of the tax issues. And that meant the taxes due to Lestran—as well as the ones due to my clan. After all, missing out on an extra source of income...

Blast! What's been happening in Barliona during the week that I have been absent?

"Welcome to Barliona," said the settings system as soon as I pushed the 'Enter' button. I couldn't explain what was going on without being in-game, so I didn't feel like contemplating the meaning of life any further. It was time to act. The settings screen vanished and the Anhurs central square rose up right before my eyes.

Shaman Mahan was back. The time had come to seek revenge.

CHAPTER TWO
RETURN TO BARLIONA

"GREETINGS, STUDENT," said Kornik's sarcastic voice as soon as I materialized in the central square. A litany of notifications began to stream past my eyes regarding increases to my reputation with the Malabar Empire, the Shamanic Council, the Emperor, the Governor of Lestran and a whole bunch of other NPCs. My castle was in a different location, I needed to choose a head of the settlement in my charge, the Guardian of my Castle's new location was waiting for me to pay taxes for using his lands...There were so many notifications that I didn't even have time to read them meaningfully enough to react.

"Greetings, teacher," I replied, swiping away the wall of text blocking my sight. I'll deal with them later.

"Come with me. They're expecting you," Kornik held out a green paw.

"Who?" I couldn't help but ask and only then understood that another class-specific scenario was awaiting my attention. If the Council wishes to meet with me, then as soon as I enter the game, a script is launched informing me that the Shamans have already been in session an entire week, deliberating how best to describe the new quest I had to do. I wish I knew what it was.

"Whoever," quipped the goblin and took me by the hand to whisk me away. Before we left the square however, I managed to hear: "Why that's Mahan! He's the one who..."

It was only upon reaching the Astral Plane that I realized that I didn't feel a thing. The cold light and sweltering abyss that made me writhe every time I'd been here earlier, were no longer there. The pressure I felt from the Supreme Spirits' presence was gone too—as well as the subconscious terror of slipping from the dividing line and hurtling deep into the embrace of the light or the shadow. I was playing with the sensory filter all the way up and I couldn't say that I was pleased with it. I got the impression that some part of me was missing—like it had been turned off because it was unnecessary, and yet it was this part that completed my being. I'd make sure to look into this issue tomorrow and see whether I could turn off the sensory filter entirely. I really wouldn't want to play with these kind of settings.

"SHAMAN!" thundered the darkness and the air around my avatar froze, triggering a system notification about a slight amount of damage taken from the heat. Before I didn't even notice this, figuring the darkness was 'nice' in that it saved me from the freezing light, but now I understood that these two elements could not be 'nice' by definition. They were the Imitators of the gods for whom both players and NPCs were hardly more than bugs. "WE HAVE BEEN MONITORING YOUR PROGRESS, SHAMAN!"

"Oh Supreme Spirits," I replied respectfully, slightly bowing my head. I had assumed that I was being taken to a council session, since it never occurred to me that Kornik could act as the messenger for the Supreme Spirits. "You wished to see me?"

"WRONG QUESTION! WE HAVE BEEN MONITORING YOUR PROGRESS, SHAMAN!" the Spirits repeated, evidently wishing me to play the 'guess the song based on one note' game. As a prisoner, these kind of encounters with their constant allusions and hints drove me nuts, so now, no longer under any restrictions, I decided to test the degree of my freedom.

"The Spirits do not wish to speak with me?" I raised an eyebrow inquisitively, focusing my gaze right between the spots of light and dark. "Why am I here then?"

"WRONG QUESTION! WE HAVE BEEN MONITORING YOUR PROGRESS, SHAMAN!" The Spirits growled once again and a notification appeared informing me that I'd lost 50% of my Hit Points. If it weren't for my sensory filter, that would have really hurt!

My tongue wanted to let slip another irrelevant question, but I decided to use my brain and think things over a bit. No one could guarantee that, goaded a third time, the Spirits wouldn't send me to respawn. Nothing bad would happen of course, but I wouldn't find out why they were so eager to see me. I mean, I have to know! If they want me to ask them a question—I figured this from their first two statements—I need to figure out what it was.

It must be somehow related to a game process, since NPCs do not deal with anything beyond the game, and therefore it should be related to Shamanism, it should be related to me and it should be related to my Way. Parsing several options in my head, I asked the dumbest of the questions that occurred to me:

"What Totem did Fleita choose?"

Boom! A white glow wrapped me from all sides as if a bright sun had exploded at my feet and for an instant I lost my sense of spatial orientation. When my eyes could again focus on the gray border between the two spheres, the Supreme Spirits began to speak:

"YOU HAVE COMPLETED ALL YOUR TRIALS! FROM NOW ON AND HENCEFORTH YOU ARE A HARBINGER! YOU SUCCEEDED IN TRAINING A WORTHY SHAMAN!"

Quest completed: 'The Way of the Shaman. Step 4. Training.'

Quest completed: 'The Way of the Shaman. Step 5. The Student.'

Once again, my vision filled with a tidy list of notifications announcing that I had earned new skills that I would have to examine in more detail later. An icon with the tooltip 'Blink' and an image of a portal appeared right in front of me. Reading the description brought a satisfied smile to my face: 'Activating this ability will teleport you to the selected location of the continent. The desired coordinates may be entered by...'

Here followed a long text about how I needed to set up my Blink, the number of players I could teleport with me, the cooldown duration, and the restriction against blinking into the new Shadow Empire as well as various other information which—once again when I had time—I would read carefully later.

"WE ARE FREEING YOU FROM YOUR TOTEM AND GRANTING HIM THE MAXIMUM POSSIBLE LEVEL AS YOUR PET. HENCEFORTH YOU CAN SUMMON HIM WITHOUT ANY RESTRICTIONS OF DURATION OR LOSS OF LEVEL IN THE EVENT OF HIS DEMISE. IN VIEW OF YOUR TOTEM'S UNIQUE HISTORY, WE RETURN TO HIM HIS MEMORY AND REINSTATE HIM AS A FULL-FLEDGED DRAGON."

"And he remains your brother," came the familiar voice causing me to turn. An enormous, four-meter long, dark blue dragon, whom I'd already seen in the game's launch screen was standing several steps before me, smiling widely with his two rows of sharp fangs. "I remember it all now!"

"So what Totem did Fleita choose?" I repeated my question over the surging wave of ecstasy in my chest. I was a Harbinger at last! I could blink all over our continent like some inter-dimensional cricket. I no longer had to splurge vast sums on scrolls of teleport! I could visit neighboring continents by blinking to their embassies! This...this was really something!

"A DRAGON!" announced the Supremes. "SHE SELECTED A DRAGON!"

My jaw almost hit the floor at the news. Fleita chose a Dragon? But how?!

"Thank you, oh Supreme Spirits, for initiating my student into the order of Harbingers. His time had come," said Kornik, barely suppressing his laughter. Considering that even Draco was cracking up, the look of bafflement on my face must have been all too evident.

"Will you blink on your own, or do I need to hold your hand like a little boy?" The goblin went on having his fun—pulling me from my deep shock. The one week I had been absent really had seen some miracles happen in the game. What'll happen if I'm absent for a month? Maybe they'd make me Emperor in absentia?

Opening my settings, I copied the castle's coordinates and pasted them into the 'Blink' input field. I took a breath and pressed the icon, dragging it while I was at it to the side—I didn't want it in front of me the entire time. The surrounding world wavered as if I had stepped through a portal, but a second later everything fell into place and I found myself standing in Altameda's main hall. That was also the first time I'd left the Astral Plane on my own two legs, instead of being kicked out of it by the Supreme Spirits of the Higher and Lower Worlds. It was a nice change, what can I say...

"Master!" sounded Viltrius' joyous yelp as the happy goblin appeared beside me, fiddling with his ears in his joy. "The Master has returned!"

"That's right. I'm back. Draco," I turned to the enormous Dragon who'd teleported to Altameda with me and was now taking up all the space in the hall, "are you always going to be so...uh...large?"

"Don't whine," grinned my former Totem and in an instant turned into a much smaller dragon, just a little bigger than what he had been as a hatchling. "Is that better?"

"That's perfect," I tussled Draco's nape automatically as if he were some large, gentle dog that I hadn't seen in a long while.

Buff received: 'A friend's joy.' +1% to all main stats for 24 hours.

"I missed you too," I smiled and gave Draco a friendly hug. No really—Barliona is quite the social game—unlike other players, if the NPCs love you, then they love you as sincerely as their AI permits it. In that sense, Barliona is perfect...

"Two Dragons embracing," sounded Kornik's voice—and, simultaneously with it, Viltrius' panicked exclamation:

"Master, I cannot prohibit him from entering the castle! My authorization is insufficient!"

My majordomo really sounded terrified, which made sense considering that he believed himself the only sentient in the entire world besides me who had power over the castle. Kornik's uninvited appearance, however, had dispelled my majordomo's illusions about the hierarchy of Barliona, giving rise to pure panic in Viltrius' very soul. I'll need to play around with the castle's settings to grant the goblin more powers—it really was no good that Harbingers could teleport in here whenever they felt like it. Plus there was the question of how Kornik had managed to discover Altameda's coordinates...

"Next time you blink, make sure to close the portal behind yourself," explained Kornik. Either I'd asked my question out loud or it was obviously imprinted on my face. "And by the way, what are you standing there for gaping? I thought that you had a million questions for me. The one time in my existence that I actually want to spend ten minutes answering your questions and there you are just standing wondering how I managed to get here. What person in his right mind would call you a Shaman after that?"

"How did Fleita get a Dragon?" I asked, once the words 'spend ten minutes' had properly sunk in.

"I'd like to say 'just like that' but it wouldn't be true. She completed her trial like no one ever has. To be fair, there'd never been a Zombie Shaman to attempt it...But that's not the point. When she re-enters this world," (these words came as a great surprise to me, since NPCs do their utmost to ignore the players' constant absences in the game) "you can ask her yourself about how she kept the wolf and calf alive, how she erected the bridge across the pit and demolished the statutes. Having earned the right to select a Totem, she went through all the available options, turned around without choosing anything, stepped out to Prontho and the Supreme Air Spirit and announced 'I want a Dragon.' I know now why you accepted her as your student—you wanted to pay us back for everything. With a Shaman like that, we'll have fun times ahead of us indeed."

"And so she was granted the Dragon?" I prompted Kornik, who'd fallen silent.

"Well try and not give to her! We had to take her to Renox, explain the situation—one of his older Dragons was just then getting ready to leave this world, so they convinced him not to and to be reborn again as a Totem. I should mention that one of his limbs was pretty hurt anyway, so in general...Well, no matter! Now your student has a Dragon and she's busy training him. And she's not dragging her heels about her own progress either—are you aware that your student is about to become a Great Shaman? And it's only been three days since she became an Elemental Shaman!"

"They spent a long time asking me what it's like being a Totem," Draco offered his two cents, not giving me the chance to open my mouth in astonishment. Fleita was about to become a Great Shaman? Mind-boggling! "And so Aquarius (that's the name he chose for himself) died in his old form and became the Zombie's Totem."

"Which is all a bit much," said Kornik.

"Why?" I went on inquiring.

"Because Zombies can't have normal Dragons," Kornik explained. "They don't have the permission. So I think when he gets his memory back, old Aquarius will be in for a surprise."

"Fleita's Totem isn't an ordinary Dragon," Draco said. "Fleita's Totem is an Undead Bone Dragon. There have only been seven such creatures in Barliona's history, and Aquarius is number eight. Considering that he is effectively a singular creature that other Dragons are terrified of...Well basically it's not only the Shamans who'll have some fun once Fleita will become a Harbinger—it'll be a ride for us too."

"And she certainly will become one eventually," I completed the thought. "She's my student after all..."

"That's what I'm talking about..." Kornik nodded. "All right, you two figure stuff out over here. If you need anything, you know how to find me. Just remember to close the portal after you blink, otherwise anyone who wishes can follow you..."

"Master, the trespasser..." squealed Viltrius as soon as Kornik vanished, reminding me that it'd be a good idea to protect the castle from such visitors. No, I won't do it just because of Kornik, but after all he's not the only Harbinger in Barliona. Geranika could do the same, and we were right beside his Empire.

"What do I need to do in order to make it so you can block visits from any sentient, including a god?" I asked the majordomo.

"I have to," Viltrius began, when suddenly his green face went chalk white and the goblin collapsed to the floor.

"Leave us," sounded a familiar voice, addressing my majordomo and Totem.

"All right, brother. I'm going to go see our father. If you need me, summon away," Draco said and dissolved into thin air. Viltrius followed him without bothering to get up off the floor. If he had already grown accustomed to my conversations with Heralds and even Emperors, then the appearance of a goddess was an even greater shock.

"Greetings, oh Eluna," I said, standing up from my chair and bowing to my visitor. Even though we had no relationship formally, I was nevertheless the subject of the Supreme Spirits of the Higher and Lower Worlds and as such it would be idiotic of me to disregard the official head of Barliona's pantheon of 'light'. As they say in Barliona, all gods are equal, but Eluna is more equal than others. And that's not a mere formality either...

"I think that's the first time since we've met that you've looked me in the eyes instead of studying my sandals," smiled the goddess.

"Times change," I replied philosophically, noting the beauty of the woman standing before me. I guess Eluna didn't have an official appearance, since I didn't recall her looking like this—every time she appears to a player, the system processes what the player wants to see and generates a new avatar for the Imitator. The players like to obsess over the goddess's perfection, compose verses in her name, go mad for her and generally behave like a bunch of fools. I'd probably be doing the same if it weren't for the fact that, this time, Eluna had appeared to me in the guise of Anastaria. A perfect copy of the woman I loved and, judging by the system's choice in the matter, continued to love. What is this—some form of manipulation?

"Eluna, before we continue our conversation, I'd like to ask you—do you have an appearance that could be considered 'natural?' I'm happy of course that you try to appear perfect for everyone, but I'd like to speak to the real you instead of a form of you. Forgive my impudence, but..."

"Shaman, Shaman," said the goddess smiling and the image of Anastaria imprinted on her face began to waver and change. "In times gone by, you could be sent to Tartarus for such words."

"Times change," I repeated and barely contained a cry of surprise—beside me stood a woman from the Blessed Visage of Eluna—a detail from the chain I'd crafted back in Beatwick. An ordinary, everyday, pleasant and smiling woman with a turned up nose and several extra kilos in her hips.

"Is that better?" Eluna asked, adjusting her clothes as well and turning them into something resembling a Greek tunic.

"A little," I managed, surprised at my earlier assumption that Eluna shouldn't match her appearance. It was so self-evident now! "You wished to see me?" I asked the goddess, inviting her to sit on my throne. By the way, I will need to order Viltrius to add some more chairs in my throne room—besides my rocking chair and the throne, there weren't any places to sit here.

"That's right, I did," nodded the goddess. "I do not want you to save Renox..."

The goddess had uttered a single sentence but she trailed off and stared silently at the fire in the fireplace. My initial reaction was a desire to argue that Renox was my father and I simply could not allow him to pass away before it was his time. However, I restrained myself and tried first to answer the great universal question of 'Why?'

First of all, the goddess had come to me personally—and I made sure to check that I didn't enjoy Exalted status with her and my Attractiveness with her was at a mere 57. Consequently, the first why is why she came to me herself instead of sending a messenger through, say, Elizabeth? Formally speaking, Eluna is not my goddess. The second why is why I'm not allowed to save Renox. Barliona had recently acquired a new Dragon—I'm thinking of Fleita here—and yet Renox, who remained unknown to most players, still had to depart. The Corp wouldn't destroy an NPC of his level without good reason—consequently there had to be some larger plan behind this choice. The third why is why...Wait! Eluna doesn't want me to save Renox! She didn't say that she doesn't want Renox to be saved in general—she merely doesn't want me to do it! Why? The only answer that comes to mind is that something will happen during my attempt to save him. Something that will affect me as a player. Erm...I don't think I put that well—something that will affect my character and make the game difficult for me. What could that be? The obvious answer was Geranika. Perhaps he has managed to acquire Rogzar's Crystal in some manner and if the player receives it, then he can kiss his character goodbye. Although—this is pure idiocy. The devs would never pull something like this. If for instance Anastaria was saddled with such an item, she'd instantly raise hell demanding that the Corporation grant her a quest to destroy the item. Actually, while I'm on the topic, I really like this idea—of slipping an item like Rogzar's Crystal into her bag. That would certainly make her squirm. I need to speak with Geranika.

"What could happen to me in Armard?" I asked and judging by Eluna's smile guessed her thoughts pretty accurately.

"You saw Rogzar's Crystal," said the goddess, "so you can appreciate what I'm talking about here. Rogzar was unique and the crystal was one of a kind as well, but Geranika has other similar crystals."

"Big deal, so I'll have to walk slowly," I smiled, and yet Eluna's melancholy smile indicated to me that her warning wasn't mere words. "Or not..?"

"Rogzar's Crystal is the weakest of the weapons in the arsenal of the Lord of Shadow," said the goddess. "The three other crystals are much more terrifying and valuable—they are called the Petrified Tears of Harrashess's Hate. Do I need to explain to you who that is?"

"The Patriarch already told me," I replied, gradually beginning to understand the gravity of the situation. The Tears of the dark son of Barliona's

Creator were a lethal thing even in name alone.

"A Tear of Hate has practically the same properties as Rogzar's Crystal—it cannot be transferred, dropped, broken or destroyed...But, unlike the item you're familiar with, the Tears block all abilities. All of them...You are the main foe of the Lord of Shadow, who was even kind to the Emperor when he made a show of handing him the sheath to the dagger. But when it comes to you, he's not playing around. I know for certain that the Tears of Hate have been activated because the entire magical ether shuddered from a wave of pain and hate emitted by these crystals. This means that they can now be given to some other sentient and then the victim will never be able to rid himself of them. You won't be able to use your abilities—none of them, including the summoning of your Totem. Shaman Mahan will die forever, becoming simply Mahan. I cannot interfere with the events of this world directly. Even this warning that I'm giving you will carry enormous penalties for me from Barliona, but you and Anastaria are important to me. I really do not want to lose you two. Think about these words, Shaman. If you go to Armard, Geranika will find a way to burden you with the Tear..."

Having finished her speech, the goddess dissolved into the air, leaving me deep in contemplation.

This isn't possible!

The Corporation would never introduce some crystal—even in the form of a Tear—that would ruin the game for a player. After all, the most a player can even be restrained for is one hour and repeated deaths lead to the 'anti-death' status in which the player is immune from other players' damage, so the possibility that a player's avatar is completely incapacitated forever is pure nonsense. An NPC sure, but not a player character. Otherwise the Corporation would be sued in a jiffy...And yet! The goddess didn't simply stop by for a visit! She's not some ordinary NPC with an average Imitator—she is one of the game's key characters and any warning from her is equivalent to a warning straight from the devs—the Tears are real, they exist and there is a danger I'll receive one.

Damn them all!

Dear Game Administrators,

Just now, at (<System_TimeStamp>), I had the pleasure of speaking with an NPC playing the role of Goddess Eluna who told me something very interesting. I was informed that...

Please explain the principles underpinning the Tear, the reasons for its appearance and how this item might affect my character.

Once my email received the 'Received for processing' status, I called for my goblin:

"Viltrius!"

"Yes, Master!" The castle's majordomo appeared beside me in a flash. I don't know what algorithms had been activated but currently this little green goblin was standing before me as straight as a nail, as if he was trying to show me how courageous he was. And this is supposed to be the majordomo of a Level 25 castle?

"Tell me what needs to be done to ensure that you have full powers over this castle. So that we don't receive any uninvited guests. I want you to immediately whitelist Kornik, Prontho and Fleita. Those three are allowed to visit Altameda. But the others, just like that Archdemon who showed up to litigate for our portal demon, must only have access to the castle if you grant it to them. I'm listening!"

"In order for me to have full control of the castle, the castle must contain at least three hobgoblins (though five is ideal), each of which shall have his own territory to guard. Only these creatures can block visitors from entering their territories, be they Harbinger or deity. However..."

As Viltrius was speaking, I was already digging around the castle's settings, looking for the hobgoblins section. If I had to hire several NPCs to ensure my safety, then...What the hell is this?!

"However, this cannot be done at the moment," Viltrius continued in a guilty tone of voice. "Your spouse stored four alganides in the castle—and hobgoblins are allergic to this mineral and refuse to enter a castle that contains it."

The button for hiring the hobgoblins, which were medium-sized furry creatures of indeterminate gender dressed in red shirts, was grayed-out. Even despite the annual cost of a hundred thousand for each hobgoblin, I was ready to hire five, but the system wouldn't let me do that...

"What is algana-what-cha-ma-call-it?" I asked the goblin.

"Alganide is a mineral mined deep in the Elma Mountains. It is used in Alchemy. It is very toxic and it emits a specific odor that hobgoblins can't stand."

"And this mineral is somewhere in the castle? Or in our vaults?"

"In the castle. It is in Anastaria's personal chamber. She brought a chest there, placed it in the center of the room and forbade me from touching it. It is that chest that contains the alganide..."

"I see. Well, let's go take a look at this chest then," I offered, getting up from my beloved rocking chair.

"Master," Viltrius squeaked once again, looking at me guiltily. "That's not possible."

"What do you mean it's not possible?" I sat back down from surprise. "You have unrestricted access to the entire castle. I own this place, remember? What could be off limits to us in Altameda?"

"The private chamber of Mistress Anastaria as

well as Master Plinto—these are both areas that you may not enter without their permission. Such are the rules of tripartite ownership."

"WHAT?! Where does it say that? Who came up with these rules? I am the rightful owner of Altameda and only I can decide who can and who cannot enter its rooms! Show me!"

The Goblin was getting ready to squeak something about the need to respect property rights, but I wasn't listening to him anymore. Anastaria and Plinto have personal chambers that I can't enter? Like hell! Shut everything down. Tear the rooms out by their roots and toss them over the castle walls. This is my territory!

"I forbid you from touching that chest!" No sooner had I burst into the room than a thought from Anastaria burst into my head. The good thing was that my rage at the thought that the girl still had something of hers in my castle and, moreover, that I couldn't touch this thing was so immense that I didn't even consider how I should respond to her. Earlier, back in reality, I wanted to just ignore her, then blow her off, then yell at her, then ignore her again and, finally, choosing none of the above, I had entered Barliona hoping to figure it out when it came up—and yet now I didn't feel like reflecting at all. What's the difference how I spoke with Anastaria if it was her fault that I couldn't hire the hobgoblins I needed?

"Oh and welcome back, by the way," the girl

added.

"*No way, this castle is mine! You can take all your junk with you!*"

"*You're mistaken, my dear, that castle is OURS. I am just as much its owner as you or Plinto. So get out of my room and forget it even exists. I won't allow you to bar me from Altameda.*"

"What's going on here?" I exclaimed as my hands passed through the chest like it didn't even exist. Smack dab in the middle of a small room with one window—furnished with nothing but a simple bed and a rug—stood a locked chest which was inaccessible to me. What was more was that Anastaria had been automatically warned when I broke into her room! That means there's some alarm here, notifying her of any intruders.

"Viltrius!"

"Yes, Master," said the goblin, pressing his ears to his head. I guess I seem pretty terrifying right now, if my poor majordomo is this scared of me.

"How did Anastaria find out that I entered her room?" I asked, trying to calm my nerves and speak normally. It wasn't the NPC's fault that Anastaria had thought of installing this thing on the lock, so I couldn't blame my servant.

"The properties of a personal chamber are basically no different than that of a Bank of Barliona. As the owner, you may enter, but you can't do anything else without permission from the room's owner."

"How can I strike Anastaria and Plinto from the list of owners?"

"We can't. Even the Emperor cannot do this. Although..."

"What?"

"You can buy out their shares of ownership. If they sell them to you officially, you'll become the sole owner of Altameda."

"What do you mean their shares?" I asked, stunned. "Altameda belongs to me!"

"That's not entirely accurate," Viltrius corrected me. "The Emperor did grant you exclusive ownership; however, as soon as you married Anastaria, under the laws of the Aristocracy, 10% of your property passed to Anastaria. You are the rightful owner of the castle and can decide where it teleports to, but Anastaria may also do whatever she wants with her territory. Aside from selling it to another sentient. The same goes for Plinto. Your blood brother also owns 10% of the castle's territory and if he showed up at the castle's gates, I could not bar him from entering. They're both owners too! Accordingly, if you wish to take full ownership of the castle, you must buy out the shares of the other owners. This is stated in the Code as well."

Well I'll be! In order to complete a quest, I gifted Anastaria and Plinto 10% of the castle. Opening the castle's properties, I launched the calculation for assessing the castle's value and couldn't help but whistle to myself when it was complete—if it were built from scratch, Altameda would have cost me 450 million gold! In my fit of largess, I had given 90 million worth of equity to two players, one of whom had been using me all along! I suppose I need to have a careful chat with the other too...What the hell is going on?!

STOP!

Take a deep breath and activate that part of the body that's responsible for reason. In humans that's typically the brain. In actual fact my largess and my lovely existence on this planet isn't what's at stake here. That's a mere consequence. What should be much more interesting is the cause of all these events—what scared the Corporation so much that it decided to gift an ordinary prisoner like me a castle worth 450 million gold? It's almost as surprising why this question hadn't occurred to me since I got the castle. Did the Corporation people really fail to consider that I might sell the castle, even if only piecemeal, pay for my release and transfer all the money out to reality? Missteps like this don't just happen on their own! This isn't some fairy tale! In which case, the question is why?

Actually, 'why' seems to be the word of the day.

"Viltrius, could you explain to me how the clan has so many members?" I asked the goblin, after blinking back into the main hall. In addition to the standard coordinates input field, the Blink spell also came with another interesting feature: It allowed me to select a specific point on a 3D model of the area around me, with a radius of several kilometers, to teleport to. Furthermore, this interface scaled very smoothly and was a cinch to navigate, and therefore also gave me the chance to study Altameda from 'within.' Seeing yet another notification in the clan chat, I remembered my surprise from the huge number of people who'd suddenly appeared in the castle and therefore decided to put aside the issue of the castle's ownership and Anastaria's room and ask Viltrius some questions.

"I don't know, Master. When Plinto became the clan deputy, he began to recruit Free Citizens..."

"Hold up. How did Plinto become deputy?"

"Well, he's not technically the deputy. He's more of an acting deputy," Viltrius began to explain. "According the Charter of the Legends of Barliona, which Clutzer and Anastaria drew up, the clan cannot exist more than three days without a deputy, a treasurer and a raid leader. When Barsina, Leite and Magdey left the Legends of Barliona and when you failed to transfer their duties to yourself, the issue of disbanding the clan came up. That's in the Charter too. So a general meeting was held and the meeting decided to make Plinto the acting deputy. Clutzer became the raid leader and Uruk became the treasurer."

"Who the hell is Uruk?"

"One of the Free Citizens who used to work for Leite in the auctions department."

"I see..." I shook my head with displeasure, opened the Charter and read it carefully, focusing on the clauses that the goblin had mentioned. Yeeeah...You really do have to trust people a lot to allow something like this to happen. The Clan Charter, which we rewrote after the clan changed its name—or more precisely which Clutzer and Anastaria rewrote—really did contain several clauses about filling required positions. Why does everything have to be so crappy?!

"I'll be back in a bit," I told Viltrius, opened my map, looked up the Anhurs coordinates and blinked to the capital. It was time to visit the guild registrar and take complete control of the clan. I can't have random players named Uruk managing my clan's treasury.

"Mahan, Hello!" I had barely assumed the duties of raid leader when Clutzer called me.

"Hi," I replied dryly, not yet sure how I should talk to this person. Clutzer was one of the ones who plotted against me with Phoenix, so it'd be foolish on his part to imagine that I'd meet him with open arms. In fact, he's probably better off watching his jaw in case my fist found it.

"I saw you returned to the game but didn't want to bother you immediately. However, since you're adjusting the clan duties, you must have time. Can you spare me several minutes? I'm at the Golden Horseshoe. Can we chat?"

"Let's chat," I replied. "I'll be there in a few minutes."

There was no point in avoiding my problems: They need to be solved right away or not solved at all. In all honesty, there's nothing for me to discuss with the Rogue—everything he had to tell me, he'd already said to me back there on the plateau in front of the Creator's Tomb. So the most precise move was to kick him out of the clan—and yet something kept me from going through with this. I wanted to look him in the eyes, even if they were just the eyes of his avatar. I wanted to look at him and ask, 'Why'd you do it?' Mulling things over a bit, I reached for my amulet and made a call. I really didn't want to go to the meeting on my own, since I couldn't be sure that I wouldn't attack Clutzer with my fists—I still had a week-and a half before the happy moment when I'd get my Spirits back.

"Yo..." came Plinto's voice. "Whatcha want?"

"Hi, Plinto. This is Mahan. I'll be waiting for you at the entrance of the Golden Horseshoe in two minutes."

"Uh...you want me to come downstairs and show you to our table?" the Rogue countered sarcastically. "We've been waiting for you two hours already. Why don't you get a move on?"

"We?"

"Oh gawd, why is everything so difficult with you? Do I really need to come down, or will you come up on your own?"

"All right, all right. Relax. I'll be up in a second."

I hung up the amulet and hummed to myself. So they were already waiting for me. Clutzer really deserves his fame as an analyst—he understands perfectly well that, one on one, our meeting won't go very well. So he invited Plinto. Hmm once again...But really, what a pair those two are! No doubt they had set up an alarm to notify them when I reentered the game and all this time they were just giving me the space to do what I needed. And it's only when I turned my attention to the clan that they decided to talk. Well, if it was time then it was time. I'm always ready to talk.

"*Are you still here, Dan?*" Stacey's thought suddenly popped into my head, forcing me to stop and clench my fist. What the hell was it now? My first interaction with Anastaria had occurred under emotionally trying circumstances, so I hadn't really felt anything except anger. Now, however, a wave of unvarnished hate all but flooded me from head to toe. If she showed up beside me—I'd kill her!

"*I'm still here, kitten,*" I replied as softly as possible. I couldn't allow myself to show Stacey my anger, hate or desire to strangle her. She didn't deserve to know my true feelings. And who cares what she'll think about me talking to her like this. From now on, this is the only way I'll speak with her.

"*Oh my darling, it's so lovely to speak with you again!*" Anastaria immediately caught on. "*Listen—how are the Legends doing? I heard that my little Clutzer's been recruiting people left and right, is that true? Have you all decided to rebuild the ruins?*"

"*You know, the Legends are doing just fine, thanks to your assistance. As for the ruins, when are you going to give that Chess Set back to me kitten? The Eye too—I wouldn't mind seeing that again.*"

"*What Chess Set, love? I don't believe I recall what you're talking about.*"

"*No matter! When we meet, I'll make sure to remind you.*" I avoided hanging up by some miracle. That bitch is having her fun too! "*What about you? How are you?*"

"*Not bad, not bad. Listen, what am I even talking about—we should meet up tomorrow! I've filed for divorce and you have to attend the ceremony. So a Herald will come for you tomorrow. I just wanted to warn you in advance. Who knows, maybe you'll be busy or something...It's scheduled for two o'clock server time. Anyway, that's it. Talk to you later! Kisses, my beloved Shaman.*"

"*Excellent, wonderful, until tomorrow,*" I grunted. There weren't any more messages from Anastaria, yet my mind had turned into an enormous hippodrome around which my thoughts raced like horses.

Until this conversation, I really had planned on

breaking all ties with Anastaria so that there wouldn't be anything that bound me to her, but now that she broached the topic herself, I wanted to hold on to our marriage with everything I had. That damn premonition of mine, suddenly awaking for the first time in several days, began to scream that under no condition could I become a divorced Earl. I'll have to dig through all the relevant laws of Barliona to figure out before tomorrow's meeting what will happen in the event of a divorce, in the event of refusing the divorce and in the event of even showing up to begin with...It wasn't for nothing that back in Narlak, I'd received the *A Noble & Healthy Lifestyle Companion*— a tome expounding all the laws and regulations of being a member of the aristocracy. Even if it was two thousand pages long, I should have time to figure out the important items. What if during the divorce proceedings, half of my property, including Altameda, would be given to Anastaria? Did I need that? No! So I'll chat with Clutzer and Plinto right now and then go back to Altameda. I'll abandon all the chores I've begun and focus on reading that book—and I won't leave the game until I figure out what I am entitled to as an Earl and what my duties are. I don't have much time—tomorrow and two days. And I'm not about to duck the meeting either—the time had come for me to change from a player who runs around a lot to a player who reads and makes his decisions objectively and judiciously.

"Please come in. You are expected," said the host, helpfully opening the front door and inviting me into the Golden Horseshoe. Once upon a time the tavern's owner used to stand here, but over the years he ceased to greet his guests personally and simply hired a player to do it. Despite the fact that it would be much cheaper for him to employ an NPC for the job, the goblin owner rejected this option: According to him, NPCs would never work in the Golden Horseshoes. Full stop!

"Would you like to order now or would you like to see the menu?" the server asked politely. Clutzer, Plinto and Eric waited silently while I made my decision. I managed to notice that they hadn't spent the last week sitting by idly—Clutzer was sparkling at Level 204, Eric was now a Master of Malabar, and Plinto boasted the red badge of a PK-er. All three remained silent as I sat down at the table, waiting for me to begin—but I too stayed silent. I nodded each one a greeting and turned to the server.

"Dish du jour and a Tartarus ale."

Having taken my order, the server left, leaving me on my own with my three former companions. Why do I say former? Because in this world, my only remaining companion was Draco. Everyone else is an acquaintance. That's enough for me.

"I suggest we don't beat around the bush," I began, sitting down, "and get to the topic at hand immediately. First of all, a question—did all three of you know what would happen on the plateau?"

"No, only I did," replied Clutzer. "I was the only one who participated in designing the plan. The others weren't in the know. They are prepared to swear an oath to the Emperor about this."

"An oath which doesn't mean anything to me if for instance knowledge of the plan was passed along out in reality," I smirked bitterly.

"That's true. You know, I wanted to meet you one on one originally, but later I understood that for you, I'll always be a member of Phoenix and it doesn't matter how much I swear to the contrary. That's normal and I don't expect any trust from you. But we made a mistake that we want to correct, so we stayed in the clan and began to recruit people. I have several ideas and I'd like you to listen to them. You can make your decisions later—for now, just listen..."

Taking a gulp of water, Clutzer waited for the server to place the plates of food before us and leave the room before continuing:

"First of all, let's go through the reasons for why and how everything was done. After that, I'll go through our options...As I already told you, I was the one who originally brought the three of us to Phoenix. I just didn't believe that a prisoner in this game could accomplish anything. It's never happened before, so I figured it'd never happen. So we joined Phoenix and began to wait for you..."

Clutzer rehashed his captivating tale about the

young analyst's entry to Phoenix and about how he went from being a simple advisor to one of the authors of a vast global strategy to acquire the Chess Set of Karmadont. In effect, he didn't tell me anything new, but I made a second mental checkmark—hearing the story for the second time no longer made me want to destroy the world. Even when he broached the subject of Anastaria, I felt no urge to tear her apart into little bits and pieces. Although—it's completely plausible that this was due to the tactic I had concocted for speaking with her. Who knows?

"That was before you left the game. Now, about what happened afterward," Clutzer went on. "Here's a link to the video. You really need to watch it."

I wasn't interested in letting them know that I knew what happened after I signed out of the game, so I opened the trade window, loaded the video file and watched the opening of the Tomb once again. There were the angels and there was Anastaria speaking with them...

Hold on...

No one can see right now what I'm looking at and in what sequence, so they think that I'm paralyzed with the shock of this revelation—and yet, I was trying my hardest to remember the angle from which I'd watched this same scene earlier. The current video was clearly taken by Clutzer, since I could hear his commentary. I was however interested in something else entirely—who had recorded the clip that I'd seen?

I couldn't care less what my companions thought, so I signed out of Barliona, got out of my cocoon, opened the link I received in my email earlier, found Clutzer, approximated where the cameraman must have been and returned to the game. Before making deals with unknown strangers, I'd like to have an idea of what resources they had at their disposal.

What can I say...When I spied who must have recorded the first video—in terms of deduction and geometry—my eyes popped out of their sockets. After all, I was perfectly familiar with this player—it was Exodus, one of the Hunters of Phoenix. I finished watching Clutzer's video, which was longer than Exodus' and which documented how Plinto went on to kill everyone on the plateau, I located the frame in which you could most clearly see the spy and paused the video.

The Level 302 Hunter, as far as I recalled, was either the leader of Phoenix's Hunters or someone very closely placed to that role. In the Dark Forest he had proven himself a good player, since he was about the only ranged fighter who could survive in seemingly any situation, so it was now difficult to accept the fact that he was the one who had shot video. Over the past week, I had lost my faith in miracles and now one thing was clear: Either this was a set-up and Exodus' video was shot for personal use and later stolen, or I was missing something important. In any event, it's now evident that I have to meet this mysterious stranger. I'll wait for a reply to my letter and see what he has to offer.

"Very nice," I quipped, letting everyone know that I'd watched the video. Fifteen minutes had passed since I opened it, and it wasn't nice to keep people waiting. "In other words they needed a deputy to enter the Tomb, and the plan was to send me to the mines..."

"That's precisely why we're here," Clutzer went on. "And this is also why the clan has so many members. We really didn't want you to return to the game and disband the clan—and none of us doubted that you would return eventually. Even if you'd kicked everyone out and remained the only member, the clan would cease to exist. And the Charter doesn't matter here—that can always be revised after all. What matters is that Phoenix would win and the Legends of Barliona would be gone."

"Are you trying to say that you began recruiting people so that I'd feel socially awkward kicking everyone out and ultimately do what you all wanted— and not what I wanted?" I asked sarcastically. As much as I disliked it, Clutzer was right: My original plan was to remain in the Legends on my own. Now, however, when there were so many people in it...I wasn't so sure...

"Among other things," the Rogue admitted sincerely. "You see, that's not all that we have to show you. Several days ago, Anastaria gave an interview which they published on Phoenix's site."

"I've already seen it," I cut Clutzer off. "Which is why I'm all the more surprised by the size of the clan now. After all, Shaman Mahan betrayed his players and became the villain of Barliona. If there's anyone who wants to join me, then either he's stupid or he's a white knight who wants to prove Stacey right and lock me up behind bars."

"You don't know people very well, Mahan, or else you forget your status..."

"My status?" I frowned, completely lost about what Clutzer was getting at.

"That's right—your status. You are Shaman Mahan, the central hero of two feature-length movies—and a positive hero at that! A player who has a unique castle, unique projections and immense luck when it comes to the game's scenarios. The guards of Anhurs still speak of your wedding with Anastaria with awe. No one had done so much damage to the capital before. And here you believe that the players will trust Anastaria in this matter? We didn't sit around twiddling our thumbs this entire time either— the forums are currently discussing an alternate version of Anastaria's account, in which you two had a serious quarrel, you left because of a broken heart and are now in the middle of a drinking binge. An ordinary old drinking binge, which any ordinary person would go on. You'll have to forgive us—we couldn't think of anything better. But then again people love their dramas and a quarrel between two virtual spouses is much more plausible, pleasant, and ordinary than what happened in actual fact. And yet, everyone awaits your return. I've already had about seven news agencies contact me today, begging for an interview—it's not like you check your mail. You're a celebrity Mahan, whether you like it or not. So everything depends exclusively on you, or more precisely on what you intend to do."

"All right, fine. But what are these two here for?" I asked, indicating Eric and Plinto. I could hardly believe the latter's silence, yet Plinto hadn't opened his mouth once like a well-disciplined boy. This wasn't the Rogue I knew.

"Oh, they're just extras. I figured that, one on one, our meeting would take a different turn. After all, I'm Anastaria's creature, her right hand man and all that. Were I Anastaria, I'd make sure to get in touch with you and ask: 'How's my Clutzer doing? He hasn't ruined your clan entirely yet, has he?' Your telepathic link is still functioning after all."

"Still?" I asked with surprise.

"As soon as you get divorced, you'll lose that ability. But once again—if I were Anastaria, divorce would be the first thing I'd go for. I'm sure that you haven't examined this subject at great length, so listen up: In order to get a divorce, both spouses need to be present. It won't happen if only one half of the cookie's there. However, there are several hidden perils which—if you're unaware of them—could cause you to lose half of your virtual possessions. And quite legally I might add. The status of an Earl in Barliona is as follows..."

Clutzer began to tell me such things that my eyebrows climbed higher and higher. It turns out that under Malabarian law adopted back during the reign of Karmadont, several layers of the nobility didn't have the right to get a divorce. Or, more precisely, they had the right, but they incurred such penalties in doing so, that it was far simpler to live out the rest of your life with a person you didn't love. These unlucky layers include only several titles—Dukes, Councilors, Heralds, Emperors and, unfortunately, Earls.

All this meant that I could lose 30% of my property to the Empire, be demoted from Earl to Baron and have the remainder of the property I acquired since entering the marriage split. And that went as much for my things as for Anastaria's. Considering that during our grand campaign she didn't really acquire anything valuable, I'd be the one on the losing end of this. And as further consequence of all this, the Ying-Yang would be destroyed and we would lose our telepathic link.

"Hmm..." I said philosophically after hearing out the Rogue. "Where'd you find all this information?"

"Several sources. At first I assumed that the

basis for the legal code would be the *Rules and Obligations of the Aristocracy*, a copy of which you should have. However, upon closer inspection I realized that this is merely a digest of decrees, laws and directives of Malabar. So I was forced to go to the source. Here, I'm sending you a file—it says the same things I just told you, only with legal citations so you can look everything up yourself."

"So what do you suggest?" I asked unwillingly, understanding perfectly well that I needed third-party advice that wasn't emotionally biased. Whether I'd accept it or not would be my own decision, regardless of what Clutzer would tell me, but I did need to hear him out.

"At the divorce ceremony, if it happens, I advise you to dig in your heels. As in 'no, I don't want a divorce,' and 'but I love her,' 'I can't imagine life without her,' and 'oh darling, please don't leave.' If you're against the divorce while Anastaria insists on it, then you won't have to pay the Imperial treasury and you won't lose any possessions. You'll be clean before the law. However, I have one suspicion..." Clutzer said slowing down, but then trailed off entirely.

"What is it?" I prompted.

"According to the rules, the husband speaks first. That is, you'll be examined first, irrespective of who initiated the divorce. They'll only ask Anastaria afterwards. And—here's my crazy idea—if you agree to the divorce and Anastaria then says 'darling, don't leave me'—and she very well might say that, then...Well, I think I don't need to explain it to you. You understand."

"She's definitely capable of it," Plinto spoke up for the first time. "She's not human...She's like a robot or something. No feelings whatsoever."

"I have a question for you too," I decided to ask, now that Plinto had entered the conversation. "Have you met her out in reality?"

"Yes, many years ago we used to go to the same school. That was before Barliona. Stacey was already a monster back then. Over the years that I've known her, I've never heard of her even going on a date with someone, much less going steady with them. That goes for Hellfire too. Everyone considered him her man, but he was little more than cover for her, so that she could avoid annoying suitors. When you two began dating, I was pretty taken aback. Stacey expressing any emotion whatsoever is something pretty incongruous to me. I reckoned she had changed—that you taught her the charm of love—so I kept my distance and didn't say anything...What came of it is what came of it..."

"All right," I said, pushing aside the million questions I wanted to ask him about Anastaria in her real form. "Let's say I agree with you and refuse to get a divorce as well as agree to keep the clan running, but did you three really only want that from me? It looks a bit one-sided, is all. Some crap happened and you feel guilty that you didn't warn me because Stacey ordered you not to, but I mean, you guys aren't really like that. By the way! After I paid my bail I had to undergo a rehab course, whether I liked it or not. The program took me five days and only because I was at Dependence Level Green when I came out. How did you manage to do the rehab course without me noticing it?"

"Simple—Anastaria is familiar with the dependence levels as well as how the process of rehabilitation can be initiated while still in the game. We spent several weeks doing a special course in game and as soon as you went absent in your crafting, we'd get the signal to sign out. It took me three days. Eric managed it in seven and Leite did it in five, if I'm not mistaken. By the time you'd crafted the Giants and the clan symbol, we were already free. Albeit under a ton of contractual obligations."

"And of course there was no way to warn me, even if in reality?" I smirked.

"When you're under observation around the clock?" Eric almost yelped, unable to maintain his silence. "There were always two or three people from Phoenix around me! Even when I went to the bathroom, the bastards! They didn't just keep us on lockdown, they corralled us like we were crazed maniacs! My wife wasn't allowed to visit me, since I could slip her some information. And all of this was set forth in our stupid contract! You think Clutzer was the only one who tried to let you know what was going on? Did you even look at the first item I crafted? The one that unlocked Crafting for me?"

"Sure I did."

"Then tell me, what did it portray?!" Eric said, still clearly agitated.

"Nothing, they were Bracers..."

"Bracers-shmacers! Did you examine the fillet?! When you gave me the Gladir, I almost said the hell with everything and told you the whole truth. I managed to keep my mouth shut at the last moment and decided to let you know through my craft. Do you have them with you, the bracers?"

"No," I shook my head sadly after checking my inventory. "Anastaria took them. They were a Rare item..."

"The fillet portrayed a battle between the Siren and the Dragon...Not even a battle, but a...First the Dragon was standing on the Siren, pressing her into the ground with his paws, but the venomous beast had twisted around and was offering a gift to her vanquisher—an apple. A poisoned apple...And the next image displayed the triumph of the Siren and the death of the Dragon...That was the only way I could tell you of the danger you were in without incurring the wrath of the Heralds, but you didn't understand a thing...Eh," Eric sighed bitterly.

"Leite was the only one who was perfectly happy

with Anastaria's offer and did everything as she commanded to a T," Clutzer continued. "Remember when he kept asking if Stacey was aware of what was going on? As I recall, you'd declared war on Phoenix and Leite had blown his cover...Stacey later remarked that back then Leite had almost lost it."

"You know, Mahan," Eric intervened again, producing the shining Gladir from his bag, as well as the belt and gloves of Crafting. "The devil knows what you'll decide, but if you kick me out of the clan, then these things will stay with me. That's the agreement that you drew up yourself. Here you go." Eric offered me the items over which players engaged in Crafting would simply kill another player. A total of +11 to Crafting is too useful in our business to be abandoned just like that.

"Okay, I'll think about it," I said, taking the items. "I'll admit that initially the idea was to boot everyone out of the clan, but now I should probably noodle on it a bit. But I'll say it again—you could have told me all of this without meeting in person. What are we all here for?"

"You're right," grinned Clutzer. "Everything we've said so far are just the hors d'oeuvres. Now let's move on to the main dish. Leaving you to choose what happens next—even if your decision is to shutter the clan—I'd like to describe several possible plans of action. Here's what I suggest..."

I couldn't help but smirk as I listened to Clutzer.

Plinto periodically jumped in with corrections, so I got the distinct impression that this plan had been cooked up a long time ago, discussed and mulled over, but never agreed upon fully. On the basis of incomplete information and the assumption that I knew more than they did, Clutzer and his warriors had concocted a pretty plausible plan of revenge. It's practically impossible to hurt an individual player in the game—I didn't count, since my case was pretty unusual—but it is wholly possible to hurt a group of players. The important thing is to know what to aim for.

And so!

First of all, we would formally declare war on the Phoenix Clan. This step would attract everyone who loved PvP to our banner. The opportunity to safely attack players from an enemy clan in the city, or rather in its 'safe zone'—without running the risk of being thrown in jail, would attract a whole mob of bored trolls.

Second of all, I had to give an interview in which I accused Anastaria of taking the Eye and the Chess Set from me without my consent. I'd also claim that she's ignoring my requests to return those items. Here I'll have to invoke the Emperor, after first demanding that Anastaria return the Chess Set and the Eye to me several times. The public must see the white aura of truth flaring around me during my performance. What actually triggers the confirmation isn't important—what's important is that it is visible. This is pure psychology—if the Emperor confirms it, Mahan must be clean! Clutzer was very happy to hear that I'd already asked Anastaria to return the Chess Set and was rejected. With that said, Clutzer rejected the idea of airing Anastaria's confession that her family had used my clan to obtain access to the Tomb. On the one hand everyone would see the true face of Phoenix—bastards without any principles who were ready to commit any evil for their own personal gain. However, from a gaming perspective, the clan would also acquire new advantages through the confession, since we'd basically be advertising that Phoenix has earned the most desired scenario in the entire game. If you want to be the best, join Phoenix and not some other clan like the Legends of Barliona or whatever, who are where they should be—in their rightful place, lagging behind.

Thirdly, we needed to hit Phoenix in its purse. Here Plinto would help us. Clutzer confessed that he had adjusted the plan on the fly as soon as he'd seen that I had received my Harbinger title. The gist of the financial blow would be that we would clean out Phoenix's treasure vaults. When I looked at Clutzer with befuddlement, suspecting that he was suffering from heat stroke, he explained further: Plinto would sneak into the castle and record the exact coordinates of the entrance to the treasure vault. It was 100% certain that Phoenix' treasure vaults were exactly like ours—located somewhere in the mountains. And here my newly acquired skills as a Harbinger would come in handy. An ordinary scroll of teleport can send someone to a concrete point in a two-dimensional coordinate grid. If the treasure vault is buried deep underground, then even if you know its location, you can only teleport to the surface. But not in my case— a Harbinger uses a three-dimensional coordinate grid to teleport. Even if it means fighting, Plinto has to break through to the vault, record his coordinates and send them to me. As soon as Phoenix calms down, I'll take both players as well as two maximum-capacity bags with me and blink to the treasure vault to relieve it of its contents. This is a one-time deal, since Phoenix will make sure to install hobgoblins in its vaults afterward. In fact, Clutzer had to admit right then and there that there wasn't any guarantee that the vaults didn't already have hobgoblins. But it was worth a shot...

And yet all of these foregoing points paled in comparison to what the Rogue proposed next—we would assault, capture and destroy Phoenix' castles...At this point, I could no longer control myself and burst out laughing. No matter how many people we managed to assemble in order to capture a castle, two Raid Parties led by Hellfire and Anastaria would smash us to smithereens. There was an enormous difference between a player of Level 350 and even, say, one of Level 250. We wouldn't even be able to approach their walls! Clutzer, however, uttered a single word that forced me to stop and think.

Armageddon.

The process for crafting this terrifying weapon—which was practically impossible to survive—was simple enough. The spell was enchanted on a special sheet of paper that grew once a month from the Alvandella tree. Every clan worth its salt had one of these trees, which would typically grow right in the center of the castle. This meant that we had to acquire one of our own. That was obligatory. Second—the scroll had to be 'charged,' which involved channeling about twenty million MP into it over the course of a day. Clutzer assured us that this wasn't a problem—he already had a gaggle of Mages that would charge our scroll. After that we'd need to go see the High Mage and have him inscribe the spell structure onto the scroll. Finally, the Emperor or the Dark Lord would need to imbue the scroll with life. This was where I'd come in handy. Clutzer planned on channeling Mana into ten scrolls over the next six months. Beside the ones we'd grow ourselves, we could obtain paper for the scrolls from the Azure Dragons and the Heirs of the Titans. No doubt they'd be happy to help, since Phoenix's dominance was a problem for everyone. Clutzer would guide the Mages, while my job would be to deal with the High Mage and the Emperor. In view of my relationships with the powers that were, it shouldn't be difficult for me to arrange the necessary audiences. As for activating the scroll after it was charged—that was a matter of technique. Plinto would burst into the castle, start a melee and receive the 'In Combat' status. He'd have to survive for a minute and then cast the wave of flame in the very center of the castle. Phoenix's castles weren't Altameda. They weren't built from Imperial Steel. Furthermore, the spell would be cast within the walls, increasing the devastation...In general, we could be sure of knocking several levels off their castles at least. And if we went so far as to detonate five scrolls simultaneously inside Phoenix's main castle (this was the number that Clutzer reckoned Plinto would have time to activate) the number of levels lost would be even more substantial. We could even block the clan's access to their treasure vault. And that would entail a severe blow to the reputation and finances of Ehkiller's clan, which couldn't help but please us. Either way we'd have to spend the next six months in preparations. Such a plan wouldn't come to fruition any earlier.

I promised the guys that I'd consider their proposals and called Viltrius to have him summon me back to Altameda. I didn't feel like saying yes or no without having first considered everything. I liked the plan of using Armageddon very much, but there was a downside—there was nothing to stop Anastaria from doing the same thing in Altameda. I'm sure that if we managed to pull this off against Phoenix, she would find my castle and set off several scrolls of her own inside of it...So I needed to think things over very well before making my decision. Take for example the declaration of war. A portion of the players would happily join our clan, looking for a fight with Phoenix. And yet the gatherers and craftsmen don't really like being in a clan dedicated to PvP. What did I need then—a clan of fighters or a clan that could sustain itself? Did I need a clan at all? There were so many questions that I didn't have answers to. This definitely wasn't what was on my mind when I entered Barliona this morning.

And then there was that visitation by Eluna...By the way! I had sent a letter to tech support!

I opened my email and smiled at the twelve million letters that had filled my inbox during the past week. Then I clicked on a special section that blinked green notifying me that I had a message from the Barliona admins.

> *Dear Mahan,*
> *Thank you for your inquiry...*

Right, we'll skip the formalities...

> *We'd like to bring to your attention that we are currently offering a new service—you may now transfer your character to a different faction...*

We'll skip this part too...

As for your inquiry, we are happy to inform you that, indeed, an item called the Tear of Harrashess was developed for the game. However, we assure you that players cannot acquire this item for their own use. The warning you received from the Imitator playing the role of Eluna was no more than a precaution taken by another Imitator playing the role of the High Priestess of that goddess. You have a unique reputation and attractiveness with this NPC, so she asked the goddess to warn you of the threat. We assure you that this item poses no danger to you whatsoever since it is technically impossible for you to receive it.

We wish to use this opportunity to recommend to you a new...

The rest of the letter was an ad offering various cosmetic improvements to my castle, so I didn't keep reading. Glancing over the tech support part of the text again, I could be sure of one thing—it was a good idea for me to be afraid. After all, no player could receive the Ying-Yang either. Only an NPC could own that item.

Thus, not having decided anything, I opened my mail and began to go through the letters. The twelve million emails that snuck through my spam filter in the past week was just too much. I don't even know how else I can set the filters up in order to sort out this torrent of information. I already have an ad blocker in place and another filter to block requests for money as well as...Excuse me?!

When I opened the list of filters to add another one, I was astonished to find their utter absence. The list of applied filters was empty, which meant that ads and other spam could now reach my poor consciousness. So it follows that during the transfer of my Shaman, all the settings were reset. No wonder I felt a bit uncomfortable in Anhurs today, surprised at the extreme activity of the players. Everyone was yelling, making noise, while the chat was bursting into little pieces...I'll have to start everything all over again. I somehow missed this part before.

"Master, there's a package here for you with a request that it be delivered to you personally," Viltrius said, distracting me from my renewed attempts to set up my email and offering me a small package.

"From whom?" I asked surprised. The fact that the package was sent through an NPC meant that someone with access to the castle had found Altameda's location, walked up to the gates, called Viltrius and handed him the package. Furthermore, this someone did all this while I was in Anhurs just now. In other words, I needed to think carefully about what I would do.

"Master Spiteful Gnum, whom you hired to repair the gates and refresh the building's ornament. He is bound to the castle, so he sent the package to you with his demons, since Altameda's location remains unknown to him.

"Thank you. I'll take a look," I said, taking the package from the goblin. Somehow I'd forgotten that my castle was playing host to one of Barliona's odder players. When I teleported the castle to a new location and blocked all access to it, I had left Gnum without work and, consequently, further development, which for a creative type like him could not fail to evoke displeasure. So I guess I could roughly guess what was in the package already. After all, besides his skillful carpentry, the gnome was also a pretty good Tailor...

This is no way to conduct business, Mahan! What the hell? I enter the game and find the castle's gone! I call Viltrius, but that green twerp doesn't pick up. My demons are in shock—they don't know that castles can teleport, no one can find you, everyone's upset and in a trance, while meanwhile my materials are rotting...Anyway! I found a way to express how I feel about you! Here's another gift from me! If you want to continue your repairs, don't bother calling me.

P.S. You know where to find me.

P.P.S. How did you manage that anyway?

P.P.P.S.S. Lol, S.S.

Item acquired: 'Cape of the Opposite.' Description: A sentient who equips this cape

adopts the appearance of those of non-traditional sexual orientations. When this item is equipped: +20 Attractiveness with members of your own gender and -40 Attractiveness with members of the opposite gender. Item class: Unique. Creator: Spiteful Gnum.

A bright piece of cloth fell into my hands, shimmering with all the colors of the rainbow. The power of Gnum's creation was so great that even holding this piece of cloth in my hands I could see my hands grow elegant like an elf's. A manicure began to transform my fingers. Dropping the cape to the floor and making sure that this was no more than an optical illusion, I ordered Viltrius to remove the cape to the treasure vault. No one's cursed me out in such an extravagant way before...

But in one sense I was thankful to Gnum—I had finally decided how my clan would develop from here on out. Yes, the clan—I decided against disbanding it, yet in my plan, the Legends of Barliona wouldn't engage in any hostilities against Phoenix either. To the opposite—my main task in the next six months, while the scrolls of Armageddon were being prepared—would be to stay as far away from battles as possible. If something happened, I'd have Plinto and Clutzer with their Raiding Parties. They'd deal with the contingencies. Instead, I was faced with a different problem—the development of different professions. And I don't mean gatherers—there were endless numbers of those in Barliona. But autodidacts like Gnum and Svard are one in a million. As long as I can maintain their interest, I want them to stay with me. And as long as they're with me, I have the advantage. This means that I have to retain their attention, and I know exactly how to do that.

After all, I have to not only destroy the main castle of Phoenix, but also try and rummage around its darker corners—and these are mere preludes that no one will notice. I want to aim my main blow at the foundations of Phoenix's budget—the sale of unique items. If I can wriggle my way into this market and push Phoenix out, the losses suffered by the clan of the fried chicken will be colossal. Which is what I need.

For now, I had to meet with Gnum and encourage him to work with me. Without players like him, I'd never achieve my goals...

CHAPTER THREE
A MEETING AND NEW QUESTS

"**M**AHAN!**" As soon as I entered her office, Elizabeth's sullen face looked up from the documents that were occupying her and brightened. "How nice of you to stop by!"

"Hi Elsa," I greeted the High Priestess and following her gesture, sat down in the chair. "I have some business to discuss with you..."

Having made a decision about my clan's further development, I understood perfectly well that I wouldn't be able to verify what Clutzer had said about the divorce at the moment—and since I needed to get some sleep too, I decided to run two more errands before signing out to reality. The first was to go to the plateau and appear before the Angels to receive access to the Tomb. The second was to see Elizabeth and ask her for advice about the divorce. I didn't trust anyone else when it came to this question.

I located the coordinates to the plateau before the Tomb in my logs, opened the Blink settings, entered the data, pushed the Blink button and...remained in place. To my immense surprise, an unpleasant notification appeared before me, telling me that Anastaria had considered her plan down to the slightest details.

Teleportation to the indicated coordinates is impossible. This location has an activated anti-teleportation crystal in place.

Fully aware that I could become a Harbinger or use my castle's capabilities, Phoenix had installed crystals that blocked any teleportation to the Tomb. It followed that I'd have to blink to a neighboring locale and reach the Tomb on my own two...well, wings. And if Phoenix is as committed as they seem to preventing me from reaching the entrance, then they'll have placed a hundred or two high-level players whose assignment it is to keep me from breaking through.

Bastards!

"Your business can wait," Elsa jolted me from my ruminations. "Better tell me something else—why is this here lying on my table."

With undisguised revulsion, Elsa picked up one of the documents from the pile before her with two fingers and offered it to me. A notification about having received a document from an NPC flashed before my eyes as a text appeared below it:

To the High Priestess of Eluna,

Oh High One, please listen to this plea of mine, for I have not the strength to bear this burden any longer. My priceless spouse, known to you as High Shaman Mahan, has variously sought ways to avoid meeting with me—as if that unearthly spark that caused the Ying-Yang to flower and burn with all the colors of the rainbow, has faded. With immense hurt in my heart, I met my husband's eyes, filled with hate, after which he pushed me away and forgot about his eternal oath...He has ceased to love me. If you believe that I am lying, summon my husband yourself and speak to him about me. Listen to his feelings. There will be no love there, only hate, anger and the desire to crush and destroy me. I admit that I am not without fault and I realize the cause of this behavior—after all, I returned to my father's clan, but if you love someone you must know how to understand and forgive. Mahan is incapable of forgiveness. I've already understood this, so I have nothing left to do but fall at your feet and beg you to annul our union. I am ready to sacrifice myself— if only I can cease to be a burden on my beloved husband. Let me suffer—so long as he gains his liberty.

Anastaria, Captain of Paladins and Paladin General.

"Tell me this isn't true, Mahan," Elizabeth said expectantly when I had finished reading. "Tell me that you don't hate your wife..."

To say that I was surprised would have been an understatement. It's one thing to file for divorce claiming irreconcilable differences—it's something else entirely to claim these grounds. So Stacey is guilty, but I'm the bastard who was incapable of heeding the feelings that are greater than actions. And it's not like I can explain to Elizabeth that it was because of Anastaria that I lost the Chess Set and the Eye—or that she used me for her own personal ends. The real world didn't exist for the High Priestess. The fact that Anastaria had switched clans—the fact that she'd returned to her father who perhaps missed his daughter, didn't mean she had fallen out of love with me. The clan that one belongs to, the colors one wears, doesn't mean anything to an NPC. Instead, the player's feelings are everything.

"Elsa, this letter is like a knife to my heart," I said at last. My initial emotions had ebbed and I managed not to swear. No one was tracking my body metrics, or at least the system didn't mention this, so Elizabeth was still waiting for my verbal response. If Anastaria had written a letter like this, then she wanted to cast me in a very unpleasant light. I doubt that they'd show me this letter tomorrow. But if I started arguing with Anastaria in front of Elizabeth, even if I had refused the divorce, my Attractiveness with the High Priestess would decrease from its current level of 100 points. Well, best of luck to you, Anastaria! I'll turn on stupid mode and act like I don't know anything. "Forgive me, I'm just stunned, stunned at what my beloved wife writes here and...No but this is some kind of counterfeit letter! Anastaria could not have written this! Elsa, are you sure that this if from her?"

"Naturally—she handed me the letter herself."

"That's impossible," I droned on, trying to gain some time and figure out where I should go next. It was evident now that if I start accusing Anastaria in Elizabeth's presence, I would hurt my relations with the High Priestess. And I really didn't want this to happen. I had to choose each word carefully and purposefully—I couldn't allow Anastaria to drive a wedge between me and Elsa. "Impossible, I tell you!"

"I was also very surprised," Elizabeth agreed. "If you hadn't loved each other completely, you'd never have gotten the Ying-Yang to bloom. The stone cannot be tricked—it heeds the deepest feelings of sentients and makes the decision of whether or not they are worthy of being together on its own. Your Ying-Yang showed that you were worthy. Could you really fall out of love over the course of two months? No, that's pure folly—you still wear the amulet...As soon as you stop loving each other, the Ying-Yang will ignite, burning away to ashes, and your abilities will vanish. Or does the amulet already not work?"

"No it still does," I assured Elizabeth and made up my mind. If Anastaria had written this letter, let her squirm before the High Priestess herself. I'll deny everything and insist that I love my wife with all my heart, and claim it's she who wants to leave me. "I propose we check—I'll summon Anastaria right now and she will explain the letter herself."

"Indeed!" Elizabeth brightened up again. "Why play a guessing game when we can ask her directly?"

"*Are you there, my beauty?*" I asked Anastaria telepathically.

"*I am, my sun. What did you want?*"

"*Could you drop by for a visit, dear?*"

"*I'll still respawn in time for the divorce, silly. There's no point in ambushing me. But since you miss me so much, summon away.*"

"The Ying-Yang still works!" Elizabeth exclaimed when Anastaria appeared in the office. It took Stacey only a second to assess the situation and a forced smile spread across her face. The girl hadn't expected this move on my part. "You are mistaken, my daughter. Your husband could not have stopped loving you. Otherwise your abilities would not work. Mahan loves you and you love him. Explain to me please what prompted this letter as well as your desire to get a divorce."

"*One-zero to you,*" came Anastaria's thought, after which she sank to her knees before Elizabeth.

"Forgive me, holy mother. My mind was confused and I made a terrible error. I beg you to please destroy that letter and punish me—I admit my falseness and repent. When I had to return to my father's clan, I spent too much time thinking about how my spouse would react and I mistook my imagined fears for the truth."

"You deserve punishment," Elizabeth concluded without a shadow of doubt. "Eluna shall decide your main sacrament. I'll say personally that I find your disunion with your spouse unpleasant. It doesn't do when two people who love each other spend time apart from one another."

"The High Priestess cannot compel us to change clans. One's membership in a given clan is not related to our relations or feelings," Anastaria replied immediately, narrowing her eyes in suspicion. I have to admit that the High Priestess's words had surprised me a great deal too—was she really about to force us to be in the same clan? That would contradict the game rules and the players' free will. And that's impossible.

"You are correct. I cannot," Elizabeth shrugged her shoulders. "I was merely expressing my thoughts on the matter—I don't like the fact that you two are living apart while still loving each other. And that has nothing to do with your clans—each sentient is free to be where he is most comfortable. What is odd to me is something else—the fact that you don't spend time together. When the full falseness of the letter came to light just now, I was very upset. I have nothing left to do but cancel tomorrow's ceremony and assign you a punishment. Well, it's not even really a punishment—

but more of a request. You are free to ignore it, since as a Paladin you do not serve the Priestess. And the same goes for Mahan—Shamans are entirely unrelated to Eluna and her Priests. However, that which I will ask you to do will be impossible to perform on your own. It requires teamwork from both spouses. Over the course of a month, you must spend no less than one hour with each other, questing, raiding, exploring or even simply speaking. The main rule is that you must work together, not separately—otherwise, the time you invest won't count. This is the only way I'll be able to ensure that you're both a single whole and capable of further deeds. Are you prepared to accept my wish?"

Quest chain available: 'Tight-knit family. Step 1.' Description: Meet up 30 times over the course of 3 calendar months, spending at least 1 hour together in questing or speaking to one another. Quest type: Unique, family. Reward: +2000 to Reputation with the Priests of Eluna, +1000 to Reputation with Goddess Eluna and the next quest in the chain. Penalty for failing or refusing the quest: -2000 to Reputation with the Priests of Eluna and -1000 to Reputation with Goddess Eluna.

"I bow before your wisdom, mother," Anastaria replied with a bow, "and I accept your wish. I will prove to you the strength and endurance of our family."

Two pairs of eyes fixed on mine, each pair expressing utterly different things. If Elizabeth was looking at me like a loving and caring mother looks at her child after having solved some problem and now awaiting the correct words from her child, then Anastaria's expressed only one thing—triumph. I was getting the impression that I had once again made some misstep that turned out to be beneficial to the girl. The sensation that I had been used yet again was so evident that it took enormous effort not to push the 'Decline' button. And yet any way you look at it, an increase in my reputation with Eluna and her Priests would be very useful to my character. A single unique item that I craft grants me 500 to Reputation, and it's not like I make one item each day or even each week, so I suppose I'll be able to tolerate Anastaria being next to me for an hour. And besides, this is a quest chain with several steps. The important thing was to smother the hate in my chest for the girl standing beside me. Since, after all, we're a loving and inseparable family.

"I accept your wish, oh High Priestess," I said, pushing the 'Accept' button.

"A very wise decision, my children," Elizabeth replied, illuminating us with the sign of Eluna. "As soon as you complete my assignment, I will personally meet with you. I will always have a quest or two to strengthen a family and make it indestructible. In the meantime, you're free to go...Although wait! Mahan, you had some business for me!"

"It's no longer important," I parried, noting the curiosity in Anastaria's eyes. There's no reason she needs to know about why I came to see the High Priestess. Then again, I guess Stacey could figure it out on her own.

"In that case, I will now leave you. You should spend some time alone together..."

"I suggest a neutral option—an hour's worth of conversation over dinner at the Golden Horseshoe," Anastaria proposed as soon as we left the temple. The girl was behaving as if nothing had happened between us and we were still in love as before. I didn't feel like playing that game.

"All right. An hour at the Golden Horseshoe will suit me fine," I replied in what I thought was a calm voice but which in fact was more hissy and unclear than I had imagined. I guess my patience was rapidly running out. Another minute and I'll throw myself at Anastaria with my bare fists, and the hell with fines and jail.

"Okay, since you're back to your old self, it's time we part," Anastaria immediately replied with the same smile. "We can begin our meetings tomorrow, around 2 p.m. server time. I'll call you. Didn't you drop my amulet?" Mockingly, Anastaria stroked my cheek. "Of course you didn't. One doesn't throw away items like that...Until tomorrow, Harbinger. Sweet dreams."

Anastaria took a quick step, embraced and kissed me and then vanished into thin air, once more performing her favorite little trick of signing out to reality. That stupid Ice Queen. Well whatever, let her have her fun—I'll have the last laugh. Although I was sure that Clutzer remained a player of Phoenix, there was some sense to his plans. I just needed to consider it and adapt them to my purposes.

EXIT!

My first voluntary exit from Barliona was so unusual that I spent a few moments lying in my capsule enjoying the sight of my ceiling. Say what you will, but a year in a fantasy world really does leave its mark. Understanding that I wouldn't really get any sleep in the turned-off capsule, I activated the ejector and toppled over the edge of the capsule. The time had come for dinner...

The phone call caught me at the critical moment of deciding why I shouldn't have to wash the dishes today. It was only two plates, a cup and a couple spoons, but I simply couldn't force myself to rinse the remnants of the food and salad. A hundred reasons raced through my mind—from the need to distribute labor among people to the recognition that I never even liked these plates and could safely toss them instead of washing them. I might as well buy new ones.

"Speaking," I picked up the phone, deciding finally that the dishes would remain unwashed and it'd be the caller's fault. Whoever he was, it doesn't do to distract me in the evenings. Like it or not, it was already midnight.

"Good evening, Daniel, could we speak?" said an unfamiliar male voice, clearly tinged with metallic notes. I got the impression that this wasn't a human but a computer, speaking to me through voice modulation software.

"We already are," I said carefully, realizing that I couldn't really blame a computer for my dishes going unwashed.

"I am calling you about our offer regarding Phoenix. We have received your response and wish to discuss the details. Could you come see us right now?"

"At one in the morning?" I asked caustically.

"It's only a few minutes after midnight," the metallic voice corrected me. "We will send a car to pick you up. It will bring you back home too. The meeting won't take long. You should be home by three. What do you say? Do you have time?"

"You know, I always welcome a chat, but chatting with someone without knowing their name, or for that matter, being taken who knows where in the middle of the night without any guarantees of safety...This is all a bit too complicated for me, so I must politely decline such an enticing offer."

"You didn't manage to reach the plateau, did you? Even the powers of a Harbinger don't allow you to jump where Phoenix doesn't want you to be—and you're okay with this?" The voice lost its metallic edge and became an ordinary male voice. Judging by its timbre, its owner was well over fifty, as I could make out notes of age in the voice. At the same time, there was a confidence of power in the voice too. "Or have you changed your mind and decided to shelve the whole idea under the assumption that Anastaria still loves you? Do you imagine that you'll make an inseparable couple? A strong family?"

Well this is a little more interesting already! Someone still unknown to me can track my actions in Barliona. This someone seems completely familiar with what I wanted to do, what I did and whom I met. The conclusion is evident—this someone has some special relationship to Barliona. Even though the caller was clearly indicating that he had violated a term of use or even a law, I knew that I had to go and meet this person. What if he could handle Phoenix?

"Send the car," I decided. After all was said and done, if they wanted to hurt me, they'd have done it long ago. And if these people knew what I was doing in Barliona, then they wouldn't have any trouble finding me in real life.

"Go downstairs, it's already waiting for you," came the reply and the caller hung up.

Maybe I'm no Julius Caesar—but still: '*Alea iacta*

est.'

"Please forgive me for such an unusual meeting," said the older man whose appearance resembled that of a prim, ossified Lord of ancient England. A large checkered suit, a bow tie, a cane, dark polished shoes reflecting the starry sky...Seeing a man like this at the shore of the same city pond that had once suffered from my bet, was quite unusual. People like this typically sit around expensive restaurants and relate tales of their exploits with young girls in their youth. "This is my only opportunity to meet you without attracting undue attention to myself."

In view of the several bodyguards I'd noticed on my way into the park, the standing of my companion was quite high. As far as I understood the outward appearance of Barliona's upper management, this person was not one of them, so I was becoming more and more curious.

We took a seat on a wooden bench and began staring at the pond in silence like two lovers afraid of speaking the first word. I recalled the powerful voice of the old man—who still had not introduced himself to me—and decided that our rendezvous was all the stranger for it—if he had so little time, why didn't he start talking?

"Tell me, Daniel," the old man finally began, half-turning to me and leaning on his cane, "what's it like to be humiliated by the person you considered to be your second half?"

"I doubt you brought me here to have a heartfelt conversation," I parried. Whoever this guy thought he was, I wasn't about to let him pluck at my heart-strings.

"Don't be angry with an old man for his tactlessness," my companion apologized to my surprise, "It's only that what the Phoenix leadership did with you, they once did to me. But in reality, instead of in the game. It was only through a miracle that I didn't lose my mind and remained myself, so I decided now to begin our conversation with that tactless question. You have suffered from Stacey's manipulations, while I have suffered from the one you know as Barsina."

The old man fell silent again, staring off into nowhere as if succumbing to the recollections of the past. A minute passed, then another, and the third one was already under way and we were still sitting there in silence enjoying the view of the nighttime park—stylized to resemble older days by its dusky lamps.

"You wanted to speak with me," when the silence became too tedious, I was forced to remind him of my presence, "and discuss something."

"Yes!" the old man perked up returning to reality. "I want to offer you vengeance for everything that clan did to you!"

"Forgive me for interrupting, but before you explain further, could you tell me what you need me for? If you can carry out the revenge yourself, then I'm not sure what I can do that you and your people cannot. I'm just an ordinary player. I don't have any relatives among the elites and any revenge I can even imagine would be a drop in the ocean for Phoenix."

"A reasonable objection," agreed the old man, "I was about to address just that. Tell me, what do you know about the Zavala family?"

"Nothing," I admitted sincerely, making a mental note to dig around the internet to find out about Stacey and her parents. If I wanted revenge, I'd need to at least know against whom it'd be.

"Hum..." the old man replied with some surprise. "You didn't bother to figure out whom you're dealing with?"

"Not yet. I suppose it's no secret to you that I'm a former prisoner, that today was the first time I entered the game as a free player and that I simply had no opportunity to look up these things until now."

"I am aware of your status, but I don't understand one thing—you began to date Anastaria and didn't bother to find out who she was in real life? Whether she has a husband, children, or all her limbs? What if she was the victim of some accident and her in-game appearance was all that remained from the way she was, while in reality she was a charred piece of meat?"

"I don't really want to talk about this right now,"

I muttered, grimacing from revulsion. In a way this was a pretty good answer for why Anastaria had refused to enter the Miss Barliona contest this year. She would've been disqualified for the discrepancy between her real-life and in-game appearances. Ugh...However I felt about this girl, I'd never wish something like this on her. It was too much.

"Don't worry. Anastaria is in one piece and unhurt, but I was very surprised by your attitude toward it all. In our day and age, information is the greatest weapon and a voluntary refusal to employ it is...very odd."

"Let's discuss oddities some other time," I offered, avoiding this slippery subject. He did have a point—I could have asked someone—anyone—to find out whatever I wanted about Stacey, but for some reason I never got around to it. Guilty as charged and I apologize for it—but I won't allow anyone to drag me around the floor like some naughty kitten.

"In that case let me tell you a bit about them. You can find out the rest on your own. Victor Zavala—you know him as Ehkiller—is one of the wealthiest people of our continent. To be more accurate, he is number 188 among the continent's wealthiest residents. However, unlike the majority of his colleagues, Victor maintains 80% of his assets in the game, making no attempts to transfer them out to reality. The Phoenix corporation, and at the moment this is a corporation, comprises the leading clan which in turn contains the management, the raiders and the best craftsmen, as well as hundreds if not more affiliate clans, like, for instance, everyone thought the Legends were. Phoenix is one of the few truly profitable clans in the game and has a financial cushion that protects it from any harm, including even the complete destruction of all of its castles. Naturally that would hurt, but it wouldn't kill them…"

"If what you say is true, then the only way to hurt Phoenix is to destroy the entire Zavala family," I said, surprised at my own words. You can't even think such things, much less say them out loud, and yet…

"I like how you're thinking but I must disappoint you—it's impossible to destroy Victor. No one knows where he lives at the moment and all attempts to find him have failed. No! We must adopt a different approach. Given the particularities of Phoenix, we have to hit them in their most cherished place—their money, and now I'll tell you how we'll do this."

Slowly but steadily like a train gathering steam, the old man began to reveal his plan of revenge, in which I was designated to play no small part. In essence, the plan was based on me playing the most important role. With all due respect to my companion, it's very stupid to concoct a plan that depends on another person. Who knew what was going on in my head really? Hell even I didn't really know.

The plan as the old man told it to me was as follows: First—I have to make it to the Angels and receive access to the Tomb from them. As soon as I manage to do this, Barsina will receive access to the Tomb too, the Angels will depart, and Phoenix will be able to enter at will. However, only I will have the 'original' key to the Tomb, which makes all of the loot in the Dungeon Unique or Legendary. If I receive the original key, Phoenix won't enter without me—it just wouldn't make any fiscal sense to do so. Consequently, a fee of one hundred million from each member of Phoenix is a very fair price of admission. Nineteen participants then is practically two billion gold...Even for Phoenix this'll be a significant monetary blow.

"It's a pretty idea," I said as soon as the man fell silent. "But there are two 'buts'! The first is that I won't be able to reach the entrance to the cave. I can't teleport to the plateau and it's sure to be guarded, so I'll be killed before I make it to the Angels. Second— why would Phoenix spend the money? No item in Barliona, not even their cumulative price, can cost two billion gold and therefore there's no reason Ehkiller should agree to pay such money. I don't know what he'll actually do naturally, but I definitely wouldn't agree."

"These are reasonable objections. I'll address them in order. As soon as you agree to our plan, the crystals will stop blocking your Blink spell. How that'll happen is my problem—but it'll happen. All you'll have to do is enter the coordinates at the Angels' location, blink in and then you'll be under their protection. As for the second point—before departing, the Angels will announce that only he who carries the original key can receive the Salva. No one is forbidden from venturing the Tomb without you, but the Salva will only be obtainable with you.

"The Salva?" I couldn't help but ask.

"That's the second part of our plan. The Salva is an item that can destroy the Tears of Harrashess. Shall I go on?"

The realization of whom I was dealing with was like an electric shock. And I don't even mean the specific person with whom I was speaking, so much as the organization that stood behind him—you can't accomplish things like this on your own. Eluna had already told me what the Tear of Harrashess was, but the fact that an ordinary player could be burdened with it after all, considering that the Barliona admins had told me otherwise...

"You will have to complete two Dungeons," the old man interrupted my thoughts. "In each one of them you'll find two parts of an item which, combined, will create a portal. The Mages will charge it and you'll be able to teleport right into the center of Geranika's castle, which currently contains four activated Tears. Your job will then be to take the Tears and slip them to Anastaria, Hellfire, Fiona and Alveona—the leading players of Phoenix. I can't tell you how you will be able to do this because that is the most sensitive part of our plan. However, as soon as the Phoenix players are in possession of the Tear, a notification will appear about the Salva and the fact that you are the only one who can find it. It's for these reasons that you shouldn't teleport to the angels before the time is right—otherwise, by the time you get your hands on the Tears, Phoenix might have completed the Dungeon."

The old man's plan stunned me with its cruelty and thoughtfulness. If I slipped Anastaria the Tear, Phoenix would absolutely play two billion to free her— the other three affected players be damned. And yet...

"According to its official description, the Tear cannot be transferred to another player," I recalled the properties of the crystal that I'd found in Altameda. "The idea of giving this item to Anastaria is a good one, but it's unrealistic."

"There's nothing unrealistic about it," smirked the old man. "You'll have to hurry and reacquire at least one of the Crastils—those orbs scattered throughout the continent that no one knows what to do with. You had a couple, but Anastaria took them, so now you'll have to obtain one from Grygz, the head of the pirates. We'll help you in this. A player who has a Crastil as well as another item that you'll find in the Dungeon, will be able to transfer an activated Tear. In fact, before it's activated, a Tear won't affect a player with a Crastil. Anastaria has a Crastil, but as soon as the Tear is activated, Phoenix won't have a choice but to pay for access to the Salva...And still this isn't all."

"There's more?"

"Salva isn't an item. It's a scroll with a recipe. A Jewelcrafting recipe. A Jewelcrafting recipe with certain requirements: 20 points in Crafting, the title of Blessed Artificer, and the ability to enter the Astral Plane. In other words, it's a class-specific scroll for the Shaman and, when the raid is done, only you will be able to read it. No one will trick anyone—if there's no raid, no one gains access to the Salva. But neither is there a guarantee that you're the only one who'll pick it up. This means that it's vital you draw up a proper contract for your raid party. I'll help you with that. After that, you activate the Tear and all four players will effectively lose their characters. That'll be the biggest blow to Phoenix—ten years' worth of grinding experience to level up their four top players will all be wasted. All of their Reputation, Achievements and skills. They wanted to destroy your Shaman so I'll give you the opportunity to destroy their characters. A two-pronged attack on Phoenix— we'll hit their money and their talent. It seems to me that this will be a worthy revenge for the humiliation you and I have suffered."

"Two billion is a very hefty sum to spend," I said pensively. "It'd be easier for Ehkiller to sell his name or kill me in real life than spend that much money. Especially once the Tears have been activated."

"You will enjoy the best security available. You

will leave this city. We will provide you with top-of-the-line equipment and high bandwidth uplinks to Barliona. No one will know where you are. The important thing is that we need your help, since the entire plan depends on your abilities."

"I won't be able to complete the Dungeon without trusted people," I continued thinking out loud. "I need people who can help me with advice at the right time, and therefore they will have to also be aware of what's going on. How many players can you give me?"

"Only one, at the moment," the old man replied sadly. "As soon as we agree to the terms of the plan, my person will get in touch with you."

"How will your manipulation of the game affect me?" I couldn't help but ask another vital question. "I don't feel like being sent to the mines once again. A chat with you is one thing—altering game data is a whole different ballpark."

"It won't affect you at all. You are an ordinary player, completing his series of scenarios. What happens in the other planes of the game doesn't concern you. The important thing is that it helps you. You won't be breaking any rules. This is why we won't be signing any papers—if something doesn't go according to plan, Daniel Mahan the player will remain unaffected."

"Do we split the money?"

"Let's wait until we get there," the old man smiled. "As soon as the Phoenix players receive the

Tear, they'll file lawsuits against the Corporation for limiting their game experience. We'll have to survive that. When it becomes clear that everything happened according to the rules and the players themselves are at fault—and that in fact there is a remedy in the form of the Salva—then we'll talk. There's no point discussing money at the moment. This by the way ensures your safety—as long as you have the money, your life won't be in danger. Certainly not from me, at any rate."

I kept wanting to ask why the old man wanted to do all this, as the fairy tale about Barsina sounded very unconvincing, but I controlled myself. What difference did it make why this person hated Phoenix so much? What difference did it make that someone was about to use me again to achieve his personal ends (and again in the dark like Anastaria). What I wanted right now was to have a chance of revenge against Phoenix for what they had done to me and my clan. If I'd have to do what someone wanted to achieve this, I was ready. I couldn't care less what ulterior ideas this person had in mind—even if it meant he'd take over Phoenix with my aid. It was all okay with me so long as those four Phoenix players would be destroyed. Even though I didn't have any beef with Fiona and Alveona, destroying Anastaria and Hellfire would be an excellent revenge indeed. I could stand to be a puppet for the sake of it.

"I'd like to know what to call you because 'old

man' or 'hey' doesn't really suit someone of your age."

"Agreed, I don't particularly like responding to 'hey,' smiled the old man, still deep in his thoughts. "But I'm not opposed to 'old man,' so let's just agree to that. What did you decide? Shall we work together?"

"We shall," I nodded. "What do you need me to do in order to begin making our plan a reality?"

"Complete two Dungeons. You already have the quest for one of them—you need to kill the Dragon of Shadow. He will drop the first half of the artifact. It doesn't matter who goes with you—take the artifact yourself. You'll recognize it pretty easily—it's the hilt of a dagger. I won't tell you the name of the item, since I don't know it, but you'll know it when you read the description. The second Dungeon will be the Dungeon of Shadow. There you'll receive the blade of the dagger and a unifier. You can find out the coordinates to the second Dungeon from the High Priestess—she'll issue you the quest as well. And that's all for now—you have four weeks to accomplish all of this. Then you'll have to appear before the Angels. Otherwise Barsina will receive the key to the Tomb and all our efforts will be in vain. Don't worry about the deadlines—my person will remind you of them constantly. Are there any questions?"

"Not at the moment, but I'm still wondering— how will you adjust the game data? The Corporation runs such a comprehensive security system that any interference with the game process is typically intercepted at the level of intent. To say nothing of the unlawfulness of such actions. It's one thing that I know about your plan. I'll already be breaking the law if I don't say anything to the law enforcement agencies. I really don't want to go back to the mines, so I'd prefer to approach all of this with a clear understanding of the people I'm working with."

"With great knowledge comes great sorrow," the old man remarked. "Don't cram your head full of trivia—that's my job. You've agreed to work with us. You don't need to know anything else. That's all for now then." The old man got up from the bench, propping himself with his cane. "The driver will return you to your home, and I expect you to complete the two Dungeons as soon as possible. Remember—you only have four weeks."

"When am I going to meet your man?" I asked, also standing up.

"Soon. A player will approach you and speak a code word. Let it be 'Crastil.' That's how you'll know that he's come from me and that you can trust him completely. We shall meet again soon, Daniel! I hope everything will work out for us..."

My return trip home flashed by unnoticed as I was buried in oppressive thought. On the one hand, the old man's offer wasn't just good—it was perfect. What scared me the most was that I saw no pitfalls, and yet there were definitely pitfalls. Life had taught me that if it seemed like nothing but roses, there were thorns lurking not far off. I couldn't see the thorns at the moment and that stressed me out. As much as I hated her, Anastaria had taught me one thing—I could trust only myself. Everyone else only wanted to use me. And now I was consciously taking this step, since the advantages were evident, but the absence of pitfalls....it just wasn't right. Things don't work this way.

Thinking in this manner, I collapsed into my bed and fell asleep...

* * *

"How'd you sleep, bunny?" Anastaria asked sarcastically, sitting down in the chair across from me. "Did you miss me?"

My nocturnal escapade didn't come without a price. I ended up sleeping in until it was almost two in the afternoon. Glancing at the clock, I almost swore out loud—I had a meeting to go to! I quickly stuffed two sandwiches down my throat and then stuffed myself into the capsule. It was very important to me that I wasn't late to our 'date'—I didn't want to give Anastaria another opportunity to have fun at my expense.

"I did, my sunshine," I grinned, noting to my surprise that I didn't actually feel any hate towards Anastaria at the moment. With a clear plan of action for the next month in my head, I no longer felt at a loss in front of the girl. In a month this doll would turn into a monument and I wasn't about to give her the Salva to regain control of herself. Anastaria would be enshrined for all eternity in Barliona—as a statue.

"Oh! You're not spitting and sputtering today," Stacey again tried to get into my head. "Did you have a good meal?"

"Uh-huh. I sure did. Stacey, I'm officially asking you to return the Karmadont Chess Set to me as well as the Eye of the Dark Widow, the Crastil of Shalaar and of Gwar, Levaar, Babar, et cetera et cetera. Oh! And the Bracers that Eric made and the Squidolphin Scales...I think that's the full list of the things you stole from me."

"You forgot to turn your video recorder on," the girl smiled back. "How are you going to prove that I'm a big ol' bitch without it? Or did Clutzer decide to play with words and summon the Emperor as a witness to your oath that I refused to return your items upon your official request. A pretty move...I'll think of something though. What do you plan on doing today?"

"I dunno, stuff," I shrugged. "You said yourself that I missed out on continental quests too often. So I guess maybe I'll try and find one. I want to get a handle on being a Harbinger—I have the powers but I still can't use them for the next two weeks. There're lots of quests and I'm short on time, so I'll find something to occupy myself with before the clan tournament begins. By the way, tell me again, when is it supposed to be?"

"In a month and a half. The Emperor keeps delaying it—first it was the Dagger. Now it's the heart of Chaos. Are you planning on saving Renox?"

"No. Eluna made it very clear to me that I shouldn't set foot in Armard. I'm an obedient person. I listen to a goddess when she speaks to me, so I'll figure something else out...What about you? Will you go to fight Geranika?"

"You know, I've been forbidden from going there too...No, this won't do. Here you go!" Anastaria said suddenly, opened her bag—which was closed for me (I'd checked just in case)—and retrieved a painfully familiar case. The very one that contained the Chess Set of Karmadont. "Everything else is contestable, but the Chess Set really is yours regardless of how you spin it. Mahan, I officially give you these items."

Anastaria placed the case with the Chess Set right on the table. A notification flashed by saying that I had received an item and instantly a 'self-destruct' timer appeared—the case was lying on the table without an owner, so the system decided that it was trash that must be destroyed. In five minutes, there would be nothing left of the Chess Set—unless I pick it up.

"Everything else, is my rightful loot," the girl smiled as soon as I picked up the case in my hands and opened its lid. Eight green orcs, eight blue dwarves, two giants, two ogres, two lizards and one king. Everything that I managed to craft by that point was mine once again—but I didn't understand how. Anastaria would never act so carelessly with items like this, which meant she had her reasons. I needed to speak with Clutzer. Damn it!

"So I guess it's pointless to ask for the Eye?" I ventured, replacing the figurines and stuffing the whole case into my bag.

"Well..." said Anastaria with a silly face. "What Eye?"

"I see. What do you want for Eric's bracers and the Crastil of Shalaar? The Bracers are the first item Eric crafted, they unlocked Crafting for him, so I'd like to return them to him...As for the Crastil of Shalaar, that's the only item that I have from Renox."

"You're scaring me, Danny," Anastaria shook her head with surprise. "You're so calm, collected, thoughtful, constructive...You don't seem at all like the Shaman that I spent three wonderful months with."

"But you haven't answered me. We can deal with the Eye later, but I'd like to decide about the Bracers and the Crastil right now. Do you want to make a deal? And if so, what do you want for those items?"

"Hmm, yeah, that's quite a dilemma you're raising," said Anastaria, watching my eyes carefully. "I understand why you want the Bracers—the first crafted item is also the first of its kind. But the

Crastil...You must know something no one else does, right?"

"You still haven't answered," I went on plying my line.

"I will give you these items in exchange for information—specifically, what you need the Crastil for," Stacey announced. "You will tell me everything and summon the Emperor to confirm that you haven't concealed anything from me. Once the Emperor confirms your words, you'll get the bracers and Crastil."

"There are many Crastils in Barliona," I shrugged, "and Eric can always make more bracers. It's not like I won't survive without them. Simply, they were originally mine and I'd like to have them back. We still have a half hour ahead of us. You don't mind if I eat, do you? I have a busy day ahead of me..."

Greetings Kreel!

I'm finally ready to take a trip with you to the cave of the Dragon. When are you going to be ready? I'll be bringing a Level 204+ Raid Party with fifty people, Plinto and several others. I figure that should be enough to kill the Shadow Dragon. Let me know when you can take on this Dungeon.

Leaving Anastaria on her own as soon as our hour of daily spousal interaction had ended, I began to put our plan in action. To begin with, I wrote a letter to Kreel, the owner of the Dragon of Shadow quest. Who knows how long it'll take him to get ready, so it was better to deal with this sooner. The important thing was to receive the Dungeon coordinates; I'd figure the terms of our venture with the Titan later. The right way to do it would be to buy the coordinates from him and stop worrying about...By the way! I can attack players now! I'll have to fine tune our contract. Sorry Kreel, I'm not that easy to deal with—and neither is life in general...

"Mahan!" Elizabeth met me as happily as ever. "I'm so happy that you're doing what I asked you and spending time with your spouse! Family is the most important thing we have in Barliona!"

"Elsa, I don't have a lot of time right now. Tell me—do you have any quests for me? I'm a bit tired of sitting in one place and I want to wander around the world and encounter some scary monsters...If Eluna forbids me from participating in the war against Geranika, maybe I'll be able to help some other way in my battle with Shadow? I don't know...Maybe someone needs me to carry some water for them?"

The High Priestess laughed at this: "Water? What an idea! That'll be a real picture—Earl Mahan carrying water for the pigs. I could sell tickets to such a show. No, Mahan, you won't need to carry any water; the serfs can take care of that. As for the battle against Shadow beyond the borders of Armard..." The High Priestess's eyes fogged over as if she was downloading information, but then went clear a moment later and Elsa continued sadly: "Of course, I have one assignment! There's been a tragedy on our side!"

"A tragedy? Let me help," I immediately offered. If the old man was right and there would be an investigation into how the Tears of Harrashess were obtained, then giving me the coordinates to the Dungeon directly was impossible and I had to receive them through standard gameplay. So first I would be issued a quest in the course of which I would stumble across the Dungeon I needed. Or, if I skip it, I'd receive a hint about its location. The important thing was to be in the right place at the right time.

"That would be wonderful of you. We recently sent a mission to the famed city of Klarg in the Free Lands. My priests took up residence on the city's outskirts, several kilometers from the village of Blue Mosses and began to bring the light of Eluna to the inhabitants of that Dukedom, when something odd began to happen—they began to lose their cows. The priests are worried and afraid that there's something in the woods! A huge favor—go there and find out what's making the livestock disappear. I'm worried about my subjects—they have hardly become adepts and already I've had to send them on such a serious mission."

Quest available: 'Lost Cows.' Description:

Cows have begun to vanish in the woods outside of the village of Blue Mosses. Find out what is happening. Quest type: Common. Reward: +100 to Reputation with the Priests of Eluna and 30 silver. Penalty for failing or refusing the quest: −100 to Reputation with the Priests of Eluna.

I have to confess that I couldn't help but smile as I read the quest description—a reward of 30 silver coins was quite the bounty! Accepting the quest and glancing at the map to see where these Blue Mosses were located, my smile grew wider—a portal would have cost me several thousand gold, were I not a Harbinger.

"You find this funny?" Elsa asked, misunderstanding my grin. "People are suffering, they're afraid, they have to spend money they don't have, and you're happy as if nothing's going on?"

"No, not at all!" I had to hide my smile and provide explanations—when you have a very high Attractiveness level with an NPC, you're constantly forced to be careful because they can find fault in any trifle. The developers find it advantageous to keep the players working for Attractiveness, so they try to lower it any chance they get. "I simply recalled a moment— you remember when we traveled to Krispa recently, the town on the border with Kartoss. Well, we encountered an enormous mob of Free Citizens from Kartoss there! Your quest simply reminded me of that happy battle, so I smiled..."

"No but I'd know for certain if there was a mob of Kartossians in Mosses," Elsa assured me. "I talk to the head of the mission every day over my amulet and she hasn't mentioned anything of the kind. When will you go?"

"Today—why waste time? I'll go to Blue Mosses and find out what's going on with your cattle there. I figure I'll be back tomorrow."

"It's decided then! I'll be waiting for your report tomorrow evening to see what you've managed to accomplish. For now, forgive me, I have to run. Business awaits!"

I emerged from the temple, looked at the small square with its pretty fountain, at the players darting here and there and suddenly a wondrous idea occurred to me. Retrieving one of my many amulets, I made a call.

"Speaking!"

"What's up, Evolett? This is Mahan troubling you. Do you have a moment?"

"You know yourself that for a partner I always do," came Evolett's immediate reply, but I cut him off.

"Let's skip the idealistic stuff for now. I'm calling because I remember you once offered me two tickets to the celebration of Tavia's and Trediol's wedding. I understand that the deadlines have long since expired, but you wouldn't be able to arrange a tour of the Dark Lord's castle for a partner? I don't even need to see the Dark Lord—I just want to see what the designers cooked up in the Nameless City. Can you do it?"

A silence ensued in the amulet, forcing me to smirk. The idea of calling Evolett had been so spontaneous that I couldn't restrain myself. It was difficult to admit it, but I liked this person and at the moment, I wanted to clarify what our relations would be like in the future. Since I was no longer going to disband my clan, there'd be a life for me in Barliona after my revenge and Evolett was one of the few clan leaders who had respectable clan resources at his disposal. It was a bit dumb of me to do this of course, but something told me that I had to do it this way. Call him up and ask him directly.

"The celebration was called off due to the Heart of Chaos stuff," the answer came at last. "If you decide to visit our Empire, I'll be happy to give you two tickets."

"Oh really? And when has the celebration been rescheduled to?"

"Either right after the Heart is destroyed, or never—what's the point of celebrating when the world's been destroyed? The NPCs aren't fond of feasts during times of plague...So in other words, it'll happen in a month and a half, no sooner."

"Wonderful! Save two tickets for me and I'll make sure to swing by for them," I assured the Priest, delicately skirting around the topic of what had happened to me on the plateau. I need Evolett for his resources and he's just made it plain that if I ask him, he'll help me out. That's enough for me.

Hanging up, I placed the amulet aside and decided to check one more thing that wouldn't leave me alone. I wouldn't have my Shamanic powers back for another week and a half, but this didn't prevent me from speaking with Kornik. I wonder if the same channel would work if I wanted to get in touch with Fleita.

"*Student?*" I sent a telepathic message into nowhere, imagining the Zombie. I have no idea how this works, so I'll just do what I know—and all I know is how to send the messages.

"*AAAAAAHHH!*" Fleita's terrified and savage scream erupted in my head. A second later my amulet began to vibrate.

"Hello!" I answered happily, knowing full well who was on the other end of the 'line.'

"Mahan! You scared me! How'd you do that?! You entered my head! I could hear your thoughts! That was cool! Let's do it again!"

A torrent of random requests began to pour from the amulet, then Fleita hung up and thoughts began to appear in my head as if I were speaking to Anastaria:

"*OLD MAHAN, HE'S NO FUN! CAN YOU HEAR ME?*"

Perhaps 'appear' is an understatement. The

thoughts filled everything around me, stifling the noise of the city and forcing me to fall to my knees with my hands clapped to my ears. I felt as if I had two megaphones screaming in both ears, amplifying the sound by hundreds of decibels.

"You're right—old Mahan ain't much fun," I replied to Fleita, still shaking from the clamor in my head, and added: *"Now stop yelling. I can hear you just fine. If you keep this up, I'll get tinnitus!"*

"Oh, I'm sorry," Fleita replied quietly. *"Can we really communicate this way?"*

"Well theoretically not, but it's not like anyone will overhear us," I quipped sarcastically. *"Now I'll be able to read all your secret thoughts and find out where you were last night."*

"WHAAAT?!" An angry roar filled my head, forcing me to grab onto my ears again. A notification popped up informing me that I'd just received the 'Dazed' debuff, and giving me pause for thought— maybe I could do the same to Anastaria? It'd be mean of me of course, but hey, it's fun to be mean too. *"Don't you dare dig around my head!"*

"Calm down. No one's going to dig around your head. That was a joke! I didn't think you'd react this way. Tell me, where are you and what are you up to?"

"What, you don't know?"

"If I knew, I wouldn't be asking."

"I..." Fleita began and our link broke off. I guess the girl's Energy had run out, since mine was halfway

depleted, and so now my student was lying on the ground somewhere, croaking something incomprehensible and scaring innocent bystanders. One major downside of exhausting your Energy was that signing out to reality and re-entering the game didn't restore it. You either had to wait or drink water. There was no other option.

"Mahan, such conversations really take a lot out of me," Fleita wheezed through the amulet five minutes later, simultaneously telling me two things. The first was that she had restored her Energy the natural way—which meant there hadn't been anyone around her with water—and second that Fleita had her sensory filter turned off. This is what surprised me the most, since underage players in Barliona weren't allowed to do this.

"Tell me, dear, how high is your sensory filter set to?" I asked the question that concerned me.

"It's at ninety per...Oh! That's not fair!" Fleita all but screamed in a bitter voice. "I wanted to surprise you!"

"I'm sick and tired of surprises," I smiled. "But you still haven't answered my question. Where are you and what are you doing?"

"I'm outside of the Nameless City, gathering mushrooms. Evolett told me that it's not fitting for a Raider to go where he shouldn't be and sent me to training. He thinks that if I'm busy picking mushrooms I won't send a Spirit of Eavesdropping to their meeting."

"Erm, what for?"

"Well I'm curious! They discuss all kinds of things there! For example, before they noticed my Spirit, I managed to hear that the Dark Legion is getting ready to attack one of the cities of the Free Lands, that they plan on expanding and become a true competitor to Phoenix, knocking them off their throne, that...Oh, I think I'm spilling clan secrets here...Mahan, don't ask me about this—I only found this stuff out by accident and in fact have forgotten all of it. By the way, did you know that Evolett has three scrolls of Armageddon? They were talking about this right before they found my Spirit, so I remember it clearly..."

"When were they talking?" I inquired, pricking up my ears.

"This morning. After that they caught me and sent me to gather mushrooms. Forty forest toadstools...Which grow at a probability rate of 3%. I've only found three so far..."

"Okay, I see. All right, once you've caught them all, call me and I'll take you with me. We'll go kill some monsters."

"Cool. With who?" Fleita wondered, but I hung up and reached for the previous amulet. So you have three scrolls of Armageddon and you just happen to mention them several moments before some Rogue or Assassin, with high level Detection, noticed Fleita's

Spirit? Well, well...

"Evolett, this is Mahan again. I imagine you know why I'm calling."

"About the tickets?"

"That's right, the tickets. Three tickets to a big old fireworks show. You know, aside from all the other stuff, I'm curious how you obtained these tickets. You didn't have them only a couple weeks ago. I remember that very well—when we were on our sailing expedition, your tickets would've come in very handy."

No doubt Evolett is not alone at the moment and therefore I didn't want to speak about the scrolls of Armageddon openly. But I couldn't not ask either—we'd almost died out there on the seas. Something wasn't tallying here.

"You're right. I do have three tickets, and I am ready to share them," came the reply. "I won't tell you how I acquired them, but I will say that I had to make new friends with some interesting people to do it. The tickets are theirs, not mine. I'm sure you want to relax a bit, so I'll be happy to give you the three invitations as a partner. Use them wisely. Write down these coordinates—I can meet you in ten minutes."

The amulet fell silent, giving me the chance to consider the news I'd just heard. Why does it have to be so complicated with everyone? Evolett had seen Fleita's Spirit from the get go, and used her to tell me that he wants to hurt Phoenix. He'd mentioned the scrolls and, if I understand correctly, the chance to take part in a small raid. And what's more is that, judging by my first call, he had expected it. Hmm...yeah...Considering that Evolett and Ehkiller were family, I'm having trouble understanding the motives of the Kartossian. Doesn't he know perfectly well what I'd use the scrolls for...Is there a dispute between the brothers then? Damn! I may as well head back to the mines and never worry about anything but ore and rats for the rest of my life...

"Have a seat," Evolett indicated an unoccupied seat. I looked around and automatically opened my map in order to figure out exactly where I was. I opened it and froze, for the normal locale map had been replaced by a three dimensional projection of the castle. The system had determined where I was and adjusted the locale representation. And because I was a Harbinger and in a castle, I had to have the option of blinking to any part of the building. I had assumed that this only worked in Altameda, but....

"The main hall of the Dark Legion castle?" I asked with surprise, realizing where I had been invited. "Open for teleportation?"

"Certainly not, but that wouldn't stop a Harbinger or a god." The Priest smiled meaningfully. I suppose that in the intervening ten minutes between his invitation and my arrival, he had told the hobgoblins, who were supposed to block my Blink, to go take a walk.

"So what's up with the tickets?" Accepting the

invitation, I sat down in the armchair. "And why three at once?"

"Three clans, three tickets," Evolett shrugged. "It's a bit easier in Kartoss than in Malabar when it comes to these things. Everyone tries to work together here."

"Okay, I'll put it a different way—why? I know that you know how these tickets will be used. You know that I know what your relationship is with Ehkiller. Why?"

"Would you like some wine maybe?" asked the leader of the Dark Legion as if he hadn't heard my question. "The best vintage from the Golden Horseshoe, presented to me by the owner himself. What I like about Barliona is its fantasy. You enter it in order to feel like a hero saving little children. I love children very much, Mahan. I'm already almost sixty and, trust me, my appearance in-game doesn't match the one in real life—this one is heavily modified. Back in reality, Evolett is an ordinary old man who wants only one thing—grandchildren. Children are more than just little people. They're what makes life worth living."

"I don't understand," I shook my head. Either I'm dumb or Evolett has confused me with someone.

"In real life my job is to help orphans find their new families. I don't place them in some orphanage somewhere, no—I find families for them, facilitate the adoption process, help them adapt and return to life. I even got a job in the mayor's office in order to obtain the power to punish abusive parents who do such terrible things to their children that..." Evolett checked himself as if it was difficult for him to even remember this, let alone speak of it. "I was very concerned about the fate of one girl in particular. I won't mention what her father did to her, but it was so bad that even the mines weren't a sufficient punishment. The girl had been broken so completely that she had become a vegetable. She was shut up within herself. The only time she showed any signs of life was when she'd panic at the approach of a man...I know what my brother and my niece did to you and can imagine how you feel at the moment. But I also know what you did for Rastilana. In real life, her name is Julia. Even if all she does now is babble about Dragons, at least she came back to life. Uncertainly and tentatively at first, but she has begun to get in touch with the doctors and has stopped trembling when they are near her...It was her flight on the Dragon..."

Evolett poured himself some wine and drained the glass in one go, as if it were filled with eighty-proof vodka. For a short while he fixed me with a distant stare and then finally went on:

"Yesterday I found out that you had returned to Barliona. One doesn't have to be a genius to know why you came back. No one would forgive what they did to you. You don't have the resources to exact your revenge, but I did want to thank you for helping Rastilana. I'll deal with my brother myself. That's all I have to say."

"A campaign to the Free Lands?" I asked another question, accepting three scrolls with the most destructive spell in Barliona from the Priest.

"Tell Clutzer to get in touch with Zlatan to hammer out the details. I want to capture a city that has nothing to do with our empires, so there shouldn't be any issues with reputation."

A silence ensued which I was afraid to disturb. On the one hand, I had nothing left to do in Kartoss and it was time to go back to Anhurs. On the other hand, I felt like a gift such as this called for some words from me. A present of three scrolls with a nominal value of six to eight million gold kind of begged for some statement of gratitude, but what exactly...so I remained silent, staring into the blazing fireplace.

"In three weeks, it'll be Allie's birthday," Evolett said all of a sudden.

"Allie?"

"Barsina. They plan on celebrating in the game as well as in reality—in Vengard. All of the Phoenix leadership should be there, as well as the leaders of their affiliated clans. Everyone will come dressed in their best clothes. Everyone will do their best to show off their status, their riches, their success...No one knows about these tickets and I hope very much no one will know until the very end. I'll be there too. I'm going to ask my Tailor to make me the best suit possible today. Do we understand each other?"

"We understand each other," I confirmed, shook the Priest's hand and entered the coordinates for the village of Blue Mosses. It's hard not to understand a person who offers you the chance to destroy the belle monde of Malabar with all its unique items. After all, Armageddon doesn't work any other way.

I imagine that if this celebration goes off the way I want it to, Anastaria will be a little vexed...

CHAPTER FOUR

BLUE MOSSES

*L*OOK IN THY GLASS *and tell the face thou viewest,*
Now is the time that face should form another,
Whose fresh repair if now thou not renewest,
Thou dost beguile the world, unbless some brother.

Message sent...

A mere thirty minutes went by before the reply I was waiting for arrived:

But if thou live remembered not to be,
Die single and thine image dies with thee.

When I reached the central square of Blue Mosses, instead of registering in the hotel or with the alderman, I simply signed out to reality. My conversation with Evolett had put me on one curious idea that I just couldn't get rid of. It was time to turn on my brain. Pulling my body out of the capsule and getting comfortable on my sofa, I sank deep into thought. Let's see what we had:

First—some secret faction was conspiring against Phoenix. This is all well and good, except that they wanted my help, meaning that I'd be in everyone's crosshairs. Given my past relationship with Phoenix and Shaman Mahan's reputation among the Barliona community, no one would doubt for a moment my desire to exact revenge and hurt the clan of the flaming chicken. And consequently the conspirators would remain in the shadows, while the full weight of Phoenix's counterblow, and there was no doubting that there would be a counterblow, would fall square on my head. An enticing proposition...what could you say?

Second—according to the conspiracy, Phoenix would pay me about two billion gold. Supposedly, this amount would guarantee my safety and security. Well I think I must be losing touch with the world around me: What would prevent the conspirators from taking all of this money from me? Even let's say by brute force. I recalled the old man mentioning that Ehkiller couldn't be tracked down in reality during our conversation. So this secret faction had promised to protect me from Phoenix's wrath, and yet its representative didn't once mention that nothing would happen to me. Does that old man really need me around as a witnesses? I kind of doubt that.

Third—tinkering with the game data. Other than mental confusion, what could explain me forgetting my earlier career? I had trained to be a software developer and clearly remembered attending re-training courses, where the teachers drilled a single notion into our brains: Hackers, whether they are virtual or operating in reality, would be punished to the fullest extent of the law. And furthermore, the law would come down on both the hackers and their accomplices with equal force. Any way you spin it, until I notify law enforcement of the information I have, I'm technically an accomplice. So even if everything goes according to the old man's plan, I won't be able to avoid the mines. And further down the line, what's to keep the old man and his people from betraying me and blaming me for the whole affair? Wasn't Marina bad enough already? By the way—I need to meet up with her already. The girl had spent so much time trying to meet with me, that it'd be impolite to delay seeing her any longer. Not to mention that she had helped me out several times by providing information I needed.

Fourth—Evolett. Maybe I'm just missing something, but why would a brother go against his own brother? He must understand that Ehkiller's reputation will take a hit if Plinto manages to infiltrate Phoenix's prettiest castle in the middle of a celebration and then detonates Armageddon in it. Even if their best players like Anastaria and Hellfire will show up to the party in outfits made by Reander, some part of the attendees will surely wear their best equipment. Especially those among them who want to become Raiders with Phoenix—even though this is supposed to be a mere birthday party, plenty of guests will bring their most powerful armor and weapons. No doubt Phoenix will charge an admission fee and then when Armageddon goes off in the middle of all this pageantry...The number of players furious with my clan will exceed all limits. And if on top of all this there are members of the Imperial family among the attendees, then...Well, Evolett's actions clearly suggest that 'we're partners and all, but I've got my brother's back—no offense.' Which gives rise to the next question—why give me the three scrolls? A single scroll would be enough to hurt Ehkiller's game-wide rep, and yet Evolett went over and beyond and provided me with all three. Why did he do this? What's in it for him? It's odd and I can't understand it.

So all in all, I have a huge number of questions that I simply don't know the answers to, and yet I'm starting to make some kind of decisions and take my first steps out of this maze. An odd sense of anxiety and foreboding took up residence in my head and was refusing to leave me for several minutes already—I must be doing something wrong and, if I go on this way, I won't be able to do anything about the consequences later.

Well damn it! Am I a Shaman or what? If I'm a Shaman, isn't it time to listen to my premonition not only in the game but out in reality? Ultimately my premonition remains a premonition, regardless of whether it's caused by my subconscious or generated by the program. Something big and, ahem, unpleasant is coming—and I need to survive it, so it's time to recall the lessons of the past and come up with a plan B.

And this is all why I posted a small poem on one very interesting forum, having first made a gross error in the text by substituting the word 'brother' for the original's 'mother.' Anyone unfamiliar with the *Sonnets* won't notice, while those who are, will think that I made a mistake. And yet both I and the person to whom this message was addressed understood its contents perfectly well—I needed to meet and all of the channels of communication might be under surveillance. According to the unspoken rule of the freelance artists who congregated on this forum, a mere thirty minutes later there were hundreds of other posts with poems that served to conceal the 'correspondence' of two specific people. Each 'artist,' (whom I too had once been), had a very limited circle of contacts, so the overwhelming mass of people simply stayed away from me, and yet I needed them since they made it much more complicated to track my conversation. When we had become 'free,' the word 'paranoia' had become fundamental to our lives and most of what we did we did under its cover. Over the past year, I had for some reason begun to trust people and throw myself headfirst into the most insane ventures instead of evaluating the situation carefully and weighing my options. So it was time to stop now and think everything over carefully. I have the time and opportunity—everything else will come.

My friend's flawless response also had its meaning: 'I understood your message and will try to arrange a meeting.' If the couplet that came in reply had contained an error of its own, the message would be clear—Sergei just couldn't do anything to meet me. There was no mistake however, so I had a chance to escape the trap that had surrounded me from all sides.

It was only once I'd regained the capacity to think clearly, or at least convinced myself that I did, that I began to realize the magnitude of everything going on around me. If there is some secret faction that can track my movements in the game, then it can just as well stay informed about where I am in reality—as they made abundantly clear to me with my nocturnal outing. In that case, I can be certain that neither phone calls nor emails are secure—the fact that I was being tracked was clear as day. This is why I sent the code phrase to my friend despite the fact that we hadn't once used it ever before. This is also why I was incredibly happy to see his reply. And this was finally why I was getting ready to go to Cafe Alventa—it was there that our agreed upon meeting was to take place.

"Who else dares challenge me one on one?"

exclaimed one of the establishment's regulars, looking over the dimly lit hall. I had secreted myself in a distant corner, ordered some beer and did my best to look like a tired player who just wanted to take a break from Barliona for a little bit. Alventa was famous among the gaming brethren for its ability to put one's brain back into its customary place, turning a denizen of Barliona into a denizen of Earth, so there wasn't anything strange about my being in this place—I needed this anyway.

"Me!" sounded the drunk voice of one of the patron's and a fairly puny guy of about thirty got to his feet. "Texas Hold 'Em, with standard rules."

"Accepted!" replied the first guy and the two cardsharps passed into a neighboring room. The screen instantly switched to their duel, along with a list of cards that each player had been dealt, yet the speakers remained silent—according to the standard rule-set, all sound and electrical signals in the room were jammed. The only thing that trickled out was a video signal, and even that passed through a system of mirrors with the camera recording the final reflection. The room in which the duel was taking place had become a unique place that granted perfect solitude to the players within. You couldn't be too careful when money was on the line.

Without doubting for a second that I was still under surveillance, I sipped on my beer and watched the game. Although, to be honest, there wasn't much to watch—the puny challenger was being handled, well, handily. It was fun to watch him do his best raising too quickly with pocket aces or bluffing pitifully with a 2-8 off suit. You couldn't see the players' faces on the screens—only the cards on the table, the piles of chips and the dealer's hands periodically flashing by, and yet all of this was enough to understand that the room was actually hosting a negotiation.

This was room's true purpose, the one it had been created for—to ensure a 'secret' meeting between two 'freelance artists...'

"Aren't you all sick of chewing your cud like a bunch of cows?" The regular's ringing voice resounded through the establishment. "Who else dares challenge me one on one?"

"Me!" I yelled and stood up from my table. It was now my turn to flash my hands in front of the camera and make childish mistakes in poker. "Texas Hold 'Em with standard rules..."

"Sounds like you're really up the creek without a paddle," said Sergei after hearing my story. He entered the room only after the regular had closed the doors, activated the jamming system and donned the fantastical helmet that kept him from hearing or seeing what was happening around him. Our secret meeting had to remain secret and Alventa's owners were utterly fastidious about this principle.

"That hardly even does my situation any justice,"

I agreed, committing another error in my game. This service had to be paid for, so the regular always won his games with the free artists, whenever they needed a meeting. You could of course come and actually play a game with him, in which case knowledge and experience really did matter, but if you were there to meet with someone, the house had to win. This was ironclad.

"You do understand that the old man is going to use you like some kid?"

"I understand."

"And his offer is illegal."

"I get that too..."

"And still you're planning on accepting his offer," Sergei concluded, when I won one more time, thus indicating that the conversation might last longer.

"Right on the mark," I sighed. "Sergei—any way you spin this thing, there's some trap here. I can't abandon my revenge—my conscience won't let me. And I won't commit everything I have to it either— what's the point of revenge if you perish in the process? The only thing left is to take the offer."

"That's all very fine and all, but I can't understand one thing—what do you want revenge for anyway? What did Anastaria do to you that you now want to destroy her avatar? By the way, I personally think that as soon as you saddle her with the Tear, Ehkiller will raise all hell with the Corporation and force them to add several items that will dispel the

Tear's effects and that won't belong to you alone. After all, something could happen to you. What if you stop playing? Or lose interest? Or anything else that might happen to you...If I had Ehkiller's resources, I would go all out in this respect."

"That's a good point," I replied pensively, folding a hand that was clearly a flush. "I won't give you an answer right now, but at least I have a reason to talk to the old man again. It doesn't really seem to me that he's thought that part through."

"If everything you told me was the truth, then they're already watching your every step. Do you even understand the amount of money on the line? Can you imagine two billion? That's too much to let you out of their sight."

"That's exactly why I called you. I need to disappear, and for real and for a long time—while retaining my ability to enter the game. Let's assume the worst-case scenario—my old man works for the Corporation and can easily trace the location of the capsule that I'm using to enter the game, so I need a proxy array of, oh, I guess seven servers might suffice."

"Seven?!" Sergei asked with surprise, looking at me like I was crazy. "Do you understand how much that costs?"

"Money's no matter—my life is dearer to me. I'll need a feedback line at every level of the array that will let me know about any unwanted guests. I have to know as soon as they start looking for me."

"Hmm, yeah..." Sergei replied, deep in thought. "I can see that your imprisonment has really rehabilitated you—as soon as you're out you're already in the middle of another mess. I'll need three days and money to get everything ready."

"Send me the invoices. I'll pay immediately. Sergei—I really don't want to do all this, but I have a serious premonition that if I don't, I'll be worse off for it. And it's not like I can go to the cops. What am I going to tell them? You see, detective, I met someone who told me this and that? I believe that I'm brilliant and unique and that someone will hack the game for my sake? I imagine they'll assign me to a nut ward before I'm done talking. And I can't simply disappear either—Phoenix is going to drone on in my head for the rest of my life. That's the long and short of it."

"And yet that doesn't absolve you of the requirement to record your message to the Corporation," Sergei parried. "You know yourself that if something goes amiss, then you'll have an ironclad alibi—since you'd notified the corporation of what was coming. Whether they react to it or not doesn't concern you, but as an honest and responsible player, you're obliged to submit a proper report about this flagrant violation that you found out about. Dan, if you don't do this, they'll sic the hounds on you later on."

"Agreed," I nodded. "As soon as you arrange a

safehouse for me, I'll write to the Corporation. Then I'll also get a chance to see how the old man responds to it."

"Okay, then I'll be on my way," said Sergei, standing up. "I don't have anything to add. We need to act and...Dan, I'm very happy that you found a way out of Barliona. Expect news and some people in three days. They'll take you to your new place of residence. Good luck to you, Mahan!"

"Good luck to you, Filin," I replied, going all in. The time had come to end our game.

"A goodie day to yar, Sire Earl!" the alderman of Blue Mosses said in his awkward Malabarian as soon as I returned to the game. I looked around and did my best to stifle a grin—almost all of the inhabitants of Blue Mosses had gathered around me, as if demonstrating that if I say all the right things, I'll be able to acquire a new quest. By default, Barliona's NPCs go about their business and don't pay any attention to the players as the latter flit about here and there, and yet since the villagers reacted to my appearance in the game by immediately gathering around me, I could safely assume that either they're about to chase me away or ask me for help. There was no third option.

"A good day to yar too, my dear Sire Casheesh," I replied, glancing at the alderman's name.

"Please call me Cash," the alderman corrected me. It's odd—I can understand what he's saying, but the way this NPC is saying it is so odd.

"How can I be of service, my dear Cash?" I uttered the standard formula for receiving a quest. There wasn't much sense in wasting time in this place, the Priests were outside of it, and yet habit becomes second nature. If I'm going to talk to the NPCs, I want to hear everything they have to tell me.

"Service? Why there is one indeed, Sire Mahan," I prepared myself for a new quest, when the alderman suddenly changed topics entirely: "Please remove thyself from this village within the next two minutes. If not, we will help thee. With pitchforks and torches."

I looked around myself at the villagers gathered around us and only now noticed that they were not at all disposed in a friendly manner. Angry faces, clubs, scythes and pitchforks in hand, several people even had huge dogs on chains—it was quite a welcoming party. They had come out to meet me like I was some notorious outlaw—they couldn't keep me from entering the village, but they could escort me out in short order. With a guard of honor and all.

"You are prepared to attack an Earl of Malabar?" I raised an eyebrow demonstratively, and turned on the aristocrat. All that I needed was for NPCs to start telling me what I could and couldn't do in the game...Clutzer, the old man, Evolett and now it was the NPCs too. Soon enough, even Anastaria would start calling in orders.

"We request that the Earl leave the village

peacefully," the alderman went on, without blushing, "Sire Baron won't be angry if we help thee leave."

"So it's like that?" I asked with even more surprise. "And you think the Baron of Klarg won't be angry if he's later examined about this episode by the Emperor of Malabar or the Dark Lord of Kartoss? Very odd."

"The Dark Lord?" the alderman froze and even took half a step back. "Sire Earl is from Malabar, what Kartoss have do with it?"

"The Dark Lord of Kartoss is a very close acquaintance of mine," I smiled, having felt my way to the beginning for our subsequent conversation. Opening the reputation chart, I highlighted the 'Dark Lord of Kartoss' entry and sent it to the alderman. The status of 'Respect'—which was about 2000 points away from 'Exalted'—is worth a lot in this game. Especially with those who hate Malabar and everything related to it. By the way! It looks like I've already figured out why Eluna's Priests are losing their cows out here!

"But Malabar..." the alderman tried to object, yet I had decided to take this situation to its ultimate end. Turning to the village gates, I said:

"I'll make sure to let the Magistrates know about my treatment in the Klarg Barony this very day. It's not merely ignorant to welcome an Earl with pitchforks: It's a flagrant offense to the aristocracy of all of Barliona. I will do as you command and depart this place, Sire Casheesh. Good luck to you."

"Wait!" The alderman switched to Kartossian. Ah! Another test? Casheesh no longer had an accent, as if Kartossian was his mother tongue. "There has been a slight misunderstanding!"

"A misunderstanding?" I replied in the same language, indicating that I am perfectly familiar with it. "Is sticking a personal friend of the Duchess Urvalix onto a pitchfork a misunderstanding?"

"The Duchess Urvalix?" Casheesh squealed in a forlorn voice.

"Of course! I call upon the local Guardian as my witness—the Duchess Urvalix, who was formerly the Duchess of Caltanor, is a good friend of mine."

My hundred points of Attractiveness with Tavia played their part now and a bright aura surrounded me, finishing off the alderman. He collapsed to his knees and howled pitifully:

"Mercy oh Master Earl! Do not allow me to perish!"

Following the alderman's lead, the rest of the village dropped their gardening implements and collapsed to their knees, begging me to restrain my wrath and not mention this affair to anyone else. They offered money and goods and even the prettiest girl in the village as a handmaid to my castle, yet I shook my head to it all, realizing that I really hate it when people beg me on their knees before me. It's simply repellent!

"Is there really nothing that will allow the honorable Earl to forget about our mistake?" When the alderman ran out of arguments, which I was quite happy to see, Casheesh addressed me with the look of a beaten dog. Stifling another urge to raise him to his feet, I replied:

"There is. Information. I need to find out what has been happening to the cows of the Priests of Eluna."

"The cows?" The alderman's astonishment wiped his pitiful look right off. "Why but that's obvious—we've been taking them!"

"Why?"

"Because our earth is no place for dirty Malabarians. They're not welcome here! Even if they are keeping the cursed ones at bay...Our Baron prohibited us from hurting the Priests, but he didn't say anything about their cows."

"What cursed ones?"

"Nearby lies an evil place. The beasts there are altered—a strange darkness surrounds them. The Priests keep the beasts away from our village, so no one harms them. But as for the cows..."

"Don't change the topic. Where is this place located?" I grasped at the thread that should lead me to the entrance of the Shadow Dungeon. Altered beasts is quite a sign.

"Right here." A map of our surroundings appeared in Casheesh's hands and he pointed to a point about ten kilometers from Blue Mosses. "It's been three years now since this evil has appeared. At first the Master Baron fought it on his own, but when the Priests appeared everyone sighed a sigh of relief."

"Then this is what we'll do. You are to stop stealing the Priest's cows and return to them all the cows you've stolen to date. You are also not to harm them in any way in the future. Now give me the map," I added, checking mine. "And if you do this, I will give you my Earl's word that no one will hear of what just transpired here."

"The word of an Earl of Malabar?"

"The word of a friend of the Duchess," I corrected myself. Looking at the villagers still kneeling before me, I added: "You may rise."

Quest completed: 'Missing Cows.'

"Accepted," said the alderman, offering me his map. "Henceforth, no one shall do harm unto the Priests. Thank you, Master Earl, for your kindness and understanding. I suppose, we will go about our business—we need to find the cows and return them. There're just so many things to do..."

"Fleita! Enough mushroom picking for today. We've got some business!"

"Finally! I was starting to think you'd forgotten your promise!"

"Viltrius will summon you in a moment and send

you to me. What's up with the mushrooms?"

"I only found half of them! These stupid mushrooms refuse to grow!"

"Whoa!" said Fleita when she appeared in Blue Mosses and glanced at her map. "And what are we doing in this bleeping corner of the world?"

The speech synthesizer that was installed in all the gaming capsules, blocked players under 21 from using obscene language, and yet everyone understood exactly what the girl wanted to say.

"If you're going to curse, I won't bring you along anymore," I said authoritatively like some grade-school teacher.

"What do you mean you won't bring me along?" Fleita asked with surprise. "Hey Mahan, why are all the locals looking at me so oddly? And what are all those pitchforks and torches for?"

"To chase you out of town with, what else..?"

"Oh! I'm always happy to see that. You didn't tell me what we're doing here though..."

"Curiosity killed the cat! You've already earned your PvP status, I see."

"Dang! I wanted it to be a surprise—attack! It'd be the last thing you'd expect."

"Uh-huh, and later you'd be writhing in pain. Even if your sensory filter is as low as 90%, that 10% of sensations isn't something to sneer at you know."

"You can say that again. Just remembering the time I used up all my Energy makes me shudder! By the way, what's your sensory filter set to? Minimal? I mean, is it all the way down to 70%?"

This question rooted me in place. NO! I completely fail to sense a difference between the way it was and the way it is now. I still feel the blowing of a cold wind, the smell of firs throughout the forest, and I'd probably feel the sharpness of the pitchforks sticking into my stomach. This doesn't seem like 30% of sensations at all...

Dear game administrators,
Please help me get to the bottom of a little issue I've been having with my sensory filter settings...

My inquiry to the developers went out that very minute. It didn't matter that I was standing in the village gates. I didn't care that Fleita was beside me shifting from foot to foot and glancing with concern at the villagers who had gathered to escort her out with pitchforks. I needed to understand why I'm still playing with my full range of sensations, as if my filter was completely off.

"By the way, student, you never did brag to me about your Totem," I recalled, as soon as we walked out of the village. "Draco told me such crazy tales about it that now I'm curious about what you managed to scrounge up."

"What were the crazy tales he told you about my little Bunny?" Fleita frowned.

"Bunny?" I stopped in surprise. "You named your Bone Dragon...Bunny?"

"It's no worse than Draco," the girl's frown deepened. "He's still very small and I only have three minutes of summoning time with him left."

"For today...There's always tomorrow. It's not like you'll do anything useful with those three minutes today anyway," I said. The girl's words only served to pique my interest further.

"All right, all right. Stop pressuring me—'show me, show me...' Well, here you go!"

A moment passed and something appeared beside us. At first I didn't even understand who or what it was—just a jumble of huge flying bones that whirled around Fleita like one of the spells that a Death Knight has. But when this jumble of bones stopped spinning, froze and looked at me—shivers ran down my spine. Two eyes flaring with a cold fire stared at me from a bare skull. The wings had a transparent magical field instead of skin to trap the air. And the four bony paws with long crooked claws looked like they could rip apart anything. Fleita's Bone Dragon was beautiful and terrible at the same time.

"Hello teacher!" came a childish voice. It was so juvenile and thin that I replied without even thinking:

"Hello Bunny!"

The Dragon left Fleita and wheeled several times around me as if examining me.

"You are so big," my student's Totem remarked and returned to the girl. "I am weary. We shall meet later."

The bony whatchamacallit vanished and an entirely different whatchamacallit set upon me with her questions:

"What do you think? Isn't he adorable? Do you have any idea how happy I was when I got him? I was squealing with joy! Mahan, you're the best teacher I've ever had!"

"Yes, he truly is wonderful," I agreed with the girl. "How did you complete the trial?"

"Oh," Fleita blushed. "Kornik asked me never to tell anyone. He says that no one should know these things. Especially my teacher," the girl's white skin reddened with a blush and the Zombie began to resemble a living person.

"So it's like that?" I feigned offense. Fleita instantly backed down.

"I can't tell you in game! But no one can keep me from doing it out in reality. Tell me your number and I'll call you tonight to tell you everything!"

"It's okay," I smiled. "If Kornik asked you to keep it a secret, let it remain a secret. Let's go and see what's been haunting Blue Mosses."

It took us an hour to reach the location we needed. At first I considered simply blinking there, but then I decided a stroll would be nice too. I'm not much of a Shaman at the moment—I can't fight and I don't know what lies in wait for us up ahead, so it's better to take it nice and easy. I'll always be able to stress things later on. When the first Level 79 Shadow Wolf attacked us, it became clear that we were getting close.

"You took me along in order to fight animals?" Fleita, who was at Level 73, asked angrily after she had dealt with the wolf. "You're exploiting me!"

"You need to grind a bit, increase your level," I replied philosophically to the girl's complaint.

"You're only Level 137 yourself!"

"Not 'only,' but 'already!' These are different things entirely. Don't relax just yet—there're many battles that lie ahead. Replenish your Mana and on you go!"

I did my utmost to help the girl, but my Spirits refused to come. I could zip around the continent all I wanted, I could chat with my student telepathically, but there were no Spirits to summon. None of the modes worked. My abilities were gone and that was that.

"Erm, Mahan, are you sure that the two of us can handle this on our own?" the girl asked in a shocked tone after she had dealt with the tenth Wolf. Stopping at the edge of another glade, we were looking at a giant Oak with a bright, shimmering entrance to the Dungeon in its trunk. We had found our Dungeon! I doubt that there would be some other in this area. That just doesn't happen. But there was this one little snag—the glade was also playing host to a pack of thirty Shadow Wolves all at Level 150.

"Not anymore, no," I muttered, glancing desperately around for some solution to this problem. This was bad, but so was the alternative. Any way you looked at it, everything was a negative. I didn't want to share the Dungeon's location with anyone. No one, at least, whom I'd played the game with. So in effect, this was a dead end, unless that is...Damn, well why not? I reached for an amulet I hadn't ever used and made a call.

"Speaking!" sounded a hoarse female voice.

"Kalatea, how are you? This is Mahan from Malabar. Do you have a minute?"

"Mahan?" the girl asked puzzled, and then added: "The Dragon?"

"The very one. I need the assistance of your Order."

"I am listening..."

We couldn't complete this Dungeon on our own. There was no arguing with that. I had brought Fleita to bolster my hand in my dealings with Evolett—one more First Kill, unique for Kartoss, would mean a lot to him. But I didn't want to invite Plinto and Clutzer with their raid parties—I'm not one to harbor a grudge but I also don't have any problems remembering what they did. And finally I had no desire or time to recruit random players. The only way I had of completing the Dungeon (which I really needed to complete) was to invite a third party that wasn't involved in the relations between the Legends and Phoenix. This left only Kalatea and her Shamanic Order.

"What are your conditions?" The Shaman asked once I had finished my tale about the Dungeon I'd discovered.

"You get a First Kill, and I get all loot apart from the gold. That gets divided by an Imitator."

"Three million per warrior for the portal just to get a First Kill..." Kalatea began, but I cut her off.

"Several months ago I asked you to verify the possibility of a Harbinger blinking to a different continent. You said it was possible."

"Okay, let's say I shuttle my group over to your continent. But in order to reach your location, we'll still need a portal. Do you have an extra two hundred thousand?"

"You don't have to blink to my continent—I can pick you up from Narlak. At the moment, that area is off limits to players—the developers are up to something in there. But I can use it to blink to the Kalragon embassy in Astrum and pick you up. What do you think of my offer? All I need is your people and their coordinates."

"Will your student come with us?" Kalatea asked after she understood how I could reach Astrum. I was a Harbinger. Considering that she had designed the Shaman class, she understood perfectly well that you can't become a Harbinger without a student. And once she'd heard my hum to the affirmative, she clarified further: "What happens if he's killed? Have you put the Death Seal on him already?"

"My student is not an NPC. She is a player. A woman."

"I need an hour to call everyone," said Kalatea after an even longer pause. "And another three hours to get everyone to the embassy. You'll also need about three hours to transfer everyone to the starting location. When do we move out?"

"Are you bringing half of Astrum with you?" I smirked, imagining how much people we could transfer in three hours.

"A Harbinger may not transport more than five people per hour. Either one at a time or everyone at once, but no more than five—however you prefer. I'll bring fourteen Shamans and one tank. That's my raid party."

"Will Antsinthepantsa come too?"

"Of course! I had reckoned that she would become Harbinger much earlier than you. I guess I was wrong. I have one more condition—I want to speak with your student."

"No problem. She's free to do as she likes. As I told you, she comes with us. Start assembling your people."

"Okay, I'll send you the coordinates in an hour. Later!"

The amulet went silent but Fleita—who had

managed to stay tactfully quiet during our conversation—immediately fell upon me with a thousand questions. So I had to tell her how I met Kalatea and who she was. When I told the girl that Kalatea is the coolest Shaman in all of Barliona, Fleita emitted a sharp gasp. What a circus! The whole thing ended with Fleita pouting to let me know that she was offended at something. All of my questions were met with a single answer: "Everything's fine!" So I calmed down and decided to leave the whole thing alone for a while. If everything's fine, then it's fine.

"Wait here," I pointed at a short oak. "It'd be even better if you signed out to reality and took care of your chores. Tell everyone that under no condition are they to bug you about anything for the next five to six hours. You will be busy getting another First Kill."

"Sure thing, *dad!*" muttered Fleita, and dissolved into thin air. No, she really must be upset about something. But what?! What is this, daycare? I tried one more time to be paranoid about Fleita, but couldn't come up with anything: Despite everything Anastaria and Barsina had done to me, I still fully trusted my student and couldn't make anything of her periodical fits. A person involved in some kind of plot simply couldn't have become an Elemental Shaman and be well on her way to becoming a Great Shaman the way she was. Logic said the opposite, but my feelings, premonition and everything else remained firmly on the side of this peculiar girl. The only truly depressing thought was that, one day, she'd become someone's wife. And a wife like her could clean your brains in about ten minutes.

The incoming mail notification rang. An icon indicating I had received a message from the admins appeared in the bottom portion of the screen and I couldn't help but crack a grin. Look at that...how prompt of them! I opened my mailbox and was about to read the reply from the head honchos of Barliona when the list of the first ten items in my inbox drew my eye. Or rather not the list itself so much as a specific letter from a sender familiar to me: Kreel the Titan.

Hey Mahan!

It sure took you a while to make up your mind! At the moment, we have completed three Dungeon levels—that is, floors—and two remain. We haven't reached the final boss yet. If you want to join us— you'll have to pay, since I can handle the Dragon without you just fine. The price of participation is five million per player.

Kreel, Last of the Titans!

Why look at that!

I even lost interest in the mail icon for the admins' reply. Kreel is raiding the Dungeon without me?! How was this possible? I thought Renox clearly let him know that he has to take me with him!

I still didn't have access to Vilterax, so I did what seemed easiest at the current moment and got in touch with my teacher.

"Kornik?"

"I'm listening to you, oh student-with-no-abilities-to-actually-speak-telepathically-with-me," the goblin quipped.

"Why did Renox allow the Titan to kill the Shadow Dragon on his own?"

"Because this matter no longer concerns you. You're not going to Armard."

"I'm not going to Armard, but I need to be the first to kill the Dragon!"

"In that case I don't understand why you're pestering an old ailing goblin instead of asking your father directly..."

"Because I can't go to Vilterax. I don't know how to get there."

"I don't understand—that's what's keeping you?" There was so much surprise in the goblin's voice that I couldn't help but sense some trap. "You don't know how to get to Renox and so you decided to distract me from my grave and solemn business? You know it has been a while since I've punished you, student!"

"Former student," I corrected the goblin just in case, but immediately collapsed to my knees from Kornik's deafening roar.

"I'll show you what it means to be a former student! Tomorrow morning I expect you to appear *before me in Anhurs! I'll show you a former teacher in action!"*

A notification appeared informing me that I had received several temporary debuffs and a handy explanation for what was going on:

You have incurred the wrath of your teacher. Speak to him to receive your punishment. Quest type: Common, Class-based.

Kornik left my head, leaving me alone with my thoughts about the eternal question: 'What just happened?' The hell with the punishment—it couldn't really be that bad given that this was a game. They'll force me to help some old lady or something like that. It ain't scary. What's interesting is why I chose to get in touch with Kornik instead of Draco? That was a bit dumb of me. If there's anyone who can tell me about the reasons for why Renox adjusted the Kreel's quest assignment, it would be my Totem.

"Come here, Draco!"

"Coming, brother."

"You called?" An enormous Dragon appeared right beside me a second later. Draco arrived in his true appearance, once again stunning me with his proportions. You can't help but tremble a little when you're staring into a giant, toothy maw that's as big as your whole body.

"I did," I replied, sighing with relief when my

Totem, or pet as the Supreme Spirits had referred to him, shrunk to a manageable size. "Tell me, why has Renox allowed Kreel to kill the Shadow Dragon without me?"

"Because you were too long taking your rest, brother. The Shadow Dragon began to grow in power. A little longer and he will join Geranika. Can you imagine what'll happen if the Emperor of Shadow acquires a Dragon?"

"Judging by the way you say that, nothing good..."

"Precisely. No one knew when you'd return and no one wanted to rush you—you'd had your share of trials as it stood. So Renox met with Kreel, presented him with the Titan Armor which can withstand the Dragon's flame and sent him into battle."

"Renox gave something to Kreel?" I echoed surprised. "Why would the Titan accept a gift from him?"

In the brief time I've known Kreel he's struck me as a bit of a role player. He wasn't simply playing with a Titan avatar—he was a Titan, with all the hate of Dragons and desire to become the first and best that came with that race. Of course, everyone gets to choose how they'll lose their minds in this life, but in my view this was too much.

"When Kreel saw the armor, his jaw just about fell off," grinned Draco. "This wasn't just an item. Renox gave him one of the nine items in the Divine

Set of the First King of the Titans."

"Divine?" I echoed surprised. "Is that some new item set?"

"No, it's just that before his death, the king was carried away to the Celestial Empire. And items that we call Legendary here are called Divine over there. I guess the word just stuck in my mind, so that's how I refer to the set. The Legendary set of Nabudhossar, the first king of the Titans, was given to him by the Ancients and others whose names have lots of letters and are hard to pronounce."

"Hang on, you said one of the nine items. Where are the rest?"

"One already belonged to Kreel—the sword, I believe. Father only had one, and it was tied to a certain class. As I recall it, he said that he knew someone who knew someone who knew someone who knew about the other items. What do you need them for? They're for Titans."

"Life's long," I shrugged. "Who knows when I might have to need to strike a bargain with Kreel."

"Oh! A plan for the future. Then okay. Listen, what are you doing here alone in the forest? And so far from Malabar...These are the Free Lands, aren't they? And isn't there some strange shadowy place nearby?" Draco twitched a little as he asked this last question. It was like the thought alone revolted him.

"We're going to do some fighting. Want to join us?"

"Like you need to ask! Who are we going to fight against?"

Having told Draco the story about how I'd stumbled across this Dungeon, I couldn't talk him out of running ahead to do some reconnaissance. The Dragon swore to stay out of any trouble he came across and dashed off to observe the Shadow Wolves. In the Totem's own words: 'That's a sight to behold!' Well, anyway, he's a Level 200 Dragon and the wolves aren't even at a hundred and fifty yet.

After Draco left, I opened my mailbox again and began reading the reply from the game admins:

> *Dear Mahan,*
>
> *Thank you for your inquiry...*
>
> *We'd like to bring to your attention that we are currently offering a new service—you may now transfer your character to a different faction...*
>
> *We wish to inform you that at the current moment your sensory filter is turned all the way up to 100% and your level of sensory perception is therefore at 0%. In order to increase your sensory perception, please visit the nearest client affairs office located at the following address...*
>
> *We wish to remind you that in the coming months there will be...*

Today was clearly not my day. Kreel, Kornik, Renox and now the damn admins! Why the hell are they telling me that I'm playing without any sensory perception if I can feel the cold wind blowing on my skin right this instant? And what about the dull ache from those debuffs Kornik blessed me with? Or the taste of the various supplies I have in my inventory? This is impossible!

Unwilling to file this in the to-do box, I penned two more letters. The first was addressed to Barliona tech support with a request to figure out why it is I'm feeling things when I shouldn't. The second letter was a little less straightforward:

Greetings Kreel!

I agree—it took me a bit longer to make a decision than I expected. Congratulations on receiving a unique item. I hope you'll manage to collect the full set. Five million is a bit too much for a First Kill. Here's my counter offer: I need two items from this Dungeon. Of my choosing. Any two I point to. I'm not interested in the money—you can have an Imitator divide it. In exchange for all this, I'll give you a clue for the next item from the Legendary item set of the Titan King. Give it some thought. If you complete the Dungeon without me—I'll keep this info to myself.

Shaman Mahan. Dragon.

Having read the letter several times and considered it from all angles, I pushed the 'send' button. Let Kreel think about what he wants to do next. Then I looked at the mass of unread letters and sighed heavily—as much of a jerk as Barsina turned out to be, at least she did her job well. I didn't feel like going through over ten thousand requests to join my clan, so I created a special folder in my mailbox where a script could dump all the offers.

Hang on, I'm being a little thick here.

Why would I need to go through this on my own? This is Barliona, after all! A world where everyone wants to make a buck. Would it really be that difficult to find some bewitching Samantha among the player community to sort my mail with a wiggle of her nose? Someone with a post-grad degree and a hundred credit hours' worth of qualifications in hiring people? Why, there must be hundreds of players like that! Why do I have to do this on my own, trying to figure out why a given player really wants to join my clan? All I have to do is grant the relevant authority to some person who specializes in this!

No sooner said than done! I saved my current coordinates and blinked to Anhurs. Any way you spin it, Clutzer is right—the clan must continue to exist. And if so, it must contain more than just me. I needed people, I needed warriors, gatherers, and craftsmen. I needed the same people that Barsina had recruited so skillfully and later shuffled to Phoenix—just as skillfully. I needed my own mob to get my back!

When I stepped out of the clan servicing center—it turns out that Anhurs has one of these organizations—I was perhaps the happiest player in Barliona. This wasn't even a center so much as an ordinary clan full of clerks who offered a complete set of clan services, beginning with management and ending with raid group recruiting based on player compatibility. I explained what I wanted and, twenty minutes later, became the happy holder of a player recruitment contract. And hardly had I signed the contract, when my mailbox sighed with relief and the girl sitting across from me gasped—all the letters begging for clan membership were forwarded to her as my new head of recruitment. Let her deal with them. I didn't change the plan for growing the clan—the priorities remained loot, crafting and security for the players occupied with these pursuits from monsters and raiding idiots. All lovers of PvP should go to other clans—I didn't need those folks. If I need someone to deal with other players, I'd do it myself or ask Plinto.

Damn!

Plinto!

Any way you spin it, I won't be able to manage without him. If he doesn't help me, all my attempts to hurt Phoenix will come to naught. There's just too great a difference in levels between us—and I only have three scrolls of Armageddon. I needed that Rogue. But I couldn't just order him to kill everyone in Phoenix without having good grounds for it. Theoretically, good relations between us would do. At the moment Plinto is in waiting mode—no one knows what I'll decide to do. Even I don't really know. So I need to take the first step and demonstrate my intentions to the Rogue—I'll invite him to the Dungeon. But only him—not Eric or Clutzer or anyone else.

"Ey! What an unexpected sight! Look at you without a security detail! I'm here suffering, wandering around the city, and he couldn't care less!" sounded a familiar voice, plucking me from my deep contemplations. I raised my head, deciding as I did so about my relations with Plinto—and encountered Spiteful Gnum standing several meters before me. "Don't you have something to tell me?"

"Altameda can fly," I blurted out the first thing that came to mind.

"I'd already gathered as much. It can fly and block my calls and also block my demons. I bet it can cross-stitch too. I don't have any questions about that. Instead, tell me something else, my dear: What the hell? Did you get my letter?"

"I got it," I grinned recalling the cape.

"And so where?"

"Where what?" I asked, baffled. Gnum's a genius—that's a fact. And he's also one of the oddest fellows I've met in my life. I wonder whether he thinks about the words coming out of his mouth or whether he goes about it the way I do—that is, thinking about them every once in a while?

"You're a bit slow on the uptake today. Where are your apologies, assurances in our long-lasting friendship and sworn promises to allow me to return to the castle? I'll take it apart brick by brick if I have to, but I'll figure out how it can fly."

"Uh-huh...I bet you will. And if you break it?" I grinned, understanding perfectly well that without additional information Gnum wouldn't be able to learn anything. Altameda can fly not because it's a special castle but because it's cursed. But why should this information be publicly available? What if some weirdo shows up and removes the curse? What'll I do then?

"Malarkey! If I take it apart, I'll put it back together again too! Where do I need to go?"

"I thought you weren't talking to me?" I reminded the gnome, still unsure how to deal with him.

"Pff! Found something to remember. You may as well remember that the grass used to be greener and the sky bluer. Where's the castle?"

"In the Free Lands. Look Gnum, the castle has a restriction in place at the moment—only I can enter it or someone from my clan. That is, not just anyone can waltz in, there are very few who can. And if you get in there and those sculptures see you, they might not take a liking to you."

"The hell are you talking about? My girls would never harm me!"

"They're, uh, my girls now, or did you forget? Altameda changed location because it was in danger. Sorry, but I'm not going to remove the restriction just for you—I don't need any extra guests in my castle."

Judging by the bleak look that descended on Gnum's face, I had upset him. And upset him gravely.

"I see," he muttered a second later. "Then I'll be on my way. If you change your mind, you can..."

"Gnum, I wasn't done," I shouted at the Necromancer's back. "You can join my clan and do whatever you want with Altameda. Within limits of course."

"Join your clan?" Gnum stopped, turned and, if his expression reflected how he felt, prepared to kill me. "You want me to grind away like an ox in the field 28 hours a day? Genuflect before you begging for resources? Meet my performance criteria indicators because 'that's what we pay you for?' I don't need that crap!"

"Look at you spouting nonsense. Gnum, the only reason I need you in my clan is to give you access to Altameda. I'm not willing to budge on that. Everything else...What am I? The son of a millionaire to pay you a salary? You can figure that part out on your own! The Imitator will pay you something, but I don't know what. Who knows how those damn programs figure out the accounts? As for resources, it's the same deal. I'll tell Viltrius that you're working on the castle and that he's to compensate you for everything and provide everything you need. If you want to work on your own projects, go ahead and do it. I could use your help."

"On my own projects? So you mean you won't spit and sputter and scream about deadlines and products?"

"Of course I will. But it won't be products, so much as like 'Hey, Gnum, say, why has Altameda stopped teleporting?' If you mess up my castle, Gnum, I'll eat you alive. You'll have to go on crafting from my Dragon belly!"

"I told you already—nothing's going to happen to your precious castle!" Gnum brightened up. "Am I going to have to sign something? As in like I hereby undertake to transfer my apartment, car and dog to this person if I use his materials for my own purposes and all that?"

"You forgot your toothbrush. I want that too."

"You've got a point. Without the toothbrush everything else's a wash. But seriously? Do you want a contract? What are the terms?"

"None," I shrugged, earning a little karma for myself. "If you want to work—work. If not—don't. What's that expression: 'I can dig, I can not dig, I can also screw something in?' That's the only term of our unofficial agreement. I have only one request—if you need something in large quantities, you have to tell me ahead of time so I can procure it for you."

"I thought you had mountains of Imperial Steel?" asked Gnum surprised. "I don't really need much of anything else."

"I did have it and now I don't. All I have left is

Spectral Ore. Phoenix took everything else."

"Spectral Ore..." Gnum echoed a little oddly. "That's uh these like glowing clumps of fog with the outline of a rock...and there's no limit to Profession level and it's not clear what recipe works for them yet? How much of that do you have?"

"I won't say a lot. To be honest, I don't recall. Two or three stacks of it for sure. I think."

"All right, I get it. Will you take Alyx too?"

"Where?" I didn't understand. "What? Who's Alyx?"

"Into your clan, where else? Alyx is Raniada. I think you ran into her one time. She's a friend of my wife."

"Why is everything so complicated with you? Your wife's friend...Wait, Raniada the new Miss Malabar?"

"Yar."

"Not even a question. Same terms as with you. In fact, let's keep things simple. Here..." I sent Gnum an invitation to join my clan. The Necromancer thought for a little and then accepted the invitation. Immediately, a small, chubby cherub in a loincloth began to whirl around him. A goblin.

"Eureka! It worked!" Gnum exclaimed. It seemed that he couldn't care less about what the projection looked like, since he did nothing to change its appearance.

"Of course it works, why wouldn't it?

Congratulations on joining our clan, yadda yadda." Opening the settings screen I adjusted Gnum's properties. "From now you are in charge of the stemware. You can accept whoever you want into the clan too. The only condition...Ah, forget it! Figure that out on your own. I'm feeling a bit lazy."

"Wait, really, whomever I want?" Gnum narrowed his eyes slyly.

"Are you going to ask me dumb questions forever?" I replied just as slyly. "Whoever you want. Nice cupid you got there. I can't even imagine what you had to do for the system to issue that little wonder."

"Yeah, well, there was this one thing...I summoned the wrong demon...misread something you see...Anyway, it's a long story, but this little goblin's pretty cool, so leave him alone!"

"I'm not arguing—I think he suits you well," I remarked when the little flying devil began to fire salvos of tiny flaming arrows all around him. "Kek and all that..."

"What now?"

"If you got a monster like that, I can't even imagine what it'll assign Svard. I bet something epic and pink."

"Pink? Why the hell?"

"Do you even remember Svard? He dresses like a clown. And he's as stubborn as a mule. Loves work like an ant. Crafty like a spider. Think about it—what could combine all these characteristics in one person? Only some pink hippo in a white toga. I can't imagine Svard getting any other projection."

"Hmm. All right, listen, I need to run and take care of some business. Where's the castle?"

"Here, I'll send you the coordinates." It was difficult to suppress my smile seeing Gnum hurry to get away from me. And I could only think of two possible destinations: either Raniada-Svard, or Svard-Raniada. There was no other option.

"All right. In that case, I'll see you later," yelled Gnum, already almost running. I finally allowed myself to smile—if the Necromancer doesn't recruit Svard into my clan, then I really don't know how life works.

Vacillating for a moment, I got out one of my amulets and made a call.

"*Moshi moshi!*"

"Hey Plinto! I have some business worth a hundred thousand million. What'd you have planned for the next day?"

"If you've decided to wipe someone out, you can forget about me. I'm not much of a Rogue for another week."

"Erm..." I fell quiet, remembering that Plinto really was one of the few players who had been stripped of their powers. Stop!

"Hang on, but then that begs the question—in the video that Clutzer showed me, I could see you killing Anastaria and Hellfire..."

"Well sure, but you're forgetting that they don't have their powers either. Those two are like giant tin cans at the moment with a huge pool of Hit Points. It doesn't help that they've pumped all their blessed stat points into Endurance and Intellect, instead of anything that would actually help them in battle. I simply cut them to pieces with a pair of good daggers and my high Agility. I didn't use Acceleration or any other bells or whistles."

"Okay, we need to talk. I still don't understand completely—you came out of Stealth, but that's a Rogue skill. Where are you now? I'll blink over to you in a second."

"Erm..." said Plinto and my whole world turned upside down and inside out: I could not recall a moment when the Rogue lacked some quick and sarcastic response to a mundane question. If he can't meet up with me, and it's clear he's not in battle, that means only one thing... "All right, blink on over. Here are the coordinates."

I quickly entered the coordinates the Rogue gave me into the Blink entry field and teleported, expecting either not to find Plinto at all or to find a portal closing quickly on a delicate ankle...

"If you tell even one person about this," came Plinto's voice as soon as I appeared beside him, "you can forget you know me. At all. You are the first player to see this. Welcome to my workshop. Oh and, pick your jaw up from the floor."

I was gaping at ten sculptures hewed from a snow-white stone. Yalininka, Eluna, a Rogue I didn't know brandishing his daggers, an intricate tree that resembled a Guardian, women, men, monsters, animals...The enormous cavern buried deep in the Free Lands was filled with sculptures which all had one pretty curious entry among their list of properties:

Creator: Master Sculptor Plinto the Bloodied

"Damn," I exhaled only once my 'Oxygen Remaining' bar had appeared.

"Yesterday I found out that there was another certificate available for a new sculpture, so I wanted to take care of that today. I figure I'll get another point in Crafting for it."

"You have Crafting?!" I exclaimed with surprise, staring at Plinto with unvarnished shock.

"Surprise!" the Rogue muttered sarcastically. "Plinto knows how to make something with his hands!"

"I can't believe it!" I blurted out, feeling like I was in a different world. "You're a Master?"

"You could always see I'm a Master. It says so in my character properties. Anyone can see it. That's why I had to acquire Stealth and Tracking Mastery. But originally I became a Master in Sculpture. You had something to tell me?"

"Yes...Well, no...Listen, why do you keep all this hidden in a cave here? These are really great!"

"Because as soon as people find out about them, the reputation of Plinto the Bloodied will be destroyed. How is anyone going to fear a player who crafts? And it's not like I care whether people see my work or not. Their mere existence suits me fine. I just can't lift my hand to destroy them, so I found a cavern, brought all the sculptures here and sometimes I come here to take a break from the outside world."

"Ah...Ahem...No this is some kind of madness! It's like I'm dreaming!" I blurted again when I began to look at the sculptures. +10 to Building Attractiveness, +5% to Castle defenders' Endurance, +32 to Building Attractiveness, +23 to...Well, it was non-stop bonuses for castles and various stats related to castles.

"So who'd you want to knock off?" Plinto reminded me about the purpose of my visit.

"No one...Tell me, how come you had Stealth back at the plateau?"

"It was a scroll. Clutzer called me on his amulet and told me that something was about to go down and I needed to be there. Then Viltrius teleported me there using Clutzer's coordinates. I hid myself and watched the show. Then when you left the game I decided to spin the merry-go-round. Stacey and Hellfire were defenseless and unprepared to fight, so I stunned them with a blow to the temple and finished them off a moment later. To be fair, their henchmen ended up getting me in the end too, but it doesn't matter—I'm up 12–9 against Hellfire now."

"Okay, I see."

"Listen, believe it or not, I have no desire to explain anything, prove anything or beg for anything. If you want to go on working together, you should revert back to the old Mahan I know—ready for any old madcap business. If not, I hope for your sake no one finds out about this cavern."

"All right, forget it. You're right. What happened, happened. I can't go back and change it, so we have to move forward. I'm considering raiding a new Dungeon but I need a high-level fighter. I forgot that you don't have your powers when I called you, but I'll extend the invitation anyway. Do you feel like spinning your knives around for a few hours?"

"When?"

"We're going in in four hours. I can bring you to the starting point."

"It's just us two?"

"No, we've got some Shamans with us. There won't be anyone else from the Legends in the raid with us."

"Heh. You're plotting some kind of mischief but you need a high-level Rogue?"

"One ready for all kinds of madcap business. I have a couple plans, but I won't be able to make them happen on my own. I'll die too quickly."

"Are you talking about what Clutzer mentioned?"

"Not quite, but something similar. I want to cast Armageddon in the middle of Phoenix's main castle."

"The castle will only drop a level, and even then maybe..."

"That's only from one scroll."

"Hmm..."

"What'll happen if we activate all three at once?"

"Hmm...I don't even know what to tell you. The clan doesn't have enough money to buy three scrolls at once, but knowing you, I'm guessing you already got your hands on them. Correct?"

"Yes."

"In that case, I'd be happy to do a fiery cha-cha-cha through Phoenix's main castle in a week's time. Do you merely want to blow up their castle or do you want to blow it up properly?"

"Meaning?" I furrowed my brow not understanding.

"For instance, Anastaria, Hellfire, the Phoenix leadership and their raiders, et cetera—do they have to be in the castle? Do you want to do maximum damage or kind of just fart and spoil the air?"

"Maximum damage."

"I got you. I'll do the planning. As for the Dungeon—if your Shamans won't be embarrassed by extra help, then I'll be happy to join your raid. Only, I'm going to pop out to reality for a few hours and tell my family."

"They won't be embarrassed. Listen, let me take

these sculptures to Altameda, what do you say? No one knows where it is beside me. And even if someone finds it by accident, it's not like they'll get into the throne room. You know as well as I that someone will stumble across this place eventually. You did, after all."

"What makes you think that no one knows where Altameda is located?" Plinto arched an eyebrow in surprise. "If you want, I can tell you the precise coordinates of my personal chamber and, consequently, the entire castle."

"WHAT?!"

"Whoa, what are you all wound up about? How do you imagine I took out old Hellfire without knowing where the castle is?"

"You put some kind of crap into my castle!" I yelled, without hearing Plinto's last words. Or, rather, not wanting to hear them. What the hell?! Why is it that when it comes to words, everyone is so good and ethical and then when it comes to actions, all you start finding are closets full of skeletons?

"Calm down. No one put anything in your castle. Viltrius would've ratted me out long ago. What do you know about a Master of Tracking?"

"I don't know shit about it! Plinto! What the hell?!"

"Here he is, our fearless clan leader—Screech. What is the world coming to?! I'd like to point out that you're the first person to learn that I'm a Master of

Tracking. Everyone thinks that I'm a Master of Stealth. I won't bore you with the details, but basically when a player reaches a certain letter of development in this area, he can acquire a very important little thing called a Mark. A Master of Tracking assigns a marker to an item or player and later he can determine its exact location whenever he likes. It's not that hard to get rid of the marker—all you have to do is have the Priests or the Emperor bless you, but who's going to bother doing that? Only those who know about this skill. I have markers assigned to you, to Altameda, and in fact to everyone I've worked with or met."

"The first time we met, back in Beatwick, you asked me where Anastaria had gone. As if you couldn't see her on your map."

"Back then I didn't have a marker on her. Before heading out to Farstead, Anastaria reset all her buffs, so the markers were erased."

"But now you know where she is?" I smirked.

"Of course. At the moment she is in," Plinto's eyes fogged over for a moment as he opened his map, "Hmm...she is several feet from another player I keep tabs on named Kreel. Simply Kreel. The coordinates are..."

"WHAT?!" I couldn't keep myself from exclaiming in surprise. Stacey was with Kreel?! Considering that the Titan was supposed to be working on the Dragon Dungeon, Anastaria was with him?! That bitch decided to betray me again and get a First Kill?!

"Oh look at how excited you are!" quipped Plinto. "Just like a jealous husband who's just discovered that his wife is out with another man."

"They're doing the Dungeon!" I yelped, still unable to get ahold of myself. "A Dungeon I really need to complete myself!"

"Have they been doing it for a while?" the Rogue inquired.

"There's two floors left."

"Then you can forget about it. Even if Kreel and Anastaria didn't assign someone to defend the entrance, you won't catch up to them."

"Why should I forget it? I could simply accept their progress and join them..."

"You think that Anastaria will share a First Kill with you?"

"Five million per player," I muttered, suddenly realizing the reason why Kreel had named such a steep price.

"They offered you the chance to complete the Dungeon for five million?" Curiosity appeared on Plinto's face. "Was that their offer or do you think that they agreed to that amount?"

"Kreel offered."

"Say, how much money does our clan have anyway?" Plinto inquired.

"36 million."

"Will you let me borrow five? I'll pay it back the

first chance I get."

"I'll trade it for the sculptures," I instantly knew what to say. "With all due respect to your authorial rights to the sculptures and all that—I could really use them. You've seen the castle—the walls have nothing on them. I'll have Viltrius hide the creator's properties and no one will know that they're yours. I can even put them in the cellar if you want."

The Rogue smirked and gave me a wry look.

"You want to give me five million in exchange for a blow to my reputation?"

"No—for the risk of one, not a blow necessarily. And, please note that that risk isn't much greater than some player stumbling across this place. Even lower, I'd say. The sculptures will be protected."

"Where will you put them?"

"If concealing their properties is enough for you, then in the main hall. If not—in the vaults or the cellars. Wherever, as long as their bonuses still apply."

"All right. Call Kreel. We'll do this together. Two more wagons for their train."

I got an amulet and called my majordomo.

"Viltrius, open a portal to the following coordinates." I looked at our current location and read the coordinates to the goblin. "Send Vimes over here. He needs to pick up some sculptures. Your orders are as follows: If you can conceal the sculptures' properties, you may place them in the hall. If not, you must place them somewhere where no one will see them, but where their bonuses will still apply to the castle. That's the first thing. Second, I'm allowing you to let Spiteful Gnum and Plinto into the castle from now on. Got it?"

"Yes, sir!" came the reply and a portal opened beside us. A moment later the Tauren emerged from it with a terrible look on his face.

"Master," boomed my head of security. "What do you need moved?"

"The statues. They have to be moved to the castle. On the double!"

The guards began doing their job, but I knew that I hadn't done everything the Rogue asked of me. Checking my mail one more time to make sure that the Titan hadn't answered me, I got out Anastaria's amulet and called her.

"Speaking!" The girl's charming voice wafted through the cavern. I could hear the sounds of battle in the background, yet hearing the girl's calm voice, you wouldn't guess that she was in active combat. One more wagon. Heh, Anastaria a wagon! If I told them they wouldn't believe me.

"Hello, my darling," I began and encountered Plinto's wide-eyed stare. I never told the Rogue about the manner in which Stacey and I were speaking to each other, and he therefore lost his customary mask of sarcasm for a moment.

"Hi baby, why are you calling me on the amulet?

Did something happen?"

"Oh I just felt like it. Listen, baby-poo, could you let me speak with Kreel please? I don't have his amulet with me and mail takes too long."

"Bunny, I don't think he can talk at the moment. He's a little occupied," Anastaria said sarcastically, "I'll be happy to pass your message on to him though."

Only knowing Anastaria well could you catch the slightest note of surprise in her voice. It was infinitesimally small, but to my tuned ear it blared at full blast: 'How did you find out?!' Of course the girl would never allow herself to show a weakness and therefore covered her words with a patina of sarcasm.

"Tell him to call me back as soon as he gets the chance. Tell him that I've sent him an offer that he can't refuse. That's it, my little wagon—hugs and kisses. Be careful not to get crushed by the boss!"

When I hung up, I encountered Plinto's mocking stare.

"You're a real mean one, Mahan. What are you making the girl panic for? Now she'll start imagining that if you don't have people of your own in Phoenix, then at least you have spies in Kreel's clan...and then she'll start guessing who spilled the beans and suspect every fifth person she comes across. Hah! I'm sure this very instant Stacey is standing there and desperately trying to remember whom she'd mentioned that Dungeon to."

"No big deal. It'll do her some good," I answered Plinto's smile with my own. "By the way, is there a chance she'll think of you? I didn't betray you, did I?"

"They already checked me several times. I'll say it again—you're the only one who knows I'm a Master of Tracking. Anastaria knows that I'm a Sculptor. She's actually the very person who suggested I develop that Profession to me. But they don't know a thing about the Tracking business."

"She knows about the sculptures?" I asked surprised.

"About my Profession, not the sculptures. We started out together after all—and in the very beginning carving marble is a great way to raise your Agility. So Stacey advised me to become a Sculptor. She doesn't know that I never quit this Profession after reaching the higher levels. She doesn't know about the Crafting either. By the way, did you know that Crafting isn't only a creative stat? You should go see a High Shaman and ask him to teach you how to use your Crafting in battle. I'll wager my right eye that the outcome will please you."

I was about to start interrogating Plinto about what Crafting gives him, when my amulet began to squeal—someone wanted to speak with me.

"Speaking!"

"Mahan, this is Kreel. I read your letter and I can only say one thing—welcome to the raid party. We're actually already done for today. We'll pick it up again tomorrow, so be online in the morning. I'll send you an amulet. We have two bosses left. If you like you can join us for the last one. It doesn't matter to me. Aren't you a bit underpowered at the moment anyway?"

"I won't be coming alone. Plinto is with me. One more wagon for our train."

"You never mentioned Plinto, but I don't see any problems with it. Let him come along. His ticket will be five million too."

"I can offer an exchange. We're about to do a virgin Dungeon, so we can make a deal in which I invite you to our raid to get you a First Kill there too. In exchange, you'll take Plinto into your raid party. I think that'll be to our mutual benefit."

"Agreed! Send me your amulet."

"Done," I replied after opening my mail and sending Kreel a way to get in touch with me.

"In that case, I'll see you tomorrow. Anastaria wants to talk to you. I'll pass her the phone, erm, amulet now."

"The answer is no," I said before Stacey could utter a word. "I'm not taking you to this Dungeon."

"But you haven't even heard my offer, kitten," said Anastaria as Kreel's chuckle sounded in the background. "Don't you want to save Renox? I can tell you how to do it."

CHAPTER FIVE
THE ERGREIS

"WELCOME TO ASTRUM TERRITORY, Earl," the tall, dark-haired man in a business suit greeted me. "In order to leave the building premises, you will have to register in this continent and learn a little about its culture, particularities and restrictions. Only after you have passed a test of our continent's culture, may you spend more than a week in Astrum. Otherwise, you shall be deported and barred from visiting Astrum for the next six months. Please try to be understanding—I was not the one who came up with these rules."

A notification appeared before me asking me to select the purpose of my visit to Astrum: As a guest or as a tourist. The length of stay indicated by the diplomat (7 days) was printed in parentheses next to the 'guest' option. The other option had no limit.

I stared with puzzlement at these buttons, trying to decide which to choose. On the one hand, I wasn't going to stay in Astrum longer than a week. I only wanted to pick up the players and go back. On the other hand, I also had two invitations to the Emperor's castle. And I would definitely want to spend some time in that location.

"I don't have time for the training at the moment," I said, choosing the guest option. "But soon enough I'll be back and I'll be happy to exhaustively study the culture of Astrum. Tell me, if I want to pick up some Free Citizens of Astrum and take them to our continent of Kalragon, do they need to take cultural studies classes as well?"

"Absolutely. Any traveler is required to familiarize himself with the culture of the continent he is visiting. This is a matter of courtesy to the sentients that inhabit those lands. Otherwise someone might come visit our gnomes and start drilling holes in the cave ceilings so that some sunlight could get in. And that's just culturally insensitive."

"But they won't incur any penalties if they spend less than seven days on our continent?"

"Three days," the diplomat corrected me. "Only aristocrats are granted a week, since no one doubts the level of their education. Commoners are granted only three days in order to establish whether they need to do the training or not. All they have to do is complete the preliminary registration and that's it."

"Thank you for the explanation," I thanked the NPC sincerely. Any way you spin it, this was my first trip 'abroad' and there was much to learn. After the straightforward registration procedure, I opened the door and took my first step onto the neighboring continent.

"Hi!" Kalatea's voice sounded right beside me. "Everyone's ready. We can start ferrying people over. Only Antsinthepantsa and I have the language packs installed, so we'll have to translate. Although wait—yeah, my tank also speaks the language of the Dark Empire, Kartoos."

"Kartoss," I corrected the Shaman. "How'd he learn it?"

"Two reasons," answered a hefty man encased in very pretty golden armor—a Level 288 Warrior. "The first is I keep track of changes to game mechanics. The last update tweaked axe throwing and I had to do the test in Kartoss, so I was speaking to their warriors a lot. This meant I had to learn the language. *Leraz galvart, Kalatea-kun?*" the last phrase, as I understood it was addressed to Kalatea, not me.

"Bjorg is asking whether you understand him..."

"Perfectly well," I replied to the Warrior in Kartossian, and was suddenly struck with a thought which forced me to ask: "Hang on, isn't Bjorg a woman's name?"

"That's the second reason," the Warrior smiled. "I've been in Astrum only five years. Before that I was in Kalragon. I've been a fan of Norse mythology for a long time, so I decided to give my avatar a strong-sounding name. Bjorg! It was only after I'd made my character and began playing that I discovered that this is a woman's name! Well, Bjork, not Bjorg, with a 'k,' but the gist remains the same. Like I give damn though. I still like it!"

"I was always sure that our continent has the best players," I smiled, offering Bjorg my hand. "Welcome to our raid, Warrior!"

"You can call me Valentine, or Val for short. I'd even prefer it."

"In that case I'm Daniel, or Dan. All right, I bet Kalatea is starting to suspect I'm going to try and recruit you."

"If I was actually thinking it, you'd already be emerging from your cocoon to wait out the next twelve hours," grinned the Shaman, demonstrating her own knowledge of Kartossian. "I already told you, Mahan, my Order only recruits the best people."

"Shamans..."

"Not exclusively. I have a tank—Bjorg here—and several Mages for opening portals, Druids, Paladins...the Order of Dragons welcomes all classes. Are you ready to start transporting people?"

"Yes. Who will go first?"

"Bjorg, Antsinthepantsa and three Shaman-Elementalists. They'll be in charge of scouting..."

"Sorry, Shaman-Elementa-what?" I interrupted Kalatea, never having heard such a drawn-out term used about my class.

"Elementalists are Shamans who use Elementals instead of Totems."

"Elementals are those huge concentrations of fire or earth or water..."

"Or air, absolutely correct. You're already beyond Level 100—haven't you gained access to them yet?"

"Erm...I probably have, but the thing is my powers have been blocked for a month. They'll be back in a few days finally. Then I'll learn all about Elementals and what wine they're best paired with. Could you share a bit of strategically important info about them? On a friendly exchange basis, let's say."

"A friendly exchange?" Kalatea raised an eyebrow. "The Legends of Barliona offers to work with the Order of the Dragon?"

"Erm...Yeeeah?" I ventured, unsure of what the Shaman was getting at.

"On behalf of the Order of the Dragon, I accept your offer," Kalatea said in an official tone and immediately, a notification appeared before me:

The Legends of Barliona and the Order of the Dragon have become allies. Please confirm this.

"It's that simple?" I asked with some disbelief, not quite ready to push the button. "Without discussing the terms of our alliance? We're allies just like that?"

It was too fast. Everything was happening too quickly. I didn't have to be a genius to understand that Kalatea wanted this for some reason—and lately,

I've developed a bit of an allergy to this kind of thing.

"Is something bothering you?" Kalatea continued to flap her eyebrows.

"Everything, if I'm to be honest. With all due respect to your Order, I must decline your offer," I added, pushing the 'Decline' button. "I am unfamiliar with the method of collaboration and I don't understand my responsibilities in this relationship, so I'd rather not risk my clan. Maybe as allies, I have to transfer 50% of all my loot daily to your Order. After all, I was the one who asked to collaborate..."

"Then it is as I have heard. Your faith in people has been crushed. Wiped out. I accept your decision. As soon as you settle your problems, I will be ready to offer you an alliance again. Let me reiterate—the Order only works with the best. You are one of them."

"Let's figure out who's who later. Valentine," I turned to the Warrior, "shall we go?"

"We shall," Bjorg replied with a smile. "Will you tell me what mobs we'll be facing?"

"None too complicated for a Warrior of your level. Wolves, foxes, bunnies and hedgehogs—all sub Level 150. The only snag is that you can't kill them. We'll need people from my continent."

"What do you mean?"

"We have this, uh, thing on our continent. It's called 'Shadow.' Creatures under its influence can't be destroyed at the moment. We're so sick of dealing with them that I can't even begin to explain it to you."

"Is that the second movie about the scenarios on your continent?" Kalatea caught on.

"The very one."

"I don't think we'll have much of a problem. Antsinthepantsa updated before she moved to Astrum. She'll go with the first group."

"Okey-dokey. In that case, let's be on our way. We don't have much time."

"Why not? Three days should be enough to complete a Dungeon."

"I wouldn't be so sure if I were you," I smirked. "The developers in charge of our continent are a bit annoying in that regard. Just take my word for it ..."

Altameda Castle has gained a leveled! Current level: 26.

Profession level increased: 'Architect Level 3.' -15% to cost of rebuilding razed buildings.

Finally, Plinto's statues had taken their rightful places! I'm sure Viltrius is currently running around Altameda, frantically dusting this unexpected surprise. And why not? There's much more prestige to be the majordomo of a Level 26 Castle instead of some sorry pile of Level 25 rubble. Silly NPCs...

"*Bunny-wunny, I am just stunned!*" Anastaria's thought popped into my head. "*Where'd you get the money? Are you still embezzling money from your clan?*"

"*A friend of mine once told me that it's not nice to use rude words with girls, so I'll simply suggest that you take a pleasant walk at a location well known to you,*" I replied with no desire to fall for Anastaria's jibes.

"*How could I go if you don't come with?*"

"*I've already told you, darling: If you want to come along to the Dungeon, give me back everything you pilfered out of my bag within thirty minutes of your switching clans and abandoning the Legends of Barliona. If you don't wish to do so, then I've already indicated the place you should absolutely go to.*"

"*I see our 'dates' aren't in vain. We've learned to express what we want,*" the girl replied in a satisfied tone. "*However, I must refuse your offer. I need the Eye, and I simply can't return the Crastils to you without knowing what they do.*"

"*What do you need the Eye for?*" I asked, surprised. "*You've already gained access to the Tomb.*"

"*The First Kill, kid, the First Kill. Or did you really think that I'll just let you have that?*"

"*If that's all you got, then stop bothering me,*" I didn't 'aggro' in reply to Anastaria's trolling and decided to end the conversation.

"*See you soon then! Don't forget—we have another date tomorrow. Our family has to remain strong and close. I'll be waiting for you at the Golden Horseshoe at noon. Kisses!*"

As much as I wanted to say a few choice words

to this...this woman...I restrained myself. My job was a simple one—locate two items, find a Crastil and the Tears of Harrashess, activate them and slip them to Anastaria and Hellfire. It'd be nice to blow up Phoenix's castle along the way, but that's already a matter of circumstance. And therefore I wasn't about to let myself feel anything whatsoever towards this...this creature. She didn't deserve it.

"The last part of the raid is ready. We can pick them up as soon as your cooldown expires," Bjorg collapsed noisily beside me. "Cool mobs you got here. You really can't kill them. We've, uh, leveled up your Fleita there to Level 90. You don't mind do you?"

"She doesn't belong to me, but thank you. It really is surprising that you can't kill Shadow mobs. So it works out that you can't just change continents just like that, huh?"

"Just like that, no. You have to go through extra training. As soon as I came to Kalragon last time, I was instantly told to meet with the Warrior Mentor in order to start a quest chain that updated my class. It's pretty interesting, but you need time for it. And we don't have any at the moment."

Nodding my assent, I blinked the other Shamans to our continent, created a raid party and set myself as its leader. Then I ordered everyone to start clearing the mobs in the Dungeon so as not to waste time and dialed Kreel's amulet. The decision to refuse Anastaria's offer came surprisingly easy to me: I wasn't going to save Renox. The developers had decided that this NPC had to die and so there wasn't any point in bashing my head against that wall. I'd wager a tooth that if Anastaria actually has some quest, it'd be impossible to complete it.

"Greetings!" Kreel was in the game as we had agreed, so my call wasn't in vain.

"Kreel, hi! This is Mahan. I'm starting our raid into my Dungeon. Are you coming with us or should I summon you for the last boss?"

"Do you think you'll complete it quickly?" the Titan asked surprised.

"I have no idea. Maybe it'll take us one night, or maybe it'll take us several months. I've never tried doing two Dungeons at once, so I'm unsure about the logistics of it all. What if we miss something and lose our shot at the boss? That goes for you as much as for me."

"Agreed, raiding two Dungeons at once seems like an interesting thing. Let's do it this way: You guys will fight your way to your final boss, while I fight my way to mine. Hopefully, we only have one monster left before we reach ours. As soon as we do, I'll call and summon you. The same goes for you. This seems like the most efficient way to do it."

"Got it. Best of luck to you, Titan!"

"Pff...Let's not be too dramatic now. Good luck to you, Shaman!"

The amulet fell silent. I twirled it in my hands for

a few moments and then tossed it back into my bag with all the other ones and got out another one. It was time to summon Plinto.

"Why don't you go yourself?" the Rogue wondered as soon as I'd invited him to the party.

"I hate being a wagon," I confessed honestly. "To watch fifteen Shamans accomplish something singular and lack the opportunity to do it myself...I could of course go take a look and see how others play the Shaman class, but...well, there's always a lot of 'buts.'"

"Suit yourself," Plinto smirked, unsheathing his Legendary cutlery. "I can't pass up a chance to wave around my stilettoes. I should suggest to the developers that they cook up a training ground for Rogues in which the player has to run the obstacle course without using a single class skill. Nothing but his own God-given hands. Everyone's so accustomed to using the same old ability combos that they've forgotten that Barliona isn't some prehistoric game with scripted mechanics. You have to be creative in it!"

"Erm..." I muttered expressively in reply.

"Okay okay," droned Plinto. "You didn't understand a damn thing..."

"Understand what?"

"I'm actually kind of barred from telling you in-game. I even have a contract with the Emperor, so I'll just repeat what I said—linking abilities into combos is simply a custom in Barliona; it isn't actually coded in. If you want to make something happen—it doesn't matter whether it's battle, the crafting of an item or a chess set, if we're talking about you specifically—then you must be creative. You have to use tools that no one had ever thought of using before you. That's the only way you can become a true leader in Barliona. Since you're not joining the raiding party, you should think about this."

"Are you talking about Crafting?" I guessed. Plinto seemed to be alluding to the fact that Crafting had some effect on combat. However, I had assumed that this pertained only to him—working with chisels to create the sculptures somehow affected the weapons his class used. But unlike him, I have to summon Spirits and don't use items to fight. Although, I do create things in Design Mode. Without Items...Hmm...

"I can tell by the wrinkle on your forehead that a thought has occurred to you and you're busy contemplating it further," Plinto concluded. "In that case, I won't distract you. You can tell me later what you end up cogitating."

Plinto dived into the shimmering veil of the Dungeon's entrance, leaving me in deep thought. Summoning Spirits and Crafting. How could I combine these two seemingly unrelated things? According to the manual, Crafting influences all professions, determines the ability to independently learn the finer points of a profession and permits the creation of unusual items. There is a percentage chance to independently discover and learn a unique recipe. What does that have to do with Spirits? I urgently needed to use my phone-a-friend lifeline.

"*Delra gantar derta est! Prakti verza!*" The amulet roared with Kalatea's voice.

"Hi Kalatea, this is Mahan," I said, ignoring the sounds of battle reaching me from the other side. "Do you have a moment?"

"What do you think?" Kalatea all but screamed.

"I'll be a second. Are Crafting and Spirit Summoning somehow related?"

"No! At any rate, I never designed anything like it—or tested it. They're two completely different things—stats that are related to crafting and stats related to summoning Spirits."

"I see. Thanks, that's all. How's it going?"

"It's not going!" Kalatea blurted out and then swore several times in Astrumian. "The Dungeon's mobs are all Level 200—it's like fighting children for us. But our inability to actually kill them is, well, killing us. We've almost reached the first boss, but all of the XP is going to Antsinthepantsa, Aozaki and your student."

"Aozaki? Who's that?"

"One of my Shamans. It turns out that she's spent time on your continent and did the skill update training. So we have another person who can speak

Malabarian. Anyway, she says that it takes five days to update your skills. Five days! They'll kick us out of Kalragon before we finish!"

It sounded like Kalatea was losing her temper a bit. I had never seen the Shaman in such an agitated state before and now had to give myself a mental pat on the back for refusing to go into the Dungeon with the others. I'm sure they'd sic all the dogs in there on me.

"In that case, I have a proposal. Take a break from the fighting, do the registration and cultural classes and in a week we'll come back there again. We don't have to complete that Dungeon today. If we have to do it in a week, let it be so."

"*Varga est!*" Kalatea ordered her raid party and returned to our conversation: "Agreed! Will you arrange our transportation to Anhurs?"

"If it's anywhere on the continent, there's no problem. Altameda is always at your service."

"Will you give us a tour?" Kalatea immediately rejoined.

"Not of the entire castle," I backed off remembering Plinto's sculptures and his desire to keep them under wraps. "There are several areas that are off limits to guests. As for the rest of it, you are more than welcome to check it out."

"All right, everyone. We're leaving! Grinding for a First Kill without earning any XP in the process is a waste of time. *Varga est! Dalran!*"

While the Shamans retreated from the Shadow Dungeon, I called Kreel and laid out the situation to him. Having received his assurance that all our prior agreements remained in place, I asked Viltrius to open a portal and transferred the entire raid party, including Plinto and Bjorg, to Altameda. Even though it was getting late, none of the guests from the neighboring continent refused a visit to such a unique place—a castle that had been the subject of an entire movie.

"Viltrius, show our guests around Altameda," I asked my majordomo, slumping wearily in my chair. "When they're ready, open a portal to Anhurs."

I had played my fill for today and had no more mental or physical energy left. It's not like the guests could do any harm to the castle. It was impossible to record Altameda's coordinates, or leave it, or catch a glimpse of Plinto's statues. Nothing was possible. They could only stroll about and gape at its sights.

"What a beautiful castle," Kalatea returned in about thirty minutes. Thirty minutes that I had spent struggling with my bursting mailbox. What a time-sink—it was already 1:30 in the morning. Clan recruitment, requests for money, threats, questions, spam, quest offers, questions about mechanics—the mailbox had it all. I was especially amused by a letter from a player named Sabantul: "Mahan! I have a treasure map that I want to sell you for 300,000." I stared at this letter for a few minutes—I'd never encountered such an extreme attempt to wheedle some money from me. Does anyone actually fall for this? I was about to enter this player in my spam filter, when my hand experienced a spasm and clicked on the 'Reply' button.

Hi! A treasure map for 300k is a bit steep. Where'd you see prices like that? I can buy your map for about ten thousand, no more. And, please note, I haven't seen your map and have no idea where you got it from. You won't sell it for 300k, so here's your best offer.

I can't explain why I wrote this letter. I had the dim feeling that I had done the right thing, so I ignored my reasoning and surrendered to the urge. I'm a Shaman after all, aren't I?

"Mahan, I'm still chewing over your question about Crafting and Spirits," Kalatea went on. "It's implausible."

"On the one hand, yes," I agreed. "On the other, who knows what the devs really coded in? As I understand it, you are the designer of the Shaman class and its main tester. But what if Crafting isn't tied to the class specifically? What if it was designed as an inter-class mechanic?"

"Impossible. You can't distribute something like that between the various classes, while preserving balance. Barliona is strict about that."

"Do you have Crafting?"

"That's not a very appropriate question to ask a

player, but I'll answer it—no. I don't have Crafting. Aozaki, however, does have it. Given that she is terribly curious by nature, I'd guess she'd already dig something up if there was something there."

"I don't have any arguments for or against this—it's just an idea that occurred to me. I haven't tried any experiments myself. If you'll permit Aozaki to stay with us and work with me on this issue, maybe we'll come up with something. Or at least, we'll make sure that Crafting and Spirits are really unrelated. It's a bit silly to discuss what's possible and what's not at the moment."

"The members of my Order are not slaves. If she likes, she can stay," Kalatea said with a slight note of aggro in her voice. I began to get the feeling that she had some issues when it came to these types of conversations. Well, the hell with her. I didn't feel like rummaging in her head anyway.

"Then we're on the same page," I replied, yawning. "Until tomorrow, then."

EXIT!

The cocoon lid slowly slid aside, unveiling the ceiling of my modest room to my sight. I hadn't any thoughts left, as if my brain had gone offline for maintenance. I clambered out with difficulty and forced myself to swallow a quick dinner/breakfast and collapsed into my bed with a soft moan. My head hurt as though a herd of horses had galloped through it—and back again. Several times. That there's the difference between a long-term immersion capsule and my budget version. I really needed to look into buying a cutting-edge model as soon as possible. Damn! I forgot that I would be leaving this apartment in short order. Somehow this had slipped my mind. I hope that Sergei will think of buying me a normal capsule. Otherwise, I'd kill him in some degenerate and very violent way.

And on this happy note, I slipped into sleep.

The next morning began for me at ten till eleven with my cocoon blaring wildly. The alarm which I had set before exiting the game was stubbornly reminding me of my date with Anastaria. Heartless piece of junk. My headache was still there, though it hurt less than the night before. Still, it reminded me of its presence with a dull hum in the back of my head. That was the last thing we needed! I really needed to take the day off from Barliona—I'll meet up with Stacey, speak with Kreel and then sign out to reality at the first opportunity. Let the Shamans deal with their visa to Kalragon on their own, let Kreel kill the penultimate boss of his Dungeon, and let Barliona go to hell—my health was dearer to me.

Hello, wanderer! Have you already been released? Good work! Let's hang out at my place tonight—have some beers and catch up. I will call a driver for you—aren't you like unemployed or something? He'll be there at six in the evening. Don't be late.

Before jumping into my cocoon, I checked the mail and was surprised to see Sergei's message. He had managed to get everything ready a day in advance! In seven hours I would be free of the strange old man and his henchmen. Then I'll be able to go on without worrying about threats to my life. And that included from Phoenix and its members in reality. I doubt Ehkiller will part with several billion gold so easily. If I were him, I'd deal with the problem in a more direct manner.

Sounds good! I'll be waiting for that ride!

"You look way too happy," Anastaria remarked as soon as I sat down in the chair across from her. "Have you finally decided to take me to your Dungeon and are about to tell me this good news?"

"You almost guessed right," I refused to submit to her jibe. "But only almost. You've heard my terms—you'll only get access to the Shadow Dungeon after you..."

"Gawd you're annoying," Stacey cut me off. "'Crastil, Crastil, Eye, Crastil.' Bah!"

"Nice special they have going on today," I wasn't about to spar with Anastaria. "I can't figure out what its taste reminds me of."

"Grygz sold me all his Crastils," Anastaria said suddenly, placing on the table all of the orbs she had collected. "As of now, I am the only player who has any. So we'll have to learn to see eye to eye."

"Oh no! What a calamity! How will I survive this

mortal mortal blow?" I replied glibly, even though everything inside of me had turned upside down. If the head of the Pirates was out of the picture, I only knew one other NPC that had this item—the High Mage of Anhurs. The next question was whether Anastaria knew about him as well...But no, there's a more important question—would the High Mage even give me his Crastil? I'd have to approach this from two angles—on my own and with the help of the old man and his programmers—this, despite the fact that I was plotting my escape from him. I had to encourage the Mage to part with his Crastil. And part with it only for me.

"I'll find another one," I added, noting that Anastaria was watching me closely. It was like she was trying to gauge by my reaction whether or not I was bluffing. "There's more than just Crastils in Barliona."

"What's true is true. Did you hear the latest news from the Armard campaign?" Anastaria changed topics.

"Erm...No...Why, what happened?"

"There's a small Malabar clan called Oblivion that's headed by a Mage named Musubi. It's basically a raiding clan. Those who don't enjoy raiding, don't hang around it too long. And so, in some utterly mysterious manner, these guys managed to break through into the city and entrench themselves in a cellar of one of the buildings."

"Great! But, uh, why are you telling me this?"

"Let me finish. The Armard mobs didn't bother to deal with them. They simply walled Musubi's raid off in the cellar. Why risk anything, after all? Those Imitators are a clever lot, what can you say. Portal scrolls don't work in Armard, and there's no way to escape. They tried a summons from the Anhurs Mages, but it didn't work. The situation seemed hopeless. Either they had to sit there and wait for the Character Stuck button to appear, or hammer their heads against the walls in the hopes of being sent to respawn."

"I'm sensing a 'but.'"

"Of course! Understanding that the costs of equipment, herbs and enchantments wouldn't be recouped by the loot they had acquired, Musubi decided to sign out to reality and begin selling teleportation right into the center of the city on the forums. There were several Mages in his raid party that could..."

"Wait up—you just said that teleportation doesn't work in Armard."

"Not exactly. Scrolls don't work and you can't teleport to a specific location in the Shadow Empire. Likewise, as it turned out, you can't summon a player from Armard, but you are free to summon people into the city. So Musubi attracted the attention of Etamzilat and Undigit, both of whom decided to send their raids right into Armard. The 'City Capture'

Achievement corrupted their brains—they wanted to be the first to complete the Emperor's order. They paid a lot of money to the Mage, and fifty of the top players from each clan teleported into the barricaded cellar. At first they didn't notice that there's wasn't a way out—everyone was getting ready for the battle ahead. But when the cellar was brimming with players from three clans, and it turned out there was no passage out of it..."

"They forced Musubi to refund the money?" I couldn't help but crack a grin, imagining the looks on Undigit's and Etamzilat's face.

"They tried, but he refused outright: 'I don't know what you're talking about, you're right in the center of Armard as we agreed. I kept my part of the bargain.' That's when Undigit made a fatal mistake..."

"He summoned the Guardian," I realized.

"Yup! He had signed the contract with Musubi in Barliona and so decided to deal with him according to the strictest interpretation of the game law. I'm guessing he figured he'd make a profit along the way too."

"And so the Guardian appeared," I prompted Stacey onward. "And a trial was held. As I understand the updated mechanics, Armard only has one Guardian."

"That's correct. Geranika appeared and was very surprised to find so many players in one of his cellars. He remarked that he'd need to investigate this riotous affair thoroughly, since no one had reported it to him before. And then he began to try the case before him. Finding for Musubi, since he really had done everything according to the terms of the contract, Geranika teleported the entire Oblivion raid party outside the city. So they didn't interfere. He even gave them some items as a reward for 'such a pleasant gift.' No one knows what Musubi got out of it, but it's been three days since anyone's seen him in-game. But that's not important. After that Geranika began holding talks with a hundred high-level players."

"In other words, there is a cellar in Armard chock-full of Legendaries?"

"Not exactly. I can't say for sure since Donotpunnik won't show me the video and I'm not one to believe things without having evidence, but, again, rumor has it that Geranika has some power similar to 'Temporary Rust.' A very unpleasant spell that takes the form of fog. An item that finds its way inside begins to lose Durability until it's destroyed. It's not hard to remove this debuff: ordinary water is enough, but the thing is you have to get the item out of the fog first. Otherwise the debuff is recast immediately."

"A hermetically-sealed cellar full of players who basically can't move," I muttered. Somehow the loss of Undigit and Etamzilat no longer seemed that funny to me—parting with equipment intended for raiding makes the raid seem a bit too expensive.

"The debuff lasts ten minutes. Ten percent Durability is consumed every minute," Anastaria went on. "It works even if the item is in your bag. How do you think they got themselves out?"

"They got themselves out?" I asked surprised.

"Of course! After all, Donotpunnik was there— and he's not one to lose what he'd worked so hard to gain. So he concocted an escape plan. I'm curious to see if you can guess what it is."

"There were two raid parties there, right?" An idea immediately occurred to me. "The easiest way is to slaughter the other raid party. I don't know about the 'Rust,' but once you respawn all of your debuffs are gone. Of course that means that someone has to survive..."

"A+ Mahan," Anastaria smiled, "and a donut as a bonus! What an intelligent little darling you are! They cast lots, chose a player who would lose everything and began to kill each other. Even combining their forces they failed to harm Geranika in any way. As a result, the Heirs of the Titans and the Azure Dragons are now at war with Oblivion. Undigit promised a thousand gold for every killed Oblivion player. That's how it is."

"Hmm...strange. I didn't figure Undigit for *such* a fool."

"Explain?"

"A thousand gold per kill that kicks the player out of the game for twelve hours. I'd get a new level so as not to lose Experience and then spend the next month signing into the game just to get killed. Twice a day at 12 hour intervals. I'd take all my equipment off too, so that they wouldn't waste time seeing who got what. Sixty thousand credits a month for doing absolutely nothing sounds like a good way to get by."

"Hahaha," Anastaria laughed. "You're a real miracle, Mahan. The clan heads have gotten so accustomed to dealing in millions that several hundred thousand spent on revenge seems like a drop in the ocean to them. And of course, for the right person, this very drop might seem like an ocean itself. I'll make sure to pass your idea along to my dad. Maybe we'll manage to make a deal with someone from Oblivion. Listen, I gotta run. Our family dinner here is done for today, but I meant to ask you, will you go to the ball with me?"

"Go where with you?" My eyebrows jumped from such an unexpected request from Anastaria.

"To the ball. I have an invitation to this one event in Shaldan Province. It'll be in four days. The ball must be attended with your second half, if you have one, and well, you're still technically it. I've been told that the Governor might spare several minutes after the ball to speak with me—and whoever is with me. I'm pretty sure your clan needs to boost its rep with one more Province?"

Hmm...Clan reputation with Shaldan Province? Did I need this? Hell, I still wasn't that sure I needed the clan, let alone the other stuff! I guess I'd already decided to keep working on it and contracted a company that would recruit people for me, but I hadn't really done anything else. At the same time, weak excuses such as not having the time or the opportunity or something else wouldn't do. If I wanted to do it, I'd definitely find the time. I needed to do something about this and as soon as possible! Either I work on the clan and become its true leader, or the Legends of Barliona ceases to exist. It's a bit crude of course, but nothing else occurred to me. It was that simple—it would cease to exist.

"Dan, I really need to run. Will you go with me?"

"Pencil it in," I decided. "You may count on me, Duchess. But only for the chance to speak with the Governor."

"Oh how nice, 'Duchess.' I can't help but recall the days we spent together, and the nights," Anastaria meowed, making me want to wring her neck.

"All right, until tomorrow then," Anastaria tarried for a second, almost jerked towards me as per habit, wishing to kiss me and dissolve into thin air, but the table intervened, thankfully, keeping her from doing this. Sighing with some disappointment, Stacey waved a goodbye and cast a portal to wherever. I suppose that'll be 1-0 for the table...

"Mahan! I've already received a report that you've dealt with the problem plaguing the mission to Blue Mosses," Elizabeth said enthusiastically. I decided to complete the cow quest right after leaving the Golden Horseshoe and, just in case, undergo the cleansing process to rid myself of any markers. Who knows how many I'm currently sporting, courtesy of Phoenix's Rogues? Maybe none and maybe I'm decked out in them like a Christmas tree! At the moment, the last thing I should do is reveal to Anastaria where another Crastil is located. I had to be the first to speak with the High Mage of Anhurs.

Quest completed: 'Missing Cows.' +100 to Reputation with the Priests of Eluna and 30 silver.

"I don't have anything for you at the moment," Elsa added with disappointment, spreading her arms. "Lately our Priests have been really on the ball, completing all their assignments. I don't even know how to keep them busy, so you'll have to forgive me."

"It's not a big deal. I don't have too much free time myself right now." Elsa, I have some business to discuss with you...Two things actually. The first is that I'd like to receive your blessing in order to cleanse myself of any Rogue markers."

"Hang on, let me check," Elizabeth interrupted me and her two eyes turned into ice. Several minutes later, a notification appeared:

Buff received: 'Blessing of the High Priestess.' +5% to all main stats. Duration: 24 hours.

"Three markers," Elsa concluded, regaining her typical appearance. "Plinto the Bloodied, Soulstealer the Grandiose and Mata Delkar."

"Ah yes, all people familiar to me," I lied blatantly. I could more or less understand why Plinto had tracked me, but the other two, Soulstealer and Mata remained a mystery to me. By the way! "Say, do you tell everyone who placed the markers?"

Plinto's always placing markers on Anastaria and swears that she doesn't know about them. And yet, practice just showed that Elizabeth not only confirms that there are markers on you, but also tells you whom they belong to.

"No, typically, I merely bestow my blessing. In this case, I was curious who is tracking a Harbinger, so I decided to look up the owners too. You said, that you had two pieces of business for me. We just dealt with one. What's the second one?"

"Do you know what a Crastil is?"

"An ornamental orb with an inscription in a dead language which no one speaks. Well, that, or there is another hypothesis that the inscription is pure nonsense."

"I need one. Do you know where I can get it?"

"As far as I know, the High Mage of Anhurs has a Crastil. The Emperor has several lying about in his treasure vaults. Several more are scattered about the continent and I think the pirates have one or two. If I remember correctly, you already should have one or two as well."

"I no longer have them, and so I'm looking for a new way to acquire one of these little balls."

"What do you need it for? They don't serve any purpose. Hundreds of minds over many millennia have tried to solve the riddle of the Crastils with no success."

"I have a theory I'd like to check. What do you think, will the Mage sell me the one he has?"

"He is one of the few remaining investigators of the Crastil, so I doubt it. But you could give it a shot. Why not? The one piece of advice I can offer you is offer him an exchange. Something that might pique his interest. Something unique."

"Unique?" I asked surprised. "Does the High Mage really like unique items?"

"Like any other normal sentient," Elizabeth shrugged. "I like to collect unique items as well. Unfortunately, I don't have a Crastil in my collection."

"And what do you have?" I couldn't help ask against my better judgment when Hoarding Hamster and Greed Toad, who'd been busy snoozing until that moment, suddenly elbowed aside my innate modesty and took control of my entire organism. Even if this was only a temporary usurpation, it was enough to force out the question. And, I was surprised to discover that in some sense I agreed with them. What if I get the chance to rummage around the stores of the Priestess of Eluna?

"You're still the same old Mahan," Elsa giggled. "I'm sorry to disappoint you—I don't have anything that could be of use to a Shaman. I'm not interested in items that have nothing to do with Eluna, and she's not your goddess."

"I wouldn't be so sure," I refused to give up. "The Amulet of the Junior Priestess doesn't have anything to do with a Shaman either, and yet, if you recall Beatwick, it was used to save quite a few lives. Life is long and sometimes things go so awry that you can only look at them and wonder how it could work out this way. Today Eluna isn't my goddess, tomorrow she is and the day after it might turn out that she's no one's goddess at all. Could you guarantee that this doesn't happen?"

+20% to Charisma. Total: 61%.

"Perhaps you're right," Elizabeth replied slowly, considering something. "Life is so unpredictable that you never know whether you'll be a High Priestess forever or you'll be exiled one day to some distant part of the Empire for something your husband did. Come along—I will show you my collection."

You have received temporary access to the private chamber of the High Priestess of Eluna. Access duration: 60 minutes.

"When they found Yalininka's body," Elsa began to explain, pausing at the first exhibit in her modest room, "there was no limit to the sorrow of the sentients of this continent. The elves refused to accept the silver wings because they considered themselves and the wings complicit in the great one's death. Then the High Priestess of the time was tasked with saving the wings as a token of remembrance of the faith healer. Even though I hadn't the right to do it, I moved the wings from the treasure vault to my office. It doesn't do for a relic like this to gather dust in the darkness."

Silently, I looked on two small silver wings and a lump of sorrow formed in my throat. Instead of the eternally young girl that everyone always depicted on statues and paintings, I was imagining the elderly and life-weary woman who, nevertheless, still had enough strength to come to the aid of a lost and confused Shaman during the last few minutes of her life. And this even though the Shaman considered himself the most cunning and intelligent persona around.

"This is the fan of Riksha'as," Elizabeth began to list the other items, but I was only half-listening, still staring at the wings. Their properties were hidden to me, but even if a player who equipped them could fly with them, I would knock him out of the air and thrash him until he'd drop this Legendary item. There are items that one is not allowed to use. They should only be revered. And I couldn't care less that this is a game.

"This is Elaine's amulet and this one of the nine Paladins of the Round Table," Elsa went on, pretending that she didn't notice my stupor. "The elven gown of Loe, the golden map of Getshak, the gloves of Naruem, the cape of Omelsi...all Legendary items of legendary Paladins and Priests of eras gone by. My collection is not so ample, but every item here has its own history. A sorrowful one and a bloody one, but one proper to the item."

"*Stacey, are you in the game?*" I made a silent call. Turning off my brain, reason, feelings and emotions, I turned to Anastaria like to an ordinary person who could help me.

"*I'm here,*" Anastaria replied without a trace of mockery.

"*I really need the Farewell Ribbon of the Great Yalininka, which I gave to Barsina once.*"

A silence ensued for several moments and then Anastaria said:

"*Summon me.*"

"Elsa, could I summon Anastaria here?" I asked the High Priestess to her immense surprise.

"Right here?"

"It doesn't matter—it could be to your public office, if you like."

"Hang on," Elsa made several motions with her hands and then said: "You can summon her here. I've granted her access..."

"It is an immense honor to enter this place, oh High One," Anastaria bowed her head, instantly realizing where she was.

"What do you want?" the girl added telepathically. *"If she sees the ribbon in my hands, I'll receive all the bonuses."*

"The hell with the bonuses. Simply give it to her," I cut her off. From a player's perspective what I was doing at the moment was incredibly taboo—simply giving a unique item to an NPC. An item that I could sell for huge amounts of money and an item that doesn't belong to me. But I knew one thing—what I wanted to do was the right thing.

"Are you sure?"

"Yes."

"High Priestess," Anastaria began, "during his many travels, my husband encountered Yalininka, who sold him this item," Anastaria produced the ribbon and offered it to Elizabeth. "On behalf of our family, I request you accept this gift."

Elizabeth accepted the ribbon in a stupor, read its properties and the poor NPC's eyes grew into two immense saucers. Naturally, it's not every day that players simply donate Unique items like this.

"I detect no pretense or ulterior motive in their thoughts," sounded Eluna's surprised voice right behind my back. "Mahan truly believes that giving you the ribbon is the right thing to do, and Anastaria truly believes that Mahan is right. This couple never ceases to amaze me! They truly do not resemble other Free Citizens!"

"Goddess," Anastaria and I said in unison, bowing our heads before one of the mightiest creatures of this world.

"In that case," Eluna continued, looking at Elizabeth as a mother looks on a small child who's received a present she's dreamed of her entire brief life. The High Priestess had still not stepped away. It looked like the Imitator had had a breakdown and crashed. "I won't do anything right this moment, or make any decisions. We shall all meet again. For now, please leave Elizabeth. She needs a little time."

Some junior Priests appeared and first ushered us out of Elsa's private chamber and then from the temple entirely. They managed this so gracefully that I couldn't think of a single objection. The temple's doors closed to the irritation of some players who were in a hurry to see the Priests, but only a minute passed before Anastaria and I remained alone on the temple's steps. What was the point in trying to break in and lose time? There's never enough of it anyway.

"Thank you," I said, carefully examining the roof tiles on the building on the other side of the square. Whatever I felt about the girl in general, she had just done me a great favor. And even if it couldn't be quantified in actual bonuses, I was dead certain that this gift would pay off for me in the future. Whether it'd be good or bad, something would come of it.

"Thanks to you," Stacey replied, examining the same tiles. "Did you see the wings?"

"Try and not see them."

"I would've never believed they were real. You couldn't even see them in that video where you met Yalininka. But here...it's a miracle!"

I didn't reply, since I didn't know what I could say. Anastaria had just given an NPC a unique item, without any questions or demands of her own. And she'd known that she'd never get it back. Still, she had given in at my request. If it weren't for the whole episode involving the opening to the Tomb of the Creator, I wouldn't have thought anything of it, but now I wasn't so sure. What did she want?

"*Where'd you run off to, sunshine?*" Stacey's surprised voice sounded in my head when I found nothing better to do than to blink away on my business.

"*The problem of the Priests has been resolved, my kitten, and I had nothing else to do there.*"

"*I understand that of course. But you could have at least returned me to the same place you'd summoned me from.*"

"*Sorry babe, I'm completely broke for time. Call your Mages and have them send you wherever you need,*" I didn't bother bringing up the mysterious Rogue markers that I'd found on myself. Why? Let her think that I don't know anything about it and that I'd received the Priestess's blessing routinely. I'd feel calmer that way anyway.

"What brings the Shaman Earl to my modest lodgings?" boomed the High Mage of Anhurs as soon as I entered his office, panting from the steep climb up the tower. Are the devs really going to keep telling me that my sensory filter is turned on after this? I almost pulled all my leg muscles struggling up those stairs.

Despite my desire to sign out to reality and get a good night's sleep after my meeting with Anastaria, I decided to stop by the place of the only holder of a Crastil known to me and try to solve all of my problems in one fell swoop.

"Greetings oh High One," I said half asleep and trying to catch my breath. I'll need to send the video of my ascent to the developers asking whether players with sensory filters should feel this way after climbing to the High Mage's tower. "I have some business to discuss with you."

"What business?" the old man adjusted his grizzled beard and sat down at his table which was cluttered with empty and half-empty vials.

"I have heard a rumor," I finally managed my breathing and stood up straight, "that you are in possession of a Crastil. I'd like to trade you something for it."

"You'd like to trade something for my unique adamant Crastil?" The Mage raised his eyebrows in surprise. "What do you need it for? Do you know something that may shed light on their use?"

"I only have a hunch," I decided to bait him along. "In order to verify it, I need an actual Crastil. I'm not asking you to give it to me forever. We can make an agreement that in a month or two, I will return the Crastil to you. I imagine that a Herald will be ready to witness such a contract."

"Hmm," hummed the Mage. "You have managed to ignite my curiosity, Shaman. Let's go over it one more time—you'd like to lease the Crastil I have and you promise to return it in two months. Did I understand you correctly?"

"That is correct."

"If your hunch proves accurate, you must tell me what you needed the Crastil for. If not, you must tell me what you wanted to check. Do we have a deal?"

"Deal."

"In that case, there is only one more small matter—what shall I receive for leasing you the orb?"

"Information," I took a stab in the dark. "You are studying the Crastils and..."

"Young man," the Mage interrupted, "I have been studying Crastils several hundred years and during this time so many people have come to me as you just did that I've lost count. Everyone wanted one thing—that I give, sell, trade, or gift him the Crastil. I don't even have to think hard to recall the last one—just yesterday, your spouse, Anastaria, offered me several truly wondrous items for my Crastil. How will you top her offer? Why should I give the Crastil to you in particular?"

So she knows about the Mage too...Not good!

"I am prepared to offer you the Chess Set of Karmadont, which I crafted, in exchange for the Crastil." I decided to play my trump card, placing the chess pieces one at a time on the Mage's desk.

The Mage froze for several moments, staring at the pieces like they were some miracle, but he quickly regained his composure and smiled:

"I have heard, I have heard," he said, stroking his beard. "The Shaman Jeweler set out on the path of the Chess Set and has already accomplished the most important thing—opening the Tomb of the Creator. No matter that you have plunged Barliona into chaos! Could such a trifle matter to the Shaman Jeweler? It's creation that's important to him!"

"Chaos?" I echoed surprised. "What's chaos have to do with it?"

"As soon as you pass the threshold of the Tomb you shall encounter the chaos of which I speak."

"Maybe in that case I shouldn't enter the Tomb at all?" I carefully asked the Mage. This news made me a little anxious. I didn't want to become the reason of some kind of chaos.

"It is too late," the old man shook his head sadly. "If you won't, some other Free Citizen will enter the Tomb. What difference does it make who opens

Pandora's Box? The main thing has already been accomplished—the way lies open."

"Esteemed Mage," I decided to squeeze the Mage as politely as possible, bringing my entire arsenal of Charisma to bear against him. "What is this chaos of which you speak? If the Tomb contains something that should not be opened, then let's not open it. But I need to know what it is first!"

"Like every other Shaman in Barliona," the High Mage shook his head condescendingly. "If there is a problem, then its source must be concealed and everything will be better. The world may end a hundred times until even one Free Citizen makes his way into the chambers of the Creator's Tomb. Geranika, the Heart of Chaos, the servants of the Nameless one—Barliona is in peril of destruction and annihilation every day. Thus, one more source of calamity will merely drown in this morass of doom."

"You still haven't answered," I went on plying my line. "How does the Tomb of the Creator threaten Barliona? And how do you even know about this?"

"It doesn't seem to you that we've strayed from our original topic?" The High Mage remained unshakable. "As I recall it, you need a Crastil in exchange for which you offered me the Chess Set of Karmadont. My response to your offer is no. I don't need the Chess Set."

"Crastils can wait, Barliona cannot. What will happen if a Free Citizen enters the Tomb of the

Creator?"

"I believe that our conversation has come full circle," the High Mage concluded, utterly unwilling to give in. "In that case, I propose we part ways. I have business to attend to."

"I am ready to give you the Chess Set of Karmadont if you tell me," I managed to exclaim before two blue guards that looked exactly like genies could drag me away.

"When will you understand?" the High Mage halted his genies with a curt gesture. "The Chess Set is only of interest as a full set, with the board included. In any other form, it is little more than some pretty and whimsical figurines, no more."

"Do you like the sea?" I uttered involuntary. I wasn't about to leave the Mage's place without a Crastil or information about what happened if I entered the Tomb, so I had to play my only trump ace.

"The sea?" the old man asked with surprise and even looked up from his paperwork. "What does my love for the sea have to do with this?"

"Like I said, I need a Crastil and information. In exchange, I am prepared to part with this item," I opened my mailbox, found a letter I had sent to myself with nothing but an attachment, dragged the attachment over to my bag and sent the High Mage a link to it. "This may not be the full Chess Set, but no one in Barliona has something like this."

The Giant Squidolphin Embryo. An item that

could easily cost fifty to sixty million if not more. A Unique vessel that must first be nurtured, taken care of, coddled. A ship that would make any clan in Barliona the undisputed master of the seas.

"I cannot accept this payment, Earl." For the first time during our conversation, instead of condescension and scorn, I heard a note of profound esteem in the High Mage's voice. "The Crastil and the information you wish to know are not worth such an item."

The Mage stood transfixed by the small cocoon in my hands, while I could barely keep myself from swearing out loud. The NPC turned out to be far smarter than me.

"I cannot give you my Crastil," the Mage went on, ignoring my state. "It's valuable to me as a reminder that not everything in this world is subject to logic and order. However, I can help you. In the process, you will receive an answer to your question about what will happen if a living creature enters the Tomb of the Creator."

The High Mage made a barely noticeable gesture and his two guards evaporated in the air around them as if they were made of smoke.

"Have you ever considered why in every city of our continent, be it in Malabar, Kartoss or the Free Lands, the Mages' towers are located in the north? The northernmost building of every city is the Mages' tower."

Really! Back when I was a Hunter I had noticed this aspect of urban design. Back then, though, I didn't give it a second thought. Perhaps this was just the way the designers preferred it? It's only now, having spent some time as a Shaman at a completely different level that I understand that nothing happens in Barliona without a reason. Any event or phenomenon not only has its own rationale, but its own history and quest chain. The important thing is to know how to bring it to light.

"This isn't mentioned anywhere," I agreed with the Mage.

"It's not. There are hundreds of theories why this is so, but only the High Mages of the cities know why it is this way. Far to the north, beyond the limits of our continent, lies an unexplored land. Every five hundred years, like clockwork, a black cloud travels from that land to Kalragon, destroying everything in its path. And it must be noted that it travels in a very strange manner—it vanishes as it approaches the coast, only to reappear some time later right beside one of our cities. Several times in centuries gone by, the ancient Mages ignored the cloud, and each time their lapse resulted in monstrous casualties. Cities vanished as if they had never existed. Along with all their residents. That was when it was decided that the northernmost building in any city should be the Mage's tower—this way, we shall be the first to suffer the blow. It is now several millennia that we are fending off this evil, and yet the clouds grow stronger every time. Last time, when a cloud appeared before Anhurs, we were forced to summon all the Mages of Malabar."

"But what does this have to do with the Crastil and the Tomb?"

"Patience, my young friend, patience. In search for a weapon against this scourge, we turned over every corner of our continent. In the northern reaches of the Free Lands, among the foothills of the Elma Mountains, we discovered a cave filled with Crastils. You've seen their inscriptions—they are mysterious and incomprehensible. The Mages thought that the words must mean something and began to experiment with the orbs in the hopes of finding a key to the riddle. That was when they discovered the Ergreis—a crystal of heavenly beauty, clear and pure like a tear. Enormous like the head of a bison. Deadly like the power of Geranika raised to the tenth power. It's difficult to say why the Creator permitted an item from a different world to remain in Barliona, especially one so deadly, but the fact remains—the Ergreis was in Barliona."

"From a different world?" I asked surprised. "Where is it from?"

"The Emperor Lait brought the Ergreis with him when he fled his world. The very Ergreis that was accidentally activated by Feeris, the great Mage of yore."

"Hang on, I'm starting to get lost. The Mages found a cave filled with Crastils. In the same cave they found a crystal called the Ergreis that had been brought to Barliona by Lait. This crystal was inactive. Some Feeris activated the crystal—it's not clear how or why—and then something bad happened. Did I get that right?"

"That's correct. Feeris and all the Mages in the cave died immediately, whereupon the deadly aura of the crystal began to radiate out to the surroundings. The Mages figured it would stop in a radius of a kilometer, then ten and then a hundred. When the aura destroyed everything living in a radius of 500 kilometers without even appearing to pause, the Mages decided to destroy the source. They couldn't teleport within the crystal's aura and griffons hadn't been domesticated yet, so they decided to set out on foot. An ordinary Hunter, who knew these lands as well as his own hand, led the campaign to the Ergreis. Today you know him as Karmadont. History is silent about how long the campaign lasted. All we know is that all its members, aside from Karmadont, perished. Three hundred and two Mages. No one knows how Karmadont managed to contain the aura of the Ergreis. What is known is that he sealed the crystal in the Tomb of the Creator. Whether the Ergreis is activated or not remains unclear to this day. In memory of the Mages who perished, 302 Crastils were removed from the cave. Over the ensuing ages, these

Crastils dissipated throughout our world, but it remains unclear what their purpose is."

"Perhaps they served as the mechanism for containing the crystal's power?"

"Perhaps—this is the only theory that has not yet been tested. This is also why I am sanguine about the fact that the Tomb has been opened. We have enough Free Mages to destroy the Ergreis. If it is activated and begins to destroy all life once again, the Free Mages will be ready for battle. But before that happens, I shall test another theory."

"'In the northern reaches of the Free Lands, among the foothills of the Elma Mountains' is a bit too vague for finding the cave," I said when I realized why the Mage had told me all this.

"Unfortunately, I cannot be any more accurate. I don't know if the cave is located in the mountains, or secreted in the ground—whether it is large or only a mere cavern. If you need Crastils, you'll have to figure out a way to find the cave. And here, Earl, I request that you leave me. My business is pressing. I must prepare for the next deadly cloud which is due in a year and a half. I must help the Free Mages get ready to fight it."

"Thank you!" I thanked the Mage sincerely—but it was on the threshold to the office that I heard the fatal phrase which turned everything inside me upside down:

"I told Anastaria this same story..."

CHAPTER SIX

FLIGHT

"**D**ANIEL?" A steely voice sounded in my phone.

"Speaking!"

"This is the Omega chauffer service. Your car is here. You are expected. A black Chevrolet."

"Thank you, I'm coming down."

Right after leaving the High Mage's office, I blinked to Altameda and signed out of Barliona. Another headache enveloped me, telling me that I had to take a break, so I took another painkiller injection. At first I was very surprised to find a complete medicine cabinet in my bathroom—however, a quick investigation put everything in its right place: The cleaning service included the restocking of any medicines I had. And if the client didn't have a medicine cabinet at all, the company would provide a complete assortment with all the necessities. Pretty convenient this cleaning service thing. I should use it more frequently.

Checking to make sure that all my devices were turned off, I put on a jacket and shut the door behind me. I hope that someday I'll come back to this place.

The heavily-tinted car was waiting in my driveway. The windows were so dark that even the setting sun couldn't penetrate them. When the door opened, I could barely contain a grin—the thickness and heft of the door demanded respect. It looked like the car was also bullet-proof. I wonder if it could take a hit from an RPG too..? Damn! What am I thinking about? I pulled my thoughts back to the dim interior of the enormous car as the doors closed automatically and I found myself in complete darkness.

My eyes had not had time to adjust when two prongs were stuck into my torso. I wanted to object but my jaw twitched in a spasm—an electric charge swept through my body.

"What the..." I began to yell, but the shock came again. And again. And again. Five brief but still very painful shocks passed through my poor body before the light came on in the car's salon.

"You make interesting enemies, Daniel," said a nondescript, balding man sitting in the front seat and pointing some kind of gadget with two wires at me. "Forgive me for the pain I caused you—it was necessary."

"What the hell?" I finished what I'd started to say.

"There were three subdermal tracking implants in you," the man explained calmly, as though my outrage did not concern him a bit. "As I understand it, you were a prisoner. The government does not release its wards lightly."

"Three trackers?" The man's words clicked in my head and I calmed down a little. In any case, I stopped struggling to escape.

"Two in your leg and one in your arm—just above your wrist. You can feel it if you like. At the moment the trackers are deactivated, but we will have to perform minor surgery to remove them completely. They are powered by your body and will reset in three hours. We need your permission to operate. If you refuse, we cannot render the service you requested and our contract with you will be terminated."

"You have my permission," I immediately agreed. The thought that there were some foreign objects inside of me was extremely unpleasant. "You said something about enemies. What do they have to do with it? I'm not sure I understood you correctly..."

"Someone really wants to know where you are," the man began to explain, entering something into his handheld computer. "This car is already being tracked. Moreover, they've attached several sensors to it to determine how many living people are in it. That's to make sure that we don't dump you into a sewer along the way. It's been a long time since I've encountered such a close watch on a subject. You've really upset someone quite a bit if they've hired pros of this caliber to track you."

"But you have a plan, correct?"

"We have everything, Mr. Daniel. However, I will require another permission from you. I will inject you with a drug called Marlacyne and you will die for two hours. Literally. At the same time, we will apply an antidote to one of our men, who was earlier injected with Marlacyne, thereby reviving him. We have to conduct a blood analysis to determine the proper dose of the drug. Your death and the revival of our man must happen at the same moment."

"You want to kill me?" I asked surprised.

"Temporarily. We purposefully didn't destroy another little bug that keeps track of your location. That one isn't from the government—someone else is keeping tabs on you. As soon as you die, we will transfer the bug to our man. Our job will be to misdirect whoever is tracking you."

"What's to guarantee that I'll survive? I've never died before."

"There is no guarantee," smirked my companion. "Besides the fact that we won't receive our payment if you don't. We are business men, Mr. Daniel. Losing money is not our line of work. Shall we begin the procedure? Or are you not ready to die just yet?"

"Get on with it," I replied, knowing full well that there was no way back. The old man will discover that I tried to flee and he'll be sure to take some sort of measures, all the way up to abducting me and keeping me in his cellar. For safety's sake.

"Place your hand on this device," asked the man,

offering me a small box with a green phosphorescent outline of a hand. Placing my hand on it, I felt a pinprick resembling a mosquito bite and the world filled with grays and vanished...

* * *

"Make yourself comfortable," a female voice sounded in the darkness. I tried to open my eyes and was surprised to discover that I felt absolutely no discomfort. I was lying on my back looking up at a light ceiling. My hands and feet were moving and my head didn't hurt. Wishing to make certain that everything was okay, I sat up abruptly and saw an attractive woman of about thirty in front of me, putting away a syringe.

"There's food in the refrigerator," she said, paying no attention that I was trying to get up from bed. "We will make sure that it doesn't run out. Next to the wall, you will find the newest model capsule," the girl pointed at the steel box. "It's hooked up and checked, but it hasn't been set up yet. You will have to do that on your own. As per your technical request, your connection will be channeled through seven extra servers. As soon as one is hacked, you will be notified. If the fifth server is hacked, you will automatically be disconnected from Barliona. The sixth and seventh servers will be destroyed. Your only contacts with the external world are through Barliona.

There is no telephone or internet line here. You do not know where you are, so it is impossible for you to reveal this information in the game even if someone were to scan your memory."

"The Corporation can scan memories?"

"We do not have evidence of their capability to scan long-term memory, but they can scan short-term memory. They've figured that out already. Please enter your digital signature here—our services cost nineteen million credits."

"You've done all this without a down payment?" I asked surprised, entering the digital signature. "What if I didn't have this amount?"

"We checked your real and virtual accounts beforehand," the girl smiled, accepting my payment. The Legends of Barliona just lost nineteen million gold. "You are a solvent person, Daniel Mahan, so we decided to take the risk. Who knows—perhaps whoever is spying on you in reality is also tracking your accounts and bank transfers. Our services are not cheap, but we are worth every credit you invest in us. The clothes you are accustomed to are in the closet." The girl waved in some general direction and only now I noticed that I was wearing some gray pajamas. "If you have any questions or you need anything, there is a phone on the table. Simply pick up the handset, and the line will automatically connect you to the Omega operator. If one of the proxies in the array you are connecting through is compromised, you will receive a notification in Barliona. We've made a minor tweak to your capsule to ensure this. What else...Oh! We have temporarily isolated the initiator of your disappearance, Sergei. The isolation duration that we agreed upon with him is three months. This too is covered in the cost of the package you paid for, so you have no need to worry about him. If you don't have any further questions, I will leave you. Look around and make yourself at home—this will be your home for the next three months. All the best."

The woman left, closing the door behind her and locking it with several locks—it was then that I noticed that there was nothing but a handle on my side of the door. I yanked it several times to make sure that I really was locked in. The apartment boasted a bathroom big enough to fit a boat in and a tiny kitchen about the size of the bathroom, an enormous refrigerator stuffed full of frozen meals and, to my surprise, my favorite beer. There was also a bedroom with a twin bed and the newest gaming cocoon available. And a closet full of various clothes, all of my size. In effect another room but transformed to a closet. And that was all! It was all I had. There weren't even any windows in this pharaohs' tomb. Given the capsule's capability of scanning short-term memory, the people who had hidden me away were keeping a very close watch over the security of my physical self.

Excellent! I could now deal with the old man as well as Phoenix from a position of power. No one could threaten me with bodily harm.

After a quick snack of several hamburgers, I climbed into the gaming cocoon and began to adjust its settings for my needs. A physiological scan, a brain scan, the attunement of the waves that would track and initiate the interface signals, the power block set-up, excrement expulsion and life support, set up, set up and more set up. I ended up messing around with the capsule for three hours, until the long-awaited notification appeared before me: "You may now enter Barliona." The good thing was that the capsule wasn't merely of the newest model, but it was also outfitted for long-term immersion, allowing me to remain in Barliona for up to six months if I wished.

This is exactly what I needed at the moment.

ENTER!

"Orders, master?" asked Viltrius when I sprawled out in my rocking throne. I needed to decide what I would focus on first. A notification let me know that my clan had lost an enormous amount of money, but that our treasury still had about seventeen million gold in it. My own personal account also had seven million lying around, so it's not like we were in the midst of a financial crisis or anything. There weren't any huge outlays coming up and we had paid all our taxes for the next six months, so I could focus exclusively on the game.

"Are there any guests in the castle?" I inquired about the Shamans that had been there earlier. What if someone was still staggering around the castle instead of undergoing registration for the new continent and updating their class mechanics...?

"No—they all left Altameda the day before yesterday," Viltrius replied with a bow.

"When?!"

"The day before yesterday," the goblin replied calmly.

"*Ping*," Anastaria's thought appeared in my head. A second went by before my head all but exploded with the girl's enraged tirade: "*Oh-ho! His majesty has deigned to return! I won't even bother asking where you've been for the past four days. Are you aware that because of your absence, I've failed the Governor's visit? Can you even imagine how difficult it was to come by that invitation?*"

Four days?!

I opened my settings and stared with astonishment at the system time. If my eyes didn't deceive me, then the last time I was in Barliona really was four days ago. Four and a half even. How much time did they spend hiding me? Or rather, how much time had I spent 'dead?' Why didn't they warn me that the procedure would take so long?

"*No one kept you from going on your own,*" I replied, not much feeling like being the whipping boy. "*You can't depend on other players in Barliona. If I'm* not around, then your invitation automatically becomes an invitation for another person. So cut the crap!"

"That's exactly the point—the bonus for us attending together is much greater than me going alone."

"So you went to the reception?"

"Yeah, I did."

"Did you meet the Governor?"

"No. He refused to see me because I came on my own."

"That's impossible! You can't be bound to a player who's not in game."

"I know. I've let the devs know and they're looking into the error. I was worried Dan!"

"I gotta go. I need to deal with some stuff."

Four days! What has happened in Barliona during this time? What has happened in reality? Are they looking for me?

A blaring amulet returned me to the game at hand. As I was rummaging for it I simultaneously opened my mailbox and sighed despondently— another several thousand letters. And another several hours of sorting them ahead of me.

"Speaking!"

"Daniel, this is Marina. Can you spare me a minute?"

"Marina?" At first I didn't quite understand which Marina, so it took me a second to get my bearings. "Mirida the Farsighted!"

"Marina," the voice on the other end confirmed.

"I think I have time right now. I'm listening."

"Daniel, what do you think of meeting today to have a chat? I've put off this conversation for a long time and finally decided that it has to happen. What do you say?"

"Let's meet," I agreed. I no longer felt anything negative toward Marina. What difference was it what she did a year ago? The important thing was what all had come of it.

"How about today in the Golden Horseshoe? I'll treat you to the best dish in Barliona."

"Deal! Around five in the afternoon, okay?"

Even though I hadn't expected her call, I had been planning on seeing Marina for a while and simply hadn't gotten around to it. It was either one thing or another. Since she'd just called me herself and offered to meet...

Hold up! How did she know I was in game? Had she dialed randomly and gotten lucky? Paranoia is of course nothing but paranoia, and yet...I should think about this.

I began to go through my mail but stopped at the fifth letter in stunned shock. I guess today is an incredibly bad day for Shamans. This was easily the last thing I expected.

Hey Mahan!

We'd like to invite you to take part in a show we are making called 'The Legends of Barliona: A failed project of Phoenix.' Anastaria, Leite, Magdey and Barsina have already confirmed their participation. We will be shooting in two days. The show is scheduled to air in a month and a half, during the clan competitions. Sincerely, Editor in Chief of ART Media.

I glanced at the letter's date and couldn't help but growl in anger—the show had already been made.

"Darling, do tell how the taping last night went..." I asked Anastaria, trying to control of my feelings. "What do they mean by 'failed project?'"

"Who knew you would abandon the game, babes? We met up, had a chat, looked at some footage and discussed why it's not worth joining the Legends of Barliona. You know, the same old stuff."

"In other words the entire gang got together and publicly discussed a clan none of you belong to— without even giving a member of that clan a chance to speak for it?" I seethed, making an enormous effort to keep from yelling at the girl. Enough is enough! It's time to stop giving her reasons to mock me by showing my emotions! I can play the Ice Queen too! Maybe I'm still hurt, maybe my emotions still struggle to erupt at every turn, but still I'm capable of harnessing them or at least trying to. Am I a Shaman or what? "Given my temporary absence from the game, the taping of the show should have been delayed. As it stands, I'll have to question its legitimacy publicly and demand that it's taken off air."

"Hmm..." Anastaria said pensively. "I swear

someone's abducted and replaced you, Mahan! I mean, where's the outburst? The fit and the tantrum? It's beginning to seem to me that you've graduated from daycare to kindergarten. That is, you've stopped picking your nose with your toe but you're still wearing diapers. As for 'temporary absence,' you shouldn't forget, darling, that I was in the clan too and that it currently exists at all thanks to the fact that I decided not to destroy it entirely. So I showed a little weakness and allowed you to save face in front of the other players. As a result I'm well within my right to discuss it whenever I want and with whomever I want."

I am the Ice Queen. I am the Ice Queen!

"You surrendered your right to speak for the Legends of Barliona the moment you quit. As the head of the Legends, I will officially declare you incapable of speaking for my clan in any capacity…"

Energy level: 30. Stop, you angry Shaman!

I sighed deeply, trying to calm my shaking. All that I wanted was to strangle Anastaria with my bare hands. I couldn't care less about the level disparity between us or my lack of Shamanic powers. I'd never felt such an intense desire to kill another person—not even during my rehab period. How could she be so low? Such a two-faced bitch? When she needed something—like for example a bonus for gifting Yalininka's ribbon—Anastaria played the role of a lamb. When she didn't have to wear a mask, she turned into a complete beast. I loathe her!

My heart was thumping in my chest and I wanted to yell, curse and tear something to pieces—to turn over the entire world and make it feel sorry it was ever born. Viltrius hid himself to avoid any trouble. The guards were diligently playing the role of castle ornaments, afraid to stir, and yet I wasn't about to take my rage out on my own people, or programs or whatever...That's not what I hired them for. A single clear idea occurred to me at the moment—I had to go and create something. It didn't matter what—as long as I could channel all of the emotions that were overwhelming me into it.

Design Mode welcomed me with its tranquil, but already forgotten, darkness, as if saying, 'Don't worry! In a second we'll show the world that it does no good to anger a Shaman.' No sooner had I formed an abstract form, swiping aside all the recipes I already knew, than it turned into Anastaria's head— disfigured by terrible lesions and scars. The image of the ideal woman had become so horrible that I was even taken aback. All of my emotions vanished in one fell swoop. There was neither hate nor love nor pity nor revulsion. As I gazed on this disfigured image of Anastaria, I realized that I didn't want to create *this*. This wasn't because I didn't want to corrupt Stacey's appearance. That didn't bother me at all. The problem was that if I was responsible for creating this, then all of my reputation with the High Priestess would evaporate entirely. Elsa would cease to exist for me—replaced by an Elizabeth who was as stock and curt as only NPCs could be.

I swiped the misshapen project aside and sighed deeply. I was the Ice Queen and therefore I had to create like one. Whatever emotions tormented me earlier had no place in Design Mode.

A new project took shape before my eyes. I reached out to it mentally, wishing to imbue it with the form of a sphere—the shape easiest to work with—but suddenly the sphere melted and Anastaria appeared before me again. Covered in lesions and scars.

Okay, start over. Time for the third project. The fourth. The fifth. Exit Design Mode. Enter Design Mode. The sixth. The seventh. Exit. Enter. The eighth.

All right...I should probably consider what's happening now.

Whatever I imagined and whatever mood I had when I began to create, I could only produce a single image—a disfigured Anastaria. If I used a recipe, the items came out like they were supposed to, but any attempt to start from scratch yielded the girl's head. This was all very strange and it quite rightfully gave me pause for thought about my own capacity to exercise self-control. Am I really incapable of managing my own emotions?

Like hell! Dear Design Mode, come over here one

more time. I have something to discuss with you. Something serious!

A disfigured Anastaria appeared before me yet again, but this time I didn't discard her. It was time to be creative.

This horrible face of the girl is the product of my current state of mind and feelings about her, and those in turn are all due to the scene preceding my recent exit to reality. I can't change any of this now, and I should accept it as a given. Yet no one can forbid me from remembering the time we had spent together. It doesn't matter that all of that was just a game to Anastaria, while for me real feelings were at stake—those emotions, those experiences were real. And that's exactly what I needed right now.

I recalled our first meeting. The girl's condescending smile, seeing yet another low-level player breaking his back to extract some ore. I remembered our first date outside of Beatwick, when we spied on the Kartossian troops from a distance: how we set up the tent, our first conversation, the laughter in the girl's eyes when I told her my story...

The image of Anastaria began to improve. Little by little the awful lesions grew smooth. The scars began to dissolve. Her shoulders straightened out and her lower lip, cleft by some terrible weapon began to fuse together, once again resembling the perfect lips of the Paladin Siren.

I remembered our haggling when Anastaria

wanted to figure out whether I was the creator of the Chess Set. Our first embrace, when the girl stood as still as a statue. Her attempt to use the Siren's venom, my kiss, the revulsion on her face, her unconcealed anger when she realized that the venom had no effect on me.

Everything I had achieved up until that point instantly evaporated. Anastaria again became horrible and disfigured, yet I clenched my fists in triumph. That's it! I understood the principles! I shouldn't remember the moments when Stacey revealed her true nature. I was an artist! I had to force myself to temporarily forget the girl's entire vileness. I had to perceive her as the ideal woman whom I had once loved.

And whom I loved to this day!

Our first kiss. Our sojourns in the Date House. The heavenly smile that played on her face when I made yet another blunder. Her embraces. Her exiting Barliona—when she'd dissolve in my arms like Snow White. The look in her stunning hazel eyes. Her voice. Her laughter. Her hands. Her voice when she'd whisper 'I love you' into my ear.

You have created a model of The Lovers' Pendant. In order to embody the real item please speak to the masters' guild. The pendant's creation will form an intimate connection between two players—allowing them to communicate

telepathically without expending Energy.

Item class: Epic. Ingredients: Diamond. The pendant requires a consensual binding between the two players. The pendant requires the two players to be married in Barliona. All players in Barliona are notified of the pendant's abilities.

You have created an Epic item. +200 to Reputation with all previously encountered factions.

+1 to Crafting. Total: 16.

+5 to Jewelcrafting. Total: 165.

Profession level increased: 'Blessed Artificer Level 5.' Quest available: 'Creator of Light.' Description: Speak with the hermit living in the foothills of the Elma Mountains. He shall help guide your craft in the proper direction. Do you wish to accept the quest?

It had been a long time since I'd seen so much system text. It had even begun to seem to me that those happy days I had spent in creation had vanished once and for all. A Blessed Artificer. I accepted the quest to speak with the hermit without a second thought, since it didn't mention rewards or penalties or time restrictions. Let it linger in my quests list. What mattered most at the moment was that I had managed to overcome myself. It's true that the mere mention of Anastaria evoked in me a savage desire to smear her across the nearest wall, but that was just blind rage. This was a conscious, deliberate and premeditated desire.

I did it!

"*A binding for lovers?*" Anastaria's thought immediately invaded my mind. "*I can't leave you alone for a second.*"

I glanced at the system time and sighed with relief—only thirty minutes had passed since I had entered Design Mode for the first time. That meant that James, one of the developers, hadn't lied to me. When I would craft earlier, they'd simply disconnect me from the game while they integrated the item I was making into the Barliona lore. Now they couldn't do this, so the introduction of the pendant to Barliona required time and approval from the masters' guild. I was certain I'd get it in any case. After all was said and done, I had gnomes of my own in the masters guild!

"*Don't worry, precious,*" I told Anastaria, staring with astonishment at my vibrating amulet. Someone wanted to get in touch with me. "*This has nothing to do with you.*"

"Speaking," the amulet wouldn't shut up, so I kicked Anastaria out of my head and answered the call.

"Yo Mahan! This is Reptilis. Do you have a minute?"

"I think so," I replied with some surprise at hearing from the kobold. I didn't even know he had an amulet for me. I don't recall giving him one.

"I've just witnessed one of those lovely events we players like to call a global notification. Something about Harbinger Mahan, Earl and blah blah blah, has managed to create some epic trinket of global significance. Judging by its properties, I could really use one of these. What do I have to do to create the pendant of my own?"

"Diamond," I replied, still in shock. That's right! The notification had mentioned that all players would receive the news of my creation.

"That's all?" Reptilis clarified suspiciously and it was only then that I realized that the Corporation had for some reason decided to hand me an absolutely unbelievable opportunity to enrich myself. If two lovers can communicate with each other without spending Energy on it, then...Let's say I charge a million gold for a pair of pendants—how many players will be ready to spend such money? I would imagine an enormous number...! Something's not right here! I don't have much faith in the altruism of the Corporation and its representatives. I don't even grant the title of Baron to whomever, since I still haven't fully understood what obligations I take on in doing so. What if I'll have to meet with the Barons I'd ennobled once a week and listen to their reports? I'd only given the title to a couple players, including Magdey, so the likelihood that I'd receive extra requirements was very high. And now there was this

Lovers' pendant. Should I charge to craft it? How will Eluna and Elizabeth react to this? After all, the family was one of the social building blocks of Barliona and only perhaps the Corporation had any right to make money off of it. Any players wishing to get their grubby hands on the family idyll would be punished to the full extent of in-game rules. That is, by decimating their Reputations and Attractiveness. Did I really need this? No, I did not. However, the idea of having to craft pendants for huge numbers of lovers also didn't appeal to me.

"You could thank me in some other way, of course, but I'll leave that up to you," I hinted diplomatically. "I won't insist. Although...Reptilis, you used to have Crastils. Tell me, where could I get some? I really need one more."

"I already gave them all to you."

"They've been temporarily removed from my possession. So I'll ask you again..."

"A Crastil...No, I don't have any more. But I could find some, if it's that important."

"It is—I can't stress it enough. If you get me a Crastil—the pendant's yours."

"There aren't any more Crastils in the place from which I, uh, temporarily removed them from—as you put it. I'll have to do some research about them to quote you a price for my services."

"What services?" I asked surprised. "I'll craft you a pendant in exchange for you finding me a Crastil.

Seems to me like a fair deal."

"If it takes me several months to find a Crastil, then I'd probably rather just go without your trinket and be done with the thing," Reptilis explained. "I don't feel like getting involved in some dubious venture. Finding things in Barliona is how I make my living and spending two months without pay on looking for a Crastil doesn't strike me as a good bargain."

"Makes sense," I agreed. "I don't even have an objection. Let's do it this way—we'll make an agreement in which you give me a week of looking, and in exchange I'll give you the pendant. For free!"

"And if I don't find anything during that week?"

"Then you'll get a pendant made from your own Diamond. I won't charge you for the labor. All you'll lose is a week's worth of searching."

"Agreed. I'll send over the contract. I won't work without it."

"Sounds good." I looked over and signed the short contract. "I have some information about the Crastils that might help your search. Here's what the High Mage of Anhurs told me..."

I related to Reptilis what I had learned about the cave of the Ergreis. It was all up to him now—if he wanted the Lovers' pendant, then he'd get me a Crastil for it. I wonder who his girl is...

When I got off the amulet, I received a new mail notification. Without thinking, I opened my mailbox, scanned several letters and sat down wearily on the ground...Oh for the sake of Karmadont!

Hundreds of players, if not thousands, had sent me letters with a single request: that I craft them the Lovers' Pendant. In exchange, they offered money, items, favors—even a ticket to an audience with the Emperor. Some of the letters weren't even offers so much as threats, but the gist was the same: Craft us a pendant. Everyone wanted the ability to communicate without using an amulet or losing Energy.

"Viltrius," I called my majordomo. "Do we have Diamonds in our treasure vaults?"

"We have two Blue, three Green, five White and one incredibly rare Black Diamond," the goblin reported.

"Bring me the black one. I need to make sure this thing works."

"As you ordered, Master," Viltrius vanished and reappeared holding a black stone in his hand. "A Black Diamond."

The chunk of black glass in my hand did not seem at all exceptional. It was unpolished and uncut and looked more like a hunk of obsidian than an invaluable crystal. The only thing that set the Diamond apart from other Jewelcrafting ingredients was that it glowed with and emitted an internal light. I'd never imagine that black light could be a thing, but the Barliona devs had somehow managed to create just this effect, even if as a mere a visual trick. I stuck the Diamond in my bag, opened a map of Anhurs, found the coordinates for the masters' guild and blinked to the location. It was time to register my invention.

"Master Mahan," the door-gnome greeted me with a bow. He was simultaneously the guard, the steward and the doorman of the master's guild. After all, if a master liked to manage the doors, why not give him some extra work too? "May I inquire as to the purpose of your visit?"

"I wish to register an invention," I blurted out the first thing that popped into my head. Registration or embodiment, what's the difference in the end? What I wanted at the moment more than anything was to slip this invention to someone else. Write down the recipe and sell it. There was no way I was going to spend the rest of my life crafting pendants.

"Allow me to examine your invention," the gnome replied in a businesslike tone. I guess this NPC was in charge of everything the masters' guild did. A surprising workload.

Wishing to get the registration over and done with as soon as possible, I opened my Jewelcrafting recipe book and offered it to the Master. Let's see what he knows about gems and settings.

"Would you look at that!" the gnome said a moment later, looking at me with renewed respect. "The Chess Set of Karmadont, the Cursed Chess, the

Novice's Amulet and so much more! You have led a productive life of creation, Artificer!"

It was my turn to be surprised. Never had one of the teachers called me an Artificer. In fact, I periodically got the impression that crafting and the creation of artifacts were utterly different things—and yet the gnome managed to surprise me.

"You know about the Artificers?" I cast my line.

"A little. There haven't been that many in the history of Barliona. A hundred or two, no more. It's very rare for an Artificer to reach the fifth rank. Incredibly rare. As far as I know, there was only one sentient who managed it before you. And that was Karmadont himself!"

"The Emperor?"

"The very one! Or do you believe that an ordinary Hunter could create the Chess Set? Of course not! Karmadont was a great craftsman. Have you seen the Imperial throne? That is his handiwork too. Let me see your book—I'll put in a registration request. Ugh. You need to embody it! You've confused me with all this chatting."

The gnome went on muttering something or other, rummaging around my book of recipes, but I wasn't listening to him. I had received a quest to meet a sentient who would tell me how to level up further. When it came to creating artifacts, that is. And yet only Karmadont had managed to reach the fifth rank. The muttering gnome had said so. There could only

be one explanation, but I refused to believe it—
Karmadont was dead. The Emperor who had created
the Chess Set no longer walked beneath the Barliona
sky. Unless...

"Ready!" the gnome exclaimed happily, returning
my book to me. "Come by in three days and I'll give
you the recipe. I imagine that by that time we'll
manage to pass all the necessary registrations."

"Is there any way to sell it?"

"Sell it?" the gnome asked surprised. "That's
impossible. This recipe belongs only to one creature in
this world—Shaman Mahan, the Dragon. No other
Free Citizen can learn it. This is an Epic recipe—it
cannot be transferred."

"At all?" I asked a dumb questions, still refusing
to believe that I was burdened with this thing forever.

"Let my hands cease to create if I'm lying to you!"
the gnome uttered the most terrible oath of the
masters' guild. These were words you didn't say
lightly, so I might as well exit the game now and
delete my character—the lovebirds of Barliona would
never leave me alone from now on. It looked like my
next several months would brim with pendant
crafting.

"I see. What else do you know about Karmadont
the Artificer?" I decided to pump the gnome for
everything he knew. If I can't sell the recipe, then at
least I can find out something useful...

"I know he reached Level 115. And that's it. The

only work of his that we still have is the Imperial throne. Supposedly it bears an inscription that mentions other works, but the masters aren't allowed to study it. May I help you with anything else?"

This was the key phrase that let me know that my conversation with the NPC had ended, so I bowed a parting and hurried to the Golden Horseshoe, not wishing to use my Blink spell. I needed to do some thinking.

"Darling, will we be meeting today?" I had walked half the distance from the masters' guild to the central square where the tavern was located when Anastaria's voice appeared in my head again. *"We lost four days, so we need to catch up."*

"Meet me at the Horseshoe in five minutes," I replied tersely. All of my emotions about the girl had gone into the creation of the pendant, and I could therefore permit myself to see Anastaria today. I really did need to complete that quest.

"You're pensive today," Anastaria remarked glibly, settling down across from me. "Has your mail boom begun?"

"Among other things, among other things," I muttered, still thinking about the Artificers. What's the difference between Crafting and Artifice? I had created many items, but for instance, I hadn't received any boost to Artifice for the Chess Set—that had only increased my crafting. Meanwhile, the Cursed Chess Set had increased Artifice—but Crafting had grown too. The Amulet of the Novice had earned me the Artificer's polarity, but the Kameamia had only increased my Crafting stat. The principle for distributing stat points for crafted items was completely lost on me, a realization that upset me quite a bit.

"Will you make us a pendant?" Anastaria continued to pry. "We spend too much Energy on our conversations. I told Kreel, that you're in the game, so he decided to storm the Shadow Dragon today. Did he get in touch with you?"

"No to both questions," I replied. "The High Priestess might consider our use of the pendants as a sign of weakness between us. She'll think that the Ying-Yang has stopped working and we've begun to use another item. Who knows what's in her head? Did you speak with Kreel?"

"About three minutes ago."

"In that case I'll..."

The first proxy server has been breached.

A notification appeared before me in the form of a bright panel with an alert text. The panel was so unlike the typical Barliona UI that it was immediately clear that this was one of the homebrewed additions to my capsules made by Omega. The same kind that mothers would use to set up reminders for their playing children that they needed to do their homework, eat dinner, clean up their rooms or stop pick their noses—thereby reminding them of their real life duties in game. My capsule just did the same thing—it was time to stop bumbling about and exit the game.

"In that case you'll what?" Anastaria asked—but I didn't feel like answering anymore. One of the seven servers had been breached. At the fifth one, I'd be disconnected from the game and the sixth proxy would be physically destroyed to prevent the hackers from identifying my location. But who was trying to find me? Anastaria? The old man? The Corporation? I opened my mailbox and quickly began to scan it, ignoring Anastaria's grumbling in the background. It's very likely that whoever was looking for me had written me a letter first. Spam. Spam. Quest request. Quest request. Sorting and automatic processing. Spam! Empty.

"Has something happened?" Anastaria asked in such a crooning, honeyed voice that my tooth began to ache.

The second proxy server has been breached.

That was fast! I forced myself to stay in Barliona through sheer force of will, wanting to see how quickly they'd get the third box too. I need to understand how much time I have after the first server is breached before I have to leave the game. Thirty seconds per server is a bit too fast. I couldn't do that even at the height of my career as a programmer.

The third proxy server has been breached.

"Say something, Dan," a note of worry sounded in Anastaria's voice.

"Sorry—I have to go. It's an emergency," I blurted out and pushed the 'Exit' button. Three servers isn't scary—the proxy array can be rebuilt. But I'm not happy to know that someone is actively looking for me—if they're looking, that means they've lost me.

My cocoon's lid slid aside, allowing me to crawl out. I walked over to my coffee table with the ancient rotary phone and picked up the handset.

"This is the Omega operator."

"Hi, this is Daniel Mahan speaking. Some unknown intruder just hacked three of the servers in the proxy array you set up for my connection to Barliona. I need a new array within the next ten minutes. Is this possible?"

"A new array can be arranged in fifteen minutes. The old one has already been destroyed. Is five minutes critical for you?"

"No, that's okay. We can do fifteen. Tell me, is there any recourse available? Against the hacker, I mean? Report him to the police for example?"

"The attack stopped as soon as you exited the

game. It is no longer possible to trace his connection. Do you wish to subscribe to an additional service that will monitor the servers you use?"

"What service?"

"We offer round the clock connection monitoring and transmit a report to the police as soon as we identify where the attack is coming from. In that case, you won't have to exit the game—the longer you remain in Barliona the better our chances of catching the attacks will be. The service costs three million credits per month."

"I'll take it," I instantly made up my mind. "Send me the invoice and I'll pay it."

"One of our associates will stop by tomorrow morning for your digital signature. Our security policy prohibits us from using the account you used to pay for your disappearance, but the new service will become effective this instant. May I help you with anything else?"

"Yes," I said, not even knowing why. "I'd like to get my hands on a Jeweler's toolkit that resembles the one that's available in the rehab center."

"Just a minute...Could you tell me which category of toolkit you need?"

"Erm...I don't understand the question."

"There are three types of Jewelry toolkits. The first and most basic is no more than a small box with wire and a rod."

"A mandrel," I corrected the operator.

"Yes, forgive me. I'm not familiar with Jewelry argot. The second set, the most popular, includes several types of fastenings and blanks for cutting gems. The third and most advanced, includes all of the above as well as a miniature anvil, molds for pouring rings and many other things. As I'm sure you understand, the various sets' prices vary a great deal. The first costs three thousand, the second twenty and the third a hundred and forty."

"I'll take the third one," I said after a moment's thought. It's amazing how adept the Corporation has become at earning money from players not just in game but in reality as well. Do you like working with your hands? Then pay us first and on you go!

"Okay. You will have it tomorrow. Will there be anything else?"

"No that's it. Thank you. I'll be waiting for the next uplink."

"All the best. Thank you for using our services."

The line went dead, so I replaced the handset and sat down in an armchair. The desire to get my hands on a Jeweler's toolkit of my own had cropped up back when I'd first seen it at the rehab center. Back then I had managed to create a very appealing ring from wire, but I wanted to see what else all my in-game abilities and skills were good for. The possibility of transferring skills and abilities earned in Barliona into reality had long been a hot topic. No doubt someone had already written their doctoral thesis on it, and yet it wasn't the theory that concerned me right now. I simply wanted to have a Jeweler's toolkit of my own. Two years ago I wouldn't even imagine that I'd calmly part with 140,000 credits on a whim. Say what you like, but if it wasn't for that encounter with Marina, who knows what my life would look like right now. I'd probably be a simple freelance artist, spending several hours a day in the game, too meek to even glance in the direction of the Imperial palace. Money sure does have an effect on people. It makes them more unfettered, independent, free. It makes them want more from life! That's the right way to put it—the more money you have, the more you want. Right! I seem to be getting carried away with all the philosophy. Before desiring something more, I had to solve several problems. As soon as I solve them, I'll be able to start thinking about my future. At the moment, my capsule awaits— a new uplink to Barliona, a new proxy array, that loathsome Anastaria, that mysterious hacker, my meeting with Marina and the raid with Kreel into his Dungeon. I don't have time to desire anything right now.

Enter!

Anastaria was no longer in the Golden Horseshoe, but no one had touched the food I'd ordered. I bet there's some period of time during which the player can exit to reality without losing his table or the food he'd bought. Pouring myself a glass of some glowing liquid, I reclined in my chair and waited for the next attack. I didn't doubt for a second that it would come. Someone really wanted to find me.

The first proxy server has been breached.
One minute.

The second proxy server has been breached.
One minute.

The third proxy server has been breached.
One minute.

The fourth proxy server has been breached.
One minute. A minute and a half. Two minutes. Five minutes. Silence.

You will be disconnected from the game in 5...4...3...

So the fifth proxy has fallen as well. For the second time today, I watched the cocoon's lid slide aside, ushering me to reality where, on the coffee table, the rotary phone was already ringing. Last time, as I recall, it was I who'd made the call.

"Hello, Daniel! This is the Omega operator. We have located the hacker and sent a police squad to their location. Your new uplink to Barliona will be ready in 15 minutes."

"You located him? But he would have been working through his own proxy array. You breached all his proxies too? Who was he?"

"That is correct. In this instance, the intruder was using an array of twelve proxies. A block of this dozen was recycled in a circuit through itself. With that said, we managed to identify the source connection—or rather, the two source connections, as there were two hackers working in tandem to find you. Their identities remain unknown to us at the moment, but as soon as the police apprehend them, we will let you know their names. We wish to apologize once again about the inconvenience and we hope that next time we will be able to identify them by the time they breach the third proxy. Good bye!"

Two hackers? A block of the array cycled through itself? What was she talking about? What's the point of setting up an array of a dozen servers if it only took 3–4 minutes to reach the most secure, second one? If anything, such an array could only elude automatic countermeasures...And a circuit block? Well, that's simply a fairy tale. If a server is breached even once, it's a cinch to determine all its open ports and corresponding connections. And in that case, the idea of a closed circuit loses all purpose. I get the impression that either Omega is keeping mum about something, or the hackers looking for me are a bunch of script kiddies. This is definitely not the Corporation. Nor Anastaria. The only conclusion that makes sense is that it's the old man. But why would he go about it so bluntly? I can't understand it. The whole picture just doesn't gel.

Enter!

Once again I found myself on my own in the Golden Horseshoe with the table and food before me. Only this time, there were no notifications about a breach. Half an hour went by until it became clear that my pursuers had left me alone. For the time being.

"Hi," I got up from the table and greeted Mirida when she was ushered in. It had been a long time since I saw her last! The Level 196 Elf was dressed in a gorgeous evening dress as if she were headed to a high society reception. I had to give the Golden Horseshoe's Imitator his due—he knew how to pick the appropriate outfit for his guests. "You look great!"

"Thank you," Marina smiled, taking the seat across from me. "The local Imitator really knows his job! Your smoking jacket fits you very well too, by the way."

I glanced at my outfit and noted its tight cut. I'd been going to the Horseshoe so frequently lately that I'd stopped paying attention to the alterations that the establishment made to its patrons' appearances.

"Cute dragon you got there," Marina smiled again, indicating my projection. My little Shaman had just finished an apple and was now licking his fingers clean. "Tell me, what do I have to do to join your clan?

Is there some competition, or do you just take applicants pell-mell?"

"Pell-mell. I see you've gained quite a few levels since our last encounter. As I recall it, you were at Level 98 back in Beatwick? Or was it 89? Either way, you definitely weren't at a hundred, while now you're pushing Level 200...How'd you do it?"

"When the high-level players started to mess around with the transformed mobs back in Beatwick, I was in the same group as you. I was gaining level after level. Before I knew it, I was at Level 130. Don't you remember the time we ran into each other at the Emperor's audience? After that, it was one quest here, another quest there. I helped Reptilis a bit and he helped me. In general, I'm not sure myself how it happened."

"Listen, I'm tremendously sorry, but I really didn't have the chance to meet up with you earlier. I was desperately short for time until recently. And in addition to that, at first I completely refused to accept that you had reappeared."

"Me?"

"The girl who caused all of this," I spread my arms. "Basically, if they hadn't stuffed me into a prison capsule, I'd still be a simple Hunter. So, formally speaking, I should thank you. Plus, you really helped me out several times after Beatwick. Especially when you warned me about the attack."

"Ah Beatwick," the girl smiled. "When I sent my

Fluffy against the Sclik, I didn't even consider the consequences. How could a high-level mob even show up in a location limited to Level 30 players? A Sclik! For him, Fluffy was no more than a morsel. If it weren't for you, I'd have to level up my little tiger all over again—as it stands, he's now at Level 117. By the way, I never told you why I came to you in Beatwick."

Here, the waiter brought in the food we'd ordered, so we had to take a break to again wonder at the culinary miracles worked by the local chefs. How they managed to create masterpieces from such disparate ingredients remained the riddle of the century. It's difficult to believe that the Culinary specialty allows someone to work such wonders that the scent alone can force a hungry player to forget everything around him. No doubt these cooks also have Crafting as well as some Flavoring attribute. On the whole, the Golden Horseshoe justified its status and (no less importantly) its prices.

"Beatwick...Imagine, it would take about two weeks to travel from Anhurs to Beatwick without a portal. I thought my Fluffy would wear out his paws from such a stroll, but he managed it. I was especially happy to see a trio of PK-ers looking for a player named Mahan for some reason. So I had to travel to the city, Farstead, I believe—since I'd just encountered that low-level Shaman there."

"How did you even manage to find me?"

"Are you familiar with a player named Reptilis

Y'allgotohellis? As I understand it, you've run into him before and even worked with him on a quest."

"Not quite a quest…Well, he wanted to kill me."

"Really? Very interesting. Honestly, I hired him to find a prisoner who'd made his way to freedom and who'd be certain to be at a compulsory settlement for another three months. He performed his job perfectly."

"Find me? Why?"

"That's exactly why I'm here. We need to talk and the Golden Horseshoe is about the only place in Barliona that is secure enough, so no one will be able to spy on our conversation—not even the devs."

"The developers? Aren't you going a bit far?" I smirked, even as deep inside, some sinister premonition reared its head.

"Dan, if it weren't that serious, I'd never try to find you to begin with. I guess I'll start at the beginning. At the retraining session where we first met, I was approached by a man of indeterminate age."

"Indeterminate?"

"He could have been thirty just as well as fifty. He was very fit, like every user of advanced long-term immersion capsules. He had an athletic built and was clearly pumped full of vitamins. Who can tell how old someone like that is? He offered me to participate in a little, as he put it, venture. He pointed at you and asked me to force you into a bet. The way he put it, he had some age-old grudge with you and he wanted to settle it once and for all."

"What did it look like?"

"If you asked me that a year ago, I wouldn't have an answer for you. Now, however, I recall blue or gray eyes and a thick beard. Mind-boggling! A year's passed since our stupid bet!"

"And what happened then?"

"They assigned me the subject of the wager— hacking the waste collector Imitator. My job was to lead you on to it. Damn it! They even issued me a scenario for talking with you, can you imagine it? This guy had calculated everything—he even knew you'd try for a truce."

"What about the idea of offering yourself as a prize? Was that yours or the scenario's?" I couldn't help but ask.

"It was in the scenario. That was supposed to be the most compelling piece of bait—the one that'd get you to agree. And it had to be voiced loud enough for everyone to hear. I did what they asked of me, received my money and didn't even consider that everything could turn as seriously as it did."

"Money? They even gave you money for it...Hang on. You said that the main goal was to hack the sewage system Imitator. Why hack the Imitator of the company you were working for?"

"But I wasn't working for it! I'm a freelance artist, what do I have to do with a sewage system?"

Okaaaay. Now things were getting even more interesting. Someone had manipulated me into hacking that sewage system. But for what?

"In the end you agreed to the bet and I went home with the money. The next day they gave me the address which I relayed to you. And that was the end of my involvement in that operation."

"What a fascinating fairy tale—but it doesn't explain why I got the address of a working system and why it was connected to the network. The sewage system used a very elaborate security system—a very effective one, but also a very rare one due to its complexity. It's hard to believe that whoever arranged the bet didn't know the network's design. Who in their right mind would connect a working Imitator to an open network? Especially the network of such an organization?"

"This is the most interesting part. You're right— the main Imitator is cut off from the network and only has one gateway to the outside world—which is synched to the communicators of three people: the CEO, the mayor and an official in our continental government. So I can safely congratulate you—a year ago you joined the cohort of the untouchables."

"Where'd you get this information?"

"I had to revisit my long-gone youth and conduct my own investigation. But that was already after I found out about the consequences of our bet. The address that they sent me wasn't at all like a standard web address. The fact that the system had only one gateway to the network was also wrong. Sooner or later, what's hidden will come to light. Unfortunately, my handlers don't seem to understand that whatever's cheap isn't always high quality, and in pursuit of savings end up endangering the security and safety of their systems. This gives rise to holes and backdoors that intruders can exploit. Although, in this case, the intruder was you."

Marina paused to take a sip and then went on.

"When the trial began, I wanted to go to the police and confess to everything. I wanted to tell them that it was all someone's ruse, that you were hacking the system for someone and not of your own free will, but then..."

"But then what?"

"Three men came to my house. They made various hints and veiled references to my aging parents and explained that it wasn't a good idea to go anywhere and try and prove anything. They explained that you got what you deserved and that eight years in Barliona wouldn't do you any harm."

"They threatened you?" I asked surprised.

"Yes. Moreover, I'm sure that they're watching me even now. The first time they came to me was when I helped you choose your name. The second time was when we met in Beatwick. Back then they told me that I might not survive a third meeting. So they asked me not to do anything stupid. Can you imagine the kind of people who have the capability to track meetings in Barliona?"

"I can—and perfectly well," I grumbled. "But it's still a mystery to me why you came looking for me to begin with. You were paid, you did your job—that's it. You've done your part."

"Because we are free artists. Because we should help each other. Because what they did to you wasn't right."

"And yet seducing a technician so that he can allow me to choose my name *is* right?"

"Yes. That was my choice. I didn't sleep with him—I only kissed him a couple times, but that doesn't count. Why not? I believe that there is cruelty in this world—and am ready to be cruel myself. But I won't stand for someone using me. Those who hired me were using me. So I decided to help you. As soon as I consider my debt repaid, I'll leave you alone."

"Have you never considered whether I need your help at all?"

"I've helped you with your name, information as well as various quests that you would've failed and therefore never become the Mahan of which all of Barliona speaks. So yes, I'd say you do need my assistance. I don't want your forgiveness—I don't need it. I reckon that by telling you who your enemies are and what they're capable of, I'll extinguish whatever debt I owe you. I'm ready to give you the information I've collected about the hacking of the waste system any time that's convenient for you. I hope that you'll have enough brains to submit it to a court so that your case can be reexamined. The entire case is so shabby that it's a wonder they even sentenced you. The only thing that's holding me back is my fear for my relatives. My visitors made it clear to me that I played a small role in this drama and that they could always find a different actor for the part. Now what about joining your clan?"

I sent Marina an invitation and assured her that we would meet in reality in the next three months. Then I blinked to Altameda. In light of this new information, I needed to think things over carefully.

And so!

My ending up in prison was no accident. Someone had plotted to imprison me in the game for many years. But for what? I had had neither enemies nor friends. I had no one at all in fact, even pets. What was the point of hiding me away in Barliona like this?

Something tells me that when I find an answer to this question, I'll find the answer to the great questions of the universe as well.

CHAPTER SEVEN

AQUARIZAMAX

"**E**VERYONE PRESENT AND READY?" Kreel's voice came over the amulet. "Then let's do it. Summoning now."

A summons notification appeared before my eyes, and I was surprised to see that it had been issued by a single player instead of a trio of Mages. Was Kreel really so lavish that he was using scrolls to teleport us over? This was a prohibitively expensive way to do this in comparison to using three Mages, but perhaps the Titan didn't know any better. But okay—he can summon us however he likes. If he prefers to burn through scrolls, let him burn through scrolls. What difference did it make as long as we reached the Dungeon?

No sooner had my new location come into focus than an enormous cloud eclipsed Barliona's bright sun.

"Hello again! This time in person," boomed the giant, offering me his immense paw. Only now did I realize that the cloud was in fact the Titan standing before me in his full battle armor. He was between two and a half and three meters tall. As for weight, well, let's just say that, seeing him, a rhino would step aside and have a smoke in envy. I'm not sure that I had the Strength to even budge Kreel—maybe only in my Dragon Form. By the way! It's possible that the Level 201 Kreel has simply transformed into his battle form and this is why his dimensions seem so daunting to me. As a Dragon, I take up almost half of Altameda's hall, so in terms of dimensions I'm no smaller. Damn it! What am I thinking about? Why would I even compare my size to a Titan's?

"Hello to you too," I said, squeezing the gargantuan paw and nodding toward the giant tower behind us. "So is that your Dungeon?"

Kreel turned his head in the indicated direction, causing some critter affixed to the crown of his helm to trace and arc in the air and in so doing leave a barely noticeable blue and white trail in its wake.

"It is," he nodded. "Flying over the tower is prohibited—you can't maintain inertia. I think they've installed a jammer in it. So the only approach is on foot from below. Here's the raid invitation. The others will arrive in a bit."

An enormous tower of white stone about fifty meters wide and a hundred meters tall loomed over the desert. The blazing sun here constantly saddled everyone with the 'Blindness,' 'Desiccation,' and 'Thirst' debuffs, which all stacked to decrease our main stats by 20%. Moreover, a notification informed me that these debuffs would intensify every thirty minutes. The tower boasted several windows about thirty meters above ground, inviting agile players to clamber up into them, yet I trusted Kreel. If he said that flying was prohibited, then that's the way it was. Besides, there was only one boss left, at the very top of the tower, so the rest of it would have been cleared.

"Why didn't you summon us straight to the top?" I asked the important question, as soon as I realized how far we'd have to climb. An ascent of a hundred meters is really a lot.

"Relax—there's a portal to the top of the tower right at the entrance," Kreel grinned. "All right. Everyone's ready. We can begin."

I noted with surprise that Plinto and Anastaria were summoned not with scrolls but with Mages after all. Or to be more precise, a single Mage. This was none other than our old friend Alisa Reyx, a Level 239 Mage who'd managed to level up one more time since our last meeting. She could summon players on her own without having to resort to two additional colleagues. Hum. Is that possible?

"Did you imagine that your clan has all the unique players?" Kreel answered my unasked question.

"No, but...All right, have you already decided on a tactic for the Dragon?"

"Yup. That's why I suggest we make everything clear right off the bat. Moni, what do you have?" Kreel turned to an Elf that had approached us. Moni the Hunched was a Level 190 Druid with an expression on his face as if we owed him several million gold.

"What's your status? Are you still incapacitated?"

I automatically tried to summon a Spirit and shook my head. I still had a day and a half till that happy moment—or, an eternity, given our current situation.

"Uh-huh. In that case listen up—you three will be the sacrificial lambs," said the Druid addressing someone behind me. I turned to see Plinto and Anastaria. "Since you won't be of any help, I won't let my healers waste their Mana on you. If you die, then you die. We'll revive you later. You'll get the First Kill even if you're dead. Any questions? No? Very well then."

"Am I to understand that you don't need any help with the tactics?" Anastaria raised an eyebrow.

"We're not a bunch of newbies here, so we'll figure it out," smirked Moni. "Although, if it becomes an issue, we'll make sure to consult with you. We don't suffer from excessive pride here or anything."

"Okay, and what if I participate in the raid in this form?" Anastaria refused to give up, turning into her Siren Form. "Will you give us a place in battle and some healing now?"

Following Anastaria's example, Plinto turned into a dark fog which materialized into a half-transparent and swirling Vampire-Cleric. It was the first time I'd seen Plinto in his Vampire Form. He made a strange impression—at once mesmerizing and terrifying. The Rogue's red eyes were particularly stunning, glowing like two rubies against the silhouette of a black Vampire.

"Hmm," Moni remarked eloquently. "What are your abilities in this form? What are you capable of?"

"Here's the description," said Anastaria, making several passes with her hands.

"So it's like that?" Moni looked at Anastaria with surprise. "This doesn't mention the cooldown. How long will that be?"

"If I understood your question, then a day. It's effective against all creatures in this world, including bosses."

"Hmm..." Moni really had a vast vocabulary. "All right. What's Plinto got? Okay, I see. This is good. And this...Are you kidding me?" the Druid exclaimed yet again. "Another day's cooldown?"

"Depends on what," Plinto's smirk gave me goose bumps. The Vampire spoke in such a completely terrifying whisper that all I wanted to do was run away, dig a hole to hide in, exit Barliona, delete my account and never return.

"The Kiss."

"A day. Also effective against everything."

"Okay...Hmm...All right...No but I understand this, but...Damn, you all are sending all our tactics planning to hell! What do you have Mahan? You're a Dragon, right? What's the latest fad among you flying lizards?"

"It's not what I have, but what my Totem has," I said, summoning Draco. "Tell this Druid about your abilities."

"As you like," said Draco, sending Moni a list of his powers. "Are we going into battle, brother?"

"We are. You'll be the main warrior. It's high time we test you in serious combat."

"Well hum," the Hunched Elf concluded and turned to Kreel: "I need about thirty minutes to set my thoughts in order and revise our tactics. There's so many new variables here, that I might even have to start from scratch. It's looking like we'll have to spend Mana on them after all."

"Kreel, you do understand that under our current agreement these descriptions of our powers won't leave this raid, right?" Anastaria reminded just in case. To be honest, this issue worried me so much that I only revealed Draco's abilities. Let everyone think that I wasn't a factor. I didn't want to reveal my Accelerations and Thunderclap yet. Something told me that the Titan didn't need to know about them.

"I will abide by our agreement," Kreel announced. "All of the information that I've received during this raid will remain a secret. And this goes for the abilities of my people that you have learned as well. A request to you, Anastaria—don't try and flatter

Alisa in the hopes of poaching her for Phoenix. Deal?"

"I can't promise that," Anastaria smiled, baring her white fangs. "Slavery is illegal in our world. If Alisa decides to join Phoenix, then I certainly won't dissuade her."

"And yet, you shouldn't persuade her to do so either."

"In the context of this raid, I will refrain. We'll see what comes later."

Kreel and Anastaria locked eyes in a stare-down contest, until the Siren again flashed her fangs.

"You can't kick me out, Titan. We have a contract that you must honor. So calm down and enjoy the game."

"Don't flatter yourself," Kreel returned Anastaria's smirk. "I'm willing to incur Eluna's displeasure for the sake of my people, so don't tempt me."

"I will reiterate—I'm honoring our contract."

"So go ahead and honor it then. We're going in! We've wasted too much time here as it is."

Kreel's raid party was extremely diverse. The highest-level player was Prospero—a Level 312 Human Healer, judging by his frame. The other warriors' levels varied from 160 to 260, with players under 200 representing the overwhelming majority. In my opinion, the party was too unbalanced. There aren't that many Dungeons in Barliona whose bosses scale to the highest-level player. And Prospero would definitely never be invited to a Dungeon raid like that, since Level 312 mobs would squash every other player in the group with a simple sneeze. Meanwhile, in Dungeons for Level 180 players, any player above Level 230 wouldn't receive any XP. But I guess this was Kreel's problem to deal with. If he wants to assemble a raid like this, then I suppose he has some reason for it.

"Judging by these gravestones, you paid a steep price for the first few meters of this Dungeon," Anastaria remarked as soon as we passed through the shimmering entrance. The place was full of transparent obelisks that you could walk through without any problem. I'd never seen anything like it.

"Assuming there were thirty of you, your raid perished at least twice here. Right?"

"No one expected a boss waiting for us right at the entrance." Adjusting his dark gray cape, Kreel didn't bother denying the obvious. "We had no choice but to deal with him the hard way."

"*What are these? Gravestones? First time I've seen something like this,*" I asked Anastaria unable to contain my curiosity.

"*If the raid is wiped out at its first attempt to complete the Dungeon, the system places gravestones for everyone. RIP and in loving memory and whatnot. They'll remain here until the Dungeon is cleared. And new ones will keep appearing when the raid is wiped. When we earned our First Kills, there used to be forests of these gravestones—so many that it was hard to see through them."*

Only after Anastaria had done answering, did I notice that the girl's voice lacked even a hint of sarcasm, mockery or condescension. She was speaking in an ordinary business-like tone that one player uses when explaining something to another. I don't think I'll ever understand this woman.

The tower's first floor turned out to be quite expansive. The ceilings were about six meters high, while the floor itself consisted of a large hall with several columns and a spiral staircase winding upward beside the far wall—with a golden portal shimmering before it. Our current objective.

"Who was here before?" I asked Kreel.

"A skeleton," the Titan replied curtly. "A huge, three-meter tall skeleton with four arms, transparent wings and a very unpleasant characteristic of summoning a wave of minions every time he lost 10% of his HP. In addition to that, he had a spell called 'Lifesucker' which he'd use any time he received damage in multiples of 10%."

"How many HP would he restore with it?" Anastaria joined the conversation.

"Five percent."

"And did the mobs reset too?"

"You mean when he passed another 10% marker? Yes. Both the mobs and the Lifesucker spell. Everything reset."

"Wanna share the video?"

"No. What's the difference how we beat him? You're not here to fight him."

Kreel stepped through the portal, ending the conversation. He had a point. We were here for something else entirely. We were here to kill the Dragon of Shadow.

"Welcome to the attic," said Kreel once the entire raid had teleported up from the ground floor. "The roof and our Dragon are above us. Moni, what's the updated game plan?"

"Hit and run. I haven't seen the Dragon yet, so I can't say anything more specific than that. We've just acquired three unexpected fighters with odd abilities who are untested in battle but who seem useful. So the short of it is that we'll start the boss fight and then see what happens."

"What stunning tactical nous," Anastaria quipped. "Is this how you beat all the bosses you come across?"

"Raynest, you're in reserves," Moni went on, ignoring Anastaria's jibes. One of the low-level Paladins nodded his head silently and sheathed his sword. Moni thought a little more and then asked Anastaria in a melodic voice, brimming with sarcasm: "What is your counsel, oh great Anastaria? How shall we vanquish our unseen foe?"

"I don't see you genuflecting. And your voice lacks reverence," Stacey doubled down.

"Damn it all!" Moni blurted angrily, waving his hand in exasperation. "How am I supposed to work like this? How?"

"I understand," Anastaria smiled. "I won't interfere."

"But really, I have no problem with receiving help. I really haven't seen the boss yet and haven't the slightest idea what he's capable of."

"Well why haven't you seen the boss yet?" I couldn't help but ask. "You guys have been here how long?"

"A week," Kreel replied in Moni's place. "In this Dungeon..."

"Bosses attack as soon as you enter a new floor," Anastaria interrupted Kreel. "If Kreel had set foot on the roof, the Dragon would've attacked him. Then the boss battle would have begun and who knows what would happen. Too many 'ifs.' Our Kreel was simply keeping our contract in mind. That's why he waited."

The smirk that Stacey directed at Kreel was so venomous, that I was shocked by the Titan's restraint. When Anastaria wanted to be the bitch, she had no rivals.

"Okay, have we chatted our fill?" When the ensuing silence began to drag on too long, Moni took the reins. "Then let's get down to business. What are you standing there for, Ugtur? Shove some coal in your boiler and full steam ahead! Prospero, you're with him. Cast some shields on Ugtur. At the count of ten, we step out onto the roof. The countdown starts now. Aden, Marlan and Potrohari, y'all are up next. Cast stealth on yourselves and slow down anything that's running around up there. Nathan, you're next. Summon your army as soon as you enter. Krolom, Pecador and Baruz—your assignment will be..."

I could barely follow Moni's orders. Aden, Marlan and Potrohari were Rogues, one of whom, as I understood, was a goblin. Nathan was a Necromancer.

To be honest, I didn't know what army this class could summon, but since Moni mentioned it explicitly, I'd guess it was worth something. Krolom, Pecador and Baruz were Warriors, whose job was to set up a security perimeter for the healers and ranged fighters who'd follow them. After that I got lost in all the names until I heard the most important part:

"Go Mahan!"

The entrance to the roof was also a portal in the guise of an ordinary staircase. As soon as I set foot on the first stair, the space around me warped and went dark. When the surrounding world returned a moment later, I found myself in the center of hell.

"Hold the line! Revive Feanor! We need more dps on the crawlers! Mahan, cast your freeze spell!" Miraculously, Moni's shouts could be heard above the terrible roar of the spells, the gnashing of iron, the screams of monsters and the swearing of players. The roof was a rather small, open platform the size of a basketball court, full of flying, crawling, hopping and scurrying monsters of Level 180. The flying mobs attacked us from all directions, even leaving the area's limits; the crawling ones kept appearing from under the area's edge; it was unclear where the scurrying ones were coming from, but no doubt they were spawning somewhere since the entire crowd of them could hardly fit on the platform. As soon as I stepped out, I was already waist-deep in mobs. At least the slain ones didn't get in the way, remaining on the roof only as projections so that we could pick up the loot they'd dropped afterward.

"*Come here, Draco!*"

"*Coming.*"

"*Cast Thunderclap the moment you get here!*"

"*Understood!*"

"We have a minute! Come on, come on! Cut down anything that's standing! Plinto! Show me what a Vampire of your level can do! Why is your damage so low? It's only 30% of the raid's total! We need at least 40%! Kreel, cast 'Breach!' Everyone—ATTACK!"

The raid leader has used the 'Thundering Shout' ability. +20 Energy and +20% to main stats for all raid party members. Duration: 5 minutes.

The mobs teeming on the roof froze. Draco looked around assertively and without asking for permission soared up into the air and banked sharply into the closest harpy, sinking his fangs into her throat. Only now did I get a chance to see who we were dealing with. The flying mobs, Shadow Harpies, had wings that seeped a gray fog as they flew. The crawling ones, Shadow Slugs, appeared endlessly from beneath the platform's edge and left a green trail behind them that seemed to be poisonous. The jumpers and runners were Shadow Gargoyles. These tried to vault over our tanks and latch onto the healers and ranged fighters. All three mob types were so mutated from their vanilla forms that only their names allowed me to tell what tribe they belonged to. I'd never call a creature that resembled a dead-humanoid covered in fog, shuffling along on a myriad of tiny spider-like legs, a slug. Meanwhile, in addition to fighting the creature, I had to fight my own revulsion at being touched by it.

The designers in charge of the Shadow expansion seemed well versed in creating abominations.

"Portal straight ahead!" yelled Anastaria when almost half of the battleground was destroyed by the Titan's Breach spell. Something resembling a black hole shot from the Titan in the direction of the monsters, sending them into nonexistence. Kreel swayed a little as if fatigued and instantly brought a flagon with a liquid up to his lips. What's this? Is he restoring his Energy? Does this mean that casting 'Breach,' as Moni had called it, Kreel had to sacrifice his Energy? An odd class, the Titans, what can you say...If you miss once or twice, you'll collapse to the ground and have to wait until someone gives you a drink. Or is this simply one of his abilities that's like this?

"Plinto!" Moni continued to direct the raid. "That portal's yours! We're done with the mobs, focus fire on the portal!"

A red portal was shimmering right at the far edge of the platform and disgorging gargoyles. One of the monsters hadn't quite managed to make it out just as Draco's Thunderclap caught him halfway through, and I imagined his legs wriggling in futile hate of my Totem somewhere in Armard.

The Mages, Hunters and other ranged fighters redirected their fire onto the portal, above which an Endurance bar appeared. Plinto, following Moni's direction, turned into a dark fog and materialized right beside the half-frozen gargoyle. The Vampire's arms transformed—they lengthened and the hands grew glittering claws—the Rogue became a man-sized propeller. Plinto's arms were moving at such a mad speed that we could hear the hum of the air he was parting. The only downside was that the Vampire's Hit Points began to fall as though in payment for his insane speed. Then the portal exploded with a loud pop, scattering the nearby monsters from the platform—and simultaneously killing Plinto, who had kept on spinning like a windmill to the last moment.

As far as I noticed, the healers had tried to heal him, but in vain—the healing spells had no effect.

"Ten seconds until the stun expires. Revive Plinto! We'll destroy the remaining gargoyles and start looking for the harpy and slug portals! Get a move on people! There's a chance we'll clear the roof on our first attempt!"

"Phew!" Draco landed heavily beside me. "I've fought my fill."

"How's it going?" I asked my Totem, carefully checking his Hit Points and status effects. What if...

"I didn't manage to kill anyone, but I did get a few mouthfuls. My jaw's a little sore. I tore the wings of twenty harpies to tatters—we'll see if they can fly again. By the way, why don't you try flying yourself? You're just standing there, not doing much...Oh! They're moving again!"

The stun from the Thunderclap expired and the monsters came to life again. The slugs crawled on while the harpies plummeted out of the air. At the same time, a light aura flashed around Draco several times indicating he had gained a few levels—the harpies whose wings he had destroyed were grounded for good.

"The slug portal is three meters below the roof!" yelled one of our Rogues. A marker immediately appeared on the new target, allowing us to see it even through the paved surface of the platform.

"Alisa!" Moni called. "Take all the ranged fighters

and focus that portal! Everyone else keep focusing the monsters! Mahan, at least smack them with your staff—every little bit will help. Stop standing there like a princess!"

I was about to do as the Hunched Druid ordered when a bulb of inspiration went off in my head. When the first portal exploded, a portion of the monsters were thrown from the platform. Draco hadn't been able to kill any of the harpies which had a hundred levels on him, but he had shredded their wings, keeping them from flying.

And I was a Dragon after all! A giant killing machine, four meters long and three meters tall! Why should I try to kill something when I could be much more effective?"

"Watch out!" I yelled, getting a running start and jumping into the mass of slugs. I began to transform while in midair and landed on the green trails of the slugs on my four immense clawed paws. The monsters immediately turned their attention to their new victim who had so graciously walked straight into their jaws. My Hit Points began to fall, so I checked that there weren't any players around me and began to spin. A new propeller appeared on the roof.

Level gained!
Level gained!
Level gained!
Energy level: 30. Stop, you angry Shaman!

"Where were you earlier?" Moni asked, when the slugs had been destroyed. For some unknown reason, the system had credited all the XP from the killed monsters to me exclusively and therefore in a matter of moments I had gained twelve levels. A Level 149 Shaman is no joke.

"What's the deal with the harpies?" I asked, drinking deeply. Even my conversations with Anastaria didn't sap my Energy as quickly as spinning in place had. If every new Level hadn't restored it completely, my heroic feat would have become a heroic self-sacrifice. I'd lucked out.

"It's the window ten meters below the roof. They're spawning from there. The Warriors and Rogues are already on it."

"Where is the Shadow Dragon?"

"Good question. Can you believe it? I wanted to ask you the same thing. Mahan, where's our Dragon?"

"He'll probably show up after we kill the mobs. Otherwise it'd be impossible to complete this roof," Anastaria approached us. She wasn't much use to us against flying monsters, so Stacey had turned back to her human form and was now examining the corpse-strewn platform in a business-like manner.

"Kreel, please tell me you have a specially-trained player who'll sort through this loot in a jiffy...If the boss shows up right now, the loot could vanish, and I'd really hate that. You are still following our contract, right?"

"When did you become so greedy?" I couldn't help but ask when Kreel nodded to Moni and one of the raiders began to sort through the loot.

"My husband taught me. Can you imagine—his greed exceeds all acceptable limits. He stole an entire castle from me!"

"Altameda was never yours to begin with."

"Tell it to Viltrius. By the way, Mahan, you and I have one unfinished piece of business. You were planning on making me a surprise, but you seem to have gotten distracted and forgotten about it. When will I get it?"

"A surprise?" For a moment, I felt utterly lost—however, when I realized what she was talking about, I felt my anger surge deep inside of me. Anastaria was referring to my promise to show her the squidolphin! Where does she get the gall? Okay—calm down. Let's remember that I'm still the Ice Queen. "Darling, I think you forgot something—the surprise was for a member of my clan. You left us, so—so sorry—the loss is yours."

"I'm always ready to come back," said Anastaria, shrugging a shoulder. "All you need to do is ask."

"What a delicate relationship you two have. You're not married by any chance, are you?" Moni smirked, still directing the ranged fighters.

"*Portal's down!*" Ugtur wrote in the raid chat, distracting me from Anastaria's provocation. There were better things to do than spar with her. "*Let's finish off the rest of the mobs!"*

When the last harpy crashed to the roof, a silence ensued. We clumped up in a group, awaiting the boss's appearance. The healers prepared their defensive spells, the tanks their damage-mitigating abilities, and the warriors their strengthening ones. Even Anastaria turned into her Siren Form, ready to use her killer spell.

But the boss did not appear.

"At the risk of asking the obvious, where the hell's the Dragon?" asked one of Kreel's mercenaries after a tedious minute.

"Maybe we missed one of the mobs?" another mercenary offered, but Moni shook his head—the 'In Combat' status had expired. All the monsters were slain.

"Maybe you missed something, Kreel?" Moni asked the Titan. "Maybe we need to sing like a song or something? Dance a dance? Make a sacrifice? What the hell are we standing here for like a bunch of idiots? Where's the boss?"

"Brother," Draco's voice sounded in my head. My Totem had been circling the platform. Kreel had begun to discuss something with Moni, and Anastaria had joined them, but I couldn't hear them. Draco's voice drowned out everything. *"What are you waiting for?"*

"The Shadow Dragon was supposed to appear, but for some reason hasn't. So we're waiting."

"*How is he supposed to be appear if he hasn't been born yet?*"

"*What do you mean he hasn't been born yet?*"

"*Well...I thought you knew. If the Shadow Dragon hatches from his egg, it'll be practically impossible to kill him. Even father wouldn't risk fighting him. Since you're all still here, then the Dragon hasn't hatched.*"

"Hold on—so the Dragon doesn't even exist yet?" I said aloud, drawing the attention of the nearby players. "Where is he then?"

"No idea," Draco landed smoothly on the platform, sat down and propped up his head with his tail pensively. "There are several options naturally. If you're looking for the Dragon egg, then he's definitely not here on the roof. He'd be somewhere deep underground on a soft cushion, but certainly not here on an open platform. That's the first thing. The second is that, if you ask me, that there portal that's hanging twenty meters above us—well, it might lead somewhere."

"Where?" As if by command, the players all looked up. Right over our heads hung the shimmering point of a portal, practically invisible against the backdrop of grim clouds.

"Well and then there's the third thing: I have an idea of how to get to that portal, of course, but there's a 'but'—it's one-way. If you go in, there's no way back out again."

"Now I see why Renox insisted I take you with

me," smirked Kreel, looking at me with renewed respect. All I could do was swear—Renox had sent me into this Dungeon to be the riding pony!

"Mahan, how much can you lift?" Moni instantly inquired.

"Two players," I muttered sullenly. "One more on Draco. We can't do any more. And you can't jump off from us, so we can't fly up to the portal and have you dive into it."

"Alisa, Prospero and Ugtur, you three are first. Mahan, how much more time is left on the cooldown for Thunderclap?"

"Ten minutes."

"Alisa, summon Plinto first—if anything happens, he'll help. After that Kreel and on down the list. Do you have Mana potions? Excellent! We'll take a ten minute break. Anyone who likes is free to pop out to reality. I'll definitely do that myself."

A timer appeared and a portion of the players immediately dissolved in thin air.

"Nice Dungeon you have here," I remarked when Kreel lowered himself down on the ground beside me. "First time I've seen a restriction on the number of flying players."

"Or Architects that could build a tower. Renox suggested I take a couple, but I assumed that I'd need them in the lower floors. It was impossible to reach the third boss after the second one without them. Mahan, I have a business proposal for you."

"I think I can guess what it is. You're a Titan when all's said and done—you need to kill the Dragon to receive some class bonuses. If the Shadow Dragon hasn't hatched yet, how are you going to kill one?"

"So what do you suggest?"

"After we complete the Dungeon, you can kill me and get your bonuses. Then you revive me and we fight a real duel. I want to know who's better—a Titan or a Dragon. A duel, as I recall it, equalizes the level difference, right?"

"Only in the Anhurs arena. To be honest, I wouldn't mind finding out what you're capable of in your gecko form too."

"Kreel, if the Dragon doesn't exist, what are we going to do with Gnum?" asked Alisa, who'd been listening to our conversation.

"You know Spiteful Gnum?" I ventured with surprise. There could be many Gnums in Barliona of course—it's no coincidence there's a tavern with this name, but still, Gnum is a fairly unusual name."

"Yes, we've crossed paths several times. I promised to summon him to the Dragon—he wanted to cut something off of him for his projects with you."

"A nice fillet of Dragon," quipped Moni as he re-entered the game. "The skin's softer there, they say. Easier to digest. Mahan, turn into your Dragon, will you? Let's see if Gnum is right."

All I could do was raise my eyebrows in puzzlement at the giggling Druid. Laughing at your own jokes is a bad habit, I've heard. Kreel seems like a serious player, so where'd he get this raid leader?

"All right, looks like no one's laughing," Moni went on, "it's all very serious, I understand. But I wasn't kidding about turning into a Dragon—break's over. The portal awaits, the troops are all anticipation and further motivational malarkey. Get on with it. Your orders are as follows: You will enter the portal and ensure that Alisa gets twenty seconds of free time. After that, you will ensure that Alisa gets another twenty seconds. And after that, you can do whatever you want."

"Moni, we have two Paladins in our raid," I suggested. "Right before we enter the portal, tell them to cast bubbles on Alisa and Prospero. Ten seconds of guaranteed immunity will be useful."

"I see you're capable of more than waving your tail around," Moni quipped wryly, and yet a notification popped up in the raid chat: "*Wake up, Raynest. Get up on the roof. We have some work for you.*"

"Everyone ready?" Moni asked one more time, after he'd issued his orders. "Then mount your mounts and full gallop ahead! Mahan, where should we sit?"

"I'd tell you where, but the skin's a bit tender there. And if you tickle it, I might buck and toss you off," I couldn't refrain, causing laughter all around. "One on my neck, the other between my wings.

There's a nave there that's a bit like a seat."

"Cast the bubbles on the count of three," Moni commanded as soon as Draco and I soared up into the air and began to wheel around the tower. The most astonishing thing was that I could distinctly make out the limit of the no-fly zone—a half-transparent cone located twenty meters below the roof and turned at 45 degrees toward the sky. A mere twenty meters from the roof and I would crash immediately. It looked like the designers really had made this Dungeon with flying players in mind. Players like me. Hmm...Like me...Doesn't this mean that somewhere in Malabar or Kartoss, or in the Free Lands (assuming Kreel is from there), there are players who can fly too? For example some Phoenix class, let's say—or Sparrow or Grasshopper. Knowing Barliona, the developers were liable to cook up any odd thing that struck their fancy.

"One. Two," Moni began to count. I banked sharply and hurtled in the portal's direction. I was carrying the healer and the tank, so I'd need to make it through the portal first. "Three!"

The shimmering veil surrounded us from all sides and when the world regained its clarity I saw an enormous hall with four torches that dispersed the darkness, set around a snow-white egg. At the same time, I couldn't feel my arms or legs—I couldn't move my wings or my tail. I wasn't even in the hall! It was as if my avatar was gone and I was watching a movie.

"Are you seeing this? Anastaria's thought occurred in my mind.

"Yes. I don't understand...What is this?"

"A cutscene for the scenario. They're about to show us the history of this place—what, why, how and who's responsible. It's been a long while since I've seen one of these."

Here, I stopped paying attention to Anastaria since the first character appeared on stage—a half-transparent shade of a phantom, barely noticeable in the surrounding murk, which only served to make it that much more sinister and terrifying. The shade flew in a circle around the egg, making several attempts to reach out and touch it with its arm/appendage—yet the four torches prevented it from coming closer. The egg remained immaculate.

"THIS IS MY LAIR!" roared a savage voice and the second character stepped on stage. In his dimensions, the Golden Dragon Aquarizamax was almost larger than Renox. He emerged in a somewhat incongruous waddle out of the gloom and forced the shade away from the torches. "NO ONE DARES TOUCH MY SPAWN!"

"Draco, I kept meaning to ask, what kind of creature is Aquarizamax? What was he famous for?"

"Nothing as far as I know. Like all the other Dragons, he served the Tarantula Lords, murdered sentient creatures by the hundreds, and refused to leave this world when the time for exile came. Nothing

special."

"You grow weak, Dragon," a sweeping whisper sounded in the hall, scaring me even though it was just a cutscene. "Soon the egg will be ours! Then the world shall behold the Dragon of Shadow!"

"THAT SHALL NOT COME TO PASS!" A pillar of fire erupted from the Dragon's maw, tearing the shade to tatters. "MY SON SHALL REIGN OVER THIS WORLD ALONE! THERE SHALL BE NO SHADOW."

"You know, Aquarium, if we keep going this way, I'll run out of warriors pretty soon." The third character in this drama stepped onstage. The Lord of Shadow, Geranika.

"MY NAME IS AQUARIZAMAX!"

"What's the difference what your name is? I need either you or your son. Choose. One of you will become the Dragon of Shadow. The other will die. Two Dragons is too much for me. I recommend you choose yourself—since I don't really feel like messing around with your child, raising him, feeding him...Too much of a hassle."

"ONE MORE STEP, MONSTER, AND YOU SHALL BE DESTROYED!" roared Aquarizamax, without however rushing to attack Geranika.

"Destroyed?" smirked the Shaman, continuing to advance on the Dragon. "You're old, weak and you haven't eaten in about two millennia, roosting on your egg here. Do you really imagine that you'll have the strength to fight me, THE LORD OF SHADOW?"

Geranika didn't shout these last words, and yet they resounded with such force that for a moment I lost my concentration. The hall's murk began to tremble strangely like a sheet in the wind and suddenly rushed onto the fast fading points of light, drowning them in the gray light emanating from Geranika's staff. Paradoxically, the illumination allowed me to see the entire scene and I realized that this wasn't a hall at all. The cutscene was taking place in an enormous Dragon's lair that merely resembled a hall around the egg. And the rest of the cave was filled with shades like the one the Dragon had already destroyed.

"EITHER YOU OR YOUR SON! THERE IS ALWAYS A CHOICE. NOW YOU MUST MAKE IT!" Geranika stopped two steps from the Dragon. Even though he was much shorter in stature, the Lord of Shadow somehow managed to look at the reptile from above. The noose of shades began to tighten around the Dragon menacingly, forcing him to take a step back. Then another. And a third—until his tail brushed up against the egg. Several times the Dragon wanted to lunge at Geranika who kept advancing, but then he'd glance back at the egg and take another step back. The Dragon could not permit himself to leave the egg alone with the host of shades.

"YOU ARE RIGHT, LORD OF SHADOW," smirked the Dragon, once he'd run out of space to retreat. "THERE IS ALWAYS A CHOICE! BUT YOU ARE

WRONG TO ASSUME THAT THERE ARE ONLY TWO OPTIONS. YOU SHALL NEVER HAVE MY SON! HE SHALL RULE BARLIONA!"

The Dragon roared and a strange aura appeared around him, pushing Geranika several meters away—after which Aquarizamax's enormous torso collapsed to the ground. The encroaching shades smothered the torches, and yet, still, they could not reach the egg. A pulsating, golden sphere had appeared around it—upon whose surface, here and there, shimmered the sigil of a Dragon.

"What's that, Draco?"

"The Last Will," my Totem whispered reverently. "The Dragon sacrificed himself to become a defender. If the sphere is destroyed, the egg will perish. They have become a single whole!"

"Argh!" roared Geranika, clenching his fists. "Why must Dragons always be so difficult? Bring me the Blackeners!"

A moment later several shades emerged from a portal, bringing with them two enormous machines that I had already seen back in Beatwick.

"Why couldn't he simply die without being a pain in the neck?" Geranika went on bemoaning his fate. As soon as the Blackeners were erected across from each other and with the egg between them, the Lord of Shadow activated them with a careless snap of his fingers. A dark vapor began to creep toward the golden sphere from the devices' long antennae, but as soon as they touched it, the sound of shattering glass echoed throughout the lair.

"How much time will the transformation take?" Geranika asked a small shade in the form of a goblin standing beside the Blackeners.

"Three years, oh my Master," whispered the goblin whose eyes were no more than two clumps of swirling fog. Another clamor of shattering glass swept across the lair, forcing Geranika to frown as if he had a toothache.

"If it must be three, let it be three. I am patient...I hate this gloom," Geranika added with undisguised revulsion. He traced a figure in the air and created a dagger similar to the one I had used to kill the players in the Dark Forest. Breaking the dagger in two parts and melting down its blade, Geranika approached the golden sphere and, swinging, plunged the hilt into it. Once again the sound of shattering glass resounded, while the silvery light illuminating the lair began to emanate not from the staff but from the dagger's hilt in the sphere.

"This should make the transformation go more efficiently," Geranika smirked. "Set up a security perimeter! Do not allow anyone to approach the egg! In three years we shall destroy the spirit of Aquarizamax and his son shall be ours! Get to work!"

Quest updated: 'Assassinate the Dragon Aquarizamax.' The Dragon has sacrificed himself

to save his egg. The Golden Dragon will hatch in a year and become the ruler of the world. If you don't destroy the Blackeners, then in a year the defensive sphere will collapse and the Golden Dragon will become a Cursed Dragon of Shadow. Make the right choice. Reward: Variable. Penalty for failing the quest: Variable.

"Alisa, start summoning our men," I whispered as soon as I regained control of my limbs. The cutscene had ended and the raid chat filled with a discussion of what we had just seen—but we had better things to do than discuss lore. The portal had brought us to the lair filled with the silver light emanating from the dagger's hilt. Black tentacles reached from the antennae of the enormous Blackeners and crept to the sphere whose golden sheen was already tarnished. It looked more like a faded sun now, occluded by gray clouds. The clamor of shattering glass no longer resounded in the cave and the Blackeners hummed at full power. The corpse of Aquarizamax, uncorrupted by the intervening years, still lay beside the sphere. However, the most unpleasant thing was that the goblin with the foggy eyes we had seen in the cutscene still remained standing beside the egg, jotting down something on a scroll and no doubt compiling a report on how his work was coming along.

The Dungeon's final boss was this undead, green

goblin. A creature whose power seemed at odds with his stature—the Level 240 Shadow goblin had four hidden abilities. His Hit Points were hidden from us as well. The only silver lining here was that no one was attacking us and we could summon the other members of the raid in peace.

"Okay—now I'll say it openly," Moni began as soon as Alisa had summoned the entire raid to the Dragon's lair and we began to discuss the tactical plan. "Anastaria, I wouldn't refuse your assistance. Four hidden abilities, an odd fine print in the quest description, and an undead goblin boss. I've never encountered this before."

"Can't say I've seen four hidden abilities before either," Anastaria said pensively, observing the goblin. "'Make the right choice...' That phrase really gives me pause for thought. The egg must be destroyed in any case. There's aren't any options about that. But how are we going to do it? What if, as soon as we destroy the sphere, the Blackeners will spawn the Dragon of Shadow? And why did they leave the goblin here? There's just too little information. It seems to me that the Blackeners haven't been placed here for no reason. The designers wouldn't simply place such obstacles here—we'll probably have to use them for cover. What remains to be understood is when. Or— what's also possible—we'll have to bait the boss behind them when he uses one of his spells, so it doesn't hit the egg. And then there's that dagger...Eh...Wish Hellfire were here."

"Our tank's no slouch either," Moni interjected.

"Yeah, yeah, I've heard that before," Anastaria replied. "The most important and, really, the only question is where we're going to try to keep the boss. There're four columns in the hall. They should serve some function too, like the Blackeners. Most likely, we'll have to lead the goblin away from the egg. I suggest we kite him in circles. Do you understand what you have to do, Ugtur? Who's going to be our second tank?"

"Baruz is a Warrior."

"Baruz, Ugtur—come over here." Anastaria produced a piece of parchment and sketched a plan of the hall on it. The diagram was so precise that even the goblin was marked on it. "First you run with Ugtur along this trajectory—then we'll determine where you should position yourself. Who can take a lot of damage temporarily?"

"I can," Kreel said tersely.

"How much?"

"Enough. I have good armor."

"Okay. Let's move on to the tank that isn't pinning the boss. The video showed a huge army of shades. There's a probability that those'll be spawning regularly. The free tank has to corral the shades in a group. Do we have any fire magic?"

"What do you need fire magic for?"

"Remember how the Dragon killed the shades?

He incinerated them. That's nothing if not a hint. We need fire spells."

"The Necromancers and—assuming we have ten minutes available—the Mages can change their affinities. Although, no—only two of them can, since Alisa won't be able to come back if she goes."

"Tell them to go and do it. This is very important."

Moni didn't bother arguing and immediately sent the two Mages back to Anhurs to change their magic affinities.

"I also recommend we form a group to focus the Blackeners," Anastaria suggested after a little more thought. "If you grant me the config rights, I'll organize the groups. Okay, everyone with melee will focus the boss. Ranged fighters will set up like this— you here, you here...Plinto, you will handle the shades. We'll need to soften them up a bit before we put them to the torch. First group—you'll position yourself here near the red mark and focus the Blackener," a red beam appeared not far from one of the columns and stretched from the ceiling to the floor. "Step out of it only on command and only in the direction of the blue marker. Everyone else help kite the boss and pour everything you have into him. Where are those Mages?"

"I'm summoning them back now," Alisa replied.

"Okay. Now, the group that'll be in charge of the shades: I'll say it again, the free tank will corral the mobs, Plinto will soften them up and you guys will incinerate them. Nothing complicated. Moni, assign some healers to them."

"You got it."

"All right. I think that's about it. A huge request to everyone—as soon as I issue an order, you have to drop whatever you're doing and do what I say. If I tell you to jump at the count of three, you jump exactly on three—not a second sooner, not a second later. If I tell you to flee or hide, you drop everything—even if the boss or mob you're fighting has 1 HP—and you do what I tell you. I assume everyone's okay with this? You won't mind if I lead the raid, Moni?"

"I'm all for it," the Druid spread his arms. "It's always a pleasure to be ordered around by a pretty lady."

"Very good. Do your Rogues have scrolls of revival?"

"Why?" Moni sounded surprised for the first time during the raid. "We have a Paladin as insurance."

"The Paladin won't be able to hide or teleport to us from a different floor of the Dungeon. I doubt he knows how to fly. As soon as the fight starts, everyone has to take part in it with no exceptions, since the boss's spells might work across the entire area of the cave. Rogues are the only class that can leave combat in Stealth and hide out in some corner. We'd frequently assign a Paladin-Healer to such a fighter to make sure he'd survive."

"What's the big deal? We'll just respawn. Nothing terrible about that. This is a one-time boss after all," spoke up one of the mercenaries, but Anastaria cut him off:

"Are you prepared to compensate me for the XP I'll lose? If the raid is revived, no one will lose any Experience, but if everyone has to respawn, we'll lose 30% of our current Level's progress. At my level, that's a steep price to pay. The amount I'd lose would be enough for you to gain two or three levels. Any more questions?"

"You assigned me to a separate group," I asked when everyone shook their heads. "Why?"

"Your job will be to stay in place and not get in the way. You have no Shamanic powers, your lizard tail won't do much good here, and I doubt you'll want to lose your Totem here either. In this fight, you'll be a wagon—and I don't want anyone spending MP on you. Sorry, but you're useless here, so I assigned you to a separate group to keep the healers from getting confused. All you can do is stun the mobs once an hour, and that's not worth keeping you alive for. Any other questions?"

Why look at that! Yet again Anastaria had managed to explain to everyone what a worthless player I was—and did so using examples and reasons. It was all so eloquent that I couldn't even object—I really couldn't accomplish much with my tail here. This wasn't the roof battle.

"If everyone's clear about the plan, we'll take our positions. We'll start at 'go, go, go.' Ready? Three. Two. Go! Go! Go! "

B E W A R E !

"Kite him to the marker! We need more damage! Tanks—the shades are spawning. Your turn, Plinto! Don't stand in the puddles! Get behind the columns, everyone! Baruz, take the boss! Now focus the shades! If anyone wastes any more Mana on Mahan, I'll kick them out of the raid!"

I was standing beside the sphere with the egg as I'd been ordered, watching the carnage unfold around me. Anastaria issued orders tirelessly, placed markers, guided the players, crawled around on her Siren's tail and smacked any healers that dared spare a healing spell on me. The boss's first ability turned out to be 'Poison Wave'—a huge green wave that instantly killed any players who hadn't taken cover behind the columns or the Blackeners. The boss cast this wave once a minute, so we had to scatter and hide over and over again. But even if a player managed to survive a wave, he'd receive the 'Poisoned' debuff, which sapped 3% of his Hit Points every second. The debuff lasted 10 seconds and it was impossible to dispel it, so the healers had to put in their all once a minute in order to restore the raid's health. I had to agree with Anastaria—spending MP on a fat Dragon under these circumstances would have been wasteful indeed.

However, there were upsides too—in my Dragon Form, the Poison Wave had no effect on me at all, and neither did the debuff that followed it. The only inconvenience were the shades that kept spawning. The tanks simply couldn't gather them in time, so sometimes I'd be attacked by some rabid mob causing me to flee in the direction of a tank. In the midst of a crowd of players the damage caused the shades to aggro someone else, while I regained some Hit Points thanks to several spells of mass healing. Which inevitably ticked off Anastaria.

B E W A R E !

"Brother, why aren't you doing anything?" Draco asked with surprise, when yet another black drop resembling naphtha fell to the ground. The boss's second spell was 'Grim Drop.' The goblin would choose a player at random, make several motions with his hands, and a dark cloud would appear above the target. Then, a drop of oil would precipitate from the cloud. If it hit the player, he'd die on the spot, while all the surviving players around him would receive a minute-long debuff of +100% damage from Poison. As soon as the drop vanished, the boss cast a Poison Wave with all its attendant consequences. By the second Grim Drop, Anastaria figured out that the damage from the Drop had to be distributed among the entire raid, while being mitigated with any defensive spell available.

"Because I've been ordered to stand here and

die," I replied sincerely. "Unfortunately, the goblin's still using poison, so I'm still alive. And there aren't any more shades. No, wait, yes there are. Hang on a second."

I ran over to the raid again, allowing a tank to take care of the shade that was chasing me.

"I wasn't asking you why you're not attacking the boss," Draco wouldn't let up. "I don't care about him. I'm asking why you're not doing anything to save the egg. The Siren wants to destroy it!"

"Well we need to destroy it in any case," I shook my head. "This world doesn't need a ruler or a Dragon of Shadow. I'm very sorry."

"How can you be so calm about the killing of a Dragon that hasn't even been born yet?" my Totem exclaimed with outrage. "What is he guilty of? The fact that he might exist?"

"Look Draco, you have to understand that this..."

"Brother, it's you who needs to understand that it's the Titan and the Siren that need to kill the Dragon—but not you! You are a Dragon! There are so few of us left that every egg has to be protected unto our last drop of blood! Aquarizamax sacrificed himself so that his son could be born. I'm begging you—think about how you could save him! What will happen if a Dragon becomes ruler of this world? I doubt that Eluna or Tartarus would allow him to do anything stupid. To the contrary—Barliona would see an era of progress, a golden age!"

"*Stacey, I have an idea. What if...*"

"No!" Anastaria replied, once I'd relayed Draco's idea to her. "*There shall be no Dragons in Barliona! I have my own interests in this. The time of the Sirens is upon us.*"

B E W A R E !

"*Do something, Brother! They will kill the egg!*"

"*Mahan, don't even think of doing anything! That egg must be destroyed!*"

"Greetings, my failed apprentice," Geranika joined the two voices already in my head, appearing several meters from me and staring with some surprise at the players fighting the boss. "I'm a bit curious—what are you guys doing here? Ah! Even Kreel is here!"

"A new target! Baruz, you're on him. Keep him pinned to the columns!"

"The target won't aggro!" the tank exclaimed in surprise when the knife he'd thrown at Geranika passed innocuously through the Lord of Shadow.

"It's a projection—ignore it!" Anastaria realized what was happening. "Get ready, the boss'll start casting a new spell in three minutes! There'll be another Grim Drop in three seconds!"

"A projection?" Geranika smirked, adjusting his jacket's lapel. All of a sudden a thick silence descended on the lair. "Could a projection do—*this*?"

The players and boss stopped in their contorted

poses. The scene looked like some mad sculptor had created a tableaux of wax figures to show everyone the deadliness of war. The lightning bolts, the arrows, the Grim Drop...just stopped. The entire cave stopped with the exception of Geranika, who began to move toward the players as casually as if he owned the place.

"As I understand it, partner, you've decided to kill my future Dragon?"

"We're not partners," yelled Kreel, regaining his speech at a gesture from Geranika's hand.

"Oh really?" The Shaman raised an eyebrow. "You were of such help in acquiring the Heart of Chaos that I'm not even sure whom I should be more grateful to—you or that insignificant creature that brought the Heart into our world. Ayrun, apprise me, what's going on here?"

The goblin dusted himself off as if some dirt had gotten on his clothes and walked over to Geranika with a self-assured stride. It was like he hadn't just lost 47% of his Hit Points.

"As you anticipated, oh Master, the Free Citizens attacked me in the hopes of destroying the egg. When the battle commenced, I notified you of the assault and began to distract them—as you ordered. I'd like to mention, oh my Master, that this has been a lot of fun. The Free Citizens learn very quickly, improvise well and act decisively. I was about to show them a new trick when you appeared and stopped everything."

"You have more work ahead of you then. How is the egg?"

"I think we can safely break the sphere—Aquarizamax's spirit has been vanquished."

"Are you aware of what awaits you if you are mistaken?" Geranika asked.

"It was only this knowledge that kept me from notifying you of Aquarizamax's demise a week ago. He is no longer. I checked everything several times and then checked it again and again—until my supposition had grown to complete certainty—we can safely destroy the sphere now. The egg will survive and you shall have a new warrior."

"In that case, I shall take it to Armard," Geranika sounded pleased. The Blackeners stopped pumping their dark vapor into the sphere, yet it did not flare gold as it had earlier. To the opposite—the sphere grew darker and turned into an ordinary, dead, foggy orb. "You have served me well Ayrun. For bearing me the good news, I'd like to do you a favor now. Ask and I shall grant you any wish you like."

"The Siren, Master. She commanded the Free Citizens and I'd very much enjoy a chance to try her in my new trial arena. Once upon a time you told me that only a madman would attempt them, so I need a volunteer. And how is this Siren not a fitting volunteer?"

"As you wish!" said Geranika and the raid party

lost one player. Surprisingly, after Anastaria vanished, the Lord of Shadow grew lean as if he'd suddenly aged 300 years—his face grew sallow and his hands began to tremble—yet the Shaman remained standing on two legs, smirking wryly at the world around him.

"Thank you, Master," the goblin mumbled reverently, bowing deeply. "Do you have plans for the others?"

"Yes, for Mahan and Kreel—but not just this moment. Transporting a Free Citizen against her will is very exhausting. You may kill them all now—I will deal with those two later. Deliver the Blackeners and the egg to my castle!" Geranika ordered the shades that had appeared. "Destroy all the Free Citizens and raze the tower. I want no memory of this place and the Dragon that lived in it to remain after you are done!"

The players' frames began to go gray one after the other—Geranika opened a portal between the raid and the egg, so the shades decided to combine the pleasant with the useful and reach the Blackeners without leaving a single survivor in their wake. As luck would have it, it was looking like I'd be the last one to respawn.

"*Brother! Do something! They will take the egg!*" Draco pleaded. I tried to move, but Geranika's 'Stop' spell remained in effect. What could I do? Stand there and look on as Barliona acquired a new epic monster?

Witness us becoming the cause of a new global event that would unite a myriad of players into one effort? The social component is the social component? We are all one and all that noise...?

Like hell!

I didn't have the strength to break Geranika's bonds—our levels were too far apart. But I did know of one creature in this world who could help me receive immunity from Geranika's spell, even if temporarily—Eluna. The goddess had promised to give me a present—why not call in the favor right now?

"*Eluna, I've rarely asked you for anything,*" I addressed the goddess mentally, "*but this right now is one such moment when I need your assistance. Barliona's fate depends on whether or not I can stop Geranika right now.*"

"*What do you want, Shaman?*" the response came immediately. "*To save the egg? I cannot promise that the Golden Dragon will bring peace and tranquility to Barliona. The Dragon that calls you his son, foretold the coming of the Golden Dragon who would enslave all the races of the world and become their Master. Is this the fate that you want for Barliona? There is no difference to me, whether the Dragon is Golden or Shadow. Were it up to me, I would destroy the egg myself—but I cannot. So I shall ask you one more time: What do you want, Shaman?*"

"*I want thirty seconds of complete immunity from*

Geranika's spells," I said—suddenly realizing what I had to do. All it took was for Eluna to mention my father and the puzzle pieces snapped into place. How is it I hadn't figured this out earlier? *"And control over my body. Just trust me, oh goddess. Have I ever failed you?"*

"There is a first time for everything. Thirty seconds, Shaman. You will have thirty seconds. After that, I will be powerless to help you. Do what you must!"

Buff received: Eluna's Kiss.

"How curious," Geranika froze as soon as a golden cloud appeared around me. "Have you decided to flee?"

"Something like that," I parried. Having no time to spend on idle conversation, I dashed to the sphere, coiled my tail around it, raising it from the floor, and cast a portal to Vilterax. The mention of Renox had made everything fall into its right place—in several weeks my father would go to his rest. That was a given that I could not change. Even Eluna has asked me not to interfere. Consequently, the head of the Dragons would die. However! My tail held the very one who would become the future head of the Dragons! Nowhere did it say that the Golden Dragon had to become the master of Barliona. No—he shall become the master of the world that he lives in. Therefore,

Vilterax shall now encounter its new leader and the poor Ice Giants, the eternal foes of the Dragons, shall fall to their knees before the Golden Dragon. But not Barliona! Why hadn't I thought about this earlier?

"Farewell all! Don't forget to write," I said, diving into the portal.

"Son?" Renox said with astonishment when I appeared on the stone platform dusted with snow. "I did not expect you to appear so soon."

"Vilterax...of course. How did I not guess earlier?" said Geranika spitefully, appearing several meters beside me.

"The enemy?" Renox asked with even more surprise. "Did you forget something here?"

"Father, he wants to take the egg of the Golden Dragon!" I yelled, anxiously checking the 'Kiss of Eluna' timer. Fifteen seconds more. There was still time, but it was fading quickly.

"What?!" roared Renox, turning to look at the Shaman—but at the same time, Geranika turned into something terrible. Black tattered wings sprouted from his back. His eyes turned red and some kind of deadly aura that destroyed all life within a meter-wide radius around him—whether vegetable or mineral—appeared around him, causing the dark Shaman to look like he was suspended in nothing. This was the combat form of the Lord of Shadow, a Level 500 sentient of Barliona. A terrifying sight.

"YOU!" A dark fog seeped from Geranika's hands

and coiled around me. For the first time since his appearance, I saw Geranika enraged. "YOU DARED TO INTERFERE WITH MY PLANS? IT IS TIME TO END THIS! THE EGG SHALL BE MINE!"

Buff received: 'Curse of the Lord of Shadow.' - 90% to all stats (including those modified by items)...

'Curse of the Lord of Shadow' has been dispelled by 'Eluna's Kiss.'

"YOU THINK YOU CAN ESCAPE MY PUNISHMENT?" Geranika took a step in my direction, melting the stone under his feet. "YOU ARE A PATHETIC LITTLE SLUG THAT I CAN CRUSH AT WILL!"

Strange sparks appeared among the fog seeping from Geranika's hands, but here Renox came to.

"You have no power in this place, Lord of Shadow," Renox said in a fairly calm voice, and yet I knew this Dragon well enough to know that he was currently at the limits of his powers. The fog and sparks seeping from Geranika's hands scattered against the protective sphere that had formed around me, Eluna's buff expired, but the situation was looking like a stalemate. Geranika could not kill me, and yet Renox couldn't do anything to him, since all his energy was channeled to protecting me. It went on like this for an eternity—although the timer indicated that only 90 seconds had elapsed. After that, other Dragons joined the contest.

"YOU SHALL NOT HIDE FROM MY WRATH!" Geranika bellowed as twenty Dragons blew their fire on him simultaneously. Another ten helped Renox hold the protective dome, protecting me from the Shadow Lord's wrath. To be honest, I had no idea what the players who were assaulting Armard were even thinking: Geranika had such vast power that a mere flourish of his hand would suffice to wipe out an army. It's odd that the devs endowed a Shaman with such power. What purpose did an enemy like this serve?

"You have no power in these lands, Lord of Shadow," Renox repeated. "Flee while you can, or you shall be crushed like a pitiful insect. At the dawn of Barliona, we killed those like you by the hundreds. Do you really believe we can't deal with you?"

"YOU CANNOT DESTROY ME, DRAGON," Geranika yelled. The Shaman's black wings resembled a bunch of charred bones—tongues of dragon fire periodically flashed between his transparent body, suggesting that not everything was okay there either, but Geranika continued to shoot the fog with its terrible sparks in my direction. What a persistent NPC!

"But I can make your immortal life a hell!"

Immortal life? That was a thing in Barliona?

"YOU KNOW NOTHING ABOUT TRUE HELL! I

SHALL RETURN, DRAGON, AND SHOW IT TO YOU!
YOU SHALL ANSWER FOR EVERYTHING!" Geranika
seethed and vanished. The protective dome around
me disappeared with him, and all the Dragons,
including Renox, collapsed to the ground exhausted.
As for me, I had to fly up into the air, since the boiling
stone underfoot wasn't a good surface to rest on.

"My son, I won't even ask how you managed to
acquire the egg of the Golden Dragon," Renox finally
summoned the strength to raise his head. "Something
else worries me—what is this sphere around it?"

"That, father, is the Last Will of Aquarizamax,"
Draco replied for me. "Geranika broke his spirit and
vanquished it, but we managed to steal the egg just in
time."

"Aquarizamax?" Renox even stood up a little
from surprise. "You have seen the Golden Dragon?
How did it come to pass that he used his Last Will?"

"Geranika. He found the Dragon's lair."

Draco began to relate to Renox what we had
seen in the cutscene, but I was worried about another
issue—how could we destroy the sphere, extract the
egg and most importantly remove the dagger hilt that
still glowed with its silvery light. After all, this was the
entire point of my campaign into the Dragon's
Dungeon.

Unable to come up with anything better, I
grasped the hilt with my paw and pulled, drawing it
from the sphere. There was a revolting 'smack,' as

though something large had been pulled out of mud and the once-golden sphere vanished, unveiling a snow-white egg.

"My son, drop the dagger. It must be destroyed," Renox immediately demanded.

"This isn't a dagger—only its hilt. I need it, father. It should not be destroyed."

"I won't ask why you need a piece of Geranika. You will answer for your actions." To my surprise, Renox quickly backed down, permitting me to keep the dagger hilt whole. "However, you should know that as long as you have this item, no sentient light or dark, will speak with you. To the contrary, they will do their best to destroy you—for, whoever carries an item of Shadow, is Shadow himself. My duty is to warn you of this."

"Destroy me? Even those who swore allegiance to me?"

"Yes. But they will be unable to do so, and will therefore quickly perish from the contradiction rendering them asunder. Their instincts will drive them to vanquish the servant of Shadow, while their duty will compel them to give their lives for their master. You cannot go to your castle—unless you want to empty it. I have warned you. Now you're on your own."

"What else is there—in addition to everyone wanting to kill me, that is? And, while we're on the subject—why aren't you or the other Dragons attacking me?"

"Because we have seen how you came by this item. So we can understand who is a true servant of Shadow and who is merely under its influence. We are Dragons after all. I am certain that you have many questions for me, but I cannot answer them right now. I must prepare the Golden Dragon for his hatching before that which we both know must come to pass—comes to pass. I need to find him a mentor and arrange training grounds for him. A new master shall soon appear in our world."

The Dungeon of Aquarizamax has been destroyed.

You can no longer receive a First Kill for this Dungeon.

Erm...HUH? I'd never seen a notification like this and something told me that Kreel would be a little unhappy. Although...wait! I'd completely forgotten about my payment for accessing the Dungeon!

"I only have one question," I managed to blurt in the wake of the departing Dragon. "Who knows where the remaining items from the Divine Set of the First King of the Titans are located? If it weren't for the Titan, we'd never even reach the Dungeon and rescue the egg. I owe him."

"In the depths of the Elma Mountains lives a hermit," replied Renox after a slight pause. "He knows where the other items are located. I have sent you the coordinates of his abode; however, I do not know how you can get him to speak with you. You will need to learn that on your own. For now, please excuse me—I have business to attend to."

Quest completed: 'Assassinate the Dragon Aquarizamax.' Completion percentage: 200. Reward: +10 Levels, +20 to all main stats, +5% to all equipment characteristics, +1000 to Reputation with all previously encountered factions.

The Emperor of Malabar wishes to speak with you.

CHAPTER EIGHT
PREMONITION

A S SOON AS THE 'QUEST COMPLETED' message faded, everything grew dark around me. Renox, Draco and the bone-chilling wind of Vilterax all vanished. Everything I was used to seeing vanished, and yet a familiar image appeared before me—the location loading bar. Had the admins really summoned me again? For what?

"Last time the table was made of metal," I said to the utterly average-looking man, taking my seat in the lavish armchair across from him.

"Last time you were a prisoner. I was risking a lot pulling you out back then," said James with a smile. He was the Corporation employee 'responsible for the recent mess that has been happening on our continent.' "Now, however, I'm acting entirely within the bounds of the Corporation's license agreement. Should I tell you which statute I'm referring to, or will you take it on faith?"

"I guess I'll take your word for it. But why am I here?"

"Why just think about it—but no, that'll take too

long. When you were released, I promised myself that I'd share twenty percent of my winnings with you. So I need your account number. Besides that, I also wanted to thank you!"

"You're still placing bets on me?" I asked surprised. "I thought I had become useless to you."

"Do you know what this is?" James suddenly produced a giant stack of documents from the desk.

"A bunch of papers. Someone in your office isn't right in the head and insists on using paper for documentation."

"Paper is more secure," James replied unfazed. "Here you go. I imagine you'll understand immediately what we're talking about."

James shoved the 500-page thick binder over to me. I looked down and made out a single clear line among the heap of cypher: 'Project: *The Cursed Dragon of Shadow*—Rules & Regulations. Project duration: 16 months.'

"The Cursed Dragon of Shadow was its own project?" My astonishment knew no bounds.

"With its own substantial budget, and enormous team of scripters, developers and designers. The only person who hasn't worked on this project in the last six months is perhaps the boss himself."

"What do you need two monsters for?"

"Are you talking about Geranika? He's not a monster—he's the ruler of the enemy Empire. We're still in a transitional period, so the players can still see him. But soon enough Geranika will be relegated to his castle and will rule exclusively through his analogs of Heralds and Advisers. At least that's what it says here. As it happens, I've gotten my hands on another document that's even thicker than this one: 'Scenario for the Development of the Shadow Empire. Volume 4 of 8.'"

"I'm not sure I follow, Jim…"

"Geez, what did I decide to work with a Shaman for? Look, you just dumped 15 months of work by three hundred people down the drain. The Shadow Dragon was supposed to be the main boss of the upcoming expansion, and yet the great hero rode in and decided to nix the whole thing."

"Are you talking about me?"

"Well who else? It's been only ten minutes since you stole the egg, and we've already had three heart attacks. The manager in charge isn't answering his phone. He's locked himself in his office. The scenario designer is waist deep in manuals trying to cook up a way to steal back the Dragon without creating continuity errors. Basically, everyone's bent over backwards, everyone's shocked, everyone's depressed and you're the only one galloping around on his horse like some d'Artagnan. I told them right off the bat that you shouldn't be allowed into the Dungeon, lest all our efforts turn out in vain. They didn't believe me. Hell, they even made fun of me. In effect I wanted to say thank you for giving me the opportunity to show up one of my more annoying coworkers. Technically, she's my boss, but she can go to...you know where. So will you give me your account number? I don't feel like looking it up in the database."

"You can't steal the egg," I mumbled, not quite buying James's story.

"Relax, we can't remove the egg from the land of the Dragons. These other worlds were created precisely to keep whatever's in them...in them. No one's going to allow our team to adjust code that's been around for years. It'd be too risky. We'll simply have to be more thorough during beta testing next time. Who could've thought of testing for a player with a really high reputation and with a race that was immune to Poison—and who in addition to this could cast a portal to a different world? But...Oh well, someone's getting canned. That's for sure."

"So how much did you win?"

"If you consider the number of idiots that lined up to make the bet at the given odds, well, forty million. Eight million of it's yours."

"Forty million?!" I exclaimed. "Is everyone who works for the Corporation a billionaire?"

"I told you, this is taking the odds into account. It was a hundred thousand to enter. That's a completely normal amount."

"I don't know. If you ask me, that's an unheard of number. Here's my account number."

"Uh-huh. Right. Got the number, said thank

you, told you about Geranika. Now I can return you where I pulled you from. Say hi to Kreel for me!"

My surroundings grew dim yet again and a loading bar appeared—all before I could react to the news that James knew Kreel. How? Did he really just openly confirm Anastaria's guess that Kreel was a member of the Corporation? One who was working on the 'Cursed Dragon of Shadow' project perhaps? I guess it's no wonder how he got his rare class then...

"The griefer's back," Moni growled from his strange chair fashioned from sand. The desert's blazing sun was already casting its debuffs on me, welcoming me back to Barliona. "He's about to sing us a song about the white buffalo."

"Is there something you want to tell us, Mahan?" Kreel's voice forced me to turn. Half of the raid was scattered around the ground, playing the role of innocent casualties, while several healers were going around reviving them. In other words, we were still in the same place where the tower had once stood. Someone had managed to survive its complete destruction and begun to revive the players. Well that's something—at least they won't lose the XP. The corpse of Aquarizamax was also here among the slain players—and so was Spiteful Gnum, bustling over and whistling some tune. Considering the size of the dagger he was holding, his current activity and the constant giggling which interrupted his tune, I really did not want to know what he was up to.

"Uh..." I spread my arms in a gesture of guilt. "Well we finished the quest..."

"You destroyed the Dungeon," Kreel pointed out.

"Oh come on! That wasn't my fault. Everyone heard Geranika order the raid destroyed and the tower razed. If I hadn't taken the egg, nothing would've changed—we just weren't destined to complete that Dungeon. And rather than scolding me, you should talk to your raid leader. Why didn't he anticipate the goblin warning Geranika? If we had blocked the call right off the bat, none of this would've happened."

"That's a lot of 'ifs,' don't you think? Sets my teeth on edge," Moni frowned.

"I have twenty mercenaries in the raid, who came along for the sake of the First Kill," Kreel piped up from the other side. "What am I supposed to tell them now? That the two weeks they spent on the tower was a waste? It wasn't like this was their quest."

"Kreel—you're talking to the wrong person again. I spent the entire battle standing there, doing nothing as I'd been told. I wasn't the one guiding the raid. And I didn't destroy the Dungeon. Send Anastaria the invoice. Let her pay for the lost time. A hundred grand to each should be enough. And if you need proof that she's at fault, you can use her own words...Erm...I don't remember exactly what she said, but she definitely took over at a certain point. No one forced her to do that. And if the Dungeon that was supposed to grant a First Kill to the players was destroyed due to her guidance, then the raid leader is the one responsible for compensation. Otherwise, why'd they create that role to begin with?"

"That's an idea Kreel!" Moni quacked, jumping up from his sandy throne. "Let me look into this issue. I have some lawyer friends."

"All right, it's decided. What about the information about the Divine set you promised me, Mahan? I was supposed to get it if we received the First Kill. The Dungeon's gone, so our contract is terminated, but I still need the info."

"Here," I sent the Titan the hermit's coordinates and a portion of the video I had recorded of Renox telling me about the set. "I don't see any point in stiffing you. If you get the Hermit to talk, I want you to tell me how you did it. For everyone's edification. If it doesn't work—sorry, the Barliona devs are an odd bunch...By the way, one of them wanted me to say hi to you. He calls himself James. He's in charge of the expansions. That's it. I got nothing to do here, so I'll be on my way. Make sure to write."

* * *

"In the name of Malabar, I shall vanquish the servant of Shadow!" screamed the guard. A wave of pain flashed across my body and a message appeared, glibly notifying me that I'd have to spend the next twelve hours outside of Barliona. They'd just sent me to respawn!

'There you have it!' I thought as the cocoon lid slid aside. Renox was right—I had no business in the cities or Altameda with the old man's present, the dagger's hilt. As soon as the guards saw me, they did their best to kill me. And if I went to my castle, Viltrius and the rest of my personnel would lose their minds from the contradiction. Did I really need this? Nope. So Altameda was temporarily off limits. On the other hand, all I had to do was complete the other Dungeon, acquire the other half of the dagger and then follow the plan. Why despair? There are plenty of locations in Barliona without any NPCs. I'll have to be patient for a few weeks. Nothing will happen to me.

Thinking such happy thoughts, I got into bed and fell asleep.

"Good morning, Daniel. It's time to wake up. Your breakfast is served," a female voice awoke me. My surprise dispelled any drowsiness in a flash. I sat up abruptly, looked around my room and saw the attractive young woman placing a hamburger, some fries and a beverage on my coffee table—along with my favorite mustard sauce. All clearly from one of those fast food joints preferred by people over a hundred (kilograms, not years, that is).

"Why such sudden generosity?" I had grown accustomed to playing completely naked in my long-term immersion cocoon and had dived into my bed without getting dressed last night, so now I didn't really feel like showing off my well-toned, unclothed body to the girl.

"We have brought the Jeweler's toolkit you ordered. On the way I stopped by a fast food place wishing to surprise you. No one likes to live off the food from the nourishment module forever. Have a seat."

"Erm..." I muttered.

"You can stay wrapped in your bed cover," the girl laughed, realizing what was going on. "To be honest, I forgot that you're a player. Our typical clients are not the kind to spend a lot of time in Barliona. I can turn away, if you like."

"As you like," I mumbled, wrapping myself tighter in the cover and rolling over, literally, to the coffee table. "What's in the burger?"

After I was left alone, I put on some underwear, sat down in a chair and heaved the Jeweler's toolkit onto my knees. My hands were trembling from impatience to tear off the shrink wrap and open the lid, but first I forced myself to calm down. It doesn't do for a thirty-year old man to tremble before such a little novelty as if he's some morally-depraved seventeen-year-old girl. And a blonde to boot.

Everything should be done judiciously, carefully and gradually—as behooves a man of my status.

The case's dimensions were quite imposing—it

was one and a half meters wide, about a meter long and twenty to thirty centimeters high. The box barely fit atop my knees, and weighed quite a bit, forcing me to give the girl who'd brought it her fair due. Still, I didn't want to open the case on the floor. The toolkit was drawing me almost on a physical level. It's odd. I'd been afflicted by such a tremor only once before—when they'd delivered my capsule for Barliona. Back then, I couldn't stay in place and kept interfering and poking around as the workers were installing and assembling the capsule. Back then my excitement made sense, since I'd waited for that capsule for almost a year, but now...I don't even know. Probably my organism wanted to see the mandrel, the wire, the instruments which had become like family to me...I had no other explanation, but that was enough to hurriedly tear off the wrapper, lift the lid and stare at the toolkit's contents.

MY BEAUTY!

How does one describe the feelings of a stamp collector who's just acquired a rare stamp? Or of a numismatist who's managed to get his hands on a singular coin? Or of an ugly guy, who's just been asked on a date by the prettiest girl in town? Ecstasy? Rapture? Nirvana? Trance? All of the above?

I was looking at the wire, the miniature anvil, the incus, the melting furnace, the pieces of metal, the mandrel, the settings for the stones, the stones themselves, the polishing wheel and I understood that

I had just learned what happiness was. My hands reached for the copper wire and the mandrel on their own and my consciousness clicked on. Purely automatically, in a regime I had developed back at the mines, I began to wrap a ring. One coil, then a second, then a third. This one was lying poorly and had to be changed. This one was good. Now we carefully remove the ring from the mandrel and begin to wrap it with a wire along its length, trying to secure the result and make the ring durable. The act of creation consumed me so fully that I looked up only when the wire that came with the toolkit had run out. My floor was littered with wire rings, yet no message appeared telling me that I had increased my Jewelcrafting by a hundred percent. Had I made some mistake? I had used the standard recipe after all, and my Jewelcrafting skill was pretty high, so something should have gone up. Had I really reached Level 12 Jewelcrafting for nothing? What a pity.

I'd need to go see Rine and ask him for another profession. Like for example, a Tanner. There're a lot of rats in the mines so it wouldn't be a problem to acquire some hides. And if anything, Kart would share some with me. By the way, I've noticed that the Rats had stopped showing up at my site, so I'd need to ask to visit someone else's. The convicts would surely share their Rats in exchange for some rings. After all, the Rats were useless to most of them. And in general, I hate the Rats. They're ugly, gray, and they're constantly darting here and there and trying to sneak into every little nook and cranny and at the same time they think so highly of themselves. Bunch of prom queens! Who gave her the right to treat me that way? For what? Everyone thinks that that damn rodent is so intelligent and shrewd, and yet somehow she fails to consider the consequences of leaving my clan. Stop. What clan? What rodent? Wasn't I just going on about Rats just now? What does...

ANASTARIA!

It was like I'd been hit by a lightning bolt. My consciousness returned and a cold sweat covered my body. Did it just happen again? I am Daniel Mahan and I am 33 years old. I'm a free man with Dependence Level Black, who hasn't completed his rehabilitation entirely and who now periodically confuses Barliona with reality. If it weren't for my hate of Anastaria, which still hadn't been extinguished, then...Why does everything have to happen this way?

For the first time since I'd been released, my lucky stars had granted me the time, opportunity and desire to think over everything that had happened to me during the last few years.

The first thought that occurred to me was that I'd been sent to prison on purpose. The hacking of the waste collector Imitator had been arranged. Someone had wanted Shaman Mahan to appear in Barliona. Obviously I'm not paranoid, but I'd notice a spy creeping on my heels. Marina had confirmed my hunch. The girls really had played a major role in sending me to virtual prison. And this begged the question of why I should trust her now? She'd appeared so suddenly and just as suddenly told me her side of the story—and then even more suddenly asked to join my clan. That's a lot of 'suddenly's.' Well, to be fair, she did provide me with a solid idea— as soon as I return to the wider world, I'll have to hire some lawyers to review my case. Good solid lawyers— not the milksop the government had assigned me. Let them figure out who's right, who's guilty and who was simply carrying the ammo belts. If they decide that Marina is guilty, I won't lose much sleep over her fate. Three months of hell called Pryke Mine taught me the main idea—everyone deserves his just desserts.

By the way, on the topic of Pryke—they'd also tried to send me back there deliberately. Anastaria's words in front of the Creator's Tomb were calculated to incite me to violence, receive PK status and be sent away to spend the rest of my sentence with a pickax between my teeth. They'd stamped me as obsolete, having first relieved me of my resources, personal belongings and friends. Why did they do this? To gain access to the Tomb? To amass further virtual resources? This was the most perplexing thing to me, since it stood apart from the general logic. Anastaria couldn't have failed to foresee that without my involvement the Tomb wouldn't be as lucrative and the loot would be worse. And yet she still hurled me against the wall like a dirty sock. Had she reckoned on making a deal later? Then why would she want to send me to Pryke? It'd be too late to make a deal then! I have trouble believing that Stacey missed this part. Something wasn't tallying here.

All right, let's put Pryke to the side, since I'm getting off topic. I need to recall everything in order. In the course of playing the game, I managed to craft the Chess Set of Karmadont, which helped me acquire the reputation I needed to leave the mines. This Chess Set instantly became a target for the Phoenix clan, which knew all about the Tomb. When it became clear that I wasn't going to join their clan, Anastaria decided to join me. By the way—why didn't I want to join Phoenix? I had no reasons for this, aside from some vague premonition that it would be wrong. If Anastaria had acted a little differently—like if she hadn't used the Sirens' Poison on me, smiled more frequently, stroked my hair a couple times—then I'd probably run to join Phoenix, forgetting all my duties to my own clan. But no! This girl, who is considered one of the top analysts in the game, did everything to ensure that the idea of joining her clan didn't even occur to me. Yet another contradiction between Stacey's image and her behavior. Why had she done this? The more I learn about Anastaria, the more certain I become that she never acts without a good reason. This means that she needed to keep me out of Phoenix for some reason. Quite an information gap here.

What follows is the scene in front of the Tomb's entrance. Now if I discount the attempt to send me back to the mines, then this scene looks a bit too...Well, were I a theater critic, I'd start yelling: 'I don't buy it!' The first thing they should've done was send me to respawn. Just in case. If the Tomb hadn't opened, then I'd be revived, since I'd remain in my prison cell and then they'd apologize, saying something like 'that was an accident, sorry, come on and open the Tomb.' But no—they left me in one piece and preferred to destroy me psychologically. Did Anastaria need to do this for the sake of race bonuses? I don't think so. It'd be much easier to slip me the information in reality so that I'd react in the way she needed. She didn't do this, which means the idea was different. What was it? I don't get it. Further—it's unpleasant to recall my humiliation, but two moments really stand out: The Ying-Yang and sending me to respawn when I called Viltrius. Let's start with the latter. A mere hour or two ago Anastaria showed me as well as a huge crowd of people that she is rightly considered one of Barliona's best strategists. Taking a boss down to 53% Hit Points without knowing a thing about him ahead of time is quite a feat. So it'd be naïve to assume that Stacey had been so taken aback by the realization that I had an amulet of communication with my goblin that she only reacted and killed me after I'd told him everything I needed to. The logical conclusion is that Anastaria wanted me to hide the castle. Again the question: 'Why?' And again the answer: 'It's unclear.' The Ying-Yang, according to Elizabeth, shows unambiguously that I love Anastaria. And that she loves me back. Otherwise the stone would be destroyed and we wouldn't be able to speak telepathically. There's no point in arguing with technology that's easily capable of determining people's feelings. Several dozen technical whitepapers confirm the capability of modern sensors to determine people's dominant feelings: fear, pain, pleasure, melancholy, etc. I don't recall whether love numbered in this list, and I'm feeling too lazy to get up and go over to the computer to look it up. Okay, it's not laziness—I'm simply afraid to find out the truth. If Anastaria doesn't love me and the software doesn't understand this somehow, then I'll be able to survive. Unrequited love and whatnot. But if she really does love me, then...No, I won't go over to the computer.

So what do we have? I managed to pay my enormous debt to the government and gain my freedom. Could I have paid it without my contract with Anastaria which penalized her and others for leaving my clan? I don't think so. If Anastaria had planned on poaching my players from the beginning, she'd never have allowed that clause in the contract to exist. And yet it was there in every single employment contract we had signed. It was thanks to these severance payments from my former clanmates that I had managed to make it out to reality. It follows that this was no accident, but a premeditated decision. Here we arrive again to our well-worn reprise of 'Why...? It's unclear.' All right, there were minuses too—beside people and the drop in ratings, I lost a vast quantity of Imperial Steel. If we factor in the items that Anastaria had taken from me, we arrive at a pretty steep price. Even though I got the Chess Set back, neither the Eye, nor the Crastils, nor Eric's first creation, nor the cards were ever returned to me. Perhaps this is all even on the balance sheet, but something tells me that my release to reality is a bit more important than some lines of software code.

And I shouldn't forget the mysterious faction that wants to hurt Phoenix. They can't do this on their own, so they've offered to serve as my instrument of vengeance. I have managed to escape their surveillance (by the way, no one's managed to track me down so far) and now I can act independently. Together, we have a single goal—to hurt Phoenix. The main plan, suggested by the old man, is to incapacitate Anastaria and Hellfire. Plan B, suggested by me, is to blow up Phoenix's main castle with three scrolls of Armageddon. In either case, we'd deliver a blow to the clan's finances and its position in the ratings. Here, all I see are advantages.

So here follows a global question—what am I seeking revenge against Anastaria for? If we ignore the slight to my masculinity—the fact that the (only) female of my pride has abandoned her male—then really nothing terrible has happened to me or my clan. It could've if I'd ended up in Pryke Mine, but it didn't. To the opposite, I'm doing quite well: I'm free, I have money and I'm famous. So what do I need revenge for? What is the purpose of destroying the character known as Anastaria? Forget Hellfire—I never liked him anyway—but Stacey...She's a symbol, and if I destroy her, an ocean of players will turn against me. I don't need a fortune teller to tell me this.

The conclusion follows quite naturally—I need to speak with Stacey. And here follows another question—why hasn't she initiated the conversation herself yet? Does she not need to have one? Even though the Ying-Yang remains whole? (I still refuse to go to the computer.) But why does Anastaria act like nothing has happened? Another cruel plan? Insanity. We need to speak—there's no doubt about that, but we would speak on my terms. First of all, I need to complete my Dungeon and slip Anastaria the Tear. Then, I need to complete the Tomb of the Creator so that I can obtain the Salva. When the aces are all in my hand, I'll be able to speak to Stacey about the reasons for her behavior.

It's decided then! One more question remains that I'm not quite ready to answer—what should I do with the Armageddon scrolls? Should I use them to destroy Phoenix's castle? Pay Barsina back for the work she did lifting my clan into the top thousand? A judicious idea, what can you say? Evolett gave me those scrolls without a single question. He even suggested I use them in a few weeks at Phoenix's official event in order to do maximum damage to their finances and reputation. What is this? The struggle of two clans for their place under the sun? It'd make sense if they were in the same Empire, but the brothers had settled at a distance from each other. By the way! I shouldn't forget that Ehkiller and Evolett are brothers! One brother taking up arms against another? Like hell!

The thing I feared the most had come to pass—I was doubting what I was doing. The idea of exacting a large-scale revenge against Phoenix already didn't seem so well-justified, although it remained attractive: If I wanted to acquire even more fame, then incapacitating Anastaria and Hellfire would be ideal for doing just that. I bet I'd make some money in the process too. Then why the hell does Anastaria keep doing everything possible to make me hate her more? The hate with which a male hates a female, as I already determined. My psychological devastation during the opening of the Tomb, the interview during my initial absence in reality, her participating in that show about my clan, her humiliating me in front of the raid. Why does she need all this? After all, she can't not understand the consequences of her actions and my feelings about them. I don't get it. Of course, I could be grateful to her here too—it's been none other than my hate for Anastaria that's brought me out of Dependence Level Black three times. Still, there's no way the girl could know this. Or could she?

Damn! I really don't understand what's going on, but I know for sure that whatever's happening isn't what I thought it was. Everything's become confused and tangled, creating such chaos in my mind that I just wanted to send everything to hell, delete my Shaman, give up the game and never enter the capsule again. I'm just not used to solving a problem with hundreds, if not thousands of variables—of which one remains a constant: I am a Shaman.

I placed the Jeweler's toolkit on the floor, stood up and walked toward the capsule in a trance. It was time to stop thinking! It's all I do lately. My job is to feel!

ENTER!

The Anhurs respawn location was just outside of the city wall, just like in all of Barliona's cities. I didn't wait around for the guards to attack me and selected a location not far from Anhurs and blinked to it.

The blue waters of the Altair—the largest river of our continent—rushed from north to south to meet the ocean somewhere thousands of virtual kilometers away. I didn't travel too far away, since right before entering my mad trance, one brilliant idea had occurred to me. It was time to deal with my clan. Having made sure that no one was about to attack me, I took a seat on the river's bank, opened the clan control panel, brought up the reports configuration screen and began to work my magic. In order to make sure that I wouldn't made some haphazard decision based on emotions, I needed a solid base of information. No one but Barliona itself could give it to me...

"Chikan, what're you gonna do when you hit Level 200?" a voice sounded, distracting me from the clan rankings. Damn! I should've made a short overflight to look for any NPCs or players in the vicinity. I wonder if this is a PK zone? But okay, it's too late to worry. I need to figure out whether Chikan and his friend are harmless or whether I should blink to another location.

"Damned if I know. Maybe I'll drop out of school, start working in Barliona full time. If things start looking bad, maybe I'll try to marry Stacy Kumin— remember her? I showed you a hologram one time. Will you be my witness if we tie the knot?"

"With Kumin? Yeah right, bro," laughed Silkodor, a Level 155 Rogue. He and Chikan, a Level 173 Paladin, were engaged in what had to be the most useless activity in all of Barliona—they were leveling up their Fishing skill. The two buddies, since this is what they surely were, were sitting not far from me, casting their lines and periodically taking swigs of some Barliona lager they had brought with them. A nice little guy's day out.

"Oh come on, John. What if some Raiders recruit me? Like the Azures or the Heirs for instance. Well why not?"

"Hah! Why not add Phoenix to the list while you're at it?"

"Ah get outta here. Just look at Mahan—he managed to do it, didn't he? He sure did. Why shouldn't I give it a shot?"

"Mahan is the Corporation's guy. Every fool knows that," Silkodor remarked flatly. "Just last night I was arguing with my Vita about who dumped who—Mahan Anastaria or Anastaria Mahan. We almost had a fight over it."

"I don't know. I read that he's an ordinary player like you and I, only he got lucky and we didn't."

"Got lucky? Like hell! You want to hear true luck? Vita mentioned this thing that happened at her job. One of her coworker's got sick."

"Meaning?"

"Meaning the guy died. For an hour. Some part of his heart gave out or something—I don't really recall. Well anyway, they managed to resuscitate him—can you imagine? Vita says that during that hour the guy only lost like 10% of his brain and he's still got a chance of living a normal life. Now that's what I call luck. But your Mahan—he's a ringer. No one's that lucky—he was there at the Kartoss launch and he cleared out the Dark Forest and got his hands on a castle and won the hottest girl in Barliona too.

Maybe only temporarily, but still."

"My Stacy is better!" Chikan objected.

"She's not yours yet. Listen! Why don't we sing a song? It's such a nice day, we might as well..."

"Hmm...All right! But give me a sec, I gotta pop out to reality."

"Are you still using that old helmet? 'Fraid the parents will start scolding you for belting tunes back home?"

"That's why I'm about to warn them not to interrupt. Five secs!"

Hanging around to hear their singing was beyond my patience, so I opened the map, chose another location several kilometers away and once again activated my Harbinger ability. I still needed to administer the clan business.

Silkodor and Chikan had confirmed my suspicion that for many players in Malabar, as well as Kartoss, Mahan was a player of the Corporation. As a result, serious players wouldn't join me. What's the point of joining a clan that'll never do anything new or interesting—since all the scenarios are already running and Mahan, the Corporate representative, is quickly fading into the shadows. Even Anastaria has left him! I need to highlight this point on my list. Let's see, where's my reports generator? I need more info...

"Eric, hi! Where are you now?" Once I decided what I'd do with the clan, I dialed the first player in my list I knew well. The recruitment firm I'd hired was populating the list with any contact they came across, so now I had a reserve of over 17,000 players.

"I'm in Anhurs, outside of the blacksmith's," the Warrior replied with some surprise. I guess I was the last person he expected a call from.

"Wonderful! I need your help. Go to the commercial quarter, find a guild named MIDCons and give their employee an amulet for me. I need to talk to him."

"Ehhh...Okay, I'm on my way. In the meanwhile, tell me, you can't do this yourself, right?"

"If I could, I wouldn't be asking you. I'm temporarily drawing aggro from any town guards—to the point that they want to kill me, not just lock me up—so I had no choice but ask you to help. Will you do it? Excellent! Tell them to call me as soon as they can! Later!"

After examining the growth curves for the clan's membership, finances, spheres of influence, reputation and rating—which for a reason unknown to me placed the Legends as the 440th clan in Malabar—I realized that I wouldn't be able to administer the clan on my own. That was a fact that I could not avoid. The clan's profits were slowly but steadily stagnating, Altameda's vaults were slowly growing emptier, while our costs were only growing. Players were joining the clan, but they didn't hang around for a long time. The average membership duration was two weeks. It took this long for people to figure out that no one paid attention to them, that no one arranged clan meetings, competitions, contests or for that matter even basic conversations in the clan chat. As a result, those who were impatient or didn't care about their projections, left the clan. There were of course the veterans, but there weren't many of them. That's exactly what I needed to change.

"Hello! This is an associate of the MIDCons guild. How may we be of assistance?" the female voice sounded in the amulet. I bet I'm speaking to a cute elf right now. She's used to using her large eyes to transfix her clients, getting them to sign documents without looking. Or rather, looking, but in the wrong direction.

"Greetings! My name is Mahan. I am the head of the Legends of Barliona. I would like to use your company's services. You do offer management services, correct?"

"The Legends of Barliona?" the girl asked, surprised. "Oh, pardon me! Yes, we offer management outsourcing for entire clans as well as particular clan functions. You may see a list of our services in our guild description..."

"I'm interested in the 'General Management' service," I interrupted the girl. "Can you recommend me someone?"

A silence filled the amulet, forcing me to check that the thing still worked.

"Excuse me, but you wish to hire a General

Manager for the Legends of Barliona?" the girl asked in an utterly stunned voice a second later.

"That's correct. And I'd like to do it as soon as possible."

"Please wait a minute. I will have to contact our management. I am not authorized to conduct negotiations for such a service. We will call you back."

Barliona is a multifaceted game in which people make money however they can. Some know how to kill monsters and therefore go on raids. Players like that make great Raiders. Others dedicate their game time to searching for something new. Others murder and rob. But there is yet another category of players in Barliona—those who have dedicated their time to making a profit. The more forward thinking players figured at the very dawn of Barliona that a game of such scope would need intelligent administrators, recruiters, psychologists and organizers. I had already resorted to a recruitment service, but the longer our collaboration went on the clearer it became to me that recruitment alone wouldn't solve my clan's problems. I needed a dedicated manager who could take charge of all the various duties. From strategy to concrete tactics to player recruitment and finance management.

The MIDCons guild was the recognized leader in management outsourcing. They managed a clan in the top 200 and managed to keep it steadily climbing month after month, a few points at a time, in the rankings. It's worth admitting that all the other clans between the one managed by MIDCons and Phoenix were managed internally. There aren't many who want to surrender the steering wheel.

But Shamans are an exception to this rule.

"Mahan?" about five minutes later, as I was growing impatient, one of the MIDCons executives got in touch with me.

"Speaking."

"My name is Arthur Kristowski. I am the founder of the MIDCons management guild. I have been told that you wish to use our General Manager outsourcing service. Could we meet to discuss this in person?"

"How about in five minutes at the Golden Horseshoe," I offered—rejoicing at the unexpected convenience of a tavern staffed exclusively by players. No NPCs! No one would attack me screaming: 'Die, minion of Shadow!' No one would cast me odd looks and try to stick a knife in my back. The Golden Horseshoe was a perfect place to meet.

Arthur Kristowski turned out to be a Level 65 Human Warrior named Serart the Kristowski. Tall, with an athletic build and slightly balding, Serart was one of those true male specimens that people frequently refer to as looking 'brutish.' Having signed nondisclosure agreements that applied to the game as well as reality—something Serart suggested—I related to him everything I'd decided in the last two hours.

"How much authority do you intend on delegating to the General Manager?"

"All of it. I need a daily report about the clan's growth. Finances, people, levels, First Kills, stores, supplies, PvP, ratings, etc. I want to see growth across all KPIs."

"In that case I want to ask you the question that will determine our subsequent conversation—what is your objective? What do you wish to achieve?"

"That's a good question that I can't answer right this instant," I admitted sincerely. "There are many ways to move forward: climb in the ratings, ensure a stable profit, have daily audiences with the Emperor. I can't quite say what I need right this instant. That's why I approached you. I was hoping you could help me formulate a goal and then help me work towards it. We could set entering the top-100 in the clan ratings as a tentative objective. We did somehow manage to reach 440th place, after all."

"I wouldn't want to get your hopes up needlessly, so I'll tell you directly that this is unrealistic. The Legends not only lack the resources to reach the top-100, they can't even make it to the top-300. Look—here is a graph of your clan's lifetime rating."

A projection of a curve appeared on the table. The curve began somewhere high up near infinity and leveled out near zero at its tail. Or so it seemed, until Serart zoomed in.

"You can see that several months ago you were

in 277th place. Then something happened and the clan dropped to the top-3000. After that there were more ups and downs and then two abrupt jumps. Yesterday and two days ago."

"Yesterday one of our players reached the highest level in the continent," I guessed the 3000 place jump in our rating. Plinto had received 10 Levels for Kreel's quest and surpassed Hellfire. Maybe by only one Level, but still he had passed him. However, I couldn't wrap my head around the other spike in our rating. I don't remember anything big happening...

"The reason isn't very important. What is, is that the clan is too unstable and its rating depends on several factors. I wouldn't recommend you focus on ratings growth right this instant. It's not hard to go up—the difficulty lies in entrenching yourself in the new place. And in my opinion, stability is more important."

"I won't argue, since what you're saying seems reasonable. Let's change the goal then. Since you mentioned stability, let's shoot for that. How can we ensure it?"

"I need information about the clan to answer that. I'll confess that I personally took this project because my company has never handled the management of such a famous clan. There are particular upsides and downsides to this, which we can discuss later, but for us this is a challenge. If you don't object, I'd like to go over the clan's chief resources and its Charter. How are you on time?"

"Given that I'm interested in transferring management duties as soon as possible, I have plenty of it."

"In that case, let's begin. Tell me, what really happened a month ago? Why did your clan's rating plummet so abruptly?"

After three hours of tough interrogation, I leaned back in my armchair. I was about as useful as a dead fish for the rest of today. In the sense that I didn't have any legs, I couldn't walk and I definitely didn't want to do anything else. Serart had angled everything he could from me. I even had to show my future manager the Giant Squidolphin Embryo so that he could decide whether it made sense to activate it right now or later. The castle, the personnel, the resources, the administration, the Charter, the contracts—Serart was interested in it all. Especially who had drawn up the clan Charter and our membership contracts.

"Thank you, I've grasped the main points. Now I'll need detailed information," Mr. Kristowski stunned me as he turned off the recording. And I do mean, Mr. Kristowski and not Arthur or Serart. There was some intangible, mysterious something that compelled me to respect a person who had so accurately processed the heaps of information I'd provided him with. "I will need access to your majordomo, the recruiting firm that you've hired to recruit players, several interviews with your deputy and officers as well as copies of documents to conduct a legal analysis. After that, I'll be able to quote you a price for our services. We typically charge 20% of the clan's monthly profit, with a cap of no more than 40 million a month. There's also a trial period of three months, during which we receive only half of this amount. I suggest we establish our remuneration right away, since I wouldn't want to waste your time or mine."

"No objections," I said, pleasantly surprised at hearing about the cap. A fifth of our profits was a reasonable amount for management, since it would only motivate the guild to work harder. Considering that the Imitators manage all the accounting anyway, there was nothing worth complaining about here. Yet even in my wildest dreams, I couldn't imagine my clan earning more than 200 million in clean profit.

"In that case, there's one last question—when do you want to hire the new manager?"

"Yesterday."

"It's that serious?" Mr. Kristowski asked with surprise.

"Absolutely. I am ready to sign the preliminary contract with you right this instant. We can sign the detailed contract with the objectives and itemized goals later this month—that'll give you the chance to familiarize yourself with the ins and outs of the clan and draw up the document properly. There's no time to waste."

"Please wait here a few minutes," Mr. Kristowski dissolved into thin air, exiting to reality. Having nothing better to do, I fell to my food and didn't even notice the time pass.

"I've told my people to draft and send over a preliminary contract. We'll sign it and you'll make me your manager. Right now, if you have no objections, I'd like to join your clan. I'm curious what projection Barliona will issue me by default."

An hour later, the Legends of Barliona acquired a new deputy head—Mr. Kristowski accompanied by a clumsy and fluffy panda as his projection.

I called Viltrius and had him kick everyone out of the main hall, including himself, and then teleported to Altameda. I sent Mr. Kristowski to meet the goblin and introduced my clan to the new deputy, triggering a torrent of astonished outcries in the chat. Then I returned to the banks of the Altair. I really didn't want to get in my manager's way.

"What's up? Are you there?" I sent a mental message to my student, but the system glibly replied that Fleita wasn't in Barliona. Lucky her! No worries or cares. Youth and adolescence! Should I write her a letter or something? She can get in touch with me as soon as she shows up in...

A LETTER!

My mailbox instantly appeared before me. I couldn't secrete the hilt of Geranika's dagger in some cavern—it'd vanish right away. And I couldn't enter any settlements with it—the NPCs would attack even if the hilt was in my bag. But what would happen if I sent it in an attachment to myself? Were the Imitators so advanced that they'd be able to sniff out an item of Shadow in my mailbox? It was worth testing.

"Greetings, my dear fellow!" I addressed the Anhurs guard, who'd lurched in my direction as if he wanted to vanquish this servant of Shadow, but then froze several steps away and fixed me with close suspicion. Judging by his blank eyes, the NPC is either downloading some update or re-formatting. In any case, I'm not being attacked...That's a start. "How can I get to the market?"

"It's been marked on your map," grumbled the guard, placing the marker. After he'd stepped a few feet away from me, the guard stopped, looked at me strangely and again lurched in my direction as if he wanted to attack me. The further the NPC was from me, the more certain he seemed that I was the nemesis of the Empire and had to be destroyed.

"It doesn't do to go strolling around Anhurs with an item of Shadow," the Herald's bell tinkled beside me. "To be sure, you have concealed it well; still, its aura percolates even through your mailbox. The Emperor wishes to see you. Please follow me."

Why look at that! So the Heralds can see the mailbox and its contents just fine. I have no idea if this bit of info will ever come in handy, but it's worth keeping it in mind regardless.

"The Emperor will admit you soon, wait here." The Herald hurried away on his business, leaving me alone in the Imperial garden. The designers hadn't cooked up anything new since the last time I'd been here, so I again admired the pretty fishes in the pond, the topiaried bushes, the carved gazebos and enthralling statues.

"Welcome to the palace, Mahan," came a familiar voice, causing me to turn.

"Princess," I bowed to the girl, not quite sure how I should behave. After Slate's temporary death, Tisha had become a real Princess. My level of Attractiveness with her was constantly bouncing up and down, so it wouldn't do to run to the girl, embrace her and tell her I missed her.

"You are carrying a terrible item," Tisha said, carefully observing me from head to toe. "What do you need it for? Since when have you become a servant of Shadow?"

"Carrying an item of Shadow does not make me its servant, Princess," I parried.

"And yet you did not answer the first question," the Emperor joined our exchange. "What do you need this item for?"

"As a keepsake. This is a trophy won in a difficult battle," I didn't bother lying and openly told the Imperial family how I had come by the dagger's hilt, including Renox's words and my decision to keep the item in my mailbox.

"If you do not remove the hilt from your mailbox within the next 24 hours, your item shall be destroyed." The Emperor said to my astonishment when I had finished my tale. "The power of Shadow instilled in this item that you call a hilt is so great that it is corrupting the minds of my postal servants. A day won't do much to them, but if you leave *that thing* in your mailbox any longer, I will order my Heralds to destroy it."

"The hilt will be removed this evening," I assured the Emperor. Now this was something worth keeping in mind. Imitators don't normally know about the in-game mail. That's something that pertains to the players—not the NPCs. And yet the guards and the Herald and Tisha and the Emperor could all clearly sense the presence of the forbidden item in my personal mailbox. Furthermore the Emperor threatened to destroy the hilt if it remained in my mail for longer than 24 hours. The conclusion is evident—the developers are trying to use an in-game method to destroy this item. They can't take it away directly—I really had earned the hilt in battle, a battle that had ruined an enormous project. Now the devs had realized what I had gotten my hands on so they're coming up with workarounds—NPCs attacking me and a 24 hour time limit. I bet they'll come up with something else by tomorrow...I need to hurry up and complete my Dungeon.

And I really have to speak with the old man or his people.

"I am happy that we see eye to eye," the Emperor said. A Herald appeared beside me and offered me a scroll with a broken seal. I took it with some puzzlement, unsure of what was going on. I wasn't about to sign anything. The Emperor went on: "Read it. I'd like to hear your opinion."

To the Eternal Emperor of all of Malabar and its subject regions.

My esteemed colleague! Let it be known to you that one of your vassals has most rudely interfered in my plans, which were several years in the making. There is no need to mention his name—we both know who this individual is. He has purloined a personal item of mine. It is impossible to return it now—your vassal has removed it from this world.

I demand compensation. The Altarian Falcon should suffice. If I do not receive it within a week, a person well-known to you will become my subject, despite our agreements about Narlak.

P.S. I don't like post scripts, but I can't refrain from mentioning my pleasure. That which I could not accomplish, has been accomplished by our mutual acquaintance. A particle of Shadow dwells in Malabar! How long will it take (do you think) for your subjects to become mine?

All the best! The Lord of Shadow, Geranika.

"Father, who is this 'person well-known to you?'"

Tisha instantly asked her father, but the Emperor remained silent. He was peering at me intensely as if expecting that some burst of sincerity would descend from above and I would solve all his problems at once. He needs my opinion? He shall have it!

"I will leave Malabar immediately after our meeting," I began. "There will be no further influence on your subjects. As for Geranika's demands, you can't allow yourself to submit to his blackmail."

"Do you know what the Altarian Falcon is?"

"No, but I prevented Geranika from creating the Dragon of Shadow, so it must be some creature that he wants to corrupt to his purpose."

"The Altarian Falcon is a scepter of power created by Karmadont himself. It was lost to history a long, long time ago. To this day, we know only its name. No one even knows what this item looks like. There isn't even an image of it. If Geranika doesn't receive the Falcon within the week, he shall do something that I dread very much."

"Father, you didn't answer my question!" Tisha insisted. "Who was he talking about?"

"Adelaide. She is alive and in Geranika's captivity," the Emperor said dryly, growing as grim as a thunderhead. It was very difficult for the Imitator to admit his powerlessness, especially to his virtual daughter.

"Mother is alive?!" The Princess exclaimed with astonishment.

"In a week's time, Geranika will corrupt her into one of his subjects and we will be forced to kill her," Naahti's expression grew even more dour. "Shadow must be wiped from the face of Barliona."

"Nooo!" Tisha's eyes became two enormous saucers, with terror dancing in their center. "Do something, father! Mahan! Surely you can!"

"The Dragon of Shadow would have destroyed many of my subjects," the Emperor went on. "Perhaps even the Empire itself. As an Emperor I am grateful to you. But as a husband, who had gained the hope of rescuing his wife..."

"Armard will fall soon," I reminded Naahti. "Geranika won't have time to do anything to Adelaide."

"We haven't the forces to take that city," the Emperor shook his head. "At first we held out the hope that the Free Citizens would be able to rout Shadow's enormous armies, but as soon as Geranika entered the battle, our faith in victory faded. The Free Citizens continue to assault Armard by inertia, and they have managed to breach its walls several times, but they could not entrench themselves and develop this breakthrough further. I sent the masters of Stealth to look for Adelaide, but they too have failed."

"You didn't send Plinto," I objected. One of my clan members could receive a quest. I needed to help him do so.

"Plinto was punished and stripped of his

powers."

"They should be back now. Plinto has a week to prove that he is the best."

"Perhaps you are right," Naahti said pensively. "I shall send him right after our meeting. But it doesn't do to depend on Plinto's agility and fortune. We need to insure ourselves."

"What do you know about the properties of the Altarian Falcon?" I asked, understanding what Naahti was getting at. "Can it scatter the clouds, stop the rivers, or subject the beasts? What is Karmadont's creation capable of?"

"Karmadont lived thousands of years ago," the Emperor smiled bitterly, stroking Tisha's hair as she wept beside him. "The scepter was lost about the same time. There is no mention of this item in all the tomes of Anhurs. We have already checked. Mahan, I can't force you to go look for something I don't properly know about myself. I can only ask you. You have a week to find the Altarian Falcon."

No quest appeared. So this really was a request of the Imitator, instead of a scenario event. Erm...Is that possible in Barliona?

After a little thought, I opened my system panel and wrote a letter to the game admins.

Good day! I'd like to report that I just received a request from the Emperor. However, I received no quest to match it. The, uh, Imitators—they're not planning on conquering the world by any chance, are they?

"I will try to fulfill your request. The Altarian Falcon shall be found."

As soon as I spoke the standard response for accepting a quest that I had not actually been issued, a notification popped up telling me that I had received a response from the game admins:

Hi! Everything's fine. The scenario hasn't been finished yet. In fact, we haven't even tested it yet and are fixing bugs on the fly. After all, we have to fix the Shadow Dragon disaster somehow...So assume that you already have the quest and the reward is 'variable.' By the way, what the hell do you need that hilt for anyway?

Why look at that! Just because you're paranoid doesn't mean they're aren't after you! While I was chilling here, the devs are trying to salvage the work they put into the Shadow Dragon scenario and therefore constantly tracking my whereabouts. Why mine? What'd I do to them? In any case, it's clear now where the Altarian Falcon—which no one's ever heard of before—showed up from: They had just made it up!

"The Herald shall return you to the city. Take this amulet," the Emperor offered me what looked like a bunny leg on a chain. "It'll conceal the Shadow item you're so attached to."

The Emperor didn't mislead me—Viltrius didn't even bat an ear when I appeared with the hilt in my bag. Mr. Kristowski had already managed to familiarize himself with the castle and had drawn up a list of preliminary measures for stabilizing the clan. He presented me with several candidates for the positions of financial manager, personnel manager, activities manager, and social media manager. Mr. Kristowski placed a particular emphasis on the need to advertise the clan and present it in a good 'gaming' light.

After I familiarized myself with the offered candidates, whose hiring would be included in the costs of the management service, I added an additional term to our future contract—Altameda's coordinates would remain hidden from everyone. Viltrius and the portal demon maintained the secrecy of Altameda's location, yet the new hires might want to take a walk around the castle where the coordinates could not be blocked. I didn't need that.

Mr. Kristowski flew back to Anhurs to recruit the new people and to terminate my contract with the recruitment firm. Meanwhile, I sat down in my favorite rocking throne and, rocking to the beat of the song stuck in my head, began staring at the nearest wall and seeing absolutely nothing. My thoughts wandered far from Altameda's halls. They circled my meeting with the Emperor, trying to understand the principle by which the devs would hide the quest in Barliona. The only existing creation of Karmadont was the Imperial throne. That's where I'd begin tomorrow. I assume the devs and scripters will be able to adjust it to my needs. That'll be the first step. The second would have to be a visit to the hermit. I need to figure out what Karmadont was really like. The third step would be to send Plinto to Armard. Let him have his fun there. The fourth and my favorite would be the next Dungeon. Tomorrow Kalatea and her Shamans would complete their adaptation to our continent and receive the ability to kill the minions of Shadow. There's only a week to complete this Dungeon, recover the missing items and head out to Armard on my own. Why should anyone take Geranika at his word? If he's already blackmailing the Emperor, he's not going to stop. The only way out is to eliminate the cause of the blackmail. That is, rescue Adelaide from Geranika!

I sorted my mail but did not find a letter from the old man or his associates. Either he'd come to terms with my disappearance, or I was executing his plan so accurately that there was no need to contact me. Or there was some third factor that I didn't know about.

All of a sudden, I felt a pang of anxiety—so sharp that I jumped up and began to pace around the hall. It was as if someone close to me was in great danger and desperately needed my help. I went through the mail and the chat logs one more time, but there was nothing that could have caused such worry. I contacted Kornik, but my teacher only made fun of my condition and announced that this was simply my Shamanic powers returning to me...and that earlier I had been blind and deaf, but now my premonition had returned and was now telling me what a worthless Shaman I was—especially for bugging my poor ailing teacher. Making sure that I really could summon Spirits again, I tried to calm myself and take control of my feelings, yet with every passing minute my anxiety grew stronger and stronger.

Guessing that perhaps this was somehow tied with something out in reality, I left the game. The cocoon's lid slid aside, I traipsed around the house, but didn't discover anything. Just in case, I picked up the handset and got in touch with the operator—everything was fine though. Since I was at it, I asked for some beer and again began to wander around the apartment. My anxiety refused to leave me even in reality. To the opposite—it seemed to be growing even stronger. Someone needed my help really badly. But who? Kornik? I had checked. Fleita? She wasn't in Barliona. Plinto? He was with the Emperor, receiving his quest. And anyway, he could hold his own easily, especially now that he'd regained his Rogue powers. So then who?

Not Anastaria surely? Impossible! Considering her relationship with me, the only thing I could feel towards her was hate. Certainly not anxiety with hints of concern.

The long-term immersion capsule features a complete set of medical sensors that keep track of its subject's organism. In the event of an emergency it would simply eject the player from the game. Out of harm's way. Worried that perhaps I was experiencing heart problems, since I'd never felt something like this before in reality, I spent half an hour on a complete medical analysis of my health. The capsule's diagnosis was unambiguous: 'cleared for orbital missions and even extravehicular activity.' So my physiology was not the problem here.

Damn! What is going on with me?

"Darling, are you ready to preform your spousal duty today?" I sent Anastaria a crude question as soon as I reentered the game. Having ticked off all the options and found no reason for my anxiousness, I decided to try the unrealistic options. I began with Stacey.

Anastaria didn't reply. The system did not announce that Anastaria wasn't in Barliona so I knew for sure that Stacey had heard me. But she didn't reply.

"Stacey, I don't want to fail the High Priestess's quest. Are we going to meet tomorrow or push it back?"

Silence reigned.

"Are you even alive?"

Silence.

You cannot summon your other half. Your other half is in a trial arena.

"Plinto, I need your help. It's an emergency!" I wrote into the clan chat when I realized that neither Plinto nor Anastaria were going to answer their

amulets. I assumed he was still with the Emperor.

Silence.

"I call upon a Herald. I require your assistance." I became desperate.

"You called me and I came," sounded the Herald's bell. "If your summons was a false one..."

"I have reason to believe that Anastaria is in danger. Real danger—not just something in-game. Can you hear me, developers? Check up on her!"

"Your summons was a false one. Therefore..." The Herald's face froze, his eyes glassed over and James's voice sounded through him:

"What's all this fuss? Why are you freaking out? What does Anastaria have to do with anything?"

"I have no idea. Yesterday she was yanked out of the Dungeon to some trial arena and today she's unreachable and I have a really bad feeling about it. Please check on her!"

"I think maybe you've been playing too long. You should pop out to reality, take a break, get some sleep."

"I just came from there. Listen, I'm not asking you to do anything crazy. Just check on what she's doing and ask her if she is okay. That second part is really important. That's all I want."

"Do you understand that this would constitute interfering in the player's gameplay? Without official permission—and I should mention that I do have permission to speak with you—we aren't allowed to interact with players."

"Can you imagine what'll happen if something happens to her?! What if she's in some closed game loop without access to the outside world?"

"Things like that don't exist in Barliona."

"Oh yeah? What about prison?"

"Apples to oranges!"

"Please, James, I'm begging you—trust me! Just trust me! If this is revenge for the project you lost, then adjust the scenario. I'll steal the egg back from Renox and bring it back to Geranika on a silver plate. Please just check on Anastaria!"

"You're not going to give up, are you? Check on her check on her...All right, we'll do it! But if we find that nothing's happened to her..."

The Herald's eyes regained their alertness and color and he completed his phrase:

"...you are hereby fined in the amount of ten thousand gold. The fine has been withdrawn from your account. The next false summons will carry a penalty of twenty thousand gold."

Collapsing in my chair wearily, all I could do was smile. The Corporation just went on making money every way it could—even one player's desire to help another. The one good thing was that as soon as I had finished speaking with James, my feeling of distress passed. Completely.

If the anxiety had been caused by something that's happened to Anastaria, I'll kill the girl myself.

CHAPTER NINE
THE DUNGEON OF SHADOW

"**M**AHAN, I'VE CRUNCHED all the data and you don't have any objective reasons to reject me," Fleita announced the next morning. "Let me join your clan!"

I hadn't received any news from James or Anastaria. I messaged Stacey several times, but either received the 'this player is not in Barliona' message or nothing at all. Anastaria had left the game without saying anything to me. A few more times I asked out loud what had happened, hoping that someone was still watching me, but there was no response to this either. The only consequence was that Viltrius brought me a mug of strong tea, evidently concerned that his master was talking out loud to no one. In view of the upcoming monumental event called 'the Raid of the Shamans' which was scheduled for the next day, I decided to leave everyone alone and get some good sleep.

"You can't join my clan," I shook my head. "The rules say that subjects of one Empire can't join a clan of another one."

"Kreel did! He has people from Kartoss and Malabar playing with him!"

"He's from the Free Lands. They allow that kind of thing over there—with a ton of restrictions of their own."

"Not at all! Evolett has several players from different continents! Aren't I in the same boat? Let's try it at least, Mahan!"

"I'm not against it, but there's one 'but'—you have to leave the Dark Legion first. Are you really prepared to risk your position in the top clan of Kartoss over a small chance that we succeed?"

"Erm..." the girl muttered.

"That's what I'm talking about..."

"I call upon the Magister!" exclaimed Fleita suddenly. "I require your assistance."

"You called me and I came," the analog of Malabar's Heralds appeared in my hall. "If your summons was a false one, you will be punished."

"I want to join Mahan's clan, but he belongs to a different Empire!" Fleita said. "The two Empires are building relationships, forging political alliances, making exchanges and conducting trade. So why can't the Free Citizens join whatever clan they wish? Why are these restrictions still around? I want the authorities to review my request and permit me to join the clan of my teacher...Please."

"Your request has been heard," the Magister replied after a moment. "It shall be reviewed by the

Dark Lord. Your summons has been deemed well-founded. May I be of any further assistance?"

"No, thank you," a broad grin unfurled on Fleita's face and—as soon as the Kartossian messenger left my castle, reminding me one more time that I needed to get some hobgoblins...after first tossing Anastaria's chest with its smelly contents...after first gaining access to it...after first killing myself from all these 'after firsts'...ahem, but so yes, as soon as the Magister left us, Fleita squealed loud enough for all of Altameda to hear her: "I told you it would work!"

"What would work?" I asked.

"I read that the two Empires are ready to work together in their struggle against Geranika, so all kinds of alliances, weddings and similar stuff is being arranged. That's why I figured that maybe I should try and join your clan. I mean, I want a projection too!"

"You risked ten thousand gold for a projection?" I exclaimed.

"How much?! Ten thousand?! Where'd you get that number?" Fleita answered just as impulsively.

"I've uh summoned a Herald falsely before."

"No way! Will you tell me why? Mahan, will you let me join your clan if they allow it? What projection do you think I'll get? I want a little Dragon too, but one that looks like my Totem."

"By the way, how's Bunny doing?" I interrupted the girl's rant.

"Well..." Fleita rubbed her nose cutely and confessed: "I kinda killed him a little. He still has three days before he respawns."

"You killed him a little?"

"We were hunting rats, a wolf showed up, I didn't make it in time...Anyway, everything we'd leveled up to that point is gone. It sucks."

"You're leveling up your Totem through hunting?"

"Well, yeah. Am I doing something wrong?"

"To be honest, yes, everything in fact. That's not how you level up a Totem."

"How then? There's nothing on the forums about it! How'd you train your Draco?"

"All right, listen up," I assumed a theatrical pose to Fleita's endless irritation and proceeded to tell the girl everything I had learned about nurturing a Totem up to that point. I didn't want to become another Kornik or Prontho. Almis's approach is more to my liking—at least he taught me something, unlike the other two green fellows.

"No way!" my student interrupted me periodically. "I can level him up to Level 20 by just playing? They grow like children? Wow! That would've never occurred to me!"

"Mahan, this is Kalatea." Our lesson was cut short by a vibrating amulet. "We're in position..."

The Dungeon of Shadow really was full of shadows. The entrance was located right in the roots of the desiccated oak, so the Dungeon's decor was accordingly decked in gloom: It seemed like the earthen walls from which the tree's roots protruded were pressing in on us and were about to collapse on our heads, and this made the Dungeon a hell for anyone suffering from claustrophobia. Instead of using torches for illumination, the Dungeon's light emanated from some kind of green and glowing bugs, endowing the players' faces with a deathly pallor.

"Bjorg, you're on point," Kalatea began to arrange the groups. "Aozaki and Antsinthepantsa, you stay with Mahan. You're his ears."

"My ears can be my own ears," I joked—happy that I had decided to spend the money on an Astrum language pack the day before. It cost a pretty penny, but it was looking like it had been worth it. Since I had two invitations to the Astrum palace, I figured it'd be nice to understand what all the gossip would be about.

"Wonderful! In that case, you can join the fourth group. What's your specialization?"

"Erm...Rephrase that question in an accessible language."

"She's asking whether you'll help heal us or help us bash everything that moves," Plinto quipped, rolling his eyes in picturesque exasperation with the dummies he was forced to work with. It's nice to be picturesque and all but in doing this, Plinto also showed everyone that he understands the language of

Astrum. Kalatea simply smiled to herself.

As I guessed, the Emperor had ordered the Rogue to infiltrate Armard. Plinto made one successful attempt, passing within the walls, but didn't stray any further. According to him, the teleportation problems remained as before and it was still impossible to pull a player out of the city, so he'd start working on Geranika and his capital in earnest only after our raid. The main info was in hand— entering the city was complicated but possible. Even Reptilis hadn't gotten that far.

"I'll be a fighter," I informed Kalatea. A small sword icon appeared in my frame and I was assigned to a group with Fleita, Kalatea and Clutzer. The group of the oddballs.

I spent a long time considering whether I should take Clutzer with me or not. I even consulted with Mr. Kristowski about this issue—what would be better for the clan? In the end the only reason that caused me to call the Rogue and tell him about the new Dungeon was the First Kill and its attendant reward. No one knows what a new Dungeon will offer. What if the reward is a +10% to loot dropped during a raid? It'd be silly to forgo a profit because of my personal feelings. My new manager reminded me that a clan head couldn't afford such luxuries.

"You guys really did a fine job clearing this place," I couldn't help but remark once we'd passed through several enormous caves without encountering a single monster. "The mobs haven's shown up yet."

"They didn't renew the Dungeon, so they haven't respawned," Clutzer explained. "If there's no rush, I recommend making several raids to get to the first boss, clearing the Dungeon as we go. This is the first attempt, after all, so the loot dropped by the mobs could be a lot tastier than even what the bosses drop."

"Kalatea, what'd you pick up during your first sally?" I asked belatedly. Under our agreement, everything but gold belonged to my clan, and I should gently remind the Shaman of this. What if she forgets?

"I don't remember. I handed everything over to the goblin in the castle," Kalatea replied. "If you like, I can send you a complete list from my logs. No? Then let's move out."

Of the thirty-five players in the Dungeon, thirty-two belonged to the extremely unpopular (on our continent) Shaman class. Tambourines, dances and songs—who wants to look that dumb in front of their friends? And yet, the more I watched Kalatea's raid in action, the better I understood just how stupid the players on our continent were.

The total Hit Points of most mobs in the Dungeons scales to the number of players in the raid. For a raid of ten, this level of Hit Points is many times smaller than for a raid of twenty. And the relationship between the raid size and the HP of mobs/bosses isn't linear, but exponential. This means you can't simply storm a Dungeon with numbers.

Unless of course you're a Shaman Elementalist.

Thus our thirty Astrumian Shamans were joined by thirty enormous, two-meter-tall elementals. Ten water healers, fifteen fire and wind fighters, and another five earthen tanks—and yet despite these immense forces, the Barliona system kept the total HPs of the mobs unaltered. As a result, we strolled along the corridor as if were a wide and vacant sidewalk, paved with the loot of fallen mobs. Now that they had received the ability to kill Shadow creatures, the elementals swarmed the hapless Level 180 mobs en masse, giving them no chance for resistance. All that the players had to do was observe the gradually growing XP bar and direct their minions at the next group of Shadow-tainted beasts.

"Boss fight," Kalatea said quietly when the raid stepped out into a huge cave. In the center of the forty-meter wide hall, flooded with green light, slumbered a two-meter tall ball of fur, seeping gray fog—a Shadow-tainted Bear.

Gar'lan Lok (Level 240). Abilities: Sweeping Blow, Fearsome Roar, Deadly Bite.

"Bjorg, you know what to do," Kalatea organized the players. "First group take up position next to that wall..."

The preparations for battle looked so smooth

and polished that the last thing I expected was the sudden feeling of foreboding. It was so unjustified—the boss was only a Level 240 with all his skills visible and familiar to us. There was nothing complicated about him and yet my premonition kept screaming that we needed some backup plan. Giving in to the urge and trying not to draw our leader's attention, I asked Plinto:

"Got any scrolls of revival?"

"Sure..." replied the Vampire, narrowing his eyes with suspicion. "What do you need them for?"

"Not me—you. Something tells me that they'll come in handy..."

"What's the problem, Plinto?" Kalatea asked, when a dialog appeared asking us to confirm our readiness for battle.

"Someone here isn't feeling so well," smirked Plinto, indicating me with a look, "but he refuses to tell us what's wrong."

"Mahan?"

"There's nothing to tell," I laughed. "I simply have a strange feeling. It's like...I can't explain it but I get the impression that we can't beat this boss right now. That's why I asked Plinto if he had scrolls of revival."

"I'm with Mahan," Fleita spoke up in my defense. "This boss isn't as simple as he seems at first glance. Something's off about him, but I can't say what."

"We'll figure it out," Kalatea hummed pensively.

"Let's see what this teddy is capable of. To battle!"

Player Aozaki wishes to revive you...

"Let's try a different way! Antsinthepantsa, summon your earth elemental. We'll distribute the blow. Bjorg, dodge the attack—he's knocking you down too easily. Let's go!"

Player Aozaki wishes to revive you...

"Clutzer, can you tank the damage? We'll add five more elementals."

"The boss doesn't even notice them," muttered Bjorg. "He doesn't spread damage to them, while his own attack is stronger depending on the targets in front of him."

"Kite him into the raid—we'll try to take the blows ourselves. Plinto, flank him in the meantime..."

Player Aozaki wishes to revive you...

"Change tactics! Bjorg, you'll be..."

Player Aozaki wishes to revive you...
Player Aozaki wishes to revive you...
Player Aozaki wishes to revive you...

"I'm beginning to suspect that we should stop

and think a little," Plinto remarked after our thirtieth revival. "I'm out of scrolls."

"What the hell kind of Dungeon is this?" Kalatea opened the staff meeting we'd hastily assembled in one of the earthen corridors. "A Level 240 boss wipes the floor with a Level 288 tank like he's a child! Even with the 'Teeth' aura cast on him!"

"Channeling the damage doesn't work. Distributing the damage to the raid doesn't work," Clutzer began to list off the tactics we'd tried. "Evading the damage doesn't work either. The only thing that's left is to somehow interrupt the attack and prevent the bear from using Deadly Bite. Or, as another option to this, we can take several Priests, another tank and have the Priests revive the tank while the other tank works on the boss."

"You're forgetting that this boss doesn't have an aggro list," Bjorg remarked grimly. "He aggros whoever he sees first, aiming his Sweeping Blow at the largest concentration of people. The second tank won't be able to aggro him. And he doesn't react to the elementals. It's like he doesn't even notice them."

"But this is just the first boss!" I stated the obvious. "According to convention, he should be the easiest."

"He's the first and only boss in this Dungeon," Plinto brought me back down to earth. "There's no way forward—I surveyed the entire cave."

"The Deadly Bite comes every thirty seconds,"

Clutzer muttered pensively, thinking out loud. "Bjorg can survive one bite if all his defensive abilities are active. He can survive a second one if we cast 'Teeth' on him and several shields...But a third—forget it. And the fourth likewise. By the fifth, Bjorg's cooldown has expired and the cycle starts over. So we need to figure out a way to survive two blows. I suggest we use a bubble. We need a Paladin for testing and...and that's it. There aren't any other options."

"A bubble won't help," Bjorg interjected. "The boss will just switch to the rest of the raid. Several Sweeping Blows and Fearsome Roars and everyone will be down for the count. Again—he has no aggro list."

"The Spirits of Protection and Spirits of Shielding don't help—they don't stack," Kalatea added. "We need to keep thinking. As for the bubble—why don't we test it? Do you have a Paladin in your clan?"

"I can recommend a good Paladin Healer," Clutzer replied when I didn't respond. "A veteran raider. Mahan?"

"From your warriors?" I asked just in case. What if he was about to suggest we use Anastaria...?

"Yeah. My deputy. Reliable dude, even if he is a Paladin..."

"All right, invite him tomorrow morning."

"Are we done for today then?" Kalatea asked, surprised.

"We need to buy more scrolls of revival and find

a way to survive two attacks. If the boss draws up the aggro list at the very beginning of battle, then a bubble will send Bjorg to the very bottom of the list. What good is he to us down there?"

"Well..." hummed Aozaki and then laughed: "With Shamans alone we won't complete this raid—but with Paladins it'd be a cinch. We take a hundred Paladins, the tank gets bubbled, everyone else bubbles themselves—except for one who bubbles whoever is being aggroed. The aggro list changes, the boss devours his prey and then turns on the tank, since he's now at the top of the aggro list. Rinse and repeat until the bear's down."

"Won't work," Clutzer shook his head. "Bubble's cooldown is two minutes. The boss attacks every thirty seconds, and his Hit Points depend on the number of players at the beginning of battle. You'll need to sacrifice half of the remaining raid three times in two minutes. After three cycles of this, there won't be anyone to fight the boss."

"Guys!" I said, drawing everyone's attention. "Let's reconvene here tomorrow morning at ten. I'll be waiting for suggestions about how Bjorg can survive two deadly blows. Thank you all, we're done for today..."

The third day of the raid ended like the previous two had—with our complete defeat. There just didn't seem to be a tactic for the bear—three different attacks which the tank had to survive. Two of the attacks did area damage, so the tank had to keep the bear's jaws away from the rest of the raid. The other attack only had a single target but one that wiped out our Level 288 Warrior. Neither slipping into the Astral Plane, nor summoning unique Spirits capable of channeling the damage to the elementals, nor any other abilities did any good—Bjorg simply didn't have the Hit Points. There was nothing we could do, no matter what we tried.

"Master, there is a guest here," Viltrius announced to my astonishment, interrupting yet another sally to the tank forums. Time kept ticking mercilessly and yet we were in the same place unable to come up with anything. Even the thought of asking Donotpunnik or Anastaria for help had already occurred to me, but I put it aside for now. It wasn't the time yet. By the way, Anastaria still hadn't re-entered the game in the last three days, as if something really had happened to her. "He wishes to see you. Shall I usher him in?"

"Y-yes," I stuttered, clearing the Dungeon and Anastaria out of my mind. Someone had found Altameda! We needed to teleport to a different location urgently!

"Your guest, Master," Viltrius said a few moments later and my visitor entered my hall as if he owned it. With each step he took, my jaw dropped lower and lower—until the tall (in Barliona terms) dwarf stopped several steps from me. An elephant could easily enter my mouth at this point.

"Let's not beat around the bush," he began. "We don't have a lot of time, so I'll say the magic word right off the bat: '*Crastil.*' Will that do?"

"M-more than," I replied.

"In that case, tell me, Mahan, what the hell are you up to?" asked Hellfire, sitting down on my throne. "You were given clear directions about what to do. The plan was explained to you, yet here you are improvising like an idiot! Have you grown weary of this life or something?"

"What improvisation?" I met the question with one of my own, gradually regaining my composure and ignoring the question about life. Hellfire was the last player I would've guessed to be working with the old man, so I needed to check everything thoroughly. The fact that he had shown up in my castle and spoken the password didn't mean much. Who knows what Crastil he was talking about?

"You were offered protection," Hellfire explained, "but you ran off in some unknown direction. It's not clear why you're wasting time. You don't have the Tears and you still haven't gained access to the Tomb. Have you done anything at all?"

"I got the dagger's hilt..." I began to explain, but the dwarf interrupted again.

"Just the hilt! In three weeks of work! Mahan, I really can't call this anything but sabotage! Are you even with us, or are you still Anastaria's lapdog?"

"Hell, don't you think you're going a bit far?" I decided to go on the offensive. I won't let anyone push me around in my castle. Especially Hellfire! "I'm doing everything we agreed on. I have the hilt, even though I didn't even have access to that Dungeon. As for getting the blade—that's in the works, even though I don't have the resources for it. Have you noticed that no one presented me with high-level players that could help me kill the boss? We've been battering our heads against the wall for three days and here you show up like a hero on a white horse and start accusing me of improvising like an idiot! Even though I don't owe you or the old man a thing, all our agreements are still in place!"

"What old man?" Hellfire furrowed his brow. "What are you babbling about, Mahan?"

"It doesn't matter," I waved dismissively, almost dropping my jaw onto the floor again. Here's another reversal! Judging by Hellfire's natural reaction, he really didn't know about the old man. That, or the Warrior was an excellent actor, which I doubt, or...or the old man doesn't manage this part of the conspiracy. Which is actually quite natural and reasonable—why send a real person to meet with me? They could've just hired some actor or had the deputy assistant of the third chauffeur talk to me. The important thing was to draw me into the plot and figure out who does what later on. So the fairy tale that the old man had told me about the conflict between Phoenix and the secret faction was just lies. The logical question is who is actually behind Hellfire and what their goals are. I don't believe that one of the best players of our continent suddenly decided to turn on the very clan that provides him with enormous funds and opportunities. That kind of thing doesn't happen. However, instead of coming to me and claiming that he'd been offered money to help me, Hellfire had made it clear that he is one of active members of the conspiracy. Why? It's completely unclear. Although...What if the old man does exist and he really does have a reason to settle scores with Phoenix? And Hellfire has just been given the information he needs to achieve the old man's goals. In Barliona, the old man doesn't even have to be an old man. I need to check this and pump Hellfire for more information! A crazy idea immediately occurred to me, so I took several deep breaths, calming my nerves and showing my guest that I was choosing my words carefully, after which I went on cautiously:

"Hell, let's try it one more time from the very beginning. We can argue back and forth for a long time, but time's exactly what we don't have. You were right about that. Imagine that you just entered the hall. Hello Hellfire!"

"Hello," the dwarf grunted, unwilling to argue with my whimsical turn. I was a Shaman after all, what else could he expect. "Crastil."

"Phoenix must fall!" I announced triumphantly

and looked at the dwarf inquisitively.

"What?" he asked after a pause, once he'd figured out that I was expecting him to say something.

"I spoke the security passphrase. You need to reply with the correct response," I said, looking at Hellfire so sincerely that the Warrior became flustered.

"Mahan, has your Shamanism made you lose your damn mind? What passphrase, goddamn it?! We got together last night and realized that you won't be able to complete the Dungeon, so we decided to help you. I was ordered to appear at these coordinates, say 'Crastil' and become your mercenary! There wasn't any talk about any passphrases!"

Serenity now! Serenity now! So in addition to Hellfire there are some other 'we' involved in all this? The idea of using the Warrior as a tank was a good one, but I really wanted to know who I was dealing with.

"That's odd," I muttered. "As it happens, I was ordered not to interact with anyone without a passphrase, and to suspect anyone with any connections to Phoenix. Sorry, but I have to suspect you too—you are Phoenix, after all. What're we going to do?"

"You said yourself that saying the word 'Crastil' is enough for you!"

"I did," I agreed, "but I was in shock. Of all the options in this place, you're the last person I expected to see. Then I calmed down a bit and remembered the thing about the passphrase. If I understand correctly, you don't know it. What are we going to do?"

"Hang on. I'll go figure it out," growled Hellfire and dissolved in thin air. I collapsed in my rocking throne and tried to still my shaking. This isn't possible! Phoenix's best player is playing against his own clan!

"No one has any idea about any passphrase." Hardly had I managed to calm my thoughts—which were racing around my brainpan like some crazed team of horses without bothering to stray into the areas responsible for logical reasoning—when Hellfire returned. "Who told you about passwords and responses?"

"The person who hired me to do this thing," I went on plying my line. "The same one who told me that I couldn't trust anyone. What are we going to do?"

"I have no idea. I was told very plainly—go to your castle, say 'Crastil,' give you this Crastil and help you with the Dungeon. Passwords and passphrases are just something from some cheap spy drama."

"You have a Crastil?!" I couldn't help but exclaim ecstatically.

"There's all kinds of stuff in Phoenix's castles," smirked the Warrior and offered me the Crastil of Shalaar, the very one that Anastaria had stolen from me. "Is this good enough as a passphrase for you?"

"I guess so," I replied, tossing the Crastil into my bag. Now I'd need to figure what to do about Reptilis. "We're making another attempt on the boss tomorrow at ten. Do you know why I need the hilt and blade?"

"Do you really fail to understand that Barliona is not the place to discuss this? If you hadn't run off god knows where, you'd already know the updated info. For now just follow the original plan. When the time comes, you'll be told what's changed. Now, let's deal with the important point: We need to hammer out the excuse for why I've joined your raid. Here's what I suggest..."

Having sent Hellfire back to the capital, I sat down in my favorite rocking throne and surrendered to complete despair. What did we have: Some weird Big Brother is watching all of my movements in Barliona, thereby breaking every last law of this world. In effect, I could even now call upon the Heralds and betray Hellfire—that is, by claiming that he received the coordinates of my castle and Dungeon from some employee of the Corporation. I had no doubts at all that someone from that organization was involved in all this. They were the only ones who could spy on players in-game. And I don't mean some low-level programmers or designers. Only security agents and members of upper management had access to these kinds of powers. That was a simple fact. Was Hellfire dumb for showing up in my castle without an invitation? No, our conversation suggests that the Warrior was a very good and thoughtful player. Did he consider that I might betray him to the Heralds? Perhaps. Was it a risk? It was. Would the people who have been planning an operation against Phoenix for several years now, slip up on such a bit of stupidity? Never. It follows that the Imitators playing the roles of Heralds are accessible to 'our' man in the Corporation. But this only further reinforces the idea that laws are being broken pell-mell. Why do this? Just to exact a revenge against Phoenix? Insanity. Why would Hellfire want to exact revenge against his clan? Stop! Why would people who could adjust game data, even if insignificant game data, need a simple Shaman? I mean, they go to such trouble to keep any unnecessary information away from me, so that I, god forbid...Oh goddamn it all!

What a moron I am! If I destroy the three leading players of Phoenix, they'll sic their meanest dogs on me! I'll become Phoenix's main target in the game as well as reality—the honor of the clan will be at stake! Its financial wellbeing! And if I don't know anything, I won't be able to betray the old man or Sergei! Only my fellow patsy—Hellfire. And yet if he too gets the Tear, I'll be hard-pressed to prove that he's in a conspiracy against Phoenix. Even swearing an oath with the Emperor as my witness won't do, since Hellfire never made any agreements in Barliona. So it follows that everything that'll happen will be entirely my doing and if there's any investigation the guilty one will be

Mahan, Mahan and only Mahan—not the old man or Hellfire or the suspicious Sergei. They want to set me up all over again, only now it's not Phoenix but their enemies—and here I am helping them do it! What a lovely life this is...

"There's a new addition to our team," I announced the next morning and introduced Hellfire. "I hope that the boss will be dealt with in short order."

"Why look at what the lizard dragged in!" Plinto muttered sarcastically. "Mahan, you didn't empty the clan coffers to hire this guy, did you?"

"Meaning?" I furrowed my brow.

"Everyone knows that Hellfire won't even go to the bathroom without someone paying him."

"The First Kill," I replied curtly. "And a share of the loot."

"Hmm..." Plinto grew pensive for a moment, then smiled widely. "That's an option. In the end, what's the difference why Hellfire has decided to bless us with his presence? Clutzer, do apprise 'Mr. Number Two Yet Again in Malabar' about our tactics."

"Has your recent bit of luck gone to your head so much that you've forgotten your true place?" Hellfire seethed, looking down on Plinto. Given the dwarf's short stature, this was no small feat, yet Hellfire had clearly put in the effort to learn this skill well. I bet Anastaria had been his tutor.

"Oh noes!" Plinto threw up his arms in mock terror as if trying to shield himself from Hellfire. "Who will come to my aid and succor?! His dwarven majesty has deigned to anger."

"Cut it out, both of you." I stepped between Plinto and Hellfire. "You're acting like a husband and wife, ten years into their marriage. You'll have plenty of time to gnaw on each other after we've completed the Dungeon. In the meantime, shut up the both of you—or neither one's going with us. I'll go pick up a tank in Astrum, if I have to. Along with a dps," I added, sensing that I'd left Plinto an opening. "Let's move out. The bear's already waiting for us."

With Hellfire along, the boss battle turned into a cakewalk. Due to the level difference, the damage that the Deadly Bite did to our new tank was much lower, and when you factored in the heavy armor, higher Hit Points and Hellfire's precision (he kept the bear from doing any damage to our raid in his berserk state) the boss turned into an ordinary training dummy—to be worked over by a series of spells.

"Are you guys going to continue on your own?" Hellfire asked quietly once the bear collapsed to the ground slain. I was about to ask what there was to continue if this had been the final boss, but realized in time that something was missing. I had received a notification about the loot we'd acquired, as well as the XP which was worth half a level, and yet there was no mention of the First Kill.

"On our own we'll be stuck here a week," I said, stumped, and turned to Plinto: "Didn't you say that there's only one boss here?"

"I was wrong. Happens to everyone," the Rogue replied nonplussed, shrugging and pointing at the wall with a new passage. "These two holes weren't here earlier."

I didn't bother asking the Rogue which second hole he was talking about. And to judge by the smirk on Hellfire's face, the dwarf, who was standing next to the new passage, also understood which second hole the Rogue was referring to. Plinto was in his element.

"Hmm..." Hellfire said meaningfully when the Shamans began to clear the way to the next boss. "Never really considered how effective elementals could be. We don't have many Shamans, but if we use Demonologists, whom we have aplenty...Not a bad idea. We should test it out."

It took us several hours to reach the next boss. The new passage led us to a small cave full of mobs, where we ended up finding a single way forward—deep into the earth along a narrow spiraling corridor, which in many ways negated our elementals. The Shamans couldn't see far enough ahead to know where to send them, so we were forced to lead with our tanks. Like in the good old days.

"Who has the key?" Bjorg asked mockingly when our further progress into the depths of Barliona was interrupted by an iron grate. Hellfire smacked the iron with his axe, hoping to see an Endurance bar appear, but nothing happened. The iron was part of the door's ornament and couldn't be destroyed.

"We need a worm," remarked Clutzer, squeezing through to the front, after which he related our adventure in the Dolma Dungeon.

"Back the way we came, everyone!" Kalatea ordered. "We need to find a..."

"No..." I whispered, stopping beside the grate and placing my face against its cold iron. "We don't need to find anything..."

I had spent the last month without my premonition telling me that something was very wrong. My mind told me to return and find another way, but my premonition said one thing—we needed to move forward. It didn't matter how or with whom— all that mattered was to keep moving.

"Mahan?" Kalatea frowned. "You know something?"

"No," I shook my head and looked up at the Shaman. "But I feel it. Tell me, what's so good about Shamans?"

"Everything," Kalatea replied, puzzled.

"Wrong. All classes are good. But what makes the Shamans stand out?"

"Heh!" gurgled Plinto. "Something tells me I know what you mean. I'm with you."

"If I'm allowed to bring companions with me..."

"What do you and what's allowed to you have to do with this? I'll be perfectly fine without you." Plinto's eyes turned into two red embers, fog shrouded his body and the space around him shivered with fear and the desire to flee. The High Vampire transformed into his combat form.

"NO GRATE IN BARLIONA SHALL BAR THE WAY TO THE SON OF THE PATRIARCH!" echoed up and down the corridor as Plinto dissolved into the air around him and materialized on the other side of the grate. I could swear that several Shamans collapsed to the ground from the debuffs that afflicted everyone around the terrifying transformation, but I didn't pay much attention to this. Not right now. "ARE YOU WITH ME, DRAGON?"

"Shamans can teleport a short distance," I explained to Kalatea, walking up to the grate and waving away the Blink input box that appeared. I shut my eyes and imagined that I was beside Plinto. Who cares if this shouldn't work—this is Barliona. Everything's possible. All you have to do is want it enough. For several moments, the world around me spun and when I opened my eyes I saw Plinto standing beside me in his human form.

"I can't do it. What coordinates did you use?" Kalatea asked anxiously. "You can't blink inside a Dungeon!"

"You don't need coordinates. You can simply teleport to the spot you need. On your own. Without coordinates."

"Mahan, this is a game! This isn't goddamn reality. Everything follows the game logic here!"

"Kalatea, you're the chief architect of our class! There's no one who knows our powers and capabilities better than you. If I can do it, so can you. Try it!"

"It's not working!" Kalatea replied angrily a few moments later. "Why don't you come back and take me with you?"

"I wouldn't do that," Plinto spoke up suddenly. "I'll wager a tooth that if you jump back to the other side, you won't be able to return. This is a classic obstacle—a grate in a Dungeon. Either you have to do something to open it or find another way around. The admins keep track of every First Kill, and they'll be happy to close this exploit for Harbingers if you teleport back. Kalatea can't hop over here not because she's incapable but because they've already fixed the loophole. I'm almost sure of it. My trick with the fog won't work a second time. Either we go on ahead together, or we return to the group and look for another way."

"You're quite the expert on Dungeon mechanics, aren't you?" I quipped.

"That's why I'm here," Plinto smirked. "So what'll it be? Rejoin the Shamans, or forge ahead together— your spirits with my daggers?"

"And my axe!" Hellfire boomed from across the grate. "Plinto set up a training dummy."

"Do you want me to sweep the path before you too?"

"It'd be nice, but my beard will do it anyway. Place the dummy."

Shrugging, the Rogue placed a training dummy several feet away from us. It was the ordinary kind of dummy that players used to practice on. Hellfire backed away from the grate and took a running start. For a moment he became a blur and the dummy beside me shattered into tiny fragments. The warrior had slammed into him at full steam.

"You're a General?" Bjorg asked almost reverently, gazing at Hellfire through the grate. "Bloody hell! You're the first Warrior General I've come across."

"What was that all about?" Plinto asked, wiping the fragments from his armor. "You just ruined my training dummy."

"You can always buy another one. When I earned my General's rank, I gained the ability to attack any target, bypassing all obstacles between us. Moats, walls, other players...grates. Kalatea, your party will have to return to the large hall. You should be able to find the main passage back there, concealed in a wall. Find it and come down to meet us. Let's go Mahan. It's time."

The portal scrolls didn't work—the system absolutely refused to let us use it to shuttle the players over. We wasted several more minutes trying to bring anyone at all over to us with no success. After speaking with Kalatea and deciding that there was nothing left to do about the current situation, the three of us descended deeper into the winding corridor.

"And this is why that grate was there to begin with," Plinto said enigmatically several minutes later, pointing around a bend. "This passage leads to the exit!"

Not understanding a thing, I approached the Rogue, saw the item he was pointing to—and at this point my inner menagerie seized control of my body. The Hamster took over the left part of my body, the Toad the right. My new animal masters hadn't yet figured out how to coordinate among themselves, so I continued to move forward stiff-legged, limping for some reason at each step and holding my arms outstretched before me. Plinto giggled, but I couldn't care less about his opinion—up ahead lay the main object of this Dungeon.

The corridor terminated in a massive oaken door, reinforced with thick steel bands. A single glance at the door was enough to tell that it couldn't be destroyed by some spell or attack. But what really drew my attention was the large golden chest that stood between me and the door—its lid locked with a massive steel padlock.

"Geranika's been here already," Plinto remarked, sitting down in front of the chest and pointing at the dagger blade sticking out of the lock and seeping a dark fog. "This what you need, Mahan?"

"Uh-huh."

"Here you go then." With one sharp motion, Plinto yanked the blade from the lock. I managed to toss it into my bag before the Dungeon shuddered noticeably.

"Oops," Plinto giggled a little nervously. He glanced at me and at Hellfire and added, "I need about five minutes to pick this lock. You're a tank and you're a healer. Don't stray too far."

"What are you talking about?" I began to ask, but the answer showed up on its own. The massive, imposing door splintered to pieces, dealing several points of damage, and the final boss of the Dungeon entered to pay us a visit. A dark-gray Hellfire decked in armor.

"A mimic with a hidden ability!" yelled the real Hellfire, immediately putting up his shield. His doppelganger mimed his action, sinking into deep defense—as new shades grew from his back transforming into two more Shadow Hellfires. "A complete raid mimic!"

The tank's Hit Points began to crawl to zero, so not losing too much time in thought, I drew my staff of Almis from my bag and began to chant:

The Shaman has three hands...

Technically, a Harbinger needs neither a staff nor a song. A Shaman of my rank is capable of working with a Supreme Spirit intermediary directly, summoning Spirits tailored to the situation at hand.

However, I'd grown accustomed to singing my song, since it helped me concentrate. I had spent a month as a powerless Shaman—a Shaman-impotent—and now, as Hellfire battled three 'mimics' of himself, experimenting with this new way of summoning Spirits seemed too much of a luxury. It was true that I had already obtained the blade of Geranika's dagger, but I still needed the unifier that would allow me to open a portal to Armard. And as I understood it, the unifier was in the chest that Plinto was trying to open. And so:

... and behind his back a wing...

Hellfire's HP pool was truly terrifying—over a million and a half. In comparison to him, my 75,000 made me look like a small child. Even though on paper my Spirit of Great Healing had a power of 56,000 points of healing, when I cast it on the Warrior, he regained only 22,000 HP. The rest was lost to our difference in levels, which didn't factor in whether I was fighting an enemy or healing a player in the same group as me.

... from the heat upon his breath...

As soon as I entered the battle, one of the Hellfires turned into a shadow and several moments later turned into a dark gray version of me. On the one hand this made the real Hellfire's job a bit easier, since now he had to deal with two parts of the boss instead of three, but on the other hand, the Shadow Shaman began to heal the Shadow Hellfires. Thus everything that the tank had achieved up to that point was wiped away.

Shining candle-fire springs...

"I need about twenty to thirty minutes," Plinto announced the happy news after a couple minutes. My Mana pool had fallen below 70% by this point and I couldn't be sure that it'd hold out for the remaining time. Ordinary Spirits of Healing did nothing to Hellfire, while the Great ones were too expensive. Like any amateur healer I didn't have any Mana potions with me, so I'd have to depend on Hellfire's Endurance and my own Energy. Or that the boss's secret abilities wouldn't activate in time.

B E W A R E !

Speak of the devil...

One of the Shadow Hellfires began to turn a bright red, like a mosquito swelling with oxygen-rich blood. Sucking in air, he began to balloon and expand. His armor began to creak, the rivets holding its plates began to pop out, the chain mail tore in half, while the eyes of the Shadow tank popped out of their sockets, threatening to explode like two over-ripe watermelons. The Shadow Hellfire looked very menacing, and yet the true tank made no attempts to run away from the expanding boss. To the contrary— Hellfire stepped up to his Shadow double, turned to me and yelled:

"Mahan! Don't let them get to Plinto! He's casting 'Explode!'"

Harsh...A mimic with the Explode spell. Did the devs even consider a way to beat this Dungeon? The mimic copies a player and all his abilities, strengthening them several times. Explode is a suicide spell used by mobs and bosses that destroys them, taking the nearest target with them—regardless of its Hit Points. If there aren't any players around the exploding monster, it destroys everything in a radius of thirty meters. So either you have to die or you run really fast. But even then there are some nuances. For example, if you have a Paladin's bubble on you, you'll survive Explode just fine. But if you don't have a Pal, forget it!

"Stacey, I need you. ASAP!" I screamed and sent a summons, without even considering that the Paladin hadn't been in game for several days. I needed her. And she was the only player whom I could summon into the Dungeon, while also the only player I didn't want to see here. But circumstances demanded it.

"I'm here!"

"Here's the invite. Hell's about to get Exploded!"

BOOM!

Scraps of the Shadow tank went flying across the entire room, passing through us and dealing no damage—and meanwhile, the original Hellfire, who had tucked his head in, remained standing in his place. Two more shadows joined the second Shadow Hellfire and the Shadow Shaman. These turned into mimics of Hellfire and Anastaria, but our Warrior quickly regained his composure and aggroed the newcomers.

"Explode every four minutes," Hellfire said instead of a greeting.

"Copy," replied Anastaria and suddenly her character transformed. Her armor, her weapons, her equipment all vanished. Everything vanished aside from two snow-white bands around her chest and hips. The girl's avatar was rendered so impeccably that for a little bit I tuned out the world around me. Despite her horrible nature, Anastaria was beautiful. There was no arguing against this obvious fact. Several moments later, her mimic changed too, adding a second naked girl to the Dungeon.

"Heeeey!" Plinto quipped without pausing his lockpicking of the chest. "Always dreamed of seeing an Anastaria striptease. Do you think they'll dance? Where do I stick my gold?"

Anastaria didn't pay any attention to Plinto's comments, nor did she ask what she was doing here or how Hellfire had come to join us. She stepped over to the wall and out of the way and began to heal the tank. Not a nod of greeting, nor a word about where she'd been, nor even a glance in my direction. Ab-so-lute-ly no-thing.

I couldn't understand what was bugging me. Maybe it was that this was further evidence that Anastaria was such an ungrateful jerk that she couldn't even thank me. But the hell with 'thank you,' a mere 'hi' would do! Does she not have the time for it or something? Like hell! I could plainly see that between casting spells, Anastaria was simply standing there like a pretty statue. Not one motion, not one look to the side—complete concentration on the frames of the players and the tank. If I hadn't seen Anastaria in battle earlier, I may have thought that all of her consciousness was invested in the fight. But that just wasn't the case!

A dim haze appeared before my eyes, while my hate of Stacey, hidden deep in my chest, began to bubble to the surface. It didn't matter that we wouldn't be able to complete this Dungeon without her help, I simply wanted to punish the girl for making me hate her again. Punish her in some way that she would remember for a long time. Burn her!

I don't remember how I turned into a Dragon. Quite simply, at one point I realized that the cave around me grew much smaller than it had been and that my body, now armored in scales, had trouble fitting into it. Plinto grumbled something unhappily when my tail almost knocked the chest over, but I didn't pay him any heed. In order to incinerate Anastaria, who remained standing by the wall, I had to turn around—but my way had been blocked by her defender: A Dragon of Shadow!

You cannot use Dragon's Breath until you reach Dragon Rank 50.

WHAT?! I can't do something? Why who will stop me? This poor imitation of a Dragon? Like hell!

You have engaged Acceleration I.

"Mahan, what the hell are you doing?! Turn back into your human form!" Hellfire shouted angrily when the Shadow Dragon's flame began to pour over him. I attacked the boss with simple Fire, which I had by default and which did absolutely nothing, even at Acceleration I it did no damage to the mimics. My own mimic, meanwhile, began to douse Hellfire with its flame, giving rise to the dwarf's indignation. I don't get it—is this bastard going to copy everything I do?

You have engaged Acceleration II.

The familiar drums began to pound in my head, but I didn't stop. I remembered that during my duel with Shiam, it had taken Acceleration IV to do damage with Dragon's Breath. Since I didn't even have this spell at the moment, I'd need to go to fifth or even sixth acceleration to achieve the same. The mimic needed several seconds to copy me, but I wouldn't give it the opportunity.

You have engaged Acceleration III.

An unbearable weight bound my body. The

drums in my head were beating ever more frequently, my eyes teared up, but my target remained visible— the Shadow Dragon. I forgot Anastaria, the Dungeon and Barliona—all that remained was the knowledge that this creature could not be allowed to exist. No one will have it easy if Geranika finds out about him.

You have engaged Acceleration IV.

The weight, the pain, and the drums were tearing me apart—at Acceleration IV everything had mixed together. The Shadow Dragon's Hit Points began to fall gradually, while the two creatures standing beside it waved their arms and tried to get in my way—yet I no longer understood a thing. I had to kill my enemy.

You have engaged Acceleration V.

"Please forgive my unexpected visit, but I just cannot permit you to destroy this new toy. I need it too much," sounded Geranika's voice, after which my consciousness checked out to its well-earned vacation. What did he mean by "I cannot permit?"

Darkness…

Dragon Rank promoted! Current Rank: 16.

New ability unlocked: 'True Sight.' Description: See an enemy's weak points. +30% to damage done in Dragon Form.

"The Dragon of Shadow..." Renox growled slowly, pulling me from the darkness and forcing me to open my eyes. Snowy mountains, Draco's pensive face, and several other Dragons circling in the distance. Vilterax! "Geranika has acquired his Dragon of Shadow. It is sad to realize that dark times await Kalragon."

"He could not have acquired him!" I tried to respond, managing only a groan. I tried to stagger to my feet, but my body refused to listen to me and even my tail refused to move.

"Lie still, you must recover. It is strange that you are alive at all—Dragons who have lost half their bodies do not typically live long. But since you are here and even arguing with me—you should survive. Form a minor circle!"

"There'll be a little pain, brother," added Draco. "Try not to scream."

Darkness...

"Well I can say one thing for certain—he's breathing," Plinto interrupted my next sojourn in unconsciousness. "Someone's even sutured his jaw back on."

"Maybe we should revive him, Stacey?" Hellfire's voice joined Plinto's.

"No," Anastaria cut him off. "He's a Dragon. If you don't need me here anymore, I'll be on my way."

Through sheer force of will I opened my eyes and caught the fading portal that the girl had departed through.

Achievement unlocked: 'The King is dead, long live the King!' You are the first to slay the Mimic King of the Shadow Dungeon (First Kill). Reward: Summon a mimic of yourself for 3 minutes. This summon may be used once a day.

Message for the player: In five months' time you will be teleported to an audience with the Emperor of Malabar...

"What happened?" Unlike in Vilterax, I could speak normally in Barliona. The two Shadow Hellfires and naked Shadow Anastaria stood frozen like statues before me—yet the boss's fourth part, the Shadow Dragon, was nowhere to be seen.

"Geranika happened," Plinto explained. "He came, he saw, he ripped you up to little pieces (and I mean literally—I'll show you the video later), he took his half-dead Dragon that you'd incinerated almost to a cinder, and then he conquered."

"But you guys are all right?" I inquired, returning to my human form.

"I don't think he had any time for us. You singed him along with his new pet. Took off ten percent of his Hit Points in a few moments."

"Seven," Hellfire corrected the Rogue. "What really ticked him off wasn't the damage, but his cape that you incinerated. Guess he was fond of it. But yeah, it was quite the spectacle when he tore you up."

"What about these guys?" I nodded at the three statues, trying to avoid the image of a burning Shaman tearing apart a four-meter Dragon with his hands.

"Good question. We were going to ask you," Plinto piped up again. "Typically the boss dies and the players get the loot. This time though, we got the loot, but the boss is still alive. Looks like a bug. You hear that, devs? You're a bunch of bunglers!"

There was no response from the admins, so Plinto shrugged and began to go through his loot:

"And so! As a result of completing the Dungeon in an accelerated manner, we have acquired the following: Plate armor—set of three. Sharp knives—set of three (for exclusive use by Rogues). An Epic piece of junk called a Unifier—set of one. Heap of gold—set of immense, and not ours anyway. And, lest we forget, a treasure chest—set of one!"

"Erm..."

"That's the chest the loot was in. Typically it vanishes, but well, typically it doesn't get lockpicked by a handsome devil."

"And what the hell do we need it for?"

"I have no idea. We can't use it to store stuff—it doesn't have slots. As I see it, the best use for it is to toss it into the bag and save it for later if I need to show off for some ladies at the Horseshoe."

"Give me the Unifier. I need that. Where's the

rest of the raid?"

"They're fighting the second boss. Just because we got the First Kill doesn't mean that all the other bosses dropped dead."

"*Kalatea, did you earn your First Kill?*" I asked the Shaman in the raid chat.

"*Yes. I can't talk right now—let's settle accounts later.*"

"Plinto, finish them off just in case," I asked the Rogue, indicating the mimic statues. "One Hellfire is enough for Barliona—no point in breeding him."

"Wait," exclaimed the Warrior. He stepped up to the mimic tank and picked him up from the ground with ease—as if the boss really had turned into a statue. "These are sculptures. I'm taking mine. You can destroy Anastaria if you like."

"Should I start cutting?" Plinto asked mockingly, looking me in the eyes. I shook my head, admitting to myself that having an exact replica of a naked Anastaria in my castle was a very attractive proposition. If this really was a sculpture, that is. I'll ask Viltrius to look after her.

"In that case, I'll help deliver her to Altameda." Whistling some sort of tune, Plinto approached the frozen Shadow Anastaria and grabbed her by the armpits. "You don't mind if I return the sculpture tomorrow? I want to check something."

"All right," I nodded, not really imagining what the Rogue had planned. It wouldn't be some perversion, would it? I wouldn't put it past him.

"Mahan," said Hellfire, once we were left alone together, "there're two issues we need to resolve. The first is when you're planning on going to Armard. The second is whether you'll make me a Lovers' pendant."

"Tomorrow and...I haven't picked up the recipe yet," I replied, trying not to look surprised. You really do discover a lot of new gossip whenever you create an item useful to everyone. The great Hellfire, the doom of all (with perhaps the exception of Plinto) turns out to be a normal person. He loves a woman and a woman loves him! What is the world coming to? "But in any case, I'll need a Diamond. Oh and also, I'm not sure whether I'll be there—as I told you, I don't have the recipe yet—but be ready to drop by my castle together with your other half."

"How much will you charge for the work? The Dark Forest demonstrated that you don't charge cheap."

"The work won't cost anything if you provide the ingredients. I can't profit from others' feelings—Eluna will eat me alive, bones and all."

"When will you pick up the recipe then?"

"I'd like to do it today," I replied honestly. I opened my mail and sighed heavily—I had received twelve thousand requests for pendants. I can't very well deny the players in their desires to speak with their loved ones, but even if I could craft a pendant a minute, it'd take me 200 hours of crafting to satisfy all these requests. A month's worth of work at a standard 40-hour work week. And that's assuming that I wouldn't receive any more requests for pendants.

"In that case, here's the Diamond. If you need us to be there in person, then don't do anything. I want to make it a birthday surprise for her."

"It's a deal. Just in case, give me her handle. Who knows—maybe that and your permission is all it takes to bind it. You do agree, don't you? As a matter of formality..."

"I agree to the binding and grant my permission to bind the girl too," Hellfire replied. He paused a bit and then went on: "Her current handle is Mirida the Farsighted. You've met before, back in Beatwick."

CHAPTER TEN
INTO ARMARD

"**H**ERE IS YOUR RECIPE**," the gnome master said in a business-like tone, offering me a small scroll. "Per the agreement, it's been registered in every jewelry catalog, so don't expect the requests to slow down any time soon. You know, in a way I envy you—such extreme demand for a craftsman is very rare in this day and age."

"Is it really impossible to transfer the recipe—or the rights or license to it—to someone else, so I don't have to make all these pendants myself?" I made another attempt to wriggle out of the 'burden' of the Lovers' pendants. I didn't have enough time to do all that work, yet I couldn't refuse to do it either.

"You're not looking forward to creating some good in this world?" the gnome asked with evident surprise. "Isn't the opportunity to unite the hearts of two lovers what every creator wants?"

"I'm not refusing to craft the pendant for the lovers that need it, especially since I'm the only one who can do it," I began to backpedal, sensing a looming blow to my reputation. "But you have to understand my side of things too. I am an Artificer. You've seen my recipe book—the Chess Sets, the Amulet, the Pendant, the Stone of Light. I make my way in crafting by creating novelties, not stamping out one and the same item according to a template. I mean, imagine if my next creation will be, say, the Chain of Immortality, which allows the residents of Barliona to survive death? The Emperor's Seal of Death is good and all, but it's even better to have an option or two. And yet instead of creating an item that's useful to everyone—not just lovers—I'll be sitting there churning out pendants. In my view, this is simply a waste of talent and resources."

The gnome fell deep in thought. Any way you spin it, my arguments were as solid as reinforced concrete—if I delete my avatar, will the Corporation really put off the introduction of this new method of telepathic communication? They're not idiots up there after all. In fact, to this very day, the powers in charge of Barliona had never once given me a reason to doubt their competence. They even managed to reintroduce the Dragon of Shadow into the game, despite the collapse of the initial scenario. It followed that there had to be some way around my problem with the pendant. All I needed to do was poke around until I found it.

"There is a grain of truth in what you say, Earl," the gnome said, stroking his beard. "There are indeed too few Artificers in our day and age, and to fetter yet another one to the workbench...But, as I have already said, you are the creator of an Epic recipe that is accessible to you alone. For this reason..."

"There's no way out?" I completed the thought of the master.

"Well there's always a way out," replied the gnome. "You could license the pendant's patent to the head Jeweler of Malabar. All you have to do is settle the financial questions of how your patent may be used."

"I don't want any payment," I immediately assured the gnome, but he simply smiled:

"But did I say anything about you receiving payment? To the contrary—you are the one who will have to pay. The Master of Jewelcrafting is a very busy gnome indeed. Surely you are aware that ever since the tremendous success of Tavia and Trediol's wedding, the nobility of both Malabar and Kartoss have sought his services. You may license the patent to an Epic item only to him and him alone. And you need to somehow compensate his time, so we'll have much to discuss indeed. Have you some preliminary offer in mind?"

That damn Corporation! I was wondering how they'd profit from in-game telepathy. I figured that it would have something to do with the price of Diamonds, which would surely surge through the roof. Like hell! They're trying to squeeze money out of me now! If you don't feel like toiling for the players' welfare, be so kind as to pay up! This begs the question: Why should I be the one to pay? If the players want a pendant so bad, why don't they pay the Master?

"I believe that a thousand gold for one set of pendants should be more than enough," I began to barter. "The Free Citizens will surely be happy to compensate the Master of Jewelcrafting for his time...indeed."

"One thousand?" the gnome arched an eyebrow in surprise. "Most Honorable Earl, who do you think we are? A bunch of dilettantes? A thousand gold will merely remunerate the Master for the time he takes to consider creating a pendant. And even then not much of it. Three seconds or so. As for the Free Citizens paying for his work, I'm afraid I must disappoint you—we will accept gold only from you. The masters' guild doesn't wish to have any problems with Eluna."

"What problems?" I furrowed my brow.

"Each pendant created in exchange for payment shall also cost 200 Reputation with the goddess and her Priests. So we wouldn't think of working with the Free Citizens directly—only through you. Now, how the Free Citizens settle their accounts with you, isn't our business. We will only be making the things. And our work needs to be remunerated. These are our terms."

"If I'm not going to charge them anything, why should I pay you?"

"Because you don't have the time to make these pendants yourself," the gnome explained calmly. "Since you need time, you have to pay for it by paying someone else. That's the way it is. Twenty thousand per pendant—that is the price for which we are willing to delay our work for the nobility."

"Five thousand," I began to barter, grasping the cunning of the Corporation's plan. I needed to check...No, it's better I ask Elizabeth what'll happen if I ignore the players' requests. What if not answering their letters causes my reputation to decrease as well?

New Jewelcrafting recipe learned: The Lovers' Pendant.

The gnome and I ended up settling on ten thousand per pendant. Ten thousand! Twelve thousand requests at ten thousand each...One hundred and twenty million gold! All of a sudden, I didn't much feel like using the services of the NPC Jewelers.

"Until you reply to a letter, there won't be any issues," Elizabeth said to my relief when I laid out my deal with the masters and my worries about the pendants. "However, if a Free Citizen personally asks you to create him a pendant, you must fulfil his request within two weeks or incur a penalty. You have created an Epic item, Mahan: Now you must live up to your creation. The master did not deceive you about the reputation—for each pendant you sell, you shall lose 200 Reputation for every 10,000 gold you make."

"Erm..."

"That is, if you manage to sell someone a pendant for thirty thousand, you'll lose 6000 Reputation instead of 200: thirty times two hundred. Be careful."

"I see," I said, disheartened, since the thought that 200 Reputation wasn't such a steep price had already occurred to me. I could've easily afforded to pay it, several times even.

"Don't worry, Mahan," laughed the High Priestess, divining how I felt. "In Barliona, everyone's assignments are scaled to their abilities. Such is the principle of our world. If the Creator considers you strong enough to create pendants for anyone who wants them, then that is the way it must be. I realize that you might think that you're being forced to do chores for the others' benefit..."

"Is that not the way it is?" I blurted out.

"Look at the situation from a different angle. You cannot charge money for the work or ask for items in exchange—their cost would be converted to gold anyway and you'd still lose the commensurate amount of reputation. However, no one says that you have to make the pendants for free."

"I don't understand, Elsa. If I can't charge anything for the creation of a pendant, how can it not be free? Unless of course..." The brilliant thought that

Elsa had been guiding me to for the last few minutes finally occurred to me.

"Yes?" the High Priestess smiled.

"Tell me," I began cautiously, afraid I'd made some mistake, "if a Free Citizen and his other half wish to establish a mental link with each other, don't they have to first test the strength of their feelings through a joint quest?"

"Go on," Elizabeth nodded, showing me that I was headed in the right direction.

"The citadel that is true love may be verified by so many different endeavors that it's difficult to even list them all. But one of the key principles of true love is the ability to work together well. The lovers must prove that they are capable of remaining together even when their weariness causes them to curse the world around them and scold each other for drawing them into whatever mad venture they're undertaking. No one needs Free Citizen couples who hate each other running around Barliona—much less ones who can argue telepathically. In fact, I bet that too much arguing will disrupt the energy field."

"That is correct, aside from the part about weariness—it doesn't do to exhaust one's other half. To prove one's readiness, a couple could put in as much as thirty-six hours of work over the course of a week for the good of, say, the Empire or the clan or Mahan himself...whoever really."

"Elsa, you're a genius!" I stuttered in shock,

grasping the opportunities available to me. Twelve thousand requests suddenly turned into twenty-four thousand pairs of hands ready to work. No doubt there would be gatherers, craftsmen and warriors among them. I had to speak to Mr. Kristowski urgently. I bet he could find a good use for them. Even Hellfire, despite the fact that we were in the same boat, would be the first to earn his pendant. The highest-level tank in the game? Excellent! I imagine Clutzer could use him. And as for Mirida? Why, hunters were useful too.

I avoided considering whether Mirida was related to my old man or not. Merely being Hellfire's girl and being mixed up in this grand conspiracy were two very different things. If she was involved—a thought that made me shudder—then everything she'd told me about how I ended up in prison was pure lies. And then...Then I would really be lost. I had to be careful.

"No longer than a week, Mahan!" Elizabeth reminded me again. "And no more than six hours per day. What they'll have to do is up to you. I have no restrictions when it comes to that."

"I have a matter to discuss with you, Mr. Kristowski." As soon as I left the High Priestess, I dialed my manager. "We have the opportunity to contract the services of a huge mass of players—and do it for completely free. Here's the situation..."

"We'll need to advertise," my manager concluded, having heard me out. "Mahan, you're not opposed to putting in some work for the good of the clan, are you? How much time does it take you to create a single pendant?"

"I don't know yet. I just got the recipe. I was about to test precisely this."

"Time frames, I need time frames. Try to make it in five minutes…"

I managed it in four. Since the players didn't have to be present during the pendant's creation, all I needed was their official permission from one and the name of the other. Hellfire and Mirida the Farsighted. After Anastaria and myself, this couple became the first in Barliona who could communicate telepathically. Noting that my Jewelcrafting bar had grown by 10%, I hung the pendant on a copper chain without bothering to consider how well Diamond and Copper went together. If anyone minded, they could change the chain. My job was the pendant.

"Hello, Daniel! This is Marina." A mere minute had passed since I created the pendant when Mirida called my amulet. "We need to talk. Let me come to your castle. I can be there in a minute."

I didn't experience any particular emotion—it seems that Altameda's secret coordinates were a secret only to me. Ordering Viltrius to usher the guest in to me, as soon as she appeared at my gates, I reclined in my favorite rocking chair and tried to get some sleep. When a girl says that she'll be there in a minute, you can safely add an hour…

"Hello, fugitive," Marina appeared exactly in a minute, forcing me to doubt her womanhood. Taking a seat in my official throne, since there weren't any other seats in my hall, she waited for Viltrius to pour her an Energy-restoring liquid and close the doors behind him before continuing: "It was quite a surprise to receive the notification about the pendant. At first I didn't even believe it, but Hell explained that you made it at his request."

"Why aren't you in Phoenix?" I asked her about the dumbest question from my list of questions. What difference did it make what clan she was in? I should be asking something else entirely.

"There aren't any projections in Phoenix," Marina shrugged, "and after what we're planning, there won't be anything at all. If the clan of the burning chicken is to be destroyed—why should I join it?"

"Never thought you'd be so bloodthirsty. How long have you been mixed up in this affair?"

"Are you trying to figure out whether our meeting was an accident?"

"Among other things. Last time we met, you fed me a pretty fairy tale—so pretty I even believed it. Now though, I think we can both agree that that was all it was."

"Barliona is not the place to discuss this. Wherever you are currently located, I propose we set up a secure line between us and have a conversation in peace this evening. Here's the server IP. Login:

Mahan. The password is the duration that I'd say I'd go out with you. Spelled out with letters, not digits. You do remember it, don't you?"

"In fact, I do—unlike some others I could name. Next question then: Why'd you come to Altameda? We could've discussed all of this over the amulet."

"Because tomorrow we will set out for Armard and we need to get ready. That's right: I said 'we.' And no need to look at me like that! We'll hammer out the details tonight. Have you tried to restore the dagger?"

"When?"

"I see. I'm guessing you didn't read the properties of the Unifier either, right?"

"Not yet."

"Well, pull it out. Let's see what the devs have laid in store for us."

'Unifier.' Description: Allows the restoration of any broken item, if you have more than 75% of the original. Required ingredients: 10 ingots of Imperial Steel, 10 pieces of Imperial Oak, 10 bouquets of Imperial Lilly, 10 particles of Light. Item class: Epic. Number of charges remaining: 3.

"I have the Imperial ingredients in my stores," I muttered pensively after reading the description. "But I have no idea what a particle of Light is or where I can find it. Any suggestions?"

"Yes, I've heard of this thing," Mirida replied,

rummaging in her bag. "If you do a daily quest for any NPC for ten days straight, he'll give you a letter of recommendation. You can then give the letter to the Mayor and gain reputation, or you can keep it, collect ten and then give them to the High Mage. In return, he'll give you a Crystal of Knowledge that you can take to the masters' guild. Or you can keep it, collect five of those and then give it to any Herald in exchange for a particle of Light. I found out about this by accident," Mirida concluded, producing five small, shining stars from her bag.

"You completed five thousand quests?!" I exclaimed with astonishment, after counting up Mirida's efforts.

"Well, as with everything else, you can skip the drudge work and simply buy the particles—but I don't have that kind of money."

"How much does one particle cost?"

"Five million. In Barliona, the price of any essential thing is a multiple of millions. It's as if the Corp doesn't know about any other number. Do you want to be able to fly? Just pay a million. Want to respawn six hours faster? Just pay a million. Want to buy a particle of Light? Be so kind and just pay five million..."

"All right, can we move on from the Corp's financial policies?" I interrupted Mirida. "Let's restore the dagger. Only, I suggest we do it outside of the castle. If we pull out an item of Shadow, all my guards will attack us."

The Unifier worked as advertised. After placing the dagger's blade on the hilt, I touched them with the Unifier, confirmed that I wanted to restore the item in question at the cost of one charge, and then went momentarily blind from the bright flash. When the stars faded from my vision and I regained my sight, I beheld a painfully familiar item, whose double I'd used to kill an immense number of people. Lying at my feet, the dagger of Geranika seeped a sinister fog onto the glade around us.

Item acquired: 'Shadow Dagger of Teleportation.' Description: Opens portal to the Armard palace in the Empire of Shadow. Item class: Unique.

The negative aura of this item was so powerful that, in no time at all, not a single green tree survived within a radius of a hundred meters around us. The earth grew black, the trees shriveled to gnarled skeletons and, meanwhile, the fog continued to seep further and further, turning the forest around us into a part of the cursed Dark Forest. It was terrible to imagine what could've happened to my castle if we'd performed the unification inside of it.

"A powerful magic," Marina remarked, shaking her head in satisfaction. "I propose we sneak into one of Phoenix's castles. I'll bring some Mages tomorrow to charge the dagger."

"Will they be from Phoenix too?" I couldn't bridle my sarcasm.

"Donotpunnik and Hellfire will come with us," Marina went on, ignoring my barb. "The four of us will manage to sneak into the needed place."

Donotpunnik? Where'd he come from?

"The five of us," I tossed in my two cents, after suppressing my surprise at the Azure's mention. "Plinto's coming with us too."

"No!" Mirida cut me off. "Until we acquire the Tears, neither Plinto nor anyone else who has the opportunity or desire to share information with Phoenix will come with us. We didn't spend all this time planning this operation only to reveal it to Anastaria's lapdog at the last moment."

"WHAT?!"

"What you heard! Plinto has always been, is and will always be Anastaria's man. Whatever he says, whatever he does—Phoenix owns him down to his little toe...Do you need proof? You'll see it this evening. Just make sure to get in touch. I mean, Anastaria's his son's godmother! Who do you think he works for? Any more questions?"

"We'll need him in Armard," I said in a hollow voice. Even though, deep inside, the last vestiges of my belief in humanity had been dashed to pieces, I still didn't want to turn on my own clan. Plinto had to save the Emperor's wife and earn us additional bonuses. STOP! Why do I believe Marina at all? After her fable about my imprisonment, she's the last person that deserves my trust. Accordingly, what she's saying about Plinto could be a lie too.

"I can see you don't believe me. Fine. I call the Emperor as my witness to the truth of my words: Anastaria asked Plinto to come to an arrangement with you not to destroy the Legends of Barliona, since, as she put it, she needed it! Further, Anastaria is the godmother of his son. I permit the system to scan my memory. When Plinto was a member of the Dark Legion he regularly received directions from Anastaria about what to do in one situation or another...Is that enough for you to trust me?" Marina asked, smiling, as the white flame of truth engulfed her for a few moments. The Emperor had confirmed the girl's claims.

"That doesn't make him a lapdog," I insisted, despite the cracks that had appeared in my trust of the Rogue. "He needs to go to Armard for something other than the Tears. As soon as we reach the palace, he'll go off on his business. If we're lucky, Plinto will aggro most of the guards and our mission will be all the simpler for it. That is, if there are even guards in Armard, I suppose..."

"Of course there are guards in Armard. How could there not be? All right, I'll think about it. Any more requests? Are we taking anyone else?"

"Do you have any issues with Clutzer?" I asked

as my heart skipped a beat. I had finally obtained a unique opportunity to discover the truth about my raid leader, so I couldn't not use it. If he works for Anastaria too, then...

"His level is far too low," Marina shook her head, clearly offering her best argument against my Rogue.

"It's quite a bit higher than yours," I parried. Did she really have nothing on Clutzer?

"He's an ex-con."

"As am I, but you're taking me."

"All right, I'll let you know about Clutzer this evening too. Anything else?"

"That's it. You, Hellfire, Donotpunnik, Clutzer and me are the squad after the Tears. Plinto's after the wife of the Emperor."

"Who?" Mirida asked with surprise.

"It's a class quest for Rogues. Even if Plinto really is working for Anastaria, let him at least help my clan."

"STOP, YOU FOOLS!" The forest Guardian butted into our conversation, appearing to protect his domain from Shadow. The enormous Oak stopped at the perimeter ravished by the dagger, hesitating to set root on it. "YOU KNOW NOT WHAT YOU DO!"

"You have a jammer for Shadow items," said Marina, ignoring him and revealing how well apprised she was. "See if it works on the dagger..."

"I think it does," I concluded, tossing the dagger in my bag. The fog vanished almost instantly, green grass began to sprout through the soil, and the trees straightened out creaking and regaining their dense crowns. In the person of the Guardian, Barliona's nature was carefully licking the wound caused by the dagger of Shadow.

"We'll talk tonight on the secure channel," Marina repeated, casting a mocking glance at the angry Guardian who was busy straightening out his trees—then she dissolved, exiting to reality.

Okay, the time had come to have a good think on the topic of 'What the hell am I getting into?' But before that, I need to set up the comm channel. I'm incredibly curious to see what Marina will have for me...

I had no problems setting up the connection. The Omega operator confirmed the address and the port and literally ten minutes later the inscription 'Meeting at 20:00' appeared on my PC screen.

There was still plenty of time until then, so I opened the internet browser and began to brush up on my history. The history of Daniel Mahan.

The doom of waste collectors...A dirty day for the imitators...Hacker v. Imitator: 1–0...

The headlines about my feat of a year and a half ago struck me with their variety, though the content of their articles didn't offer much more substance. If you ignored the incessant anti-Imitator propaganda, there wasn't really much there—some guy did something, was punished and imprisoned so that others wouldn't ape him. The outrage and calls for blood had lasted only the first week until I surrendered myself. As soon as my trial began, everyone calmed down and forgot all about me. Which is a good thing—I'd rather not be remembered as the guy who trashed the city for the rest of my life.

What made me most nervous, however, was that Marina wasn't registered as a freelance artist anywhere. There were plenty of Marinas in the circles of those who looked for exploits in Barliona, but not one of them resembled the beauty that appeared at training 18 months ago. Moreover, the Corporation's official list of participants to the retraining for that ill-fated day contained no mention of a Marina either. Either she was never invited or she bypassed the official registration or I'm missing something here. A basic search unearthed Marina's previous training and the courses she had completed. After all was said and done, I had used precisely this information to develop my hack—and yet all the courses were marked as lasting until 'TBA.' Following the hack of the waste collector, Marina vanished from the web, turning into a ghost. On the off chance that I would recognize her from a photo, I combed through a list of anyone doing any retraining whatsoever on the day of our wager. Of these 138 women, some were registered as freelance artists and some weren't, yet not a single one of them looked like my acquaintance. Marina did not exist.

This begged the next question: What's going on? In our day and age, it's as difficult for an individual to vanish from the web as, say, sneak into a bank's central vault. The Imitators automatically recognize faces on any uploaded photos and embed links to personal pages on social media. Marina's page was utterly blank, virginal, as if no one had used it since its creation. Did Marina really have no friends? Did she not go to any parties that inevitably generated mountains of holograms, videos and similar dross— that would immediately be reshared by anyone involved? That can't be possible, and yet according to the web no one had seen Marina in the past year.

That cannot not worry me.

My hands reached for the communications device of their own volition, projecting a list of Corporation employees to my screen. Two million, three hundred thousand employees throughout the world, ignoring the cadres of freelance artists. An intimidating number! Our continent only had four hundred twenty thousand of them, of which seventy-two thousand were occupied with technical matters. That's a bit better. There were over a hundred Peters in this list, but even here a deep disappointment awaited me. Not one of these faces resembled Petruccio as his coworker had referred to him. God damn. What the hell kind of a day is this? No Marina and no Petruccio! Although the latter surely must be around here somewhere. No one would let some random stranger place prisoners in their capsules. And yet this person was not among the current personnel on the Corporation's website. Okay...What was Peter's partner's name? Damn! I have absolutely no idea!

STOP!

Current personnel!

What if Peter is no longer employed?

I didn't manage to find a list of the Corporation's former employees, but I did come across another no less interesting article: 'Technician commits suicide.' A black and white photograph of Peter, dressed in an oversized sweater, looked at me from my screen, as though asking: 'Why me?' According to the article, the guy had jumped off an office building as a result of a messy breakup—and spattered some innocent passersby in the process. These passersby turned out to be busybodies who sued the Corporation and were awarded damages for the inconvenience. And here the tale of Peter, a good guy and friend, came to a meek end.

Yet another thread that could have led me to Marina had been torn and torn so completely that there was no way for me to follow up.

I spent another while aimlessly looking at photos of Corporate employees, peering into the faces of the lucky few who led lives that were difficult but carefree. I managed to unearth a photo of James Boaster, manager of the innovations department. In his photo he looked a lot older than his avatar. I also stumbled across my old mentor, the one who had guided our small team in our assault on Barliona seven years ago. Dr. Samuel Provo, PhD, was now a senior specialist in the Corporation's department of IT security. I recognized him by the familiar look of condescension on his face, as if he'd seen the entire world and decided that he was the only source of reason and logic in it. Finally, I peered for a bit at Mr. Peter Johnson, the head of this entire mess. He looked like an ordinary person, not very tall, slightly doughy and balding. An average middle-manager type. It's hard to imagine that behind this unassuming face lay concealed a powerful analytic mind and the title of the most influential person on our planet. A long, long time ago, he had bet everything on his capsules and ended up becoming the...

Connection established...

The notification tore me away from my examination of the various actors behind the scenes of our world. I didn't allow my computer to transmit the video uplink, limiting my broadcast to audio, but the others didn't bother to play hide and seek. The screen split into four quarters, one of which remained black—that was mine. The other three frames were occupied by Marina, a young man of between 25 and 30, and Donotpunnik—old and in a wheelchair.

"Mahan, why don't you turn on your video

uplink?" Hellfire spoke up first, his fingers clicking through a rosary's beads. "I prefer to see who I'm talking to."

"Hell, how old are you anyway?" I blurted instead of responding when I realized that Hellfire, despite the years he'd spent in Barliona and his high rank, really was very young.

"Twenty-seven," the warrior replied proudly, clearly considering this one of his chief achievements. "I began when I was 15."

"Let's skip Hellfire's glorious past," Marina interrupted. "We have more important questions to discuss. Mahan, will you tell us why you ran off?"

"Didn't feel like sharing Petruccio's fate," I replied honestly.

"What Petruccio? What fate?" Donotpunnik creaked.

"It doesn't matter," Marina cut him off, then added: "But I understand your motive. Okay, we'll skip this topic and return to the one at hand. The Tears of Harrashess."

"The Tears can wait too," I interrupted Marina. "I've accumulated too many questions. If I don't get some answers to them, I won't do a thing."

"Ask away then," Donotpunnik smirked. "This is precisely why you can see us as well as this lovely girl."

"I'm sure my reasons for wanting to hurt Phoenix are familiar to everyone," I began. When all three nodded to the affirmative, I went on: "However, I'm utterly baffled by why Hellfire and Donotpunnik are here. When Hellfire suddenly appeared in Altameda, I thought that he'd been sent by Anastaria, who'd somehow managed to infer the situation from the scraps of info available to her. But it turns out that Hell, the second-ranked player in Phoenix, is actively pursuing the destruction of his own clan. Maybe it's me, but I'm picking up a little cognitive dissonance here—a surge of paranoia, if you will—and I'm beginning to imagine Anastaria grinning behind old Hell's back."

"In other words you have no qualms about me?" Donotpunnik smirked again. "And while you suspect that Hell is Anastaria's spy, you don't do the same for Plinto?"

"Plinto is a separate question. I'd like to get an answer to the question at hand first. And I wouldn't mind finding out your reasons for participating in this either, Marina. You know what I'm referring to."

"Then I will begin," Donotpunnik offered. "One way or another, this is my plan and I'll be the one to describe how it'll work. I've been plotting how to destroy Phoenix for the last five years. They were untouchable from the outside. In terms of resources, Phoenix exceeds my Azure Dragons by orders of magnitude."

"I thought the Azures were Undigit's clan?"

"Undigit is as much the head of my clan as

Plinto was the head of the Dark Legion. A temporary shell. A screen. I'm content to make the decisions and have Undies deal with the paperwork. Let the boy have his fun. Now then. It wasn't possible to destroy Phoenix from the outside, so I decided to do it from within. For that, I needed my own people inside the clan. Three years of searching led me to Hellfire and Marina. The former had a lot of authority in Phoenix, the latter had access to the developers. We conceived a plan and spent two years developing it to its logical conclusion. Phoenix will be deposed in short order."

"I still haven't understood the reasons for Hellfire's involvement."

"Tell me, do you know how many intercontinental clan competitions Phoenix has won in the past five years?" Hellfire spoke up.

"Zero?"

"Bingo! The players of other continents are busy developing their characters, leveling up, conquering new heights. At the same time, Phoenix has become a swamp that swallows everyone in it, turning them into self-satisfied and condescending morons! There is no such thing as a free ride! How many times did I tell them that they had to focus on the game instead of the game around the game? But Anastaria just laughed in my face. *My* face! The nonsense of a half-crazed boy—that's how she dismissed every proposal I came up with. She never took me seriously at the clan meetings, laughed at me, mocked me and whenever I was about to give her my reply, she'd hide behind her beloved daddy. When Donotpunnik offered to act as intermediary between me and the Smoldering Pine clan from the Celestial Empire, I was happy to agree to his terms. I won't reach the heights I deserve as long as I stay in Phoenix. The clan shall suffer the punishment for its mockery. And that is precisely why I'm here."

"Marina?"

"No need to look at me like that! Between these two, I'm the least involved. In the course of my everyday job, I earned some contacts among the Barliona developers. Herbert approached me with an offer to participate in this venture. I agreed to the incentives he was offering and so here I am."

"Herbert?"

"I prefer to be called Donotpunnik," wheezed the old man. "I've gotten quite used to my handle over the last ten years."

"So who was the old man that introduced me to the plot?"

"A hired actor," Donotpunnik explained. "An ordinary actor. I didn't know what condition you were in after your release and decided to play it safe. We cooked up a story about a bloody revenge motivated by the sorrows of an old man. Basically we had to do whatever it took to get you to work with him—and abandon any plans of reconciling with Anastaria. Now that you're clearly with us, I see no further reason in hiding."

"Onto the question of my imprisonment then. Marina?"

"It was the only option I had to ensure that the people with the skills I needed remain in Barliona," Donotpunnik explained in the girl's stead. "So I engineered events in a manner that would land you in prison."

"What?!"

"Who were you before your imprisonment? A freelance artist earning forty thousand credits a month? A hacker jealously guarding his talents? A player who'd managed a measly 86 levels in three years of gameplay? Do you really prefer the young man of back then—one in the full flower of youth but without any opportunities for development—to the man you are today—one of the most promising Shamans of our continent? Now you're the head of an enormous clan with as many unique items and bonuses as a pine has needles. A financially independent person with the ability to hire a security firm at will. Don't you like this? Well so and there you have it! There's no need to grandstand and play the victim. Half a year in the mines was merely your down payment for the fortune you now enjoy. Enjoy your new life!"

"In that case, why did Marina show up and feed me a fairy tale about our bet? Why suggest that I ask lawyers to reexamine my case?"

"Because a certain someone couldn't trust his allies and escaped their protection," Herbert said tersely. "Did you think that Phoenix would let you go so easily? After everything you had done? Hah! Anastaria's people were watching you from the moment you were released. They led you on like a rabbit! It's dangerous to speak openly in Barliona—when the investigation begins, they'll dig up all your conversations. Hence the fairy tale as you call it. We needed you to get used to the idea that Marina is a part of your clan, that she is someone you could trust. It would've worked too, if it weren't for the pendant. You weren't supposed to know that Hellfire and Marina were dating. So I decided to reveal my hand and speak with you openly. I was tired of constantly adapting my plans to fit your exploits."

"Why me?"

"Because you were the first. We only found ten people capable of following the way of the creator and becoming Shamans. Three gave up, two didn't pass the final mine, four never created anything and you were the only one left. That's why we're talking to you right now and not some other guy."

"You sent another nine people to prison?!"

"This is war!" Donotpunnik cut me off. "There must always be casualties in war. You understand. No one barred them from making the same journey as you. They didn't make it, so it's not even worth thinking about them!"

"This isn't a war. This is some kind of madness!" I muttered in shock. The brief time I'd known Donotpunnik I considered him a decent person, but now I was realizing that I was talking to a madman. And he wanted us to work together? Like hell!

"This is war, kid. A true war, and it's time you decide whose side you're on. If you're not with us, you're against us."

"Are you threatening me?"

"Our conversation is starting to get off topic," Marina spoke up, before Donotpunnik could answer. "No one is threatening anyone. We have a common goal that we want to achieve. You've heard our motives and we understand yours. We won't be working together for long, merely until we give the Tears to Phoenix's leaders. Let's try and be constructive. Daniel, do you have any further questions?"

"Three Tears won't mean much to Phoenix," I said, trying to squash my anger.

"This is precisely why we've increased their number to thirty. After activation, you'll hand one Tear to Hellfire. His stats will double and he'll be able to convince Ehkiller to equip his best Raiders with them. You'll hand them the activated Tears and at that point the Phoenix clan will become the best in the world. You can charge five hundred million per tear. Lastly, you'll cite the help that Hell has provided you with as the reason for why you've given him one for free. Are there any questions?"

"Why would you want to make Phoenix the best clan in the world?" To be honest, I was pretty surprised. "I heard a completely different description of the Tears, which suggested that they do immense harm to the players that possess them."

"The Tears cannot be unequipped," Donotpunnik explained. "Let them be gods temporarily. It'll only be temporarily. After we've made sure that all thirty have equipped the Tears, we'll use Geranika to activate the Tears' other properties—the ones you've already heard about. At that point, all of Phoenix's Raiders will be incapacitated. All of their majesty will crumble and all their heroes will become mere dolls. That will be a mighty blow indeed!"

"Phoenix will complain to the admins."

"Good! There will still be the Salva. That's why we need you."

"There's only one thing I don't get—how are you going to make sure that Geranika does what you want? Any step the developers make is checked several times. Their own security service will eat them alive. I like your idea, but it seems that it's doomed to fail from the outset. And I don't feel like joining a project that's doomed from the start."

"You're right about the security service. They could easily throw a spanner in the works—if of course we don't have our own people among them," Marina smiled. "Think about it, Daniel. How do you think we found you? Who knew that you had the premonition you have? Who could arrange it so you were assigned the Shaman class?"

"Hello, wanderer!" The black quarter of the screen began to waver and a new member of the anti-Phoenix conspiracy came into focus. Samuel Provo, PhD. The mentor who had taught me everything I knew. The same mentor who had once betrayed me.

"You?!" I blurted out.

"Why, whom did you expect? Santa Claus? Santa Claus wouldn't send you a faulty technical portal in Dolma! You thought someone had just left it there? Hah! That was my first successful attempt at modifying the game. Beatwick, the Dungeon, the title of Earl. I led you like my own son, providing you with everything you needed and helping you overcome the obstacles you encountered. I never forgot what you did for me, Daniel, and now I'm doing everything I can to settle the debt I owe you. Soon the day will come when we will be even."

"Now do you understand how serious we are, Dan?" Marina raised an eyebrow. "We've almost completed the entire journey. There's not much left and we need your help. We've laid all our cards on the table. All that's left is to deliver the final blow!"

"Plinto. What about him?" I managed with difficulty. To say that I was shocked wouldn't be saying anything. A senior security specialist is far from an entry-level position in the Corporation. If he's in on this plot, the scale of the conspiracy must be immense indeed.

"He's been with Anastaria from day one. Once upon a time he was in Phoenix, but Ehkiller and Evolett decided that it'd be better to turn him into a hell-raiser and unite all of Barliona's riffraff behind him. That's how he became the head of the Dark Legion."

"He sends reports about your clan to Ehkiller regularly," Hellfire added. "How many, where, who, what and why. In vivid detail. How do you think I have the coordinates to Altameda? You think I found out from Dr. Provo? Why run the risk? Plinto spilled them like a good lapdog. The last six months you've been surrounded by players from Phoenix, Mahan. Anastaria's said several times that the main goal is to open the Tomb and strip you of everything. How much did you lose on the Imperial Steel? Tens of millions! If the opportunity had presented itself, Anastaria would have taken it for free, but there were limits even for her. Clutzer, that is."

"Plinto's coming to Armard with us," I said, stubbornly ignoring the facts before me. "I need the bonuses that he'll get there. And I don't care if he's Anastaria's man. Those bonuses will be mine."

"One of my Rogues will go with him," Donotpunnik agreed. "To be honest, I forgot about the Emperor's wife. Thanks for the reminder. I'm not opposed—Plinto will help us earn the bonuses that'll allow us to beat Phoenix too. Furthermore, three of my Mages will activate the portal and, as soon as we get the Tears, they'll start to summon our men to Armard. Only mine—I'm not about to share that loot with anyone else."

"I don't agree. I couldn't care less about your clan's relationship with Phoenix, but think for yourself—when the investigation gets going, and you know it will, some genius will be sure to notice that the Emperor's wife was rescued by both clans—while even though I was the one who cast the portal to Armard, only some Azure Dragons went with me. Any intelligent person would suspect foul play and start digging further. It's your call, of course, but I would only go there with both clans after signing some kind of contract. In my view, that'll insulate us from any unnecessary prying or investigations."

"I'll think about it," grunted Donotpunnik. "What do you need Clutzer for?"

"I don't know," I replied honestly. "I simply feel that he'll come in handy tomorrow. Won't the Rogue's stealth shroud help us stay hidden?"

"I purchased scrolls of stealth for the very purpose."

"Let him come," Samuel intervened. "It's better not to argue with Mahan about this. If his premonition tells him he needs to bring the Rogue, it's better to bring him. It'll be cheaper in the end."

"Sam, I have a question for you too. Of the

things I've earned and achieved in this game, what were you involved in? I mean, my premonition, the chess set or the other items I've crafted?"

"None of the above. I can't intervene in the gaming process to that degree. I can only help indirectly. Adjust this, loosen that, boost the probability of something happening, delay a Herald—that kind of thing."

"In that case," I said, trying to conceal the trembling that had fully spread across my body. It was a good thing that I hadn't turned on my video channel! "I'm done! We'll meet tomorrow."

"Mahan, what do you need three scrolls of Armageddon for?" Donotpunnik asked before I could disconnect.

"I don't know yet. I was planning on setting them off inside Phoenix's castle, but I'm getting the impression that three scrolls won't be enough. If I had another two, I'd smash the castle to smithereens for sure. You don't have an extra one by any chance?"

"You want to set them off inside the castle?" Donotpunnik frowned. "It's an interesting idea, but how are you going to activate them. You'll have to be in battle for a minute before you can cast them, and during that time Phoenix's defenses will destroy you and anyone with you."

"Plinto. Even if he works for Phoenix, he owes me. This will be his payment. No matter how elaborate the castle's defenses are, Plinto should be able to hold out a minute. I'll strengthen him with buffs, load him up with scrolls of healing and send him in to cause a ruckus in the castle. But three Armageddon's won't be enough to raze it down to Level 1. I need two more. Don't you want to knock Phoenix off their perch, Donotpunnik? Destroying their main castle will go a long way to doing that. I'm certain they have remote storage vaults..."

"Which they'll lose access to until their castle reaches Level 20 again!" the old man smiled revoltingly. "You shall have two more scrolls tomorrow morning. No one's ever set off five Armageddons at once before...An explosion that big might even kill the Emperor himself, let alone knock down some castle! But there's something else that concerns me—why would Evolett give them to you?"

"I didn't ask him personally, but I'd guess that the brothers had a falling out."

"Yes," Hellfire spoke up, "at our meetings lately, Killer hasn't missed a chance to trash Evolett as hard as he can. I think Mahan is right—something happened between the brothers."

"Too bad for them then. If there aren't any further questions, I suggest we start getting ready for tomorrow's mission. Dr. Provo, please check one more time that the Tears are at the proper location. Marina, your warriors will have to be ready and..."

Connection lost...

Oh boy!

What had I gotten myself into?! What stage of insanity does one have to be at to spend five years on planning the destruction of an enemy clan?! To sink immense resources into this plot, find the people you need, arrange the imprisonment of ten innocent poor bastards, only to discard the nine that turned out useless, adjust the game's code—and all for what? To earn first place in the clan rankings? To satisfy Donotpunnik's ambitions of world domination? To find a new clan for Hellfire?

So what are Samuel and Marina working for then? For money? I couldn't even imagine how much you'd have to pay them for something like this. If someone finds out that they're involved...

Erm...

What a good idea it was to run away! Why did they suddenly reveal the other two conspirators today? Why reveal to me that they had hacked Barliona to achieve their desired result? Wasn't I about to become useless to them? As soon as Phoenix buys the Tears, Shaman Mahan will become useless! Not even that—I'd become a nuisance at best and dangerous at worst—someone who knew too much. What happens to dangerous people? They're discarded to oblivion! The kind of oblivion that causes them to forget themselves too! Hadn't they openly told me that I'm a pawn that has just about completed the task it was needed for?

And yet I had escaped from their sight. They

wouldn't find me!

And yet at the same time, although they know that I'm hiding from them, they seem so completely calm about it as if I'm right there within arm's reach...It can't be!

"This is the Omega operator."

"I'd like to move to a new location. What do I have to do?"

"Your request has been received. Tomorrow our associate will get in touch with you to discuss the details."

"I want to do it today!"

"Unfortunately, it is impossible to arrange a relocation today. We do not have a residence prepared for you. Please wait until tomorrow."

This simply can't be!

"Put me in touch with the police," I made a final attempt to check my hunch. "I need to verify my current status."

"Unfortunately, we cannot fulfill your request. The police desk for general inquiries operates between the hours of 9 a.m. and 6 p.m. The desk has closed for today."

"Call the emergency line! It's always operational."

"Please accept our apologies, but that is not possible. Our company will be fined for a baseless call, negatively impacting our reputation. You are not in any danger at the moment, so there is no reason to worry. Were you told something on the closed channel that gives you cause to worry for your life?"

"I want to leave. Right this instant!" I almost had a panic attack when I realized that I was trapped in these four walls. "I am terminating our contract!"

"Pursuant to item 14.3 of the current Contract, you may leave our custody only 24 hours after you have issued the relevant request. Your request has been received. We ask that you wait until tomorrow, so that we may arrange your proper release. Thank you for using our services. All the best!"

"I won't get into my capsule tomorrow!" I barked angrily into the silent handset. "You can forget about that portal!"

Despite the rancor in my voice, the only reply was silence. Neither Donotpunnik nor the operator replied to my threat.

Well they can go to hell tomorrow instead of Armard. If they don't want to play nice, I'll play mean. With this thought, I slipped away into sleep.

* * *

"Good morning, Daniel," the girl's voice awoke me. "You have submitted a request to terminate our contract. Please tell me, would it be convenient for you to terminate it right now? We will transport you to any location you choose. Thank you for using our company's services, and please accept our apologies for the conduct of our operator yesterday. He was not authorized to refuse your request for termination and relocation. Please sign here and here," she offered me a tablet, "to confirm that our services have been duly performed. We will send you an invoice within three days."

Oops!

"Hold on," I began to backpedal, "I was upset yesterday and maybe said something I shouldn't have. Can I step out to the street? Even for a minute?"

"As our client or as our former client?" the girl clarified.

"As a client."

"In that case, please give us five minutes. We must ensure your security...Right this way," the girl said after a few minutes. "Over here."

The door of an ordinary apartment building in which I had been living led me to a likewise ordinary courtyard. It could have been in any neighborhood in the city—a playground full of children running here and there. Their mothers, chattering about this or that, and a surly street sweeper kicking up the dust with his broom. It's strange to think that humans have grasped the deepest secrets of the mind, but the streets are still swept by street sweepers in yellow vests. Capsules, high-speed networks, Imitators...A long stick with branches tied onto it—this is the instrument of the true son of humanity.

"Daniel, excuse me for interrupting, but we need to head back in. Will you be terminating our contract?"

"No," I shook my head, understanding that I wasn't trapped in the cellar of someone's house but living calmly on the third floor of a typical apartment building. "But I'd like to change locations. I suspect that the current address is known to people beyond your organization."

"Do you wish the new residence to be equipped in a similar way?"

"Yes."

"We will need two days to get everything ready. In the meantime we can tighten your security—if you suspect that your location is known to someone. What do you think?"

"I'm all about it!"

"Understood. Your request is being processed. I'd like to apologize once again for the conduct of our associate. It will not happen again. We value long-term collaboration with our clients."

ENTER!

"Everything's ready, Mahan. We can begin." No sooner had I entered the game, than Donotpunnik got in touch with me. Whether or not he knew where I lived didn't matter. In two days I'd vanish for good and not even show up in Barliona. I'd spend a month or two reading books and getting a tan on some beach. I'd find a girl and live the high life. It's incredibly easy for a thirty-three year old to entertain himself. Barliona isn't the only interesting thing in the world. "Summon Plinto and Clutzer—they're coming with us. I'll send you the contract between our clans in a second. Read it, study it, and sign it. We're about to make history..."

Achievement unlocked: 'Armard is no place for newbies.' You have reached the palace in the capital of Shadow. Speak with the Emperor to find out what your reward is.

You have received a ticket for two to an audience with the Emperor. You may claim it in any branch of the Barliona Bank.

"Cast the shroud of stealth, Clutzer," Donotpunnik ordered, carefully examining the area that our portal had brought us to. The small meeting hall, in the middle of which stood a rectangular table with an armchair at its head, was illuminated by a dim torch. The air here was so stale that it was evident that this place was used very infrequently. If it had ever been used at all.

"Plinto, Unpal—you know your objective. Get to it. Mirida—make us a path. You three," Donotpunnik turned to his Mages, "hide yourselves and pretend you're statues. Do whatever you like, but the portal has to survive until we return. Off we go!"

The two Rogues dissolved in thin air, setting off in search of the Emperor's wife, while we moved to the hall's exit, concealed under Clutzer's shroud of stealth. In theory, an NPC would be able to see us only if he came within arm's length from us. How the shroud actually works in practice, no one knew, since no one had tried to use it against Shadow in a Shadow palace. According to Donotpunnik, it wasn't possible to sneak into Armard under the shroud, but the rules should be different in the palace. At least, I really hope they are...

I wouldn't exactly call Geranika's residence beautiful or unique. All the walls were bare stone that no one had ever finished with plaster, and what little ornament there was, was wholly perfunctory. The part of the palace we were in lacked anything that didn't have some rational function. Even the torches illuminating the corridor we were sneaking along were arranged in a manner that allowed them to illuminate the largest area possible with the least amount of torches.

"We're in the upper levels," Marina remarked when the corridor led us to a second hall, which unlike the first one had windows. Armard stretched out before us like in the palms of our hands. In the distance, by the walls we could see the flashes of spells going off. The players were trying to capture the capital of Shadow by storm. "We need to descend."

"The loot's a bit underwhelming here," Clutzer wrinkled his nose, not forgetting to maintain the cloak. "Can't even pry anything loose."

"Agreed. I never figured the devs for ascetics."

"Why decorate a place that no player will ever visit?" Hellfire theorized. "Even if the players managed to enter Armard, no one would come here. They wouldn't have the guts."

"Does that mean that there may be loot down below?" Clutzer asked hopefully. "What are we standing for? Who are we waiting for?"

We passed through another two empty chambers before we found an open door with a staircase descending beyond it. Judging by the broken lockpicks lying on the floor next to it, Plinto and Unpal had already been here.

"Here's your loot," grinned Hellfire, indicating the fragments to Clutzer. Then, he grew serious and asked: "How is your lockpicking skill?"

"Seventy-two levels until I reach Apprentice level," Clutzer confessed sincerely. "I could handle this lock, but I'm not sure about the ones beyond it. I imagine that..."

DONG!

The palace resounded from the deafening tolling of a bell. Even the walls shook.

"*Donotpunnik, your Rogue is as dumb as a bag of dumbbells!*" Plinto announced in the raid chat as Unpal's frame went gray—the player had been sent to respawn. "*You should kick him out of your clan for being an armless moron. He actually tried to kill*

Geranika! Go down the stairs, it'll lead you to a corridor. Geranika's hall is straight ahead. The guards have been alerted, so be careful. The guard nearest to you is directly next to the exit from the stairwell. To the left. A big old stone fellow of Level 300. The shroud of stealth should get you through. I'm going to keep moving."

The enemy has breached our palace! Rally the defenders of Shadow! Guards, awake from your ancient slumber! The palace must be defended! Rally the defenders of Shadow!

CHAPTER ELEVEN
THE TEARS OF HARRASHESS

"**W**E NEED TO DESCEND TO THE DUNGEON," Marina typed in the raid chat. Like the rest of us, the girl was pressing herself to the wall in the hopes of dissolving in its stony embrace and thereby ensure that the squad of Level 300 iron hulks who were now wandering all around the palace would pass us by without notice. The guards tarried a few moments beside us as if they had sensed something, but then went on with their patrol. If avatars in Barliona had hearts as accessories, ours would have burst from the tension. But everything turned out okay—the shroud of stealth that Level 228 Clutzer had cast over us did its job flawlessly. Given the nearly 100 level difference, all the mobs had to do was loiter and sniff around us a little longer, yet they had moved on. I can't even imagine what would happen if we stumbled across some Level 350 monster. Donotpunnik's scrolls were Level 180 and wouldn't have an effect, and Clutzer's shroud wouldn't work against such high-level boys, so all that'd await us would be a long a tortuous wait to respawn.

"*Do you know where the exit is?*" Hellfire asked.

"*If you need to go down, you'll have to go through the throne room with Geranika,*" Plinto replied from some nook in the palace. He was on his own now. "*Be careful in there—it's full of 'old timers.' In fact, let me help you get through it—if we use my shroud of stealth, only Geranika will be able to detect us. But we haven't come here to fight him anyway. Right, Donotpunnik?*"

"*All right,*" Donotpunnik agreed unwillingly, exchanging an uneasy glance with Marina. "*We'll wait for you at the entrance to the throne room.*"

"I'm already here," the Rogue whispered right behind us. "There aren't any survivors left in the dungeon, so I figured I'd go check out the upstairs."

"You already went through the entire dungeon?" Marina asked with concern.

"In the immortal words of Mahan—uh-huh. If you sneak past two Level 400 guards, you'll reach the Armard treasure vault. They haven't yet relocated it beyond the palace walls. The gold and gems are inaccessible, but the items...Everyone shut up! I'm casting my shroud."

Another cavalcade of guards turned the corner; however, with Plinto's shroud now over us, they didn't even sense anything and walked straight past.

"Let's hug it out friends!" Plinto embraced me and Marina, and only then replied to Marina's questioning glance: "The closer we are to each other, the less chance they'll have of detecting us. Level 400 guards won't see me, but they'll sense you two if you're at the edge of the shroud. Do we really need that? I doubt it, which is why I recommend hugging it out. Get in here, Hellfire. I'll make sure to take a selfie later: Plinto and Hellfire, BFFs four evah."

"You know where you can take your selfie, right?" Hellfire growled glumly.

"Yes! In fact I was planning on framing and hanging it in there..." Plinto replied glibly, drawing an angry scowl from Hellfire. The strange thing was that I had grown accustomed to Hellfire's impassivity. In my view, the Warrior was utterly unshakable, and yet there was something deeper that linked him with Plinto—something that forced Hellfire to hear the Rogue's jibes. Moreover—he actually heeded them. And growled as a consequence. Was it possible that Hell was jealous? His reaction didn't resemble anything else. Surely this was run-of-the-mill envy of Plinto's new position as the highest-level player on our continent. The Rogue had stripped Hellfire from the title that Hell had proudly borne for the last five years.

"Ladies, let's figure out our relationships on our second date," Donotpunnik intervened tersely. "Plinto's right. We need to stick close together."

"Hear that, team? Huddle up," Plinto echoed once again sweeping Marina and me into an embrace. "Hugsies!"

"Shut up, Plinto," said Donotpunnik. "Your job is to lead us through the throne room. Stop clowning around."

The Armard throne room was an awesome sight. What had happened to the Spartan furnishings of the rest of the place? A sumptuous, alabaster throne stood in the center of the chamber with Geranika looming upon it. The throne was surrounded by a crowd of subjects, humanoid sentients all wrapped in lengthy gray cloaks, standing ankle-deep in a plush carpet with an abstract ornament. I say humanoid because they generally seemed to have two legs and two arms. Yet the color and shape of their wrists, peeking from their cloaks, bore no resemblance to human hands—even if from a distance the overall shapes of their bodies were human enough. But only in part. Some of them had so many appendages that my eyes couldn't keep up with all their myriad, tireless contortions and begged to look away. Others were simply a roiling morass of tentacles. Ten, twenty, thirty—the exact number of appendages was impossible to count, since they'd appear and vanish beneath the cloaks. These Level 450 fellows were called 'Hadjeis' and I made a mental note to look up some information about them. It's worth knowing who would be Geranika's Advisors and Heralds, after all.

"Your Lordship has summoned me and I have obeyed." The Hadjei's voice sounded like Styrofoam being rubbed across clean glass. Just as revolting and irritating, it caused a shiver in my body and made me want only one thing—to run away from its owner. And to add injury to insult, it immediately cast debuffs on anyone within hearing range, which slowed movement, increased weariness, accelerated Energy expenditure, and decreased main stats. Reflexively, I reached for my staff so I could summon a Curing Spirit, but Plinto pressed me to himself tighter, keeping me from moving. The look that the Rogue gave me was so expressive that I decided my afflicted status could wait.

"Geranika's aggro radius is twenty meters, so he won't notice us if we stick to the wall," Plinto wrote in the raid chat.

"What news of my Dragon?" Geranika asked majestically, almost imperially. A single glance at the Shaman was enough to tell me that James Boaster hadn't lied to me. Geranika really had become a new Emperor. From now on the players would have a different enemy—the Dragon of Shadow. Geranika had played his role to a T.

"He is still being nursed back to full health," squealed the Hadjei, "only slower than we had planned. He spent too long in the Dragon's flame. We have restored forty percent of his scales, but we lack the resources to continue."

"WHAT?!" Geranika hadn't raised his voice, and yet his silent roar made us freeze like statues—a minute-long 'Stop' debuff waved at us cheerfully. "You dare tell me that I haven't the resources to restore my Dragon?!"

"Yes, your Lordship, I do," the Hadjei replied unfazed. "We have exhausted our reserves of Imperial Steel—one of the main ingredients for forging Dragon Scales. We need too much of it to make a single Scale. Both of our mines are working around the clock, but the resource is simply too scarce. At this rate it will take us seven years to restore the Dragon."

"What do you propose?" asked Geranika, narrowing his eyes. "You wouldn't dare appear before me without having a plan."

"Your Lordship, I propose we purchase the Imperial Steel from the Free Citizens. There are plenty of Free Citizens in Malabar and Kartoss who couldn't care less about their reputations with their Empires."

"And what will we offer in return?"

"Gold. The Free Citizens love gold. We need three hundred thousand stacks of steel."

"But that's...Do we have that much?"

"Yes, your Lordship!"

"Send out the messengers and spies. Ensure that the Free Citizens hear our offer this very day," Geranika decided. "Gold is useless to us. When I have my Dragon, both Empires shall fall on their knees and beg me to take their treasures. What about the prisoners?"

"Nothing. They refuse to talk. I request your permission to torture them."

"I need them alive," Geranika shook his head. "It's much nicer to negotiate with the Dark Lord when I hold all his aces in my hand."

"You never negotiated before."

"Before, I wasn't..."

"Brother!" another sentient burst into the throne room, scattering the guards like bowling pins. We had only snuck halfway through and so pressed ourselves to the wall again, freezing for the moment. Shiam! "The Foe is in the palace!"

"You're a bit late, Shiam," Geranika smirked. "The fool had the temerity to hide himself in the throne room. I have destroyed him already. Myself!"

"No, brother! I'm not talking about some stray Rogue or even a crowd of Rogues—if there are even any in the palace. In fact, I couldn't care less about anyone—except for the Foe!"

"The Foe?" Geranika frowned. "You mean *the* Foe?"

"Oh yes!" Shiam replied sadistically. "I mean the Foe. You know who I mean. The shades have told me that he is hiding in the palace."

"Sounds like there's a fluffy teddy waiting for you, Mahan!" smirked Clutzer. *"They're about to start hunting the Dragon!"*

"Then the prophecy is coming true," Geranika remarked, rising from his throne. "The Vampire is in the palace. Lock the gates! I will personally scour the palace from top to bottom! Thank you for the news, brother!"

"Plinto?!" We all turned to look at the astonished Rogue, who was still pressing Marina to himself and hadn't yet shut his mouth from shock. A moment passed as Geranika and his people filed out of the throne room and shut the doors noisily behind them. We were left alone.

"I have an idea—let's send our Mages further away from here," I offered, drawing everyone's attention away from Plinto. "If Geranika finds them, we won't be able to teleport to this palace anymore. They'll place guards in every room and then we can forget about sneaking in here again. Would we really want that?"

"What's the difference?" Clutzer asked. "If they find the portal, they'll alert the guards anyway."

"Only players can see that portal," Donnotpunnik explained, agreeing with my idea. "All right. I've told them to leave. We'll leave the battle for the palace till tomorrow."

"All right, there's nothing for you all to fear anymore," said Plinto, pensively glancing at the closed doors. "You can make it the rest of the way with Clutzer's shroud. Damn it! There's no way that there's only one exit here!"

The Rogue cloaked and began to scurry from wall to wall. I could be mistaken, but I was sensing a bit of anxiety coming from Plinto—it's not every day that the Lord of Shadow decides to hunt you personally. According to Plinto, there were Level 400 guards below us, who should have run off to look for the Vampire in the palace, thereby clearing our way. Good luck to them all! Even Geranika's advanced Imitator hadn't guessed that the Vampire was a mere arm's length away in his own throne room.

"Check it out, Mahan," Clutzer whispered, pointing at Geranika's empty throne. "Do you think Geranika will be miffed if we carefully expropriate that scepter?"

"What a roundabout way to put it," I replied in the same whisper, approaching the alabaster throne. "Just say what you mean: 'Let's gank that there stick.'"

"This way, Mahan," Donotpunnik gestured at a concealed passage beside the far wall, but I didn't hurry to follow the Death Knight. Clutzer's right—it's unforgivable to visit Armard palace and not pick up a souvenir. Geranika's scepter was little more than a small iron crop with a bulb for a pommel. It looked very out of place in this sumptuous throne room. There were no gems or ornaments or inscriptions on it. A simple rod that could come in handy if you wanted to whip someone. Surely Geranika wouldn't miss it!

Item acquired: Scepter of Power. Description: Hidden. Properties. Hidden. Item class: Relic. Restrictions: Level 500+. To read the properties, please speak to the Creator.

"Mahan, I think you need to get out of here quick," Clutzer scratched his head when the entire palace resounded with an enormous:

DONG!

The Relic has been stolen!

"Why me?" I managed to inquire to no one in particular, as Clutzer pushed me to the door leading to the dungeon.

"Plinto, shroud him!" he yelled. "Geranika's about to show up! I'll lead him out of the hall!"

Not thinking too long, Clutzer engaged Acceleration I and rushed to the door.

"WHO DARES?!" This time Geranika did raise his voice and I was immediately bolted to the floor, frozen like a granite statue. Out of the corner of my eyes, I noticed Clutzer darting for the door. Had he managed to escape or not? "STOP HIM!"

"Mahan, didn't your parents teach you not to take other people's stuff?" Plinto's mocking voice sounded right in my ear. Geranika's special spell was 'Stop.' An ancient RPG spell that simply paralyzed everyone and everything. I'm afraid someone forgot to tell Plinto, however. In any event, the Rogue didn't care that he was the only player, aside from Clutzer who had slipped out, who could still move. Grabbing me like a doll, Plinto began to carefully retreat in the direction of the treasure vault, still maintaining his shroud of stealth over us.

"Do you know what you and I are about to do?"

he went on whispering, risking detection by Geranika. "We're about to betray that trio back there," the Rogue nodded in the direction of the three frozen statues— Hellfire, Donotpunnik and Mirida.

"*Why?*" Since I couldn't even speak, I had to type my question into the clan chat.

"Because otherwise, we're all goners," Plinto replied. "You shouldn't've taken Geranika's scepter. Oh, no. That was like a really, really bad idea."

"Your Lordship!" One of the Hadjeis circled the hall and stopped beside the frozen players. "There are more intruders here!"

"And now we will descend," Plinto decided, when Geranika looked over at the trio.

"*What the hell, Mahan?!*" The raid chat was filling with not very positive messages, so I dragged it further away from my immediate vision and relaxed. Plinto was calmly carrying me down the stairs and Geranika's debuff looked like it would expire in a few minutes, so I had plenty of time to think things over. I wonder what Donotpunnik is freaking out about. Did he say I couldn't steal anything? No? Well then he can go take a walk.

Donotpunnik's, Mirida's and Hellfire's frames went gray, showing that Geranika didn't waste too much time on them. The only question that remained was how he'd dealt with them—whether they'd respawn with some debuff or without it? If the trio still had some malus on them when they came back, they'd eat me alive. Little toe and all.

"Clutzer survived!" Plinto grinned when Geranika's Stop expired and I regained the ability to walk. "Three minutes forty seconds and he's still kicking. That a boy! I'll need to work with him a little more—he's going to be Rogue rookie of the year at this rate. Say, Mahan, what'd you need that iron rod for anyway?"

"It's a trophy," I grumbled. I didn't feel like admitting to Plinto that our plan was cracking at the seams. In fact, he wasn't supposed to know about the plan at all, lest he tell Anastaria everything...Oh to hell with all of them!

"Plinto, I have a question. But could you promise to answer it honestly and completely?"

"Unless you're planning on asking my account number and PIN—shoot. When you start a conversation, you always ask some dumb question. If you want to ask me how I can move despite Geranika's Stop spell—I have the Patriarch's tooth. I can't be stopped."

"What's the difference how you avoided the Stop? I want to know something else. I've heard that you are Anastaria's man. That she's your son's godmother. That you worked in the Dark Legion entirely on her orders. That you joined my clan because Anastaria asked you to. That you reported daily to Phoenix about my clan. That you..."

"I see. That I am Anastaria's lapdog. Is that what

you wanted to say?" Plinto smirked, and yet there wasn't the slightest note of laughter in his tone. I had never seen the Rogue so serious since...well, I'd never seen him so serious and composed at all.

"That's it. That's exactly what they said you were."

"And by 'they' you mean Hellfire and Donotpunnik. The two people that Anastaria has relied on the most over the past five years. Doesn't that seem strange to you?"

"...?"

"I won't beat around the bush. Everything you just said is the truth. Stacey really is my son's godmother. I really was, am and will be her person, since it was Stacey who brought me into this game. I really did join your clan at her request..."

"I was the one who let you in," I objected, but Plinto was quick to parry:

"You were played like child. Anastaria arranged a small scene with the phoenix reins—which were supposedly owed to me. You showed up and simply bought it. Do you really think that I didn't have five million gold? Mahan, I never thought you were so naïve. Stacey asked me to look after you and protect you from any danger, so that you could craft in peace."

"Craft?!"

"Quiet! Don't forget where we are. You were issued a simple objective—craft the Chess Set and thereby the entrance to the Tomb. That's why I was asked to join your clan. In effect, that's why I didn't go to Kartoss."

"In other words, you're like them," I said in a mournful voice, striking Plinto from my list of trusted people. Lately this list had really grown sparse—currently, there were only three names on it: Draco, Fleita and myself. If my student betrays me too, then...

"Let me repeat my question—two people that Anastaria has relied on the past five years, betray me to you. As Anastaria's spy, if I understood correctly. You don't find anything strange about this? And this is all done in such a particular way, that I can't do anything but admit that they're right. Donnotpunnik has always articulated his thoughts in a way that makes it difficult to get at the truth. Anastaria considers you to be a smart person—so, think, why would they need this?"

"To protect me from knowing too much," I forced out, glancing into the first room: mountains of gold, gems and chests. If the Tears are in here, I'll spend a long time looking for them.

"What caring little mommies. They think of nothing but how to take care of their little darling."

"Plinto, you..." I stuttered because it was very difficult to speak. I had believed up until the last moment that he was with me simply because he was with me—like Portos who fought simply because he fought. The truth had turned out much more banal and unpleasant, so now I didn't know what to say. The most repulsive thing was that my mind had grasped that Plinto was a traitor, while my premonition went on screaming that I could trust the Rogue. That he'd never betray me. A repulsive feeling indeed.

"One more time. Try to use your head, Mahan. Just consider why Donotpunnik and Hellfire would want this. What difference does it make how I ended up in your clan? Think about why the others told you about it."

"Why did you stay in the clan after the scene in front of the Tomb?" I asked Plinto, finding the strength to push past my emotions. Barliona is a game with real money and therefore betrayal is about as natural here as the sun's progress across the heavens. You can't make a lot of money without either. Everyone betrays, the only question is what triggers the betrayal. For some, it's titles, love, the desire to stand out, money, items…Whatever. And every traitor accepts his own criteria for betrayal. The criteria that he's willing to come to terms with. I need to come to terms with Plinto and my feelings about him. I'll think about the others later.

"Why'd I stay?" Plinto smirked. For a moment he remained staring at the wall, as if looking for an answer there, and finally he went on: "Because that was the right thing to do. Because both you and

Anastaria need to be saved. That very evening I went to see Anastaria and I asked her a simple question: 'Why?' Do you know what her answer was? Keep in mind, if Anastaria finds out about this, I'm done for. Her answer was a fit, a tantrum, a freak out—from which I could make out only several coherent phrases: 'I'm a bitch,' 'I betrayed him,' 'I don't feel good,' and 'I love him.' Was she acting? Possibly. But it was then that I decided to help you remain in the game and force you to consider the situation. It's not up to me to tell you about how contrived and inauthentic the events in front of the Tomb were—you have to see them for yourself. You asked yourself why Stacey acted the way she did. Could she not have warned you? She could have. But for some reason she didn't. What's the next logical question? That's right— 'Why?' And then you return to your first question: Why did Hellfire and Donnotpunnik tell you about me now?"

"Was it you who leaked Altameda's coordinates to Phoenix?"

"No, Mahan. You're sick and need help."

"Yes or no?!"

"No, it wasn't me. You might as well know, oh great conspiracy theorist, that the coordinates of the main clan castles are public information. Not for the entire public, of course, but certainly a portion of it. That's precisely why main castles are generally used as a base or headquarters but never as the storage facilities. When you gain the access, stop by the Imperial library and glance in the 'Castles' book, one of its last pages. I think you'll be very surprised to read about your Altameda in there. And the castle's coordinates are automatically updated after every jump you make. In any case, that's how I found your castle after you ran off."

"Why didn't you tell me this earlier?" I asked surprised.

"Because you never asked," the Rogue shrugged. "I've been playing much longer than you and know a whole host of things that you'd never even think to ask. If I were to start telling you everything I know, we'll be here for years. Do you have that much time? Oh, this one's locked!"

Plinto produced his lockpicks and began to poke around the keyhole. I was standing over him and, given that I had a moment, began to think. Any way you spin it, Plinto's right—I need to consider what Donnotpunnik needed me for. He could easily pull off this entire operation without me. And yet not only was I let in on the secret, but even introduced to the main conspirators—thereby demonstrating their utter faith in me. It's as if Donotpunnik knew that I wouldn't run to the police and would stay with him through the end of his plot. But why trust me so much? Let's assume the worst: It's Donotpunnik who ensures my safety and has no reason to worry about me going to the police. The incident with the Omega operator supports this. And yet, they immediately offered to move me wherever I liked, and allowed me out to the street. I could have yelled or asked for help. I could have been recorded by some camera. If Donotpunnik is the one ensuring my safety, then I have trouble understanding him.

"When's the last time you spoke with Stacey?" Standing there silently waiting for the Rogue to unlock the door was getting tedious, so I decided to dilute the waiting with some conversation.

"When you summoned her to the Dungeon. She's currently in rehabilitation—she only shows up in Barliona for a few hours a day. You can't really talk to her much. It's surprising you even managed to reach her."

"She's in rehab?"

"Yes, something went wrong as she was doing a quest and she got locked in the game. I don't know the details. All I know is that the whole ordeal really took a toll on her. There are all kinds of legal types from the Corporation hovering around her, trying to mediate the conflict...It's actually starting to look kind of terrifying. I heard that even Johnson himself came by with apologies and offers of compensation. But I won't lie—I don't know the truth. Got it! Let's see what this door has to offer. Okay, behind door number four, we have a...Oh, no way!"

I entered the room behind Plinto and froze with my mouth ajar. Even Plinto, who had seen one or two things in his day, hummed with surprise upon reading the properties of the item we had discovered—what was there to say about a simple player like me? In the center of a square hall, upon a one and a half meter tall plinth lay a bright red pillow bearing a small heap of crystals, radiating a sulfurous-yellow light.

'The Tear of Harrashess.' Class: Unique Artifact. The owner of the Tear receives the 'Lament of Harrashess' buff: +1000% to movement speed. +10000% to all main stats. +10000% to Hit Points, Mana and Energy regeneration rate. +10000% to Experience and Reputation earned. +90 to base Attractiveness. Ignores level difference when calculating damage and healing (does not apply to PvP). May not be sold, dropped, stolen or destroyed. Effects do not stack. Status: Inactive, unbound to player.

"Thirty Tears," Plinto uttered slowly, moving toward the plinth like a zombie. "Anyone who owns one of these crystals will be a god in Barliona! So this is why you guys came here? Donotpunnik and Hellfire want godmode?!"

"That's one way to put it," I replied in shock. If Geranika doesn't do anything with the crystals, then Barliona really will witness the coming of a new pantheon—thirty new player-gods who can deal with any opponent with a mere nod. After all, there'd be no difference in levels to reckon with! A player with a Tear could take on Geranika while still at Level 1 and simply throw slippers at him. "But they're not for you or me."

"What do you mean?" Plinto asked, but immediately understood: "You know how to give someone a Tear?!"

"Yes," I replied, and praying to all the devs of Barliona responsible for this glitch, swept all the crystals into my bag. The time had come to see whether the Crastil worked or not.

"How do you feel?" Plinto asked with mock worry. "You don't feel like devouring the world, do you?"

"You know, nothing's changed," I replied with surprise. "The crystals don't affect me."

"I assume I shouldn't count on one?"

"Why? Here," I got out one Tear and offered it to Plinto. I could complete the Tomb without the Rogue, so I could release him after I got the Salva. Someone had to be my lab rat, after all. Plus, a short stay in reality would do Plinto good. He could go do some shopping and consider who he's really working for.

You are giving a Tear of Harrashess to another player who does not have a Crastil. Do you wish to bind and activate the crystal?

Yes!

"Whoa!" whispered Plinto when his HP bar suddenly dropped halfway without actually decreasing the HP he currently had. "Mahan, I owe you!"

"We'll settle accounts later," I replied. "Let's get out of here."

"*Clutzer*," Plinto wrote in the raid chat to the Rogue who, surprisingly, still hadn't been caught! "*We're leaving! Get out of here if you can.*"

"*All right, I'll do my best. Though, I can't last much longer—my Energy's almost gone. A minute, no more.*"

"*Good luck then*," I added. "*Let me know when you return. I'll take you to Altameda. We'll think about what to do next.*"

"Listen," smirked Plinto, looking me up and down. "Tell me again how much you weigh? This little idea occurred to me..."

We covered the distance between the treasure vault and the portal room in under a minute. Plinto heaved me onto his shoulder, shifted up through his Accelerations straight to Acceleration V and paying no attention to Geranika or his howling Hadjeis sprinted the distance as fast as his legs would carry him.

"Mahan?!" I caught the astonished exclamation of the Lord of Shadow when we tore through the throne room. The Lord of Shadow tried to stop us, but his Stop had no effect on Plinto, while I spent the rest of our escape staring at a strip of Plinto's chain mail—

I didn't have a tooth of the Patriarch.

"Daaamn. That was close," muttered Clutzer, meeting us on the other side of the portal. He had made it after all! "I did more work today than I ever did at the mines...Say, is it me or is that tree giving us a dirty look? He's starting to freak me out. That'd be one for the ages—we escape the palace of Shadow only to get crushed by some Guardian."

At the edge of another blight of Shadow surrounding the open portal, milled an enormous Oak—the local Guardian was making a show of his displeasure with the damage we were doing to his forest. Not wishing to anger the high-level mob unnecessarily, I deactivated the portal and as I did so, Clutzer offered me a canvas about a meter by a meter in size.

"What is this?" I asked with surprise, brushing the fog from the canvas. The Armard throne room that we had just been in, the alabaster throne, the crowd of terrifying and strange Hadjeis, Geranika beside the throne trying on his crown...It was like David's Coronation of Napoleon or something...

"This is a canvas painted by a great painter of Shadow, entitled 'Ascent to the Throne'. Geranika's the one ascending, if I were to guess. And no need to stare at me like that! When you're darting from hall to hall in fear of your life, you don't have time to examine the loot you encounter. I was just tossing whatever came across my path into my bag! You should think about how you can clean the Shadow from the painting. That's your problem now."

"Earl," the Herald's bell rang, preventing me from coming up with a worthy answer to the bungling thief, "the Emperor wishes to see you urgently. Please follow me."

"By myself?"

"Yes. As for Plinto and Clutzer, I advise they go speak with the Rogue trainer in Anhurs. As I understand it, Masters who have managed to infiltrate Armard and survive thirty minutes of battle there, are eligible for a worthy reward. Please enter the portal, Earl."

I had nothing left to do but submit to the Herald's demand—and yet when I emerged on the other side of the portal, I couldn't stifle an astonished exclamation. I had been invited straight to the Malabar throne room. Emperor Naahti sat on the throne, while none other than Geranika stood before him, arms crossed and a very dour expression on his face.

"Greetings!" I began with an immense grin, when it became clear that neither the Emperor nor Geranika would speak with me first. And if Geranika was glummer than a cloud, the Emperor radiated with such a contagious smile of his own, that everyone around him was infected with the same positivity and elation. I, for one, submitted to this feeling entirely.

"Return my scepter, thief!" Geranika roared

instead of a greeting. Only now did I realize that this wasn't the actual Lord of Shadow but his projection. I doubt Geranika is so naïve as to surrender himself to the Emperor's mercy. Even for the sake of the scepter of power.

"You summoned me, your Highness?" I decided to ignore Geranika. It's not like our relationship could get any worse, and I didn't feel like explaining things to the dumb AI.

"Tell me, did you really steal Geranika's scepter?" the Emperor managed to stifle his grin and asked his question in an utterly ordinary voice.

"I wouldn't use the word 'steal,'" I hedged just in case. Who knows what kind of issues the Imitator of Malabar has with stealing. "I expropriated it. I am holding on to it as a trophy. That I received on the field of battle. Choose whichever option you prefer."

"You stole it!" The ordinarily imperturbable Geranika was having a bad day today. I hadn't seen the Lord of Shadow so worked up since the Dark Forest.

"How do you wish to use it?" The Emperor followed my example and began ignoring Geranika.

"I don't even know," I confessed, producing the scepter from my bag. In a blink of an eye, I was surrounded by twenty Heralds holding Stones of Light in their hands. The Emperor did not want the influence of Shadow to spread in his castle. "What is this for?"

"I have a throne, without which, I lose power," the Emperor explained. "This scepter does the same thing for the head of the new Empire. Without this item, Geranika shall die in two months. This is why I'm asking you—what do you intend to do with that stick?"

"Judging by the fact that I'm here, I'm going to have to give it back?" I guessed.

"I would put it differently," Naahti parried. "Exchange it, do a good thing for the Empire, save an innocent life. Choose the option you prefer."

"I agree to an exchange," Geranika muttered grimly. "You shall have her back. Return the scepter..."

Only now did I realize the reason for the Emperor's elation. Without bothering about my opinion of the matter, he'd already dispensed with the scepter as he saw fit, exchanging it for his wife. Whether I wanted this or not didn't interest the head of Malabar in the least. The devs couldn't permit the enemy Emperor to die, so I was being confronted with a simple fact—I had to return the scepter. Like hell! Hamster and Toad puffed up their chests in defense of the lawfully pilfered item, so I had nothing left to do but ask:

"Excuse me, Your Highness, but I have not yet agreed to the exchange. In my view..."

"What do you want?" Geranika looked over at me. "Items? Knowledge? I cannot give those to you, since you do not belong to Shadow. Money? That's not even funny."

"I'd like to visit your palace," I smirked, coming up with what I figured would be the most annoying payment for Geranika. "I want you to give me a tour, at the end of which I'll be brought back home safe and sound. We'll take a stroll around your palace, see how things are arranged in it, take in the sights, the sculptures, the paintings. They really are beautiful—I can even prove it."

Not giving it much further thought, I produced the canvas Clutzer had expropriated.

"Check out the artistry, the brushwork, the composition, the grayscale..."

"YOU STOLE MY ONLY PORTRAIT?" Geranika really lost the plot here.

"You'll have to return that too, Mahan," the Emperor said, openly laughing. "I can't spare ten Stones of Light on guarding a single painting. What do you say, my regal brother," Naahti turned to Geranika. "Will you arrange a tour for my subject?"

"You have no greater Foe in this world than me, Mahan!" Geranika took ahold of himself and became the imperturbable Ruler once again. "By the power granted me by Barliona, I guarantee Mahan's safety during the tour of my palace. I guarantee that he will be returned unharmed. But the very instant he returns, I will begin my hunt of Shaman Mahan in earnest! Pitiful fool, I will do everything in my power to make Barliona your personal hell. You have the word of the Lord of Shadow!"

"How am I going to get to your palace?" I asked, ignoring the threats.

"The dagger will open a portal to Armard one more time. After that, you may as well throw it away—I will disable its power."

"Your Highness," understanding that I wouldn't get anything else from Geranika, I decided to turn to the Emperor. What if I manage to get something from him too? "The deal with Geranika is more or less settled. I would like to also discuss..."

"You will receive my complete support," the Emperor cut me off, understanding what I was getting at, "including complete access to the palace. Will that suffice?"

"Yours or the Empire's?" I inquired, my heart skipping a beat. Receiving the Emperor's Exaltation isn't just an enormous bonus for the clan, it's...well, Mr. Kristowski would carry me on his shoulders.

"Mine and the Empire's," Naahti didn't bother bartering. "I will never forget the hero who returned my Adelaide to me."

"In that case, I propose we make the exchange!" I said triumphantly and held the scepter and the painting out to Geranika's projection. "How shall we do it?"

Achievement unlocked: 'Friend of the

Emperor.' Your Reputation with the Emperor of Malabar has reached Exalted status.

Achievement unlocked: 'Peer of Malabar.' Your Reputation with the Malabar Empire has reached Exalted status.

Access to the Malabar palace updated. Current access: 100%.

New achievements and notifications sparkled all around me, the clan chat overflowed with the celebration of players, my amulet was bursting from incoming calls, yet I remained standing in the throne room, watching the Emperor bend lovingly over his wife, quietly whimpering to myself.

What am I doing?!

Why do I need these adventures with the Emperor and Geranika? This is like a feast during a time of plague! I have 29 deadly items in my bag, which I need to urgently hand to Phoenix's players, and here I'm losing time hanging around the castle, eking out new bonuses. What the hell for?! I need to think about my personal safety, about the fact that I'm breaking the law, about the fact that if this affair comes to light, I'll spend the rest of my days in the mines. But instead of all that, I'm busy scheduling a tour of Geranika's palace and reveling in my ability to piss off an Imitator. An ordinary program! What is wrong with me? Why aren't I thinking about the important issues when they're all I should be thinking about? It's decided then! It's time to stop beating around the bush and occupy myself with the deliberate destruction of Phoenix. I would deal with Donotpunnik, Hellfire and the devs they'd bought later. Producing my amulet, I hesitated a bit and, surprised by this very hesitation, made the call. The show must go on!

"Speaking!"

"Ehkiller, this is Mahan. I'd like to see you. I have an offer you can't refuse..."

"We can't deal with it over the amulet?"

"No."

"All right. I'll see you at the Golden Horseshoe in ten minutes." To my surprise, Ehkiller agreed to meet me without a hundred preconditions. "Is that good for you?"

"Perfect. Thank you."

The amulet fell silent, but I fiddled with it for a while longer, and then called Plinto. According to Donotpunnik's plan, Hellfire was supposed to be the shining example of a player with a Tear, and yet he'd still be resting for the next four-five hours, cursing me with every bad word in his vocabulary. At the same time, using Plinto for the same purpose seemed much better to me—since I'd given the Tear to one of my best fighters, surely Ehkiller would have nothing to fear from the crystals. I'd never risk Plinto after all! Or so they'd think...

"That's how things stand," I concluded my brief

presentation on the Tears of Harrashess, which included a demonstration of my Rogue's new stats. Ehkiller had sat through it silently, without asking a single question, which, to be honest, made me very nervous: What if all my efforts were in vain and the entire plan was doomed to fail? Donotpunnik had insisted on using Hellfire for a reason, after all.

"I call upon a Herald. I need your help," said Ehkiller, making me want to jump to my feet. Instead of jumping at the chance to secure the Tears for his clan, the head of Phoenix was summoning a Herald? What was this nonsense?

"You called me and I came," the Emperor's messenger started his typical song and dance.

"I accuse Mahan of using prohibited items!" Without giving the Herald a chance to finish, Ehkiller pushed me further into a state of utter bafflement. Everything was going not at all how I planned it! "The Tears of Harrashess should not exist in Barliona. They break the game balance!"

"Your complaint has been received," the bells vanished from the Herald's voice, indicating that the Imitator had been replaced by a real person. "Esteemed Ehkiller, I must inform you that Mahan acquired these items in due compliance with the game mechanics and without breaking any rules. The Tears were introduced to the game for the NPCs—players were not supposed to be able to use them, and yet what happened—happened. We are forced to reject your complaint. May I help you with anything else?"

"If I acquire the Tears, they won't change their characteristics..."

"I am not authorized to make such decisions. At the moment, we are processing the strategies that arise from the introductions of the Tears of Harrashess into the game. We do not have those results yet."

"That wasn't a question. That was a statement. Pursuant to section 244, item 2, the characteristics of any item acquired for money shall not be altered by the Corporation in a unilateral manner."

"I repeat, I am not authorized to make such decisions. My job is to inform you that there are no TOS violations associated with owning the Tears."

"In that case, thank you. I'd like to speak to someone who has the authority to discuss this matter. All the best—I no longer require the assistance of a Herald."

Ehkiller took a sip from his mug, allowing the Herald time to leave, and then asked:

"Why'd you come to me?"

"Because Phoenix is the only clan in Malabar that could be interested in such items. Sure, Etamzilat or Undigit would also be happy to purchase a couple Tears, but I don't want to spread them among the clans. I don't feel like making everyone stronger—one faction's good enough for me."

"So why don't you use them yourself?"

"For what? To let the top-10 clans poach all my players as soon as I've given them the Tears? Like hell! The recent happenings were quite enough for me, thank you. There's nothing more valuable in Barliona than gold."

"You've changed, Mahan," said Ehkiller, with a slight dose of mockery and even condescension in his voice. "The Shaman I knew before didn't need money."

"The Shaman you knew was handily and quite cynically destroyed by your own Phoenix clan. I'm a product of your actions. So enjoy."

"What do you want?"

"I have 29 Tears. Considering the bonuses that the Tear grants, I think a billion gold per Tear should be the right price."

I don't know myself where I came up with this number. I should have probably gone no higher than five hundred million, but for some reason, a half-billion turned into a cool billion. Something in Ehkiller's look told me that he was ready to spend that much, as long as I pushed him right. And importantly, I wouldn't do this now. Now my job was to sell the goods, which is basically what I was doing.

"Too much time in this game is harmful to one's health," said Ehkiller, letting me know that my offer was unacceptable.

"Well if we were to speak honestly, I don't care who I sell the crystals to," I shrugged, demonstrating my complete detachment from the current situation.

"Either Phoenix or the Smoldering Pine from the Celestial." At my mention of the clan from the other continent, Ehkiller narrowed his eyes, as if he was trying to burn a hole in me. "My goal is as simple as a cork—the opportunity to earn a bunch of money had presented itself, and I'd like to use it to the utmost. Therefore—a billion per Tear. If I don't hear an answer from you by tomorrow, I'll be reaching out to the Celestials. And then to Astrum. I imagine I'll have no trouble finding other willing buyers."

"You're playing with fire, Mahan. What do you think will happen to your Tears if I speak to the Corporation about them? Such items should not exist in this game."

"I acquired them fair and square. If someone wants to change something, then the laws of our world remain as before. I'll fight for my billions. Perhaps I'll be able to earn even more if I hold an open auction."

"I need time to think things over. I'll let you know in two days. Can you wait that long?"

"Sure. We'll meet here in two days. Oh, I forgot to mention! If you do decide to buy the Tears, then I'll need to give them personally to whoever's going to equip them. Only I can give them to someone. Such is the right of their first owner. Later!"

Nodding my farewell, I teleported to Altameda, sat down in my rocking chair and clenched my fists from joy. Killer was mine! Either I don't know the head of Phoenix at all, or tomorrow I'll be twenty-nine billion richer! When everything's over, I'll need to give Donotpunnik and his gang their cut. Even if they hadn't mentioned money, I figure it'll be fair that way. This is their plan; I'm merely the one doing the work.

The next two days flashed by in a blink of an eye. My mood was so ideal that even Hellfire's and Donotpunnik's scowling mugs—when they showed up again at Altameda—had no effect on it. It turned out that the Lord of Shadow had saddled them with a debuff after all, and now their base stats were cut by half for the next month. Naturally I was very sorry that I'd messed up their plans, improvising as I was wont to do, and I agreed that, again naturally, Ehkiller might not agree to the deal I had offered and that a billion could really have been too steep a price—and yet when Donotpunnik grudgingly held out two scrolls of Armageddon, my good mood returned. Phoenix wouldn't get away from us this time.

And then the two days were up and at long last the awaited moment arrived:

"Mahan, this is Ehkiller. I agree to your terms. Let's make the deal..."

CHAPTER TWELVE

EPIPHANY

"**O**UR PARTNERSHIP is beginning to cost me more and more," smiled Ehkiller, sending me the contract with his signature. Mr. Kristowski had spent three days studying the document in detail, consulting with lawyers and economists, until it became clear that the contract was completely solid. Phoenix would take a loan of twenty-nine billion gold from the Bank of Barliona and transfer it to my account. Not my clan's account—mine. Here Ehkiller was unshakable—his pride forbade him from buying the Tears from another clan. From a player was okay, however. In my view there was no difference. I could easily transfer the money from my account wherever and whenever I felt like it.

"Looks that way, doesn't it?" I replied in the same tone, placing my digital signature onto the document. That's it! Now I could hand the Tears to Phoenix—it was too late to renege on the payment. The contract had been registered and transmitted to all the relevant agencies.

The five days between my meeting with Ehkiller and our little signature ceremony had been quite strange. An inexplicable euphoria had filled me from my head to my toes, demanding constant activity. I ran around all of Anhurs, helped Mr. Kristowski manage the clan, held several clan meetings, promoted several of my players recommended by my manager to Officers, met with three prospective raid leaders and held discussions with them and other potential Raiders. I had so much energy that I didn't even pop out to reality the entire time—I was simply too busy. Perhaps the enormous amount of money rearing on the horizon had completely rerouted the energetic flows of my organism. I was interested in everything, I wanted to learn everything, participate in everything and meanwhile my brain utterly refused to consider any negative thoughts. The roles that Donotpunnik and Hellfire were playing? Why who cares when a careless and leisurely life lies just ahead...

"When do you want to transfer the Tears?" Ehkiller inquired.

"Right this instant if you like," I replied impatiently. I still couldn't sit still, so I preferred to deal with the transfer of the Tears as soon as possible.

"Okay," the Mage agreed. "Do you need to prepare somehow to do it?"

"No, I only need the players who'll be receiving

them. Nothing complicated about it."

"In that case, I invite you to my castle. I'm sure you've never paid us a visit before…"

Evolett, Hellfire, Fiona, Pwner, Ehkiller himself and another twenty-three living legends of this world…Had I found myself in such company three or even two years ago, I'd probably just turn into one of the lovely statues that decorated this castle. They were all great warriors in their own right. They were unflappable warriors. They were warriors who knew how to slay mobs and clear Dungeons like no one else on our continent. It was true that in PvP, not one of them would stand a chance against Plinto, but the majesty of these players lay elsewhere. The First Kills!

The players approaching me one after another received their Tears and as they did so their faces, perhaps with the exceptions of Hellfire and Ehkiller, became frozen masks. During the first minute of the ceremony, the hall was filled with noise and hubbub from those who had not yet received their Tears. Yet, by the time I'd handed the Tear to the third person, the cacophony had died down and given way to a deathly silence, punctuated only be me rummaging in my bag.

"One Tear left," I turned to Ehkiller, asking him whom I was to give it to. Anastaria had not been among the present and I knew very well who the last Tear was for, but I decided to toss the ball into Phoenix's court. Let them deal with their problems themselves.

"You will have to transfer it in there." Ehkiller gestured me towards a small door behind the throne. His personal office. Shrugging my shoulders in puzzlement and surprised by such odd secrecy, I headed into the office. Anastaria wanted to have a chat one on one? Well, let's have a chat then.

You are giving a Tear of Harrashess to another player who does not have a Crastil. Do you wish to bind and activate the crystal?

Yes!

"Leave us, Feanor," Anastaria said to the Paladin who had just received the last Tear I had. The player's face had become a mask of shock at the unexpected gift, yet Phoenix's newest Raider found the wherewithal to nod and leave the office.

"You didn't take the Tear," I remarked, playing Captain Obvious.

"Have you decided to exact your revenge through money?" Anastaria asked, drilling me with her look.

"Have you decided to seize the moral high-ground about my wanting to make some money?" I didn't feel like being in her debt and replied along the same principle that she herself had taught me. A question for a question.

"Bankrupting someone and profiting from them are utterly different things! I should've destroyed you and your clan entirely."

"History doesn't deal with the subjunctive mood very well," I grinned. "Should have. Could have. You didn't. It's me who did what I did, and I don't regret it. Yes, I helped make twenty-nine players of Phoenix the gods of Barliona. But I also ensured my clan's future for the rest of eternity. I guess my price was too low since Ehkiller agreed to it in a mere two days. I should have quoted two billion per Tear and pumped your clan dry. As they say, the payment makes the debt pretty."

"Have you signed the contract?" Mirida wrote in the clan chat.

"Yes."

"Wonderful!"

"I made a mistake," Anastaria said with unvarnished hate in her voice. "I should have destroyed you completely. Without mercy. Without leaving anything. You think you won? You think that the friends that have helped you hide will save you? Don't be naïve. It's much easier for me to come to terms with Donotpunnik and work with him to dump you where you should be—in the sewage system. Enjoy the money, Mahan. Go to the Dating House, buy yourself an Imitator, have your way with it. 'Cause as of tomorrow, I'm dealing with you for real!"

"That's why you invited me here?" I raised an eyebrow. "To tell me what a bad person I am for daring to earn money from your clan? You know,

Stacey, I always considered you intelligent, but now the person I'm talking to is a loser. You've already lost. Take that as a given fact."

"WHAT?!" screamed Anastaria, jumping to her feet. At first I thought that her reaction had been caused by my words, but her next phrase revealed that it was something much more serious: "WHAT DID YOU DO TO THE TEARS?"

Donotpunnik had moved to the next step of his plan!

"I, uh...I'm not sure I know what you're talking about," I said, even though I couldn't help but grin. The Phoenix castle would acquire twenty-nine new sculptures today. Too bad Anastaria wouldn't be among them.

"Mahan, what the hell?" Plinto asked in the clan chat. *"The Tear's altered its description and even the Patriarch's tooth has no effect on it! I can't move at all, like not even a muscle..."*

"Mahan! What. Have. You. Done. To. The. Tears?!" Anastaria continued to yell, advancing on me like grizzly.

"It's looking like we won't be able to hold a productive dialog here, so all the best." I didn't feel like bickering, so I opened the Harbinger's Blink input, entered Altameda's coordinates and teleported back to my castle. When Anastaria's enraged it's better to stay out of her way. Even if I'd never seen her quite that angry, I could imagine perfectly well how that scene would play out.

"You won't get away from me so easily!" Anastaria yelled at me telepathically, and I was forced to reject a summons from her. *"What have you done with the Tears, Mahan?!"*

"Clutzer, this is Mahan. I have some business for you." Blocking Anastaria's messages (Stacey had taught me how to do this too), I got in touch with the Rogue. "Do you have a Paladin at the moment?"

While Clutzer was figuring out why I needed one and whom he could sacrifice, I smiled to myself—the destruction of the Phoenix clan had been set in motion. The attack was proceeding on all fronts.

* * *

"Fire at will!" Someone yelled as soon as I emerged from the portal. Lightning bolts, arrows and even axes and swords came flying from all directions—traps activated under my feet—and yet the welcoming party's revelry all came to nothing. The bubble around me was doing its job.

"The Creator has appeared!" the black angel said triumphantly, kneeling before me.

"The time has come to pass the Original Key!" echoed the white angel, likewise kneeling and offering me a small silver key. "It is yours from now unto eternity!"

The lightning bolts kept zapping me from all

sides, but now, instead of the bubble which had expired, they were bouncing off a new shield cast by the angels. It looked like the developers really wanted to make sure that the key would be given to whoever had created the Chess Set and opened the Tomb, since this is the first time I've seen NPCs temporarily protect one player from another. The local residents of Barliona don't typically get involved in player interactions, deeming them unimportant.

"The Entrance is open!" As soon as I took the key, the angels stood up, looked somewhere above my head, forcing me to turn and see an enormous crowd of players who were trying to kill me. Phoenix had really splurged on security. There were at least two hundred high-level warriors here, who were all now trying to destroy me as hard as they could. I don't know what the angels did, but a moment later the area before the entrance to the Tomb was empty. All of the players had been destroyed!

"We are no longer needed here. Only you shall complete the Tomb with the 'Original' status! Only you shall have access to the Salva! May the Creator live forever!"

Two bright stars, the angels soared into the sky and dissolved in its blue expanse. The job was done! Phoenix had received the Tears, Barliona had heard the word Salva spoken, I had received the status I needed and Ehkiller still owed me twenty-nine billion gold. The court that I would have to petition about his debt (since Phoenix would surely refuse to pay now) wouldn't care that the Tears' properties had changed. The contract stood and the contract had to be discharged. Please be so kind as to pay Mahan the money you owe him under the law.

The only upsetting thing was how fast the Tears had been activated. We could have given Phoenix a few days to feel like gods—the blow would have been all the greater. But if Donotpunnik decided it was better now, then he had his reasons. The important thing was that I'd accomplished what I wanted—my revenge against Anastaria and her clan had succeeded.

As I exited to reality, I felt like a hero coming home. Once again the feeling of triumph that had filled me the last five days returned to me and I wanted to scream and embrace the entire world in my happiness. I had no desire to return to Barliona, so I decided to do what I did best—create.

Anastaria once told me that the real masterpieces of Jewelry happened when the creator was ears-deep in his emotions. Even if she had meant in Barliona, I felt like trying it in reality. I had a Jeweler's toolkit and a ton of time. My future looked promising, so why not make something beautiful?

Heaving the enormous toolkit onto my lap, I opened the lid and sighed with disappointment— during my last fit of creation I had used up all my copper wire. Looking around my room and finding not a single ring on my floor—I guess the maid had picked them all up—I decided to see how well the casting furnace worked. If I don't have wire, I can make some myself right now! Aren't I a Jeweler?

No sooner said than done! The Jeweler's toolkit moved to the table while I began reading the instructions. All right, what do we have here?

"Light the burner and carefully bring the flame to the furnace..." That's clear enough. First I have to melt the copper to make the wire out of. Then I can extrude it just like in Barliona.

"Place several pieces of metal into the crucible and..." That's the preparation instructions. This is clear enough too.

"Heat the metal until it reaches a liquid state and then carefully pour it into..." This is much more interesting. The flame in the furnace was so intense that the copper melted in a matter of moments. There were several molds in the toolkit for pouring the melted metal into, starting from wire and ending with some kind of square, but I chose the one of the ring. Let this be my first cast (instead of wire-wrapped) creation. The important thing was to carefully pour the copper into the mold, without spilling any of it onto the table. That's it! Now I can work on the gem— since we're dealing with a cast ring here, a gem is mandatory. This ruby looks very attractive. I'll use it.

I'll use a prong setting, so I have to cut the gem into the shape of a round, multi-faceted ruby. Ugh—

okay I can't work with this Jeweler's toolkit. I need Design Mode. *Enter!* Hello, familiar darkness—it's been a while. Okay, I'll project the ruby in Design Mode along with the ring I just cast. Polish a facet here and another here. Make an adjustment here and unite it with the original. Excellent! What's with the ring? Hmm...It didn't come out too great—it's much harder to cast rings than wrap them from wire. I don't need such a crooked, ugly ring. I'll throw it out and start from scratch using a projection.

That's better. Two perfect parts of my current creation appeared before me—the ring and the faceted ruby. All that was left to do was to merge them together, connect them with the material and embody the thing into reality. Here goes...

When I opened my eyes, I saw one of the prettiest ring's I'd ever created in Barliona in my hand. The copper had been replaced with white gold, which along with the ruby created such a lovely interplay of light around this item that I could barely look away. I wonder what its properties are...

??? ???. Description: ;)("(#;$??*):*. Stats: +10% "(*@*#&!, +10%)(")!+/. Restrictions: (*"_#;??") 350"?*;_

What the...

"Daniel, are you okay?" a worried voice asked over the telephone. "Your vital signs are falling from nominal."

"Thank you, I'm okay," I whispered in shock, still looking at the ring in my palm. It had properties! "I'm just a little anxious."

"If this happens again, we will be forced to conduct a medical evaluation. We cannot allow our clients to feel bad."

"I'm okay," I repeated. "Please don't worry."

"Okay. We wish to remind you that we will soon be withdrawing the funds for our services from your account. All the best."

Hanging up the phone, I collapsed in my chair and began to stare at the ring. There weren't any doubts—it really had characteristics. They were secret, garbled, encrypted, but they were there!

How was this possible? This was reality!

Try to use your head, Mahan...Consider why Donotpunnik and Hellfire would want this. Plinto's words tore through my mind like lightning, forcing me to structure everything to some still-ethereal thought. My body wanted to jump and to fly, but I forced myself to stay sitting, to think.

Consider why Donotpunnik and Hellfire would want this.

Why had they been so confident in revealing their plan and the other members of their conspiracy to me? Why did they show me that my former mentor was involved? Why did they even include me in their conspiracy at all?

The answer swept across my body like an electric wave: Because they were sure that I wouldn't say anything to anyone! Because I'd never run away from them! Because I'd be with them always, wherever I fled!

Because I'm not out in *actual* reality!

A ring with nonsense properties can only be created in one place—a virtual subspace connected to Barliona. I'm in a mod of Barliona designed to look like the reality I know! A virtual cul-de-sac that Provo set up just for me...

This time, instead of an electric shock, my body simply went hot. I began to sweat all over. This wasn't the first ring I had crafted! I had made my first ring during my rehabilitation! Why hadn't I considered how improbable it was that the Corporation would release a person who had just spent a year in a capsule after a mere three days of rehab?

And another shocking suspicion followed the first, entrenching itself in my mind: Sergei, who supposedly arranged my escape, had done it all in three days. If he had asked me to do the same, could I do it in the same amount of time? Erm...I really doubt it. In fact, I'm sure that I couldn't. So why am I asking this question only now?

Stop! How would the people who arranged all this know that I would turn to Sergei? They knew the passwords, meeting places, our agreements...

Provo again! The mentor who'd taught us

everything! He's the one who'd drilled the principles of security into us and...

"During that hour the guy only lost like 10% of his brain and he's still got a chance of living a normal life..." I recalled the words of Silkodor the Rogue, which I'd heard on the bank of the Altair. And as this recollection waved at me cordially, another wave of cold sweat swept across my body.

"Your death and the revival of our man must happen at the same moment."

According to those who'd hidden me away, I had spent four hours in a state of clinical death. If I was to believe Silkodor's girlfriend, I should currently be little more than a bowl of petunias—without a brain, without consciousness, without memory.

My thoughts began to gallop, getting tangled, contradicting themselves, but constantly recalling surprising details that I hadn't paid attention to.

Omega's hesitation to release me as soon as I demanded it: They needed time to render the outside street. They'd even put in a street sweeper with a broom! It was looking like they'd sized me up pretty well—as soon as they gave me a taste of liberty, I immediately decided to turn back and head inside. Hadn't they promised to transfer me to a different location...two days ago?!

A personal visit from a Corporation representative named Alexander: He was the one who showed me the interview with Anastaria—so that I'd burn with the desire to seek revenge against Phoenix. From that point on, they didn't have to render any new streets. I had become consumed with my revenge and stopped noticing the discrepancies around me.

My sensory perception: If I've actually been in the same capsule I was imprisoned in, it becomes clear where my sensations are coming from. In the prisoner's capsule, my sensory filter had been turned off! Everything would read normal to the developers and admins monitoring the signal that Provo had doctored. But for me, my time in Barliona after returning had become a living torment.

The meeting with the old man: Donotpunnik claimed that the old man had been an actor, but now I realize that he was nothing but an ordinary Imitator. It's just not possible that there wouldn't be any people in the completely safe and well-lit central park. Especially on such a pleasant summer night. Even at midnight, there's always couples hanging out there, hipsters, hobbyists...

Stop!

Consider why Donotpunnik and Hellfire would want this.

Hellfire had made his position clear—he was sick of doing nothing on our continent, and the oddest thing is that I believe him. Meanwhile, for Donotpunnik who had spent five years and several billion credits on this operation, the first place in the ratings...

We wish to remind you that we will soon be withdrawing the funds for our services from your account...

Why, I had personally given them permission to withdraw from my clan and personal accounts! What a moron I am! If Donotpunnik is using me, then he'll have access to my account, which will have a balance of twenty-nine billion credits in a few days. You could easily sacrifice one, two, even three lives for that kind of money—hell, you could easily raze half the city for it! And I gave Donotpunnik's people the keys to it myself...

Blast! What to do? I need someone's help urgently! But whose?

Every step I take in Barliona is tracked. That's a simple fact—if I'm really in a virtual subspace at the moment, then my body is lying somewhere in the depths of a prison. Since I had never left the capsule to begin with. Who am I going to ask for help? The police? They don't exist for me. Heralds? Provo and his people will merely adjust them. They already showed me what they were capable of. A complaint to the admins? Even if it makes it through, what would I write? That I suspect that I've been kidnapped and imprisoned? Inside a mod of Barliona? Madness.

But the main thing is how convenient all of this is! As soon as I become useless, they'll simply disconnect me from Barliona and that's it—Shaman Mahan would simply cease to exist! What does

Donotpunnik need me for? I'm just an extra witness. And so is Hellfire now, by the way. The Warrior got into this whole affair for the sake of a clan transfer. He was supposed give the Tears to his clanmates and now that I'd already done this, Hellfire had suddenly become useless too.

The Salva!

The Salva could save me! I could leverage it to force them to return me to reality unharmed. I could promise to sign a non-disclosure agreement with them...

Then again, what does Donotpunnik need the Salva for? He's already received his money—or he will soon enough. All the Salva gets him is a little more gold on top of what he's already earned. But I doubt they'd allow me to live in exchange for several billion. It's much easier to remove the Creator's binding and complete the Dungeon using the might of the Azure Dragons. They could get a First Kill too while they're at it.

Could Phoenix help me? No, I don't think so. Anastaria will only be happy if I vanish. After what she did to my clan, I...I froze and addressed myself in the third person: "Mahan, tell yourself please, what did Anastaria do to your clan? Why *are* you so angry with her?" Seems like a simple question, but it was the one I really didn't want to answer. Stacey helped build my clan, she helped us acquire immense bonuses, provided me with intelligent people like

Barsina and Magdey, and helped Leite set up the clan finances. Should I be angry at her for this? Or maybe I should be mad because she stole those items from my bag? After everything that happened during the opening of the Tomb, there was no guarantee that I wouldn't delete the Shaman. I could have easily done so! And to be fair, after my return—rather, after I'd been returned to the game—Stacey gave the Chess Set back to me, since it belonged to me, but she kept the Crastils. Just in case—since I needed them.

Damn!

Another cold sweat broke across my body. For crying out loud!

Anastaria *knew me!* She knew that I would work with the enemies of her native clan! This is why Hellfire was the only one to invite me to Phoenix! Anastaria didn't even consider me a human in the beginning! I could even recall our first kiss outside of Beatwick! The revulsion on Stacey's face told me a lot more than any words could have. And yet, after that everything went according to plan—we began to interact. If Anastaria knew that I was under constant watch by a third party—and that at the same time, I don't really have anything to do with them—it becomes clear why she never told me about her plans...so that Donnotpunnik wouldn't find out about them! If I found out that I was under surveillance too early, I could have been disconnected and they could've moved on to the other candidates. Didn't they say that there were nine others? But no! Anastaria didn't betray me! Now it's clear why Stacey always responded to all my requests immediately—because she still cared for me!

It follows that the scene in front of the Tomb was an attempt to prod me out of the game? Either send me to the mines, if I lost control, or out to reality having first supplied me with a sufficient amount of funds. The players, the buying up of resources— Phoenix had invested over a hundred million in order to purchase my release and in doing so foil Donotpunnik's plans. But it hadn't worked!

So then why did Stacey keep needling me the entire time? Why do those interviews, why make the stupid claims she made, why use our meetings to annoy me?

Hello reason. I've missed you. Emotions! She wanted me to become aware of my emotions! So that I could return to reality and, wishing to channel my emotions into something productive, create some kind of item. After all, I was a creator! Stacey wanted me to realize that I was in my own personal virtual reality. She was looking out for me!

Right. So it follows that asking her for help is also pointless. How long will I survive in a disabled capsule? An hour? Two? If the oxygen is cut out of the nutrient solution pumped through the long-term immersion capsule, I'll have at most ten happy minutes of swimming. Followed by drowning and a hypothetical afterlife. I need a way out!

James!

A saving thought flashed in my mind and I snatched at it. Several times when I did something unthinkable in Barliona, my consciousness had been transported to a special area where I met with the head of innovation. As far as I recall, James had mentioned that I was in a closed environment, which wasn't inside the game...which could not be monitored by standard means...which couldn't be eavesdropped on.

That's a chance!

If right this instant I do something that no one expects, James will want to see me again. I would be transported to him and I will be able to ask for help, betraying Provo, Mirida, Hellfire and Donotpunnik. I don't see any other way to survive. Could I trust James, or was he on the take too? A good question, which I can't answer. I'll have to risk it, since otherwise I have no more than two days to live.

By the way, if I'm right and I'm in a virtual subspace, then my kidnappers have been doing the right thing—my desire to do something hasn't left me and if it weren't for the ring, I wouldn't have considered what was going on. It feels like they've pumped me full of some amphetamine that makes me want to move and move instead of thinking.

Like hell!

If someone naïvely imagines that they've won,

they're gravely mistaken. I will absolutely think of something that'll earn me a meeting with James. In the end, Donotpunnik himself had said: *"An explosion that big might even kill the Emperor himself, let alone knock down some castle!"* Now I'll just have to come up with a suitable target...

Geranika!

The developers are heaping all their hopes on the new enemy Empire, so they are sure to take my destruction of him as a challenge. James will definitely want to have a word with me if I pull off something like that! So...I have the portal to the palace and I have the scrolls, but where will I get my minute of combat? I can only detonate the scrolls a minute after battle has begun, so what I need to figure out is how to survive. And the only player who could help me is currently standing still somewhere in Barliona, cursing me with everything he has. Clutzer! That Rogue managed to survive longer than ten minutes in Geranika's palace...Could he repeat this feat? Why not?

Okay—Clutzer starts a fight, granting us the 'In Combat' status, I wait a minute and set off the scrolls. No, that won't work. I need to survive the explosion too! I need to meet with James and tell him everything! A Paladin and his bubble! That's the only way to accomplish what I have in mind!

My desire to act finally overcame everything, so I jumped up from my chair and ran over to the capsule.

Donotpunnik thought he was cunning? The time had come to disappoint him.

ENTER!

"Clutzer, I need you and three Mages here ASAP," I ordered the Rogue as soon as I appeared in Barliona. "We're about to make history together."

"I need five minutes. Do you need anyone else?"

"No, I'll do the rest myself."

I tarried a moment and made my decision:

"Stacey, I need your help. Right this instant."

Even though there was no reply, I sent the summons to bring Anastaria to my location. I really needed a Paladin. If my suspicions were accurate, Stacey was still on my side—along with Phoenix. All that remained was to prove it to everyone as well as myself.

"Yes?" Once again, Anastaria didn't ask why I needed her and simply appeared beside me. It was like our last awkward parting had never happened.

"Here's the situation. I did what you were pushing me to do for a long time and I wasn't very pleased with the outcome. In fact, it shocked me a great deal."

"And what have you decided to do?" Anastaria turned on her Ice Queen mode and looked at me condescendingly. The tower of my suppositions began to sway, but I quickly set up some extra supports and replied:

"I have a portal to Geranika's palace and his

permission to take a small tour. I want to make a little outing. Would you like to go with me?"

"You summoned me to go on a tour of Armard?" Anastaria's eyes narrowed with suspicion.

"Of course," I smiled in response. "What could be better than such a lavish trip? I have another small favor to ask though—remember the battle of Altameda? When I challenged Phoenix and all your clans? Phoenix gave me players and I was forced to ask them to do something. Basically, I'd like you to do the same thing."

"Are you sure?" Stacey asked after a moment's thought.

"Yes, absolutely. It's the only way out that I can see."

"Then I'm with you," Anastaria the Ice Queen melted away becoming Anastaria the Goddess of War. "When are we going?"

"Right this instant. We'll wait for Clutzer to arrive and then we'll go. I imagine Geranika's beginning to miss us already."

"Mahan, am I having a deja vu? Or are we really going back to Armard?" grinned Clutzer with an evident nervous note in his voice. Using Altameda, I transported all of us to an uninhabited location, produced the dagger and asked the Mages to charge it with Mana. While Anastaria hadn't ever seen this ritual, Clutzer knew very well what was coming.

"Of course we are! Armard is our kind of place!

Once you set foot in it, you never want to leave. You managed it once and I'd like to rectify the misunderstanding. Besides, Geranika and I have an agreement that I'd feed him a couple players every day."

"If it's like that, I'm all about it. What do you want us to do?"

"I need a minute of combat."

"Whaaat?"

"What I said. I need a minute of the 'In Combat' status. And you're the one who's going to give it to me."

"Erm...Am I missing something? You would only need that minute to..."

"When the time comes, you'll know," I interrupted Clutzer, keeping him from blurting out the rest of his sentence.

"Not a problem! If you need a minute, you'll get a minute. What's Anastaria here for? The bubble?"

"Uh-huh," I hummed, approaching the opened portal. "The blessed bubble."

Shutting my eyes and praying that the people watching me hadn't yet figured out what I was up to, I dived into the portal. How tired I am of teetering on the razor's edge...

"Check it out—they've painted the walls," Clutzer noted in a business-like tone, emerging from the portal behind me. "The palace is coming along nicely. Maybe they'll even splurge on a rug next time."

"There won't be a next time, *thief*," sounded Geranika's voice. The portal popped shut loudly, cutting off our retreat, yet Anastaria had made it through in time. The walls began to waver like melting wax and in a few moments vanished entirely, leaving us right across from Geranika and his alabaster throne.

"You promised me immunity," I managed to say before a pair of Hadjeis appeared behind each of us.

"Yes, but not to anyone else," Geranika countered. He waved his hand and a dozen tentacles wrapped around Clutzer. The Rogue's HP began to fall and the current status of our party changed. We were in combat. "I do not forgive."

"You need a minute?" Clutzer wheezed, turning to me. "You shall have it!"

"Anastaria, how did you like our trial arena?" Geranika asked Anastaria, paying no attention to the Rogue. At his words, Stacey shuddered noticeably and, most surprisingly, took my hand utterly reflexively. As though seeking support.

"It seems not very much. You surrendered! The great Anastaria surrendered!"

Geranika was relishing every passing moment, every word he spoke, every second of Clutzer's torment and Anastaria's terror—it was as if he wasn't being controlled by an Imitator at all, but by a real person, a cruel person. Had his recent loss warped some of his algorithms, increasing his levels of aggression by orders of magnitude? Or was it my presence that was making him respond so oddly?

Forty seconds remained.

"You promised me immunity," I reminded him again. "But now you're breaking your oath!"

"I'm not breaking anything, Shaman! This world shall be mine! You were constantly getting underfoot and now that your friends are in my hands, I will do everything in my power to bring them an unforgettable pleasure. The trial arena that Anastaria managed to escape from will seem like paradise in comparison."

Anastaria clenched my hand even harder. The girl was beginning to shake from terror, yet the Paladin in her did justice to her class. She remained standing and despite the evident desire to exit to reality, awaited my order. I don't know what had happened in that trial arena, but Stacey had clearly suffered a great deal there.

"Geranika, before you destroy my friends," I decided to stall for time, "tell me, why do you need to do all this? Why do you want to be the master of this world?"

Ten seconds left.

"Because it is mine! Because this world is weak and must be ruled by the strong! Because there is no one in Barliona stronger than me! Only the Creator's oath limits me from seizing power, but the time will come when my armies..."

"Stacey, cast the bubble!" I yelled, activating five scrolls of Armageddon at once. "Good bye, Dark Shaman!"

Level gained!

Level gained!

Level gained!

In the flash and ensuing blindness, the only thing I saw the same line repeated again and again:

Level gained...

I tried to count my new levels, but I gave up on the first hundred. The promotions were rushing in endlessly and I had nothing better to do than to swipe them aside, clearing my vision.

You have killed a Hadjei. Reward: +1000 to Reputation with all factions of Malabar and Kartoss.

You have killed a Hadjei. Reward: +1000 to Reputation with all factions of Malabar and Kartoss.

The new level notifications were followed by twenty notifications about the Hadjeis I'd killed. Geranika'd never see those fellows again. I even feel a bit bad for him.

"You cannot defeat me!" Through the bright light blinding my eyes, I heard Geranika's voice. He'd survived! Five scrolls of Armageddon hadn't been enough to kill this boss! What a monster the devs had created!

"We'll see about that." James still hadn't appeared, so I aimed at Geranika's voice and summoned my Spirits. I couldn't aim at the Lord of Shadow directly, so I did the simplest thing I could—I summoned a Spirit of Mass Destruction. "We shall see..."

Level gained...

You have killed Geranika, the Lord of Shadow. Reward: ???.

The blindness dissipated and realizing where I was, I collapsed to my knees. Not a trace remained of the Armard palace. In fact, nothing at all remained in a radius of two hundred meters—with the exception of the Lord of Shadow's alabaster throne. At its foot, prone on the ground, lay the mangled body of the Lord of Shadow himself. The arms and legs were gone. His clothes had burned off with his skin. Several spikes had impaled his torso and yet Geranika had by some miracle survived the explosion...Survived to be finished off by just about the weakest Spirit I could have summoned.

"Okay, you did it," a calm voice sounded behind my back. "But why?"

I turned and encountered Clutzer's eyes. He was alive and in one piece, wearing the same clothes.

"Who are you?" I asked, stunned.

"Deputy head of the internal security service of the Barliona Corporation—Major General Alex Hermann. I will repeat my question—why did you blow up Geranika?"

"I need help. Save me..." I managed to get out before the surrounding world began spinning, surged, narrowed into one point of light and vanished. Before losing consciousness, I managed to see a blinking red light and the closed lid of a cocoon a few centimeters before my face. My chest heaved with a sharp pain and all I wanted was a breath...

I had been disconnected from Barliona.

* * *

"How is he?"

"His condition is stabilizing, vital signs are reaching nominal. His brain's what worries me— Daniel didn't sleep for over nine months."

"Try to pull him out. We need him."

"We're doing everything we can. Maria, why is he moving? Did you forget to administer the injection?!"

* * *

Forty-two developers, thirteen administrators, eleven forum mods, six operatives from information security (including my former mentor), two scenario designers, thirty-two freelancers—the scale of the operation that

Donotpunnik had organized was terrifying. Hellfire, Exodus, seven 'Uns' from the Azure Dragons, including Donotpunnik himself—everyone ended up in the defendants' dock. Every conspirator save two— Mirida the Farsighted and me.

"Unfortunately, we didn't make it to her in time," Alex Hermann explained to me at the hospital. "After the crystals were activated, Donotpunnik had no use for her and she was deemed obsolete. As for you, the Corporation has no issues with you. You were acting within the game's rules. I mean, we could of course find some issue to pursue, but we won't."

"How did they manage to trap me in virtual reality?" I asked just about the biggest question I had. My entire plan was based on a single postulate—some hacker had done the impossible. But the longer I thought about it, the less likely this seemed to me. A breach of such scale was simply impossible!

"Back in Dolma you entered the technical portal and were sent out to reality, remember? Constantine, one of the technicians working on the capsules, had been paid off by Donnotpunnik, and therefore instead of a standard prisoner's capsule, you were immersed in a version modified by several hackers. They could monitor you, control you, even disconnect you if they needed to. When it became clear that you'd end up in reality, they disconnected you, cooked up a virtual subspace and then had you wake up in it. Since Donotpunnik never anticipated this would happen and the work was done hastily, the end result had several bugs. As I understand it, they were the reason you realized what was happening."

"Why were you in Dolma?"

"I wasn't in Dolma. When you entered the portal, we received a message that someone was adjusting the codebase. The code changed twice in your vicinity within a short amount of time—the portal and the teleportation to Beatwick—so we conducted a probe, which ended up giving birth to the Clutzer you knew. We recommended the original prisoner be released. If it matters to you, half a year ago he ended up in Barliona again—for theft, again. At the moment he's gathering grass. Meanwhile, we began to monitor your capsule and, as soon as you were disconnected, we pulled you out."

"I drowned!"

"There were risks involved, I won't argue with that. However, we had to not only identify the circle of conspirators, but also obtain ironclad evidence that they intended to commit murder. We'd never find Marina after she was disconnected—her body was cremated, so we waited long enough for Donotpunnik to kill you. We're working closely with the police, so we had to amass the evidence they needed."

"Using my life," I said grimly.

"Among other things. But yes, using your life too."

"So what's next?"

"Nothing. Barliona's been offline for a week now. The Corporation is suffering immense losses, but Mr. Johnson has made it clear that we must identify everyone involved before re-launching the game. No one has ever infiltrated our organization so deeply. The intruders breached our IT security through and through."

"Why are you telling me all this? Isn't this a secret?"

"Daniel, I like you very much as a person. You have something that people in today's day and age tend to lack—a faith in other people. First you believe in a person, then in everything good and kind about them and finally you're disappointed when they betray you. This is a very unique quality for a grown man—in fact, it's more common to children. As for confidentiality and secrets...One more secret won't kill you, will it? Now, get yourself ready. We need to stop by the police and lodge a request to have your case reexamined. In Marina's apartment we discovered irrefutable evidence that you were framed. We'll head to court immediately after stopping by the station. As of today, you are a witness..."

It took the court one and a half days to read the sentence. Donnotpunnik received a life sentence in the mines without possibility of parole. My former mentor got twenty years with eligibility for parole in ten. Hellfire and Exodus got ten years each. All the other conspirators, whose names I didn't know, got between two and eight years. My case was reexamined. I was declared not guilty and compensated all the money I had spent paying for my release. My hundred million was returned to me, yet the Corporation insisted that I void my contract with Ehkiller for the Tears. I didn't mind. A hundred million would be enough for a carefree old age. However, the damages that the Corporation had to pay Ehkiller did not end there. It turned out that the head of Phoenix had mortgaged a majority of his in-game assets for close to nothing in order to amass the collateral for the bank loan. Meanwhile, during the time that Phoenix's players had spent incapacitated, they had violated hundreds of contracts, the damages for which were withdrawn from the clan treasury. The Corporation had to compensate all of this, covering Phoenix's losses over and over again. And yet the largest damages were paid for Anastaria. As I understood it, at the end of the battle in the Dragon Dungeon, she had been sent to a closed-off level and blocked from communicating with the outside world, even with me. They had turned off her sensory filter and started to kill her again and again. In a particularly violent way. Stacey had no way of getting out—the trial arena did not allow the player to leave the capsule. I can't even imagine how much money Mr. Johnson had to pay Ehkiller, but the sum certainly had a tail of ten zeros at least.

"Daniel!" called Victor Zavala, as I was

descending the stairs of the court building. That's was it! The case was closed, all the Barliona data had been reset, the scenarios had been rewritten, and most importantly, Geranika had returned to Barliona. Without a third Empire, the Corporation didn't see how to develop our continent further. I was promised fantastical sums in compensation for adjusting my character's data, and yet I'd only see it in a few days when Barliona was re-launched. "Allow me to have a word with you!"

"I'm listening!" Anastaria's father was an ordinary person in reality. You'd never pick one of the wealthiest (and in light of the recent compensation, the wealthiest) players in Barliona out of a crowd of ordinary citizens.

"Let's take a walk." Victor—or as I was used to thinking of him, Ehkiller—nodded at the boardwalk running past the courthouse. "I have to beg your forgiveness. Until the very last moment, I believed that you were mixed up in this thing. Were it not for Anastaria's faith in you, I don't even know how it would've all worked out."

Ehkiller's security detail shadowed a few steps behind us, but I paid them no attention.

"You see," Ehkiller began to explain when he understood that I wasn't going to say anything. "My clan and its position in the game have been targets for a long time. I knew that Exodus was spying on us, but I didn't realize that the rot had penetrated so deeply. Even Hellfire...I was happy when you showed up with your Chess Set: Finally, we would be able to enter the Tomb of the Creator. And yet, it quickly became apparent that the Tomb was a trap. It contained something that would radically lower the stats of our characters. That was when it became clear that you're either the unwitting instrument of Donotpunnik (although I didn't know I was dealing with him then)—or that you were the enemy himself. We developed a plan according to which Anastaria would infiltrate your clan—but then the unexpected happened: She fell in love with you. No need to look at me like that. I know my daughter! Your actions showed that you were nothing but an instrument, which meant you had to be manipulated carefully. Stacey developed a new plan—the one that we ended up putting into action on the plateau before the Tomb. We had to make it so that you would leave the game and returning to reality, ruin the plans of your puppet master. But here was where the most surprising thing happened—you never appeared in the rehabilitation center. All our data suggested that you would be at the highest dependence level, and yet you were nowhere to be found. And I mean that in the physical sense, since the documentation stated that you had successfully completed your rehabilitation and returned home. It goes without saying that you never appeared at your house either, and that's when we understood that you had been abducted and that your kidnappers were planning on using you further. So we had to adjust our plans yet again. Against her best instincts, Stacey worked to irritate you—to make you aware of your emotions so that you would realize the artificial nature of the world you'd been locked in. In the end, she accomplished this. Your emotions allowed you to create the ring and save yourself. I won't tell you why we couldn't warn you about the danger you were in, or why we avoided conversations about reality—that's all immaterial now. I only want to ask you to do one thing: Give Stacey a second chance. Even though she worked to destroy your relationship, she loves you. Please trust this old man. I can't make you understand me, or to understand her. I'm simply asking. Just give her a chance..."

Ehkiller sighed heavily, turned and slowly, like he had aged a great deal, walked to the car that had been trailing us. The father had done everything he could for his daughter. It was now the kids' job to figure out what they wanted.

EPILOGUE

SEVERAL DAYS LATER, the doorbell in my apartment rang. Barliona had gone live again, but I had absolutely no desire to revisit its marvelous world. It was like a portion of me had been extracted and discarded like some useless piece of waste. A small portion—but an important portion! I slowly walked to my door and opened it without even checking to see who it was. If it was some maniac, well, he could make himself at home!

Instead, Anastaria stood at the door, nervously fidgeting with a small purse in her hands.

"May I come in?" Stacey asked. Unlike in Barliona, in reality her voice was a bit hoarse, making the girl 'realer' and all the more desirable. It made her that little portion of me that I had been missing. Shaking my head to dispel the thoughts racing through my mind, I stepped aside to let Stacey pass and said:

"Come in. Would you like some tea?"

END OF BOOK SIX

Want to be the first to know about our latest LitRPG, sci fi and fantasy titles from your favorite authors?

Subscribe to our **NEW RELEASES** newsletter:
http://eepurl.com/b7niIL

Thank you for reading *Shaman's Revenge!*

If you like what you've read, check out other LitRPG books and series published by Magic Dome Books:

An *NPC's Path* LitRPG series by Pavel Kornev:
The Dead Rogue

Level Up series by Dan Sugralinov:
Re-Start

The Way of the Shaman LitRPG series
by Vasily Mahanenko:
Survival Quest
The Kartoss Gambit
The Secret of the Dark Forest
The Phantom Castle
The Karmadont Chess Set
Clans War

Dark Paladin LitRPG series by Vasily Mahanenko:
The Beginning
The Quest
Restart

Galactogon LitRPG series by Vasily Mahanenko:
Start the Game!

The Bard from Barliona LitRPG series
by Eugenia Dmitrieva and Vasily Mahanenko:
The Renegades

The Neuro LitRPG series by Andrei Livadny:
The Crystal Sphere
The Curse of Rion Castle
The Reapers

Phantom Server LitRPG series by Andrei Livadny:
Edge of Reality
The Outlaw
Black Sun

Reality Benders LitRPG series
by Michael Atamanov:
Countdown
External Threat

The Dark Herbalist LitRPG series
by Michael Atamanov:
Video Game Plotline Tester
Stay on the Wing
A Trap for the Potentate

Perimeter Defense LitRPG series by Michael
Atamanov:
Sector Eight
Beyond Death
New Contract
A Game with No Rules

Mirror World LitRPG series by Alexey Osadchuk:
Project Daily Grind
The Citadel
The Way of the Outcast
The Twilight Obelisk

AlterGame LitRPG series by Andrew Novak:
The First Player
On the Lost Continent
God Mode

Citadel World series by Kir Lukovkin:
The URANUS Code
The Secret of Atlantis

**The Expansion (The History of the Galaxy) series
by A. Livadny:**
Blind Punch
The Shadow of Earth

Point Apocalypse *(a near-future action thriller)*
by Alex Bobl

The Sublime Electricity series by Pavel Kornev
The Illustrious
The Heartless
The Fallen
The Dormant

You're in Game!
(LitRPG Stories from Bestselling Authors)

You're in Game-2!
(More LitRPG stories set in your favorite worlds)

**The Game Master series by A. Bobl and A.
Levitsky:**
The Lag

The Naked Demon by Sherrie L.
(a paranormal romance)

More books and series are coming out soon!

In order to have new books of the series translated faster, we need your help and support! Please consider leaving a review or spread the word by recommending *Shaman's Revenge* to your friends and posting the link on social media. The more people buy the book, the sooner we'll be able to make new translations available. Thank you!

Till next time!